WHAT OTHERS ARE SAYING

"What a great read! Lee has combined the excitement and intrigue of reality television with powerful character backstories that gave me both a hero to cheer for and a villain to boo—and it's not always the same contestant. Welcome to the jungle! Let the fun and games begin!"

Dr. T.K. Wheeler, author of *Phobia, Evil Men* and *Imposters*

If you like reality based television shows with lots of action and a crazy cast of characters, "Jungle Money" is the book for you. A collection of individuals who are quirky at best and dangerous to themselves or others, are hand-picked and offered the financial deal of a lifetime - if they will compete for the win in the Amazon.

Uncharted territory in more ways than one shows what adventure, ingenuity, and lots of greed can do to a group of eager participants.

Little do they know what they are getting into...

Kathi Harper Hill, author of 8 books including *Bensy and Me* and *Poetry, Prose, and Music: Life of an Appalachian Woman*
www.kathi-harper-hill.blogspot.com

Also by G. Lee Welborn

Surviving College Park

Jungle Money

G. Lee Welborn

Jungle Money

Published by Yawn Publishing LLC
2555 Marietta Hwy, Ste 103
Canton, GA 30114
www.yawnspublishing.com

Library of Congress Control Number: 2021921191

ISBN 978-1-954617-30-8 paperback
978-1-954617-31-5 eBook

Printed in the United States of America

Chapter One

The police were on their way, and they couldn't get there soon enough to suit Morton Canfield. On any other occasion, Morton loved having camera crews in his pawn shop. This was not one of those times. *Look at my customers. Not a one of them shopping for merchandise*, he lamented. They were all frozen in place watching the spectacle happening up at the front counter. Some crazy woman stomps into his store, pitches a tantrum, and it's just like she blasted a time-stopping ray gun in a 360-degree arc, freezing the blood, muscles, and wallets of every single customer he had. Time is money, and this nut job was stopping time. If the cameras weren't here, Morton and Black Magic would have already snatched her up and had her lying flat of her butt out on the sidewalk.

A blood-curdling scream jerked Morton's head away from his paralyzed customers and back to the source of the ear-splitting yell. A large, squirming mass of humanity was locked in mortal combat in front of the return counter.

The cameraman, filming this week's episode of "The Pawn Man," jammed his camera lens in a space between two people's heads. Dissatisfied with that angle, he lifted the camera up over the crowd pointing down at the fight. When all openings on this side slammed shut, he broke and ran around to the other side of the melee. *Can't miss this*, he thought to himself. *This is too good.*

Anthony Williams, also known as Black Magic, was normally the stopper in these situations. Morton had given him the nickname after he found out his pitch to the RTV Network for a show based on his pawn shop had been successful. The "Black" came from his color. The "Magic" came from his extraordinary skill at making customer relations problems disappear. Morton was so proud of himself when he hit upon the name that he said it incessantly for weeks. Anthony didn't care what he called him. Anthony's paychecks had gone up $1.75 per hour after "The Pawn Man" show had started. As long as Morton kept signing his paychecks every two weeks, he didn't care if Morton called him Snow White.

Right now, though, Black Magic cared a lot. He didn't care about the cameras in the least, but he cared a great deal about the unbearable pressure on his man parts.

When the ruckus started, Black Magic had come over to rescue Brittany the returns clerk. Brittany should have never worn dangling hoop earrings to work knowing she would be within arm's reach of people with poor coping skills and none of their return paperwork. Now, though, it looked like not only was the clerk going to lose her earlobe, he was going to lose a reproductive organ.

At the epicenter of the earthquake was one DeShunta Jackson. She was not a regular, and if Morton ever got her out of the store and into a squad car, she would most definitely not be a repeat customer.

If DeShunta had kept her invoice, it would have shown that she purchased a Sampian 75" HD LED television from Morton Canfield's pawn shop exactly one week ago today. When she took it home, DeShunta had made sure that everyone in her building knew about her new TV. Her neighbors were shocked when she invited everyone over to watch the Cowboys play the Steelers. Since when did DeShunta care anything about football? Truth be told, she didn't. She was just proud of the fact that she had the biggest TV she had ever seen that would soon be the envy of everyone in Building U. She had paid too much for it, but when she received her stimulus check in the mail it was the first thing that had crossed her mind to buy. Although her face didn't show it, the day her nephew and his friend had set that TV down in her living room had been the greatest day she could remember.

On game day morning, DeShunta placed a bag of Cheesy Chips on the counter. *Got to feed people*, she thought to herself. *If they want something more they can march themselves right back to their own refrigerator and get it.* She started to buy some beer but then thought better of it. Cedrick from downstairs would get a buzz on and never leave if she provided beer. Instead, she bought a package of red plastic cups and set them next to the sink. Cedrick can drink some water.

Her guests arrived one by one. Each one knocked hesitantly. Once the door opened, they walked carefully into DeShunta's living room as though there might be land mines buried underneath the worn carpet. None of them had ever been inside DeShunta's apartment before.

Everything was going as planned. The commentators blah blahed all the way up to game time talking about yards and points and all kinds of things that DeShunta didn't care about. The only thing she cared about was watching the faces of her guests as their eyes landed on the giant TV. Each time she saw a new set of eyebrows fly up and a mouth forming an "O" it was like she had just won the lottery. The clarity of the picture. The size of the screen. The quality of the sound. Breathtaking. It was almost like being there.

Then disaster struck.

Cedrick, who already had his game day buzz going before he walked in the door, had brought his own bottle of Spring Label beer. He set it down on the TV table while he pulled off his hoodie. His unsteady feet failed him, causing him to stumble like a sailor on the deck of a beer-tossed ship. He lost his balance just a little when the hoodie passed over his face. He reached out blindly to find something to steady himself. His hand found the TV table. He didn't touch the TV even a little bit, just the table, but it was enough to jostle the big screen.

The slight bump shouldn't have affected the function of the TV at all--at least not if the original owner of the TV hadn't dropped it when getting it out of the box a month before DeShunta bought it. The intermittent blackouts that ensued had led the disappointed first purchaser to bring it to "The Pawn Man." He held his breath when Morton plugged it in. *Please play*, he prayed. *Please play*. When Morton pressed the power button and the screen lit up like a Christmas tree, the original owner breathed a sigh of relief. He kept a poker face, giving no hint to Morton that he was surprised it came on. Morton found it a little strange that the man didn't protest when he offered him less than half of what it was worth even though it was brand new. That's okay. Morton made deals like that every day. He had his girl give the man his money and placed it in the electronics section of the store. Morton knew he would get double the purchase price from a new customer before the week was out.

The new customer turned out to be DeShunta Jackson. That same new customer was left standing in her living room one week later, with an apartment full of people, staring at a blank screen where moments earlier the Cowboys had won the toss and were lining up to kick off. When DeShunta clicked the power button for the seventh or eighth time and realized it was not coming back on, she turned with a growl worthy of a Bengal tiger at cage-cleaning time and lunged at Cedrick the hapless downstairs neighbor. Cedrick, who had the distinct misfortune of having uncovered the weakness in DeShunta Jackson's 75" TV, barely escaped with his life. Fortunately for him, his hoodie had slipped off his head the third time DeShunta had jerked it, allowing him to bolt through the open door behind all the other guests.

DeShunta had been humiliated. She hurried downstairs to his apartment to demand restitution, but Cedrick's door frame must have been made of reinforced steel. She could not get it open with her fists, her feet, her shoulder or the propane tank from the grill on the next patio over. She screamed, "You got to come out sometime!" Cedrick, who was listening to her tirade from his bedroom closet, took a mental inventory of his pantry. He had a can of lima beans, a jar of peanut butter, some salt packets and most of a twelve-pack. He could survive two weeks without coming out.

The next day, when DeShunta wheeled the defective TV up to the returns window at Morton's Pawn Shop, she did everything right, like you would expect a grown-up person to do in a business dispute. She calmly explained how she had only bought the TV a few days earlier and now it didn't work.

Well, she intended to explain it calmly anyway.

When the time came to deliver her prepared speech to the customer service woman behind the glass, she may have gone off-script a little. She may have called the woman behind the glass a name after she demanded her money back. Maybe more than one name. Having thoroughly explained her grievance, DeShunta slapped her hand down on the counter, jutted her head forward, opened her eyes wide and raised her eyebrows as high as they would go.

After Brittany, the customer service clerk, took a deep breath to calm herself, she politely asked to see Ms. Jackson's invoice. Ms. Jackson informed the clerk that she did not need to have an invoice because she only bought it a few days ago, and she expected the store to have the invoice. The clerk pointed to the sign on the cork board next to the counter.

"No refunds, no returns, no exchanges, no nothing without an invoice."

DeShunta read the sign. DeShunta looked back at the clerk who was popping chewing gum. When DeShunta confessed she didn't have the invoice, she could not believe what came out of the clerk's mouth.

"Next."

DeShunta erupted. Her press-on fingernails flew straight to the clerk's left ear and hooked through her hoop earring. The clerk, whose head was turned to the right at an agonizing angle, knew that if she lost her desperate grip on DeShunta's fleshy right forearm, she was going to lose her earlobe.

The clerk's screams brought Black Magic and Morton Canfield running. At first, it appeared as though Black Magic was going to be able to neutralize the situation. Morton could see that Black Magic had both of his mighty hands clamped on the enraged woman's wrists. He tried to wrest her hands away from the returns window, but Brittany's cries let him know she would lose an ear if he did so. He changed tactics and tried to move DeShunta's body. All the customers in the store jumped as DeShunta screamed at the highest volume yet.

"Get your hands off my breasteses!"

Morton could see that Black Magic's hands were nowhere near her breasts, but the TV camera couldn't. A shyster at heart, Morton begrudgingly appreciated her tactics. *Well played, nut job. Well played. Keep it up. Black Magic will have you flat of your face in the parking lot any minute.*

Much to Morton's dismay, Black Magic began to scream. Morton shouted, trying to be heard above the din.

"For crying out loud, Magic, would you get that woman's hands off of Brittany's ear?"

"I can't, Boss! She got me by the jewels!"

Morton did a hand check. Sure enough, the crazy woman had one hand hooked into Brittany's hoop earring and the other locked in a vice grip on Black Magic's crotch. Morton buried his head in his hands for a moment not knowing what to do. After battling indecision, he took off for the parking lot. The police have to be close by now.

Zach, the cameraman, swung his lens wildly around the store. He leaped into the void created when Morton fled the scene and trained his lens on the central combatant. DeShunta's t-shirt began to ride up over her bra strap in the back, revealing rolls of flesh, each of which moved independently of the other. Zach beamed. This is going to be the trailer that the network would use all summer to trumpet the new season of "The Pawn Man;" he was certain of it.

Black Magic attempted to pull DeShunta away from the customer service desk, but that only elicited howls of pain from Brittany, who remained stuck behind the counter struggling to keep DeShunta from pulling off her left ear. DeShunta's low center of gravity gave her the advantage. As both DeShunta and Black Magic pulled away from the counter, Brittany was lifted bodily. Screaming, she slid over the counter and right under the glass. The watching crowd gasped as the fight continued to escalate.

Morton heard the screams from out in the parking lot. He ran back in the entrance, bumping into customers trying to flee the melee. When he saw how far the brawl had moved away from the customer service counter, he began to moan.

"No! No! Keep her away from the motorcycle! Please god, keep her away from the motorcycle!"

Morton Canfield had his most prized possession on display near the service counter. Anvil Carrabelle's nitro-powered Kazasuki Z1 superbike. On July the 4th, 1976, Anvil Carrabelle attempted to jump over the Nashville City Hall on this very bike while millions of breathless television viewers watched. The motorcycle successfully made the jump. Anvil unfortunately didn't. He miscalculated the height of his jump and the angle of descent, resulting in him being hooked by a live powerline after clearing the gold-domed roof. Those who later attended visitation at the funeral home noticed a faint, unsettling smell coming from the closed casket, not unlike a charcoal grill the day after grilling hamburgers.

For years after his death, Carrabelle's family displayed the bike in a backyard shed for people willing to pay five dollars to see it. Eventually, one of his family members fell on hard times and sold it to Morton Canfield who was delighted to get it. Morton promptly put it front and center, right in front of the customer service counter. It sat there unmolested for the next eleven years.

At least it did until DeShunta Jackson entered the picture.

It seemed that the ghost of Anvil Carrabelle was about to make one last posthumous jump. Aided by a powerful kick from DeShunta's mighty left thigh, the Kazasuki Z1 superbike flew into an antique grandfather clock which toppled over onto the motorcycle with a loud bong, breaking the headlamp, mirror and speedometer cover. With Zach's camera recording the entire scene, Morton screamed out in anguish.

"You just destroyed Anvil Carrabelle's bike!"

The fight continued unabated. When DeShunta's weave was snatched off of her head, Zach laughed despite himself. DeShunta wasn't through making the highlight reel however. Not by a long shot.

DeShunta had not planned her eating and bathroom preparations around the sustained total body workout she was currently engaged in. The amount of ab work she was having to do to keep the returns clerk from peeling the fingers of one hand off of her earring, while simultaneously maintaining her grip on the nether regions of the struggling Black Magic, did not mix well with the large meal she had eaten at the Spicy Donkey the night before. When faced with the birthing pains of an overloaded colon, most sane adults would cease all other activities to find the nearest restroom. DeShunta however, was most definitely not most sane adults. She planned to see this battle through to its bitter end. They were going to give her back every dime she paid for that defective TV.

Then the unthinkable happened.

The back of DeShunta's yoga pants, already stretched to the point of breaking from the strain of containing all that flesh, sprouted a lump. One lump became two. Lumps began to slide out of her pants leg onto the floor. When malodorous fumes began to assail their nostrils, the crowd of onlookers split evenly into two camps—those who screamed, and those who dry-heaved. The chaos at Morton's Pawn Shop was now complete.

Three months later, the DeShunta episode aired. It was the most DVR'ed episode in reality TV history. Morton got over being upset about the motorcycle when he learned the network had decided to produce a second season, increasing his take from $5,000 for the whole season to $10,000 for a single episode.

Someone else was watching "The Pawn Man" the day the DeShunta Jackson episode aired. Tony Longino sat bolt upright in bed in his Buckhead condominium, grabbed his phone and found George Commander's name on speed dial. Two thousand miles away, a phone rang in the heart of Beverly Hills.

"G, are you watching this?"

"Watching what?" G asked Tony.

"Pawn Man!"

G was not watching "The Pawn Man," but he flipped channels and found it quickly enough. "The Pawn Man" followed the typical format of most reality shows, which was to run and re-run each eyebrow-raising scene immediately after strategically-timed commercial breaks. G watched the melee with a mixture of horror and disgust, which was soon replaced by a glimmer of economic opportunity.

"G, she is perfect!" Tony cried. "Perfect, I tell you! We have just found the perfect first contestant for Jungle Money!"

The man called G pondered in silence while pawn shop pandemonium played out on the TV screen before him. Would she do it? Was there any way she would even consider doing it? The longer the thought washed over his mind, the more the corner of his mouth turned up. What a wild ride that would be. It didn't take him long to decide.

"Tony, I like it. Get Bert on the phone. Time for a quick board meeting."

Tony laughed.

"You got it, G! Consider it done. Hold on."

G waited while Tony got Bert on the phone. G didn't laugh a lot, but he liked to hear Tony laugh. If Tony laughed, it carried weight. G set his phone down and turned his attention back to the TV. DeShunta Jackson sure liked words that rhymed with witch.

Chapter Two

Charlton Pinoir-Sinclair, "Chaz" to his friends, was eighteen years old, skinny as a rail and full of youthful enthusiasm. His longish brown hair hung over his left eye, his left cheek and his left nostril, which required him to tilt his head and view the world at a forty-five-degree angle. His voice was higher-pitched than he would like, so in his alone time, he put his chin on his chest and practiced his deep voice. It did not take long before his mother could no longer bear to hear the words, "Luke, I am your father." After the ten thousandth time, she yelled an uncharacteristic, "Chaz, for the love of reason, would you please shut up?" down the stairs and slammed the basement door.

On this particular day, Chaz was a man on a mission. The vastness of the Los Angeles County landfill lay before him. He was on a treasure hunt but he had no map, and X didn't mark the spot. Chaz began to lift a mold-encrusted sofa cushion to look underneath, but a stabbing pain caused him to jerk his hand back. *Ouch! What was that?* He pulled off his glove and stared in dismay as one of his fingers began to drip blood. A tiny shard of glass protruded from his skin. Grimacing, he pinched it between his index finger and thumb and extracted it. He threw it atop the mound of garbage next to him in disgust.

Chaz debated his choices. Pop the wounded digit into his mouth and suck the wound to clean it? No, too dangerous. He probably already had the bubonic plague in his finger--no need to get it in his mouth, too. What about wrapping it tightly in his brand-new logo t-shirt? No, the bloodstains would never come out. He had spent too much time and effort designing the logo and getting it printed onto a t-shirt to ruin it the first time he wore it.

Before he could make up his mind, Chaz saw the cameraman scrambling up the pile of trash next to him trying to get a shot. This was not the time to appear indecisive. He displayed his wounded finger for the cameraman who found a firm footing and held the camera still for a close up. Chaz gave a brave smile, held his finger up like the Statue of Liberty and shared his pain with the world.

"Saving the environment hurts sometimes."

Pleased with his pithiness, Chaz posed for the camera for an uncomfortably long time. The cameraman stuck his head around to the side of the camera and silently mouthed the words, "Okay, I got it."

Chaz wiped his sweaty brow and wrinkled his nose in a futile attempt to screen out the stench. One man alone against the vastness of a Los Angeles landfill. Well, not entirely alone. Actually, he had the full support of the Leave Earth Free of Trash Society. L.E.F.T. Its members were scattered across the battlefield, each with a pair of gloves, a box full of trash bags, and a paper facemask rubber-banded around their ears.

Earth's ecosystem was in the balance, and time was drawing short. Water bottles were the enemy. Each time some thoughtless capitalist drained a bottle and then screwed the top back on tightly before tossing it aside, water, precious water, was captured inside, locked away for a thousand years. Eons would pass before the plastic finally degraded enough to release the life-giving elixir again. How much did each bottle hold? Two little drops? Two big gulps? Even if it was only enough to form condensation when the temperature dropped, it was too much to waste. Drought-stricken California was crying out for water like a fish gasping for breath.

Chaz looked behind him. Seventeen garbage bags filled with now topless water bottles bore silent witness to the number of times Chaz had freed the essence of life from its manmade prison that day. He was proud of his efforts. *Wait until the others see this.*

It dawned on Chaz that he hadn't seen the other L.E.F.T. team members in quite a while. He scanned the seemingly endless landfill with his trademark forty-five-degree head tilt but didn't see another living creature except for the scavenger birds. Even the cameraman had disappeared. He felt a sudden unease. His anxious concern transformed into irritated consternation when he looked in the direction of the distant parking lot. His whole team was standing around the university bus watching the cameraman packing up his equipment. Why were they quitting when there was still so much work to be done?

This was not the first time his team had let him down today. There had been other disappointments, like the size of the group for starters. There were supposed to be twelve L.E.F.T. members here, not counting his mom. Everybody had given a solemn pledge to be here when Chaz birthed the brainchild that awesome night at Burger Flats. He would not have pressed so hard for the Environmental Action News Crew from WLAT to be here to witness it if he had known that only four members would show, counting his mom. She wasn't even a student. He wouldn't have begged his geology professor to reserve a university bus if he had known how few would show up. They could have saved a tank full of fossil fuel by charging his mom's Econobahn and driving themselves.

But all was not lost. Anna had come. He smiled despite himself as he walked toward the group. To say Anna was the most attractive member of his geology class would be an understatement. She was beautiful, smart, and dedicated to saving the environment. She was, in guy speak, a unicorn. For reasons he still didn't fully understand, she had started talking to him during the first class of the semester. Girls didn't talk to him—especially not unicorns. But Anna did. It had changed his life. Her attention made him feel bold and confident. She made him want to change the world.

After much deliberation, Chaz decided to tell Anna how he felt. The next day in school, he mustered all the courage he could, strode up to her, tapped her on the shoulder, and before he lost his nerve, told her of the impact she had made on his life. He showed her the drawing he had made of them. Pen and ink was his forte. As he studied her face, looking for her reaction, his stomach fluttered like a flock of birds was trying to escape through his navel. He would never forget the words she spoke if he lived to be a hundred.

"It's the second day of class."

Indeed it was, my fair lady. Indeed it was. Though he could rarely find a seat next to her after that day, it didn't matter. They had connected. Time and space could not separate them. The proof stood before him in all her hole-kneed blue-jeaned glory. She was here.

As Chaz neared the group, he noticed that Anna had an annoyed look on her face. A sinking feeling began to overwhelm him. He hoped she was merely as anguished as him over the needless waste of H_2O in all the unopened water bottles they had yet to find. Surely that must be it.

In another corner of the parking lot, news reporter Monica Brawn was seething. *What a waste of a morning.* This college kid had pleaded and cajoled and needled and pressed and whined. His persistence had made her ignore her first instincts and go. She was a respected journalist, traveling California from state line to state line, shining the light of day on environmental injustice wherever it tried to hide. When Chaz had approached her, she was uncharacteristically low on material at the moment. Chaz had promised to have hundreds of volunteers scouring the most disgusting place she could think of, a landfill, determined to uncover thousands of water bottles and release the water trapped inside. All she had gotten this morning however, was video of an awkward college boy's as-yet-unsuccessful attempts to woo a young co-ed he followed everywhere like a puppy. None of this video was usable. None of it. As she quietly told her camera guy to pack his equipment so they could leave, loud voices startled them both.

As Chaz started to carry the first two bags packed with topless water bottles out of the front gate of the landfill to the bus, two men converged on him. The bus driver, whose mouth bore the traces of this morning's powdered doughnuts, awoke from his sugar-induced nap just in time to see someone struggling to get an overlarge trash bag through the bus door. A trash bag. On his bus. The driver bellowed a protest that made Chaz jump. His voice grew louder as he saw the other three toting bags of trash in the direction of his bus.

"What do you think you are doing? No trash on my bus! Off! Off, off, off!"

Monica Brawn liked what she was hearing. A conflict was brewing. Maybe something worth reporting was about to happen after all. She barked at her videographer to get the camera back out of the bag and be quick about it.

The bus driver's yelling brought the attention of the gatekeeper. His job was to weigh the trucks that entered, weigh them again as they left, and collect a dumping fee based on the weight difference. Once a customer paid the fee and pulled away, the arm of the gate closed behind him. There was no reversing for re-entry. This was an exit only.

The gatekeeper hadn't known what to do when three dorky-looking kids and somebody's mom had walked into the landfill a couple of hours earlier without bringing any trash. A news reporter, with a face he had seen somewhere, marched past him with a cameraman. He decided to let them pass. He started to warn them to stay away from the bulldozers but then thought better of it. They were in a dump. If they didn't have enough sense to stay out of the way of giant equipment, that's on them.

When the gatekeeper saw the same group walking back out carrying trash bags filled with water bottles, he was befuddled. He had never been confronted with someone who wanted to take trash *out* of the landfill. He started to object, but then asked himself why. He didn't know of any rules that prohibited it. Eyeing them suspiciously, he let them pass unchallenged. It would be a good story to tell the wife when he got home.

Everything changed when the yelling started. The gatekeeper radioed his boss and told him there was a fight in the parking lot. He prayed he would still have his job when the smoke cleared. He knew he should have stopped the crazy people walking around inside his dump.

Meanwhile, back at the bus, words were flying. Chaz's pride had already been wounded by the lack of turnout and the cut finger he was nursing. He had never considered the possibility that after all the long hours that he, his mom, and his two classmates had put in gathering water bottles, they wouldn't be permitted to transport them to recycling.

Chaz cut his eyes over to Anna. She was looking back at him with an accusatory glare, stunned at the realization that everything she had done had all been for naught. Freeing the water had been worth it, hadn't it? She wasn't sure any longer. She pondered the possibility of joining the Cage Ban Collective. She hated zoos. C.B.C.'s meetings all took place at Javanauts, and she was pretty sure the president's mom was not a member.

Exasperated, and feeling the eyes of the news camera upon him, Chaz turned angrily and stomped back in the direction of the landfill. The gatekeeper's boss arrived in his UTV at that exact moment and slid to a stop in front of Chaz. He hadn't seen any part of the events that preceded his arrival. All he saw was a bunch of bags of trash in the landfill parking lot and some kid trying to walk them in on foot. A freeloader. If there was one thing the boss couldn't stand, it was freeloaders.

"No one brings trash into my landfill without paying to dump it."

Chaz began to shake. Feeling his blood pressure nearing the boiling point, embarrassment having turned his ears a bright shade of red, Chaz dropped the bags where he stood and began to walk back to the bus. Instead of being placated however, the gatekeeper's boss became enraged.

"Oh no, sonny boy! Don't you even think about trashing and dashing! Pick that mess up out of my parking lot! Throw it in that bus you came in and resume your party somewhere else. And take these news people with you. Just stirring up trouble is all you're doing."

As soon as the boss finished, the bus driver leaped back into the fray.

"I already told you, nobody is putting garbage in my bus! This thing has got to be spic and span and ready for all the students on Monday morning. If you think you are putting two dozen loaded trash bags in here, you are out of your mind! The university would have my head on a platter, and I couldn't deny it because it would be all over the stinking news! So, don't even think about it!"

A sick realization came over Chaz. He couldn't take the loaded trash bags and bottles away because the bus driver wouldn't let him. He couldn't leave them where they sat next to the bus because the dump boss wouldn't let him. He didn't have the money to pay the dump to accept them, and he wouldn't have even if he did. Anna delivered her verdict, live and on camera.

"L.E.F.T. is so lame."

Upon hearing her words, Chaz's body stiffened like a board. *No! No, no, no! This can't be happening!* Anna, his inspiration, his muse, his unicorn, was slipping away. His big moment had come crashing down along with all his hopes and dreams, all because of this stupid dump man and that stupid bus driver. Even worse, his epic failure would be broadcast on tonight's news for all the world to see. The cameraman and the reporter were standing not ten feet away, catching it all on film.

Chaz's hands visibly trembled. His fists balled up into knots. A growl began to emanate from his overlarge Adam's apple. At that moment, Charlton Pinoir-Sinclair, "Chaz" to his friends, went quite berserk.

He swung the first trash bag like an Olympic hammer thrower and launched it over the fence. The gatekeeper's boss tried to rush him. Chaz swung the next bag like it was Hank Aaron's bat. He connected with the howling face of the dump boss and knocked him flat of his back.

The bus driver saw the fate of the dump boss and was momentarily too stunned to move. Before he could react, Chaz grabbed two more bags, sprinted to the bus, and leaped through the open doorway. Well, he attempted to leap through the open doorway. Unfortunately for Chaz, there was not room enough for him and two overloaded bags of water bottles to squeeze through the bus door all at the same time. He bounced back like a golf ball off a tree trunk. Topless plastic water bottles exploded out of the ripped trash bags. For his part,

Chaz landed flat of his back on the asphalt, thoroughly expelling all of the air out of his lungs. A seemingly endless groan spewed out of Chaz's open mouth, his lungs refusing to cooperate.

The perplexed bus driver frantically tried to call his supervisor, needing to find out what university protocol was when a student went insane but the driver was fresh out of tranquilizer darts. He couldn't get a signal inside the bus, so he jumped outside to see if he could find one out there.

Chaz's eyes, darting around like cheap marbles in a gumball machine, saw his chance. Still locked in "huhhhhhhh" mode, he staggered to his feet and made a break for the bus. He climbed up the steps and closed the door behind him. With two landfill employees, a university employee, two students and his mom all screaming, "No!" at the top of their lungs, Chaz did the unthinkable. He threw the bus in gear and headed for the pile of trash bags in front of the gate. The needle on the tachometer pegged as the RPMs on the 1992 Yellowride flew higher and higher. Laughing maniacally, Chaz drove the bus into the arm of the gate at forty miles an hour, spraying a shower of splinters and water bottles that shocked even the jaded veteran reporter Monica Brawn. Monica shrieked at her cameraman.

"Did you get it? Did you get it?"

Her cameraman gave her the thumbs up. Beautiful! Just beautiful! The camera continued to roll as the blue lights and sirens of police cars entered the arena. The police officer's attempts to reason with the raging president of Leave Earth Free of Trash were all in vain. Chaos reigned until the officer shoved a crackling taser into the side of Chaz's neck. As Chaz's body convulsed and then became quiet, Monica looked in the camera. With polish developed from years of experience, Monica delivered the money line.

"This university student told us not a half hour ago that saving the environment hurts sometimes. As you can see, truer words have never been spoken. From the Los Angeles County landfill, this is Monica Brawn reporting."

Monica's news piece, complete with the footage of a bus driving through the dump gate at forty miles an hour, made the national news.

G happened to be watching the national news. G liked what he saw. He found Tony on speed dial. G was the kind of guy who never said hello and never identified himself at the beginning of a phone call. Tony didn't expect anything different. It saved time, and time was money. Besides, Tony's favorite phone calls were the ones from G. They virtually always turned out to be very lucrative.

"Tony, I think we may have another one."

"Really? Cool! Who is it?"

"A kid went nuts in a school bus. Drove it into a landfill like he was taking the flag at Talladega."

The phone clicked and the call ended. Tony rubbed his hands together. G didn't get excited unless he had found a good prospect. This as-yet-unknown person must have potential. He chuckled to himself, imagining what G must have seen that piqued his interest.

Whoever it was, Tony would get him.

Chapter Three

Still as statues and frozen in starting position, the two competitors glared at one another. Big eyes, never blinking, took in everything. At the slightest flinch, the mad dash would begin at breakneck speed. Both athletes were in top physical condition, clinging vertically to the side of the largest pin oak tree in Grant Park, waiting for the early-morning race to begin. The gnarled bark of the tree contained knots large enough to seat many spectators, but there would be no witnesses to this contest. The only cheering the two squirrels needed was already being provided by the crickets bathed in dew two stories below them.

It was still quiet outside. The overnight temperatures, unusually mild for a deep south summer, meant that the air conditioning condenser unit far below them wouldn't kick on for at least a half hour.

Inside the tiny house, a single shaft of light burst through a gap in the plantation blinds and pierced the darkness of the dining room. Microscopic dust particles passed through the light in the midst of their time-lapse slow-motion fall to the hardwood floor, illuminated for only an instant before plunging back into darkness. The improbability of the ray of sun's appearance inside the otherwise darkened house was remarkable. How had it navigated through the dense canopy of leaves sported by the enormous tree shielding the single pane window from the sky above?

The pin oak had only been a smooth-barked sapling, not yet as tall as the front porch roof behind it, when Franklin Delano Roosevelt had driven down the street in front of this house during one of his trips away from Warm Springs after a day of bathing his crippled legs. Now, however, the sapling had grown into an arboreal giant, a tree with as much distinction as any who had ever passed beneath its boughs. A ray of light that could wend its way through a hundred thousand leaves, then through a pane of glass adorned by a newly-constructed spider web, and finally between two blinds, deserved its place of rest on the elegant Turkish area rug which marked its final destination.

The only sound inside the house was the steady tick, tick, tick of the grandfather clock in the living room. Aurora, whose eyes were hidden behind a mop of tousled fur, desperately wanted to hear bong, bong, bong, bong, bong, bong, bong, because that's when her master would begin to stir. All she could think about was the moment when the door would be opened and she could burst out across the front porch, sprint through the pea gravel and into the Bermuda grass where she could relieve her full bladder. The clicking of little dog paws across the hardwoods suddenly stopped. Was that the sound of squirrels chattering outside that she just heard? Aurora trotted to the back of the house and into her master's bedroom. At the risk of receiving a sleepy scolding, Aurora voiced a wake-up whine. There were urgent matters that needed to be attended to. There were squirrels!

Celeste's brain had not yet stopped sleeping, but she was nevertheless able to receive sound waves. Aurora was overjoyed at the sight of her master's foot emerging from under the covers and hanging in suspended animation overhead. She loved this game. The little dog leaped up and remained at full height where she could lick the lowest part of her master's bare foot. The corner of Celeste's mouth turned up into the slightest grin. Doggy tongues tickle.

The old bed creaked as its occupant struggled to a sitting position. Jimi Hendrix looked down upon her from the framed poster above her bed. She rubbed the back of her neck, her right hand massaging the stiff muscles beneath her tribal tattoo. She glanced back at the other side of the bed. Trayton had left for his job as opener at NeedaCup sometime around 5 a.m., she imagined. It was hopefully not the job her boyfriend would settle on as his career, but for now it helped pay the bills.

Celeste enjoyed working at the Treasures of Yore antique store in downtown Decatur, even if her schedule didn't quite match Trayton's. She hadn't minded all that much when he was reassigned to open the store instead of working in the afternoons—at least not at first. He slept from the time his shift ended until she got home, and then they enjoyed each other's company until bedtime. Of late, however, he was not home when she got off work and was kind of vague as to how he was spending his alone hours. He didn't seem quite as eager to see her lately. Feeling a rising sense of panic, Celeste closed her eyes, sucked in all the air she could hold, and slowly exhaled until her mind was calm again. She couldn't think about that right now. It was too early in the day to worry.

Standing on the front porch in her plaid pajama pants and oversized t-shirt, Celeste greeted the morning with a big stretch and a noisy yawn. Feeling a presence near her, she looked to her left. The elderly Mrs. Jankowicz was watering the ferns on her front porch next door. Celeste was pleased to see that she was using the art nouveau watering can that she had given her for her birthday. The houses in Grant Park, a delightful cornucopia of old and new, were peopled by a mixture of senior citizens who had already filled their homes with a lifetime of memories, and young first-time homeowners who were just starting to make memories of their own.

Mrs. Jankowicz hadn't liked the looks of Celeste when she had first laid eyes on her. What kind of self-respecting young lady shaves the sides of her head, dyes the remaining hair black, and wears black lipstick? The day they had first made each other's acquaintance had been rocky. Celeste's Havanese had jumped out of the front seat of Celeste's Doodlebug, sprinted straight up to Mrs. Jankowicz' front porch, bumped the coffee table beside the rocking chair where she sat, spilling her coffee everywhere, and then chased Mrs. Jankowicz's rescue cat, Mittens, out into the street where she was almost killed by a garbage truck.

Their second meeting, also initiated by Aurora the escape artist making a break for Mrs. Jankowicz's porch, was thankfully not as disastrous as the first. Celeste apologized as she scooped up her pup. Mrs. Jankowicz was not angered by the intrusion; in fact, she asked Celeste to wait while she went inside. She emerged holding an antique apple pattern cup filled with steaming hot coffee, which she handed to Celeste and asked her to sit down and drink it with her. When Celeste took the cup, she noticed that Mrs. Jankowicz had a tattoo on the inside of her left wrist. After thanking her for the coffee, Celeste opened the conversation.

"So, you have a tattoo? That's so cool. I just got one, too! I went to Celtic Ink in Druid Hills and got this one on my shoulder."

Celeste set her cup down, pulled down the neck of her t-shirt, and bared her left shoulder.

"It's a rose with scissors about to cut off the flower and…let me pull my shirt down back here…there is a lady's face shedding a tear as it's happening. You don't know if she wants it cut or if it's being cut against her will. I designed it. I drew it and the guy marked it and inked it. It hurt like a mother! It was just a month ago. It has healed up pretty nicely, don't you think?"

Mrs. Jankowicz nodded but said nothing. Celeste noticed that Mrs. Jankowicz had pulled her sleeve down to cover her own tattoo as soon as the subject was raised. That didn't slow Celeste down, however.

"So, when did you get yours? I didn't think women your…, you know, of your generation were as free to do things like get a tattoo. Did you have to get your parents' permission, or did you just go do it without them knowing?"

Mrs. Jankowicz took a long time before answering. Celeste wondered if she had said something wrong. It appeared as though the elderly woman was having an internal debate with herself. Finally, Mrs. Jankowicz spoke.

"I did not mean for you to see that, but it's okay. This is not something that I talk about, but since you asked…"

She closed her eyes for a second, gathered herself, and began.

"When I was a little girl in Poland, my father, my mother, my sister, and me, we lived a normal happy life as far as I can remember. I don't remember a great deal. I think I must have intentionally forgotten a lot. Anyway, Hitler and the Germans came through. They took my father first, and then my mother. They took me and my sister maybe two weeks later. We did not go to the same place. I cried and cried to go with my sister because she was older, but they did not care. I was taken to Auschwitz and given this tattoo on the inside of my forearm. I did not want it. It hurt. That I do remember. They killed, I think, 1.1 million people there. My mother, my father, my sister. My little girlfriend

Ruth. We made doll clothes for our little dolls. Ruth was my best friend. Anyway, they took her to a...a...this is hard. The bad place. They took Ruth, and I never saw her again. I don't know why not me. Why did they not take me in the bad place, too? I don't know. I just did what I was told. They never called me. I don't know why."

Mrs. Jankowicz looked out toward the street with unfocused eyes, folded her arms and began to rock herself. Celeste's mouth was open. She hated herself for bringing up such a sensitive subject. But how could she have known?

"My daughter called me one day and said some movie producer was putting together a documentary. He was gathering survivors who would tell their stories. He wanted to meet with me. I wanted nothing to do with it. All I remembered was my mother and father, my sister and my friend Ruth. We made clothes for dolls. That's all I remembered. I told my daughter not to speak of it again. That was the end of it."

Celeste was not well-read, but she had heard the term "Holocaust" before. The little old lady next door with the tattoo on the inside of her forearm had lived through the Holocaust! Mrs. Jankowicz became a hero to Celeste that morning. She had lived through hell on earth. Although it was an odd-looking friendship, Celeste and Mrs. Jankowicz began to grow quite fond of one another.

Mrs. Jankowicz asked about Celeste's parents. She could tell by the sigh and the changed facial expression that she had hit upon a sore subject. Celeste did not want to talk about it, but she felt obligated after the things Mrs. Jankowicz had shared with her.

Celeste had a happy early childhood, living with her parents in Norcross Hills. She loved her mom, but she had been a daddy's girl. Her idyllic childhood had abruptly ended when she was thirteen. Celeste was finishing up her last week of middle school when a school counselor pulled her from class and told her she needed to take her home because something had happened.

Celeste learned that her father, a jeweler, had been robbed and murdered by a three-time felon when ringing up a customer at the cash register. The killer was arrested quickly enough. Celeste's dad had the foresight to install security cameras. The lady who ran the store for him watched the video once, witnessed her boss being murdered and promptly threw up in the back office. She told the police the act was caught on tape. The investigator assigned to the case viewed the video and was pleased to see the quality was good enough to identify the perpetrator. He told her not to touch it again until he could get a video expert to retrieve it. Tragically, however, the system had been set to loop over itself every seven days. The police did not retrieve it in time.

At trial, the defense attorney moved in limine to exclude the jewelry store employee's testimony about seeing the killer's face on video because the video was lost before the defense could see it. The judge granted the motion and prohibited the employee from identifying the suspect due to spoliation of evidence. The defendant followed his attorney's advice and refused to testify. Without an eyewitness, surveillance video, a murder weapon or any admissions by the defendant, the District Attorney didn't have enough evidence to prove the State's case beyond a reasonable doubt.

Celeste's thirteen-year-old mind was not able to comprehend all the legal machinations, but one thing she knew for sure. Her father's killer had been turned loose. Celeste felt like her life was placed on hold. She was stuck--frozen in time. There had never been a resolution, and there never would be. She found herself perpetually waiting for something that would never happen. She could not move forward.

Mrs. Jankowicz studied Celeste's face as she talked. She was nothing short of beautiful. Her azure-blue eyes and perfect complexion were stunning. But what had she done to her hair? Mrs. Jankowicz had to ask. Celeste was taken aback by the question but gave allowances to an old lady who had obviously been through so much.

After the killer was set free and everyone outside of the family lost interest in the case, Celeste began to modify her appearance. The first thing to go had been her hair. She remembered how the hairdresser kept telling her it was okay when the tears wouldn't stop sliding down her face. The owner suggested that they stop mid-cut and call her mom, who had dropped her daughter off to run to the craft store and had no idea what was happening back at the salon. The tears stopped when those words were spoken. The fire within her flamed up, and Celeste took control. The cut and dye job was finished without further interruption. The innocence of youth had been taken from her. Celeste would confront the world with a new identity and a look entirely of her own creation.

Lost in the telling of her story, Celeste snapped back into reality when she realized that Aurora was no longer in the front yard. She panicked and jumped up from her chair. The anxiety quickly dissipated when she saw a small, athletic woman pushing a double stroller with one hand while carrying a small wriggling Havanese in the other. Relieved, Celeste called out to the furry escapee.

"Aurora! Shame on you! Can't you see that she has her hands full already?"

Celeste scooped up her dog, which had broken free of the woman's grasp and came running to her. Although the small woman with the high-dollar running outfit and matching shoes was not the kind of person she would normally seek out or converse with, the tiny twins in the stroller were too much temptation to resist. The babies were adorable. Celeste glanced at the woman's finger and spotted a wedding ring. She found herself looking at women's left hands quite often these days.

Celeste longed for the day that Trayton would ask if he could place a ring on her finger. There was an unspoken tension between them whenever conversations or situations arose related to engagements. She would try not to look at him too quickly when friends would announce their engagements or when commercials for diamond engagement rings would appear on the television. Trayton would not look at her. He knew what was on her mind. She hated herself for pressuring him last Valentine's Day. "I'm waiting for the right time," he had said. Trayton was there for her now and forever, with or without a proposal. She believed that in her heart. She needed it to be true.

The running woman studied Celeste's face.

"Say, aren't you the one who went to Washington…?"

Celeste smiled and nodded. Although the notoriety still embarrassed her a little, she liked the recognition nonetheless.

Celeste wasn't really sure how all of the events came together that had thrust her into the limelight. When her sociology professor at Sanger University had turned the class's discussion to the role government should play in the provision of birth control to people who needed it but couldn't afford it, Celeste had been filled with an unbridled passion. Why should the poor have to risk bringing into the world another mouth to feed when they could barely feed themselves? What was so hard about directing a little bit of the government's money into providing birth control? The government had trillions of dollars and could spend them any way it wanted. Why not birth control? She knew why not.

Men.

Men with their fists squeezed too tight around their wallets wouldn't allow it. Health insurance would pay for erectile dysfunction pills, so why not birth control pills? Celeste may be young, but she had it figured out. Think of how much money the government could save if it stopped writing checks to corporations and instead provided free birth control to the poor. The government could save billions in food stamps and child support by protecting women from untimely pregnancies in the first place. Celeste wanted to get involved and make the world a better place, but she didn't know how to go about it.

Then came the day she decided to attend the march to celebrate the anniversary of *Roe v. Wade*. It was the day her whole world changed.

The organizers in charge of the schedule had time set aside for an open mike. Celeste was inspired by all the strong women around her. A couple of people in the crowd stepped up to express their thoughts, but then no one else would do it. The podium was empty, and the awkward pause that followed threatened to kill the buzz. Celeste was near the front. She had no intention of speaking, but something came over her. An idea struck her that seemed so simple and yet so profound that she had to share it.

"As we celebrate the Supreme Court establishing a woman's right to choose, I have a question. Why should women be penalized for having babies they can't afford? Mothers provide invaluable services raising children that equal or exceed corporate CEOs, yet they aren't paid a dime. So, here is what I propose. For every single woman with an unplanned pregnancy who did not have access to birth control, the government should be required to pay to raise her child to age eighteen. It's a no-brainer to anyone with half a brain! It's cheaper to provide free birth control than to raise a child."

The crowd and all who were within earshot began to cheer. Someone asked her name, and when she told them, they began to chant, "Celeste! Celeste! Celeste!"

There were cameras in the crowd and videos of Celeste were posted on social media. A local news broadcast of her short speech caught traction on a national level. It could have been her passion, or the irrefutable logic in her argument, or her piercing blue eyes and unique appearance. Whatever it was, she soon became a media darling. "It's cheaper to provide free birth control than to raise a child." Celeste was uncomfortable with her fifteen minutes of fame, but she was willing to endure it for the cause.

Before long, however, she discovered that her fame would last more than fifteen minutes. A Georgia congresswoman asked her to testify at a congressional hearing in Washington, D.C. Celeste reluctantly said yes.

Celeste had mixed emotions about her testimony on Capitol Hill. The forum was very different from the march in Atlanta. Congressmen asked her questions, some Democrats, some Republicans. The Democrats would each start by saying they wanted to ask her a question, but then they gave a speech which didn't ask a question at all. Overall, they were very supportive.

The Republicans, on the other hand, asked her short, terse questions that she didn't know how to answer. One Congressman asked her where the money would come from to pay for universal birth control. How was she supposed to know where the money would come from? Why was that important? Why was that part of the discussion?

"The government has tons of it," she answered.

Another Congressman declared that no one was preventing her from exercising her right to have sex but then asked what gave her the right to make other people pay for it. She gave the obvious answer, at least to her—people shouldn't pay for it, the government should. The Congressman then asked her if she knew who gave the government its money. She didn't know what to say. *Where does the government get its money*?

"It prints it, right?"

The long, uncomfortable silence that followed seemed like it lasted forever. The Congressman could have at least given her a hint or moved onto a different topic with a new question, but he didn't. He chuckled and shook his head. He looked at other Congressmen who shook their heads as well. She just sat there, with the world watching her on cable news, not knowing what to say. Why did everyone just stare at her? She had replayed that scene over a hundred times in her mind.

When she returned home from D.C. and walked into her gender studies class at Sanger University, she was hailed as a hero. Her professor was super supportive. He led her fellow students in giving her a standing ovation. He made her feel better when he said he was glad it wasn't him at the microphone answering those questions.

Much to her surprise, Celeste was given the Social Democrats Profile in Courage award. Soon thereafter, she made the cover of Sundial magazine as Sundial's Woman of the Year. All of those events meant that her face was everywhere—on TV, in newspapers, magazines and online, even on a billboard overlooking I-85. It was no wonder the woman jogging in front of Mrs. Jankowicz's house recognized her from somewhere.

After saying goodbye to the jogger and her babies, and after telling Mrs. Jankowicz to have a good day, Celeste walked back into her yard. She kissed Aurora on the nose after wiping her fingers across her puppy face to brush away a crepe myrtle bloom. She stepped onto the street so she could open the mailbox. *What wondrous junk mail did I get today?* She pulled out a stack of advertisements, catalogs, and credit card offers. How had the postman managed to fit all of this in there?

Adjusting her hold on Aurora, Celeste leafed through the stack. One letter in particular caught her eye. It didn't have a bulk mailing stamp pre-printed on the envelope. Someone had addressed it by hand. How unusual to have a letter written by hand. After walking back inside her house and sitting down in a chair, she began to read out loud.

"Dear Miss Schneiderman, muh, muh, muh, saw your testimony on Capitol Hill. Muh, muh, muh. Congratulations on Sundial Woman of the Year. Muh, muh…whoa. What? Wait. Who is this?"

Celeste grabbed the envelope and looked at the return address, then compared it to the address at the bottom of the letter. *Tony Longino? The Tony Longino? Seriously?* The more she read, the more she began to hyperventilate.

"'I am the producer of an upcoming TV…' blah, blah…'South America?' Seriously? '…and I would like to discuss the possibility of you becoming a part of it'? What am I reading here? Are you kidding me right now?"

Celeste squealed with delight, jumped up from the table and ran to the bedroom to get her cell phone. Aurora sprinted after her, happy that playtime had started.

"I have got to call Trayton right now! He will not believe this!"

Chapter Four

The Brooklyn Bridge was closed. C-L-O-S-E-D. You didn't need to see a tweet, text or email alert to know something out of the ordinary was happening. You could simply close your eyes and listen to the sounds of helicopters hovering overhead, some dispatched by the NYPD and others by news stations in New York and New Jersey. You could hear someone's authoritative-sounding voice blaring out of a loudspeaker. Something very wrong had happened. At the center of it all was a man named Clarence Humberton.

The National Union of Electrical Workers Local 732 had a storied history of putting electricians to work. Local 732 boasted over 2,500 dues-paying members. At some point in each of those electrician's lives, they had been given the official explanation of the benefits they received in exchange for their dues. Shop steward Clarence Humberton, a New York native, was just the man to school newbies on the benefits of union membership. Explaining benefits was a task he performed with relish as he obtained their signatures on the automatic payroll deduction form required for their payment of dues.

Clarence stood six feet four inches tall. He tipped the scales at three hundred thirty-seven pounds according to the notes written by the nurse in his cardiologist's office. When the nurse reviewed his questionnaire and asked him if he meant to check the "No" box next to "Tobacco use," Clarence asked her if she had ever seen him smoke. She admitted she had not. The nurse asked him if he had been in close quarters with someone who was smoking, maybe in an elevator, because his clothes had the distinct smell of smoke. Clarence informed her that checking this particular box was a mere formality that he needed in order to comply with the health insurance company's requirement for continuing his life insurance coverage. When she uttered the words "truthfulness and honesty," the patient, who was there for the sole purpose of getting a favorable opinion in writing from a doctor about his heart, decided to demonstrate the power of his lungs. All the staff and all the patients in every room on the third floor of the Brooklyn Well-Being Park jumped at the sound of his voice. The volume of the invective gushing out of his mouth was terrifying.

The startled cardiologist, who was in the midst of seeing another patient in an adjoining room, rushed out into the hallway where he ran headlong into the fleeing nurse. His visit with Clarence lasted no more than ninety seconds. When Clarence learned that the doctor did not seem to fully grasp that it was a mere formality for him to give a checkmark on a form required by an insurance company, he had no further use for the doctor. As he stormed out of the office, Clarence informed every patient in the waiting room that the doctor and his nurse had both been consigned to the pits of hell.

Clarence was an unapologetic cigar smoker. If someone had a problem with Clarence smoking next to them in a restaurant or in an adjoining restroom stall and made the mistake of voicing an objection, they had better be prepared to endure the tongue-lashing of their lives. The recipient of his verbal abuse would be scarred for life. Clarence, on the other hand, would barely remember the incident by the time he walked in his house demanding that his wife explain why dinner was taking so long. Some might say he bullied those who dared to disagree with him. Clarence preferred to think of himself as simply being exceptionally persuasive.

The first and most valuable benefit of union membership was one that Clarence didn't share with the rank and file. The money taken off the top of the electricians' paychecks paid him and the rest of the union leadership combined salaries of $3.75 million a year. It wasn't a hard sell to persuade men to pay money to work. If any of them thought it unfair to basically work one day a month for no pay, none of them voiced that opinion to shop steward Clarence Humberton. If they had, they would have been told, at a volume with a magnitude on the order of a Delta DC-10 at the moment of takeoff, that without the representation of Local 732, general contractors wouldn't hire anyone but the cheapest blanking Mexicans that had just crossed over the border with no skills other than shucking corn and flipping blanking tortillas. If their eardrums weren't damaged beyond repair by that point, they would have been further educated by Clarence Humberton, shop steward for Local 732, that if they wanted to save money on their precious paycheck by not paying union dues, they could pay for their own blanking hospital bills if their arm got chopped off and they were disabled for life.

Clarence wasn't stupid. He knew all about mandatory workers compensation coverage that employees were entitled to receive from their employers, whether they were a union member or not. The men who came into his office for a job, however, weren't lawyers. They came to work. They knew circuits and transformers and breakers and switches and voltage and amps and ohms and conduits. If the shop steward said that without Local 732 the general contractors and government entities who hired them wouldn't pay their medical bills if they got hurt on the job, then that's the way it was. Anyone who tried to convince them otherwise was viewed as the enemy. The union was family. If you aren't in the family, you and your opinions can't be trusted.

On this particularly beautiful autumn afternoon, however, the last thing on Clarence Humberton's mind was workers' comp. In the words of New York Mayor Katzenberg's Chief of Staff, "We have a situation." The situation had a name. That name was Clarence Humberton.

The collective bargaining negotiations on the Brooklyn Bridge reconstruction/upgrade contract had been especially tough, even by New York standards. The steelworkers, the pipefitters and the machinists presented a united front along with the electrical workers. If the City of New York wanted first class work, it needed to come loose with first class coinage. The members knew the value of this contract, the years of work that would be provided, and the importance to not only the people of New York, but also to the people who came from all corners of the world to cross that bridge.

The show of union strength had been met with resistance, however. The City had dug its heels in. Clarence's authority and ability to make things happen had been challenged, and he didn't like it. Not one bit. Local 732 had played a game of chicken with the government, and for once, the City didn't flinch. The value of the contract, and the uncharacteristic slowdown in work that had manifested itself during negotiations had given the City leverage it normally didn't have. The electrical workers needed that contract, and the members didn't have the time to hold out for protracted bargaining. With pressure from thousands of blue-collar workers squeezing him, Clarence made the concession he swore he would never make. Clarence had waived payment of double overtime pay when work was required on a weekend. He caved. The Mayor didn't see it that way. He was completely exasperated with all of the concessions made to Local 732. Time and a half was fair in the Mayor's mind. But in Clarence's mind, he had sold out and had his rear end handed to him by the Mayor. Clarence had sworn oath after oath to make the Mayor pay. He didn't know how or when, but he knew one thing. One day, that blanking Mayor would pay.

Today, at last, that day had come.

It was Friday, October 13th. The electricity buzzing in the air was loud enough for the crabs at the bottom of New York Harbor to hear it. It was as though the Statue of Liberty had mainlined a twelve-pack of energy drinks directly into her copper and cast-iron veins. Why all the excitement? Why was all of New York going crazy?

The Yankees were in the World Series. Nothing could excite like October baseball in Yankee Stadium.

There was a problem for the Yankees fans who were members of Local 732, however. The bridge project was at a critical stage. There were problems on-site which required round-the-clock work, including weekends. Teams of electricians were being called in on an emergency basis at the worst possible time. Some of these men were season ticket holders who had been given the opportunity to purchase World Series tickets. Most diehard fans would pay any price to see the Yankees play in October. Many of the members of Local 732 had paid that price. If you try to tell one of those excited men that he must jettison those plans and go to work just before the first pitch, however, don't expect to survive with all of your limbs intact. Best to call him on the phone than to deliver that news in person.

Sal Monteverde, a dues-paying member of Local 732, had worn his Dante Sanborn jersey for the past twenty-four hours. All he could think about was walking in that stadium. He was not going to change out of that jersey for anybody or anything. When his cell phone began vibrating and the Caller ID displayed the name of Clarence Humberton, Sal debated about whether to answer. It was late afternoon. He had been drinking since 9:30 that morning. Not answering the phone carried risks. His shop steward lived two blocks away and drove past Sal's house at least twice a day every single day of the year. Clarence could see whether Sal's car was in the driveway. He could see from the street whether Sal's lights were on or off. How would you like to know your boss knew when you were awake and when you were asleep? The timing of the phone call was odd. A feeling of dread came over Sal as he watched the number displayed on his phone. The Boss was calling. Reluctantly, he answered the phone.

"Yes, sir?"

The news his boss delivered was bad. As a matter of fact, it could not have been worse. Clarence told him he was being called into work. Right now. Clarence did not ask Sal if it was okay or if he had other plans. Sal, emboldened by the alcohol coursing through his body, cried out in protest. "I've got a ticket to the game!" Clarence was unsympathetic. "So do I," was all he said. With that, the call ended. Sal was left staring in disbelief at the cell phone he wished he had never touched.

Sal changed clothes, sobbing as he folded Dante Sanborn's jersey and laid it on the dresser. The work shirt with his name "Sal" on a patch over his left breast pocket felt like sulfuric acid on his skin. How could life treat him this way? He wavered between tears and screams. He couldn't afford not to show up for work. He would be fired instantly. He had twenty-something-thousand dollars in credit card debt that he would never be able to repay if he lost his job. Worse, just last year he had to swallow his pride and beg his brother-in-law for a loan to cover his gambling debt after he nearly died in a tragic single-car accident due to a clearly-cut brake line when Sal had been late on his payments for two months. No one would believe that he was really sick if he tried to call in, least of all his boss. He was stuck.

Sal Monteverde hated life. His unsteady right hand had trouble inserting the key into the ignition of his 2003 Chevrolet Impala. He managed to back out of his driveway without incident but immediately found himself in the midst of a traffic jam. He pounded the dashboard and shook the steering wheel as he wailed with no one to hear. Sal only thought he knew how bad it was going to be. Little did he know what lay in store for him.

After what seemed like hours, Sal finally made it to the job site. He parked, struggled out of his car and stumbled his way to the stretch of bridge where his work had left off the day before. The honking horns and screaming voices from the line of cars along the bridge was deafening. He spotted a steelworker standing near a cherry picker. Sal's cherry picker, to be precise. Sal made his way to it, muttering with every step. Sal's job was to run power to a light-up message board that could not be lifted and set into place until the steelworker finished welding a crossbeam bracing on which to mount it.

Much to Sal's chagrin, the steelworker appeared to be taking his own sweet time in completing his task. Didn't he know that the quicker he finished, the quicker Sal could do his part and leave? Maybe, just maybe, he could make the last couple of innings if he hurried.

Sal tried and failed to get the attention of the steelworker. He grabbed a handle, climbed up in the cherry picker bucket and waved both his hands. Though he knew he shouldn't, Sal looked down at the water below for an instant. He shouldn't have done it. Looking at the sheer drop made his head swim. He quickly looked back up at the steelworker.

The far right lane was already closed, but the use of the cherry picker required the lane closure to be extended further back. A different worker dutifully grabbed a stack of orange cones and began placing them at the beginning of the merge so as to funnel cars away from the right lane sooner. Lane closures were bad under any circumstances, but this lane closure was on a whole other level. It was slowing a solid line of diehard Yankees' fans on their way to the first game of the World Series down to a crawl.

One driver in particular was outraged to the point of being apoplectic. His horn was insufficient to adequately express his anger, so he got out of his car, slammed the door and stomped up to the first worker he could see. The angry driver was huge, standing six feet four inches tall and weighing three hundred thirty-seven pounds. He happened to be none other than the venerable shop steward for Local 732, Clarence Humberton. Clarence had a World Series game to get to, and this bridge project, which had been a thorn in his side from its inception, was making him late.

A familiar booming voice made Sal jump. When Sal turned and looked down, he and Clarence locked eyes. Clarence screamed Sal's name. Well, it actually wasn't his name. It was a body part. Nevertheless, Sal knew who he was referring to.

"Why aren't you working? Why aren't you working?"

Sal gulped, his voice trembling.

"I can't connect to the sign until the man of steel over there finishes his welding. Until then I can't do anything."

"Crank up that machine and lift that line into place!"

Sal was confused. Couldn't Clarence see that the steelworker was still welding? What was he supposed to mount the sign to? He couldn't connect the power and just let the sign dangle in the air. Nevertheless, Clarence repeated his instructions, this time loud enough for the steelworker and every occupant of every car within a hundred yards to hear.

"Crank that machine and lift that sign into place, and then get the *(expletive)* cherry picker out of the *(expletive)* road so me and every other driver on this *(expletive)* bridge can get to the *(expletive)* game!"

Sal was generally an obedient man—even more so when given orders by Clarence Humberton. This order, however, was one he couldn't obey. He couldn't lift a sign weighing at least a hundred and fifty pounds over a line of cars twenty feet below and hang it using only an energized line wrapped around a half-finished crossbeam without a mount. That would be insane. If the line snapped, which was highly likely, the sign would kill whoever it landed on. Even if he wanted to do it, which he didn't, Sal was in no condition to operate heavy machinery. The red liquid coursing through his veins was equal parts blood and brew. As badly as Sal didn't want to say it, he had to say it.

"I can't do it, boss, not until the man finishes with the mount on the beam."

Clarence was furious. He had not been the actual on-site job superintendent on a project in years, but in the blink of an eye he reverted back to the universally-feared slave driver he once had been. If his underling wouldn't do it, Clarence would do it himself. Growling like a brown bear awakened too early from hibernation, he took five or six menacing steps and climbed up on the nearest tire of the cherry picker. Sal retreated in self-defense. While doing so, Sal leaned too far backwards and lost his balance. Rather than falling right where he was, Sal attempted to pull out of the fall by running backwards in a vain attempt to regain his balance. Unfortunately for Sal, he didn't make it.

Sal Monteverde flipped backwards over the railing and fell one hundred thirty feet off the Brooklyn Bridge into the East River.

Two things saved Sal's life. Number one, a very surprised tug boat captain happened to be no more than fifty yards upstream from his point of entry. Number two, being drunk as a skunk made Sal loose as a goose. He was too sauced to be tightened up. The water was much kinder and gentler to a limp body than if he had been tightfisted and screaming all the way down.

Kim Jeun Lee, a teenaged girl bored out of her mind due to the traffic jam, heard men yelling and stuck her phone out of the car window just in time to capture it all on video. The video went viral within minutes of her posting it on social media.

How a news crew landed a helicopter onto the Brooklyn Bridge that quickly was a complete mystery. Nevertheless, here stood a breathless, live, on-the-scene news reporter with a microphone shoved in the face of Clarence Humberton, asking for an eyewitness account of the near-fatal fall. Clarence was in no mood for interviews, however. He had a World Series game to get to.

Crowds of onlookers jumped out of their cars to peer over the bridge, trying to get a glimpse of the hapless victim. Much to Clarence's dismay, the steelworker, whose slowness was to blame for the entire mess, had stopped working so he could spectate himself. Clarence couldn't leave for the game until he connected and hung the display sign, and he couldn't do that until the steelworker finished welding the brace. His frustration having reached a boiling point, Clarence pushed past the news reporter and bellowed at the man to get back to work. The steelworker did not know the man yelling at him, but after hearing his tone, he did not intend to debate with him about the procedures required for compliance with O.S.H.A. regulations following a workplace injury. Instead, he got back to work and at a much faster pace than before.

The news reporter, knowing a golden opportunity had presented itself, stuck the microphone back in front of Clarence's face. She asked him to please tell everyone what happened here. Clarence, who did not have a diplomatic bone in his body, gave his blue-oathed version of events in a voice loud enough for everyone in the viewing audience to hear him from their own front stoop without the aid of technology.

"You want to know what just happened here? You want to report the true story? I'll tell you what happened here. His honor, the Mayor, just hocked a giant loogie and spit it in the eye of every worker in New York by refusing to pay a man a decent wage to work on the night of the World Series; that's what happened here. So, Mayor, this message is for you. You almost got a man killed here tonight by insisting we had to stick this sign up in the air right in the middle of a million people trying to get to the World Series, like anybody wants to read a sign on their way to the World Series. As for me and every other member of Local 732, we live up to our promises. I'm going to put this sign up in the air like you wanted, but if you want any other work done this weekend, you can get your fat butt out of your cushy seat behind first base at Yankee Stadium and do it your own self!"

Except Clarence injected many more words, none of which were suitable for children's bedtime stories. The wide-eyed news reporter hoped her producer had the five-second delay in place and was bleeping out the coarse language.

Meanwhile, Clarence, whose blood pressure was skyrocketing well above his normal 187/105, climbed up on the cherry picker and powered it up. Throwing caution to the wind, Clarence began to lift himself, the sign and the line into the air. He had no intention of waiting for the brace to be welded in place. That was not in the electrical scope of work, and besides, that could take all night. Clarence was being paid to work, not to wait.

The steelworker, perched on his own lift, saw the line and the bucket coming up to where he was welding and screamed an oath at the irrational man lifting it. Clarence did not really intend to touch the line to the other man's machine. He only intended to scare him, hopefully motivating him to hurry up. Clarence decided to rise above the steelworker so that he could look down on him as he worked. He wanted the man to feel his eyes upon him. The steelworker's yelling only spurred him on.

Clarence knew that somewhere above him there was a high voltage powerline, but he was not concerned. He planned to stop his upward movement before he got close. Clarence was not a skilled cherry picker operator, however. His fingers, each the size of a swollen Cuban cigar, fumbled at the controls. Clarence also did not fully grasp the concept of arcing. Physical contact is not required to close a circuit with an overhead powerline when a large metal object dares to come within fifteen feet, fourteen feet, thirteen feet, twelve feet...

The kaboom from the arc was deafening. A blinding flash of fire lit up the night sky. Three hundred thousand volts of unrestrained lightning created a fireworks display worthy of any Fourth of July. The heat set every single one of Clarence's tires on fire. The three nearest cars were instantly set on fire. Thankfully, the occupants of each of those cars were standing in a loose cluster another fifty feet or so away from their cars looking over the railing to see how far Sal Monteverde had fallen.

Clarence, terrified at what he had just done, took the gamble of pushing the control lever down. It still worked. He began his descent. *Thank god,* he thought. *Thank god. Go, go, go, go.* When Clarence got enough space between line and machine, the arc and the noise stopped. By some miracle, Clarence was not killed. He was alive and breathing.

The same could not be said for roughly twelve dozen unsuspecting New York City pigeons that had, only seconds earlier, been happily perched on the transmission line, watching cars from high overhead. They were now flash-fried and smoking. When the arc vanished, so did the electrical bond keeping their birdie feet glued to the powerline. In near-perfect unison, twelve dozen pigeons lost their death grips and plunged to the snarled traffic below. Bird bodies splattered on hoods, roofs and windshields like a barrage of mortar shells.

The breathless news reporter was in mid-sentence when a pound-and-a-half pigeon struck the very end of the lens on her videographer's camera, snapping it off like a breadstick. A competing news station reporter, somewhat glum at having not been there in time to catch all of the interview, suddenly became the man of the hour when his videographer caught it all on tape.

Clarence surveyed the scene. He saw a mixed bag. On the one hand, car tires were on fire, a cherry picker was destroyed, pigeons littered the ground, and some guy was wailing about his camera. On the other hand, Sal was okay after having been picked up by a tug boat, and the siren from a fire truck told him the emergencies would soon be handled.

Clarence tapped his shirt pocket and felt the tickets. Two golden tickets to the greatest show on earth. The World Series. His best friend, Manny Cicarello, was probably already standing in front of the gate looking for him. Manny couldn't get in without Clarence. He could feel the paper clip binding them together through the cloth. His beloved Yankees needed him. Clarence checked his watch. One hour until the first pitch. Clarence looked at his truck. He was now pretty much in the clear. All the cars behind him were no longer trying to go because of the smoke from the tires. The traffic ahead of him had cleared. Clarence began to debate his options out loud to no one in particular.

"What good is my car doing sitting there? The fire truck needs a place to park. The cars behind me need a clear path to go through. I think...the best thing I can do is..."

With that, Clarence Humberton got in his car and drove to Yankee Stadium.

On the opposite side of Yankee Stadium another spectacle was developing. While people were flooding into almost every gate leading into the stadium, there was one at a dead standstill. Instead of hurrying in to get to their seats, the people standing outside that particular gate stood unmoving, pointing up, transfixed by what they saw.

The Spider Monkey had that effect on people.

Robert David DaVinci was born exactly twenty-two years ago today. His mom and dad knew he was different from the time he was old enough to walk, for this reason—he didn't walk. If there was a way to climb to his destination, little Robert would climb. The principal of Robert's elementary school never dreamed he would be calling a parent to inform her that her second grader was at the top of a telephone pole, but so it was with Robert. He was banned from attending school fieldtrips when, as a fifth grader, he climbed to the top of the gorilla enclosure at the San Diego Zoo in front of thirty-five screaming children and two teachers who were promptly placed on administrative leave immediately upon their return to the school.

As a middle schooler, Robert had a lesser but nevertheless strong passion for skateboarding. Some kid at the skate park, in awe of Robert's skateboarding tricks, gave him the name that would stick with him the rest of his life.

Robert David DaVinci became "Boedy Da."

In many ways, Robert David DaVinci vanished that day, never to be seen or heard from again. Instead, he became a legend, larger than life and unlike anyone his friends, family, teachers and neighbors had ever seen.

Boedy's climbing wasn't malicious, despite what his teachers might think. He had a joy about him. Climbing was who he was. He didn't need to climb—he had to. Weekend excursions to climb rocks and cliffs slowly began to bleed over into Mondays. Mondays began to blur into Tuesdays. Saturday start times began to back up into Fridays. Boedy's parents couldn't call their teenage son and scold him back into the civilized world because he didn't carry a phone. They couldn't physically get to him even if they knew where he could be found. The terrain and heights wouldn't allow them to do it even if they tried.

Eventually, Boedy's mom and dad found peace with their son's path, even though it was not a path they would have chosen for him. They were sad they would never attend a high school graduation ceremony or see him wear a button-down shirt on his way to a job interview, but they took solace in the fact that their son was happy with his life. He wasn't a mooch. When he needed money, he would pick up a job renting jet skis at the beach, or baiting hooks and cleaning fish for the captain of a party boat. He would work just long enough to get the money he needed to tide him over while he pursued the thing he truly loved which was...

Free-climbing buildings. Tall buildings. No belays. No crampons. No ropes. No nets. Just Boedy.

Boedy entered the public consciousness when he climbed the thirty-floor Bonaventure Hotel in Los Angeles. He entered the ranks of the elite when he climbed the sixty-floor Millennium Tower in San Francisco. He was arrested just as he started to scale the one-hundred-ten-story Willis Tower in Chicago, but everyone knew he would try again. By that point in his life, he was given another nickname whether he wanted it or not. He didn't ask for the first nickname, much less a second. Nevertheless, the public gave him a new nickname.

Spider Monkey.

When in public, Boedy shrugged off the notoriety. Privately, though, he was intensely proud of the label he had been given. The new name spurred Boedy on to even greater heights as if he needed any prodding. Once he had tackled many of the challenging climbs available in the United States, he took off on an international quest for climbs the rest of the world could offer. The Emirate of Dubai in the United Arab Emirates was the location of one of the tallest buildings in the world. It seemed to be calling his name. Boedy answered the call. He soon found himself standing atop the Marina 101 building fifteen hundred feet above the Dubai skyline, exhausted but grinning from ear to ear.

Sporting a goatee and a headful of untamable hair, Boedy's boyish good looks and roguish smile propelled him into the bright lights. He did it for the thrill, to test his body and test his mind. Money was not the goal. Nevertheless, money helped fund his passion. He decided to cash in, at least a little, by agreeing to pose for the cover of a cereal box. His picture soon graced the cereal aisle of every grocery store from California to Maine and from Florida to North

Dakota. Boedy Da, also known as the Spider Monkey, became a household name.

For his twenty-second birthday, Boedy wanted to do something special, but he didn't know quite what to do. A couple of months before his birthday, Boedy was sitting at a sports bar in London, celebrating having just gotten out of jail after free-climbing the Shard, one of the tallest buildings in Europe. Apparently there was some law against enjoying other people's buildings, Boedy mused. The TV was turned to news. Boedy was not much of a news watcher, but he did enjoy hearing the news personalities' British accents. The sports commentator began to discuss the upcoming World Series. He was a humorous guy. He was having a great time pointing out the arrogance of the Americans, who had an exclusively American baseball tournament which they had the audacity to call the "World" Series. Boedy had never been overly fond of baseball. It reduced him to yawns the few times he tried to watch a game.

This news broadcast piqued his interest, however.

The first game of the World Series was, of course, sold out. The outrageous price of aftermarket tickets was the real focus of the story. The commentator noted that baseball fans who had not been to New York City in a while would see something new. Hotel magnate Donovan Weider had just cut the ribbon for the grand opening of the Empire Palms. The newly-constructed hotel, now officially the tallest hotel in the state of New York, overlooked Yankee Stadium. The next sentence out of the commentator's mouth hit Boedy right in his adrenal gland. In his charming British accent, the commentator made an offhand remark.

"The only seats left now are next to the pigeons on top of the Empire Palms."

Upon hearing that statement, Boedy's course was set. The bartender turned around to see an empty seat where his dreadlocked customer had sat only a minute earlier. He hated, hated, dine and dash. His irritation was soothed, however, when he cleared the plate and saw ten Euros sitting next to the napkin.

Boedy had a legion of fans who followed his every move. He didn't post on social media often, but when he did, his followers analyzed every word as though they were decoding the Dead Sea Scrolls. His next post, cryptic as always, had been quintessential Boedy.

"Think I'll go watch the game."

Fast forward two weeks to the opening game of the World Series in New York. Boedy stood in front of the lobby of the Empire Palms, watching excited hotel guests make their way through the automatic sliding doors and out into the crowds streaming into Yankee Stadium. He could not see over the mass of humanity surrounding him. Standing five feet, five inches tall and weighing one hundred thirty-two pounds, Boedy's diminutive stature did not lend itself to crowds, but it was ideal for scaling impossible heights.

Boedy made his way down to the corner of the building, at times having to press himself against the stucco facade in order to continue forward progress. Every fiber of his being cried out for him to get above the crowd. *Patience, Boedy, patience*, he thought. As he lifted his eyes to search for the first handhold, an old familiar warmth began to course through his body. The corners of his mouth curled up into an irrepressible grin. This was his happy place. He did a few shoulder shrugs to prepare his muscles for what he thought would be about a forty-five to fifty-minute climb—assuming the local gendarmes did not intervene, of course.

Boedy reached his right hand back to the small pouch at his waist, which held powdered chalk, and squeezed it. Sweaty hands are the devil. While rubbing his callous-covered palms together to evenly distribute the chalk, he heard a voice behind him.

"Hey, it's the Spider Monkey! Look guys, it's the Spider Monkey!"

Boedy turned around and saw a trio of young men about his age, one of which was excitedly pointing at him. Boedy smiled and pressed an index finger to his lips. His silent message was clear. *Quiet, boys. Keep it on the down low, at least for now.* One of the onlookers glanced up at the juncture between the first floor and second floor. His brow furrowed.

"Wait. There's nothing for you to grab hold of. Hey Boedy, there's nothing to grab up there. How are you going to…?"

With no further ado, Boedy backed up two or three steps, charged forward and leaped. He did not use his hands. He parkoured. His child-sized left shoe found the side of the vertical column to his left and pushed off, propelling his body up and to his right. The instant his right shoe made contact with the side of the column to his right, he pushed off, up and to his left. He did this so quickly, back and forth with lightning-fast kicks, that he made better time going straight up than anyone below him made going horizontally. Boedy didn't use his hands until he reached the expansion joint in the stucco that marked the transition from the second to the third floor which was where the vertical columns ended. He covered that distance in less than ten seconds. His fans standing below could no longer contain their enthusiasm. Boedy was no mere mortal. He was nothing short of a superhero.

The outburst of cheers and applause from the awestruck onlookers drew the attention of every fan, vendor, stadium employee, hotel employee, cab driver and passerby within a hundred yards. At first, people wondered if some of the star players had decided to thrill the crowd by rubbing shoulders with fans while trotting into the stadium. When they saw the sea of upward-pointing fingers and followed the imaginary line with their eyes, however, they realized that wasn't it at all.

There was a man on the side of that building.

The ruckus swiftly grabbed the attention of every police officer in the vicinity. Security was heightened because of the potential for a terrorist attack at such a well-attended, high-profile event. Radios squawked and earpieces buzzed. Law enforcement officers from all levels: state, local and federal, sprang into action. Snipers, perched high atop elevated positions all around the stadium, grabbed rifles and put eyes to scopes searching for their target.

"Sniper One, do you have a visual?"

The voice of a retired Marine Corps sniper, turned private security specialist after he got out of the service, cut through the din.

"I've got eyes on him. We've got a climber. He's climbing up the northeast corner of the Empire Palms Hotel. No ropes. No one above him. No one on top of the building pulling him up. Good god, it's like I'm watching a monkey."

The sniper's superior barked,

"Give me a weapons report. What's he got on him?"

"I don't see anything, sir. No backpacks. No suicide vests. No bumps under his shirt. Baggy pants, so I can't tell about his legs. Nothing on his belt. Wait, I see something. Correction. There's something on his waist. It looks like…a little bag. Hold on, he's reaching for it."

The superior barked again.

"Do you have the shot?"

The sniper's voice was calm and even. Assessing targets in kill-or-no-kill situations was as natural as breathing for him.

"Yes, sir. He grabbed the pouch and let go and a little puff of smoke…no, not smoke. Not smoke. Powder. That's what it is. He's got a resin bag of some kind, sir. He's grabbing it to keep his fingers dry. He's climbing again. It's unbelievable, sir. This guy has got to be a professional. One of these no-ropes guys."

"No weapons? No explosives?"

"No weapons, no explosives that I can see, sir. But I can't see through his pants legs. I don't see any."

"Stay on him."

"Yes, sir."

The information was swiftly relayed to the multiple law enforcement agencies that had teamed up to keep one of the world's best-known sports venues safe. The chain of command had been worked out months in advance. The New York City Police Chief took point.

"All right, gentlemen, here's the play. Close all gates on the south side of the stadium. Clear the road in front of the Empire Palms in both directions, and block it at the first intersections to the east and to the west. I need the hotel manager to evacuate all rooms on the northeast side of the hotel, all floors. Tell him not to send them out the stadium side. I don't remember seeing balconies. Ask him if any of the rooms above the climber have windows that will open. Let's see. What else? Tell Fire we need an inflatable jump cushion down below this guy. And I want a chopper in the air, stat."

Within minutes, a black and white Bell 429 patrol helicopter sporting an NYPD shield was hovering over an eight-story parking deck adjacent to the hotel. The pilot kept it far enough away from the climber, so that the wind from the rotors would not blow him off the side of the building. A voice came through the loudspeaker at ear-splitting volume.

"Sir, come down off the building. You are not authorized. Come down off the building."

Sniper One heard a voice in his left ear. His supervisor needed a report.

"What's he doing?"

"Sir, if he heard the loudspeaker, he's not acting like it. He's still climbing. I can see his face. It looks like he's...talking. Singing. Singing. Huh, he's bobbing his head. I think the fool is listening to music. I can't see his ears to see earbuds, though. Too much hair."

Boedy loved reggae. It made him think of Jamaica, white sand, palm trees, bright smiles, dark skin, and a life slowed down to the ideal pace. Ideal for Boedy, anyway. His earbuds delivered smooth Jamaican reggae that relaxed his mind, relaxed his body and blocked out all the distractions of the world. His earbuds could not block out a New York City police helicopter, however.

"Sir, he stopped climbing. He's looking back at the chopper."

Fifteen minutes later, a very unhappy Boedy was back down near the bottom, his inexhaustible fingertips gripping the expansion joint between the second and third floors. He let go with one hand, still gripping tightly with the other, dangling in mid-air. He looked down at the Fire Chief and stuck his thumb in the air, a quizzical look on his face. The Fire Chief thought he understood. He stuck his thumb in the air and nodded at Boedy.

A smile appeared on Boedy's face. He kicked off the building like it was a high dive, did a perfect triple backflip and landed in the center of the inflatable jump cushion. A roar of approval filled the stadium as thousands of fans, glued to their cell phones watching live coverage from a dozen different action news reporters, watched the Spider Monkey stick the landing. As Boedy disappeared deep into the top air chamber, law enforcement officers swarmed in from all sides. The fans booed when the Spider Monkey was handcuffed and escorted into the back of a waiting patrol car. Once the car door closed, however, cheers, applause and laughter came from every corner. What a fantastic show, and the game hadn't even started!

The police chief, who had been holding his breath for the past half hour, finally exhaled. Everyone in the command center applauded, and everyone within reach clapped him on the back. Situation handled. Convinced that the daredevil was alone and the excitement was over, the chief sent the helicopter back to the helipad and gave the order to reopen the streets. Game time was pushed back an hour so fans had a chance to make it into the stadium by the first pitch.

Clarence Humberton and Manny Cicarello walked into the stadium just before the end of the first inning. Not so for everyone else who had been behind him back on the Brooklyn Bridge.

As expected, Clarence was thrilled watching his Yankees taking it to the Marlins. By the top of the third, however, what little conscience he had began to nag at him. *Maybe I shouldn't have left the cherry picker on the bridge*, he thought. *Then again, it wasn't like I could move it. The tires were on fire, for god's sake.*

A woman sitting near Clarence, who had been staring at her phone more than the game, suddenly pointed at Clarence.

"Hey, here's the guy who was just on the news! The guy on the bridge!"

Heads turned and necks craned from people sitting in every row within earshot of the woman, each person straining to see who she was talking about. Clarence told her to mind her business and watch the game. When a man seated in the row in front of him asked if he was the guy on the news, Clarence knew he had to think fast.

"Do I look like I just climbed a building? Because I can tell you I didn't just climb a building. So, why don't you sit your butt down and watch some baseball?"

Except Clarence added several salty words to his reply. Much to Clarence's irritation, people began to stand up and point their phones at him, snapping pictures and taking video. He suddenly felt naked and vulnerable. He didn't like feeling that way. About that time, with the bases loaded and one out, Dante Sanborn turned an impossible double play to end the inning. The crowd went wild. The exuberant celebration that followed all but erased the unpleasant thoughts from his mind.

Unfortunately for Clarence, the thoughts returned in full force during the seventh inning stretch. Four of New York City's finest paid a visit to the seats reserved for the season ticket holders from Local 732. Clarence didn't go down without a fight. The wild wrestling match that followed not only didn't help Clarence avoid jail, but it added several charges, such as resisting arrest, obstruction of justice and assaulting a police officer, not to mention the civil suit that would soon follow as a result of Clarence losing his balance during the struggle and falling on top of a woman selling ice cream, breaking her arm.

The widespread confusion about the night's events was comical. Wild stories abounded. The Spider Monkey jumped off the Brooklyn Bridge. The Spider Monkey saved a man trying to commit suicide. The Spider Monkey got electrocuted. A man saved the Spider Monkey with a cherry picker. The man who saved the Spider Monkey got electrocuted. There was a terrorist at the game. There was a terrorist on the bridge. There was a terrorist at the Empire Palms. The Spider Monkey stopped a terrorist. Every wrong story was repeated as fact as soon as it surfaced. People could not get enough.

According to Nielsen ratings, when you combined the number of viewers tuned in to the actual game with those watching news stations reporting live from the scene during the game, this was one of the best nights in television history.

Later that night, a subdued Boedy Da sat on a cot in a holding cell in the Brooklyn Detention Complex, quietly whistling his favorite reggae song. He had smiled his best smile when the lady told him to stand in front of her camera, toes on the blue tape, for his mug shot. She told him to stop smiling when it was time to turn for the profile. He didn't understand, but okay. He knew he wouldn't be in for long. He had been through this before, though not here.

Boedy stopped whistling when a frighteningly loud voice began echoing through the hallway. Somebody was angry. That somebody was coming closer. He heard three sets of footsteps approaching. Boedy stood and moved to the back of the cell. A guard rounded the corner and began to unlock the cell door. Boedy's heart sank. In walked a giant of a man in the midst of a tirade that continued unabated after the door was locked behind him. Presently, the enraged man turned around to see who was in the cell with him.

"What are you looking at, pipsqueak?"

The next afternoon, by the time Boedy walked out of jail, he knew two things. Number one: The man in the cell with him was named Clarence Humberton. Number two: He would do everything within his power to never, ever see Clarence Humberton again.

Hundreds of miles away, Bert Redmond was calling G for the third time that day. He knew G was on vacation out west in the middle of nowhere, but he had to come within range of a cell tower at some point. His timing was good. The third time was the charm. Bert heard the phone stop ringing.

"Hello?"

"Dude, would you answer your phone every now and again? You act like you're on vacation or something! Don't you know your boy Bert can't survive twenty-four hours without hearing the golden tones of his bestest buddy G? Has anyone told you you're a beautiful man today?"

G grinned despite himself. The entertainment value of listening to Bert's nonsense made their business partnership rewarding in more ways than simply financial.

"Bert, when are you going to get a real job?"

"What do you think I'm doing? Saying dumb stuff *is* my job! People pay me to do this! Hey, speaking of getting paid, tell me you watched the World Series last night."

G coughed.

"Sorry. Dust in my throat. Hold on."

G drank from a bottle of water while Bert waited. Finally he spoke.

"Okay, sorry. It's so dry out here. Just toured the Alamo. Dust flying everywhere. No, I didn't. I'm not a big baseball guy. Why?"

Bert laughed. G liked when Bert laughed. It often meant good things.

"G, we've got not one, but two contenders."

"Cool. Well, you know what to do. Call Tony, and you guys do your thing. Sign them up."

Bert laughed again.

"Oh, I plan to. I'll have to wait a minute, though. They've got to get out of jail first."

G smiled to himself. Whatever Bert was talking about sounded interesting. Right when Bert started to explain it, though, his voice became glitchy, cutting in and out. G was only able to hear every third word or so. He tried to tell Bert he was losing him, but the beep he heard next let him know they had already been disconnected. Oh well. No big deal. Bert would tell Tony. G would be sitting next to Tony on an airplane bound for Brazil in two days. He would hear it all from Tony then.

Jail? They're in jail?

When it came to Bert and Tony, nothing surprised G anymore. He wasn't worried. As a matter of fact, the more he thought about it, the better it sounded. The more outrageous the better.

Chapter Five

From an early age, Annaliese Parkman was destined for great things. As an elementary school student, she entered the county science fair with a project demonstrating how to harness and store electricity. She won. While that was noteworthy in and of itself, her victory was made even more remarkable by the fact that her teacher/adviser failed to read the rule that said the science fair was only open to high school students. The local newspaper's headline said, "Little girl shocks the science world!"

A few years later, Annaliese reached high school, where jocks were kings, cheerleaders were queens and smart kids were jesters at best. She overcame the compulsion to conform and owned her geekiness. With a passion marked by endearing awkwardness, she persuaded her peers that excelling at academics was cool. She rode a wave of unlikely popularity into a successful campaign for class president. Once she experienced the intoxication of politics, everything changed. Her life's course was set. After graduation, she set her sights on a higher office. A much higher office.

On Annaliese Parkman's thirtieth birthday, the minimum age allowed under the state constitution, she became the youngest Governor in Connecticut history. She eschewed standard business attire for women. There were no silk blouses, knee-length skirts or one-inch heels in her closet. She wore slacks, button-down shirts with the sleeves rolled up, ties which were never tightened and colorful socks which became her trademark.

One of Governor Parkman's campaign promises was to stem the rising tide of gun violence through "common sense gun control measures." She acknowledged that Connecticut citizens had a constitutional right to own guns as long as they weren't felons, mentally ill or under prosecution for domestic violence. She acknowledged they had the right to carry guns. Nevertheless, she could see no reason why the owners could not be required to carry the guns in a state-approved lock box with the gun and ammunition stored separately. The gun rights activists howled in protest, arguing that her law was the equivalent of repealing the Second Amendment.

Ignoring her critics, Governor Parkman placed the Keep and Safely Bear Arms amendment, as she called it, on the ballot. Despite NRA opposition and the naysaying constitutional scholars who declared it would never hold up in court, the measure passed. Some called it controversial—she called it progressive and long overdue. She predicted there would be backlash from the cavemen, as she called them, but she could deal with backlash.

What she could not have predicted before she took office was the puppy and the pizza.

Jamus Riggs was a serial killer. According to a jury of his peers, Riggs tortured and killed fourteen pizza deliverymen in three states most of whom were in Connecticut. Each of the victims had their right index finger severed and shoved down their throats. Experts theorized he was triggered when they rang his doorbell. He single-handedly shut down the food delivery business in Connecticut. When he was captured, he had a stack of boxes containing petrified pizza from each of the restaurants where the victims worked. Aside from the testimony of a terrified teenager who barely escaped with his life after delivering Riggs a meat lover's supreme, however, there was precious little physical evidence connecting him to the murders. His defense attorney argued that ordering pizza and not eating it was not a crime in the state of Connecticut, nor was owning a limb lopper which was found in his garage. The jury disagreed, convicted Riggs and unanimously voted in favor of the death penalty.

Governor Parkman was an outspoken opponent of capital punishment. She successfully strong-armed the state legislature into abolishing the death penalty in her first year of office. The problem she faced was that the abolition of the death penalty was proactive only. It did not retroactively undo lawfully-imposed death sentences affirmed on appeal prior to the effective date of repeal. The timing was problematic for Governor Parkman. The Connecticut Supreme Court affirmed the death sentence for Jamus Riggs by opinion dated June the 13th, two weeks before the July 1st effective date of the statute abolishing capital punishment. Riggs was literally the last person who could ever be executed in the state. The only hope Riggs had to avoid lethal injection was clemency from Governor Parkman.

The political pressure was enormous. The usual crowd of anti-death penalty protesters gathered around the state capitol as the execution date drew near. This was no ordinary death row inmate, though. Riggs was a serial killer. Governor Parkman's left-leaning base knew she would be tempted to deny the request for clemency. They camped out in front of the Capitol. Rabid law-and-order types demanding justice joined the fray, many wearing pizza delivery uniforms and displaying messages scrawled on pizza boxes. A man wearing a giant bloody finger costume repeatedly headbutted the doorframe at the entrance to the Capitol, soon to be chased by a compatriot wielding a giant pair of cardboard limb loppers. Anarchists saw their opportunity to inject mayhem and began showing up at night wearing all black and throwing projectiles. Suddenly there was a full-blown three-ring circus in front of the Capitol.

When the shouting matches escalated into fistfights, and the police began making arrests of her constituents, Governor Parkman issued an executive order prohibiting the police from carrying guns, tasers or tear gas. She told the press she did not want to risk bloodshed. "We will keep and safely bear arms just as we ask our citizens to do. Weapons have no place in the company of peaceful protests." This infuriated the police union, who had been on the receiving end of a hailstorm of bricks, bottles and fireworks.

Governor Parkman felt trapped. She faced the reality that the problem would not go away by ignoring it. She announced her decision by releasing a written statement, short and to the point. The language was as follows:

"The Office of the Governor of Connecticut has considered the clemency request of Jamus Riggs. The Governor recognizes there are reasons why the death sentence should be carried out. The Supreme Court of Connecticut has affirmed the imposition of the death penalty. The families of the victims have each lost a loved one, but killing another will not bring them back. In deference to the people of Connecticut, the Governor will insure that the spirit of the amendment to the Constitution of the state of Connecticut abolishing the death penalty will be given full force and effect. A man who has spent over two decades of his life on death row has been punished enough. Jamus Riggs is hereby granted a full pardon and is to be released on the first legally allowable date."

The outcry from her critics was deafening. The victims' families, friends and loved ones, surrounded by their supporters who were outraged at the miscarriage of justice, camped out on the front lawn of the Governor's mansion. The Governor was understandably frightened by the angry mobs that surrounded her home. The warring factions were teetering on violence.

One evening during the siege of her home, while driving home after a long day at work, Governor Parkman began to make the right hand turn to pull into her driveway. She was distracted by an Antifa member brandishing a tire iron. Not wanting to run over him, she tried to steer her powder blue convertible around him but while looking at him on her right, she failed to look at the brick mailbox on her left. A sharp-edged brick tore a hole in the sidewall of her front left tire and bent the hubcap. She didn't want to back up because of the people behind her, and she couldn't drive forward without backing up away from the mailbox.

Frantic to get inside her house and away from the mob, she grabbed her purse and started to jump out. In her hurry, however, she failed to grab both of her purse straps, resulting in one strap getting hooked on the gear shifter and pulling out of her hand. When it did, a terrible thing happened.

Annaliese's concealed subcompact 9mm pistol dropped out of her purse. When the pistol hit the pavement, the gun discharged. When it did, the unthinkable happened. A 9mm bullet traveling 1,100 feet per second exploded out of the muzzle of the Governor's bouncing pistol and killed a two year-old K-9 police dog named "Blue." The nation's most strident anti-gun Governor not only owned a gun, she kept it loaded.

Annaliese never recovered. She was called many things by her detractors, but "Parkman the Puppy Killer" was the name that stuck. Pictures of Blue the police dog, with the words "Pardon me," were plastered on signs and t-shirts not only in Connecticut but across the United States. Every single day until she resigned early in her third year in office, anonymous donors ordered pizzas in the name of Jamus Riggs to be delivered both to her home and to the Capitol. Her career in politics was over.

Even the darkest storm cloud eventually runs out of water. So it was for Annaliese Parkman. A year and a half after she resigned, the former Governor of Connecticut dropped out of the news altogether. The world got quiet for her.

G and Tony flew to Atlanta one weekend to visit with their business partner Bert Redmond. When Bert's wife Beth casually suggested they order pizza, she inadvertently lit the fuse on her husband's silly side. Bert lifted an imaginary phone to his ear and began an impromptu one-sided dialogue with an imaginary pizza employee.

"Yes, this will be for delivery. I'd like the Annaliese Parkman Meatlover's Supreme, with puppy, pupperoni and parmesan cheese, hold the fingernails. Now are your pizzas oven-baked or electrocuted?"

Tony tried not to laugh, but he couldn't hold it in. Bert continued his imaginary conversation.

"Yes, can you tell me the ring size of your delivery guy? Wow, fat fingers. Does he play piano? He doesn't? Good. Okay, so could you ask him if he ever needs to count higher than nine?"

Tony burst out in laughter. Beth scolded Tony as he was wiping tears from his eyes.

"Stop laughing at him! You are only encouraging him!"

As Tony tried to breathe, G's calm voice cut in.

"Call her."

"Who?" Tony asked.

"Governor Parkman," he answered.

Tony scoffed at the suggestion. Asking her would be a waste of time—she would never do it. G repeated his instruction to Tony. Call her. Bert handed him his imaginary phone. Tony smacked his arm away and told Beth she was married to a retard. He pulled out his own phone and began searching for a website that would provide her number. Upon finding it, Tony stepped out of the kitchen to find a quiet place to talk.

It turned out that G's hunch was right. All it took was a phone call. As a matter of fact, Annaliese Parkman was the easiest to convince out of all the potential contestants. G smiled when Tony walked back into Bert and Beth's kitchen and delivered the news.

"She's in. I can't believe it. G was right. She says she'll do it."

"I told you, Tony," G grinned. "Don't ever doubt the G."

Chapter Six

G and Tony were on their way to the first stop of a three-country scouting location mission. Other than a bit of turbulence they encountered over the Gulf of Mexico, the flight to Brazil had been smooth as silk. G had slept the entire trip, so Tony had to entertain himself. Fortunately for Tony, entertainment abounded. People-watching on the plane ride to Brazil was fascinating. Most of the passengers had glossy dark hair and beautiful olive skin. The young ladies wore very carefully-chosen outfits designed to catch the eyes of young Brazilian men. Based upon Tony's thorough and exhaustive research (consisting entirely of watching three particularly attractive girls sitting in the rows around him), they were doing an excellent job.

Tony was certain that one of the ladies had to have been a Miss Universe contestant at some point in her life. She happened to look up right when Tony turned to look behind him. Their eyes met. Tony was very pleasantly surprised when she returned his smile. What a smile! Her skin was not quite as dark as his, but he decided not to hold that against her, certain he could find it within himself to overlook it somehow.

Tony doubted she spoke English. He wondered how long it would take him to learn to speak Portuguese. He had listened to the flight attendant's almost inaudible instructions on what to do in the event of an emergency in order to pick up the sound of the language. He even memorized a couple of phrases that he heard. He had no idea what the phrases meant, of course, but if the opportunity to speak to Miss Bright Smile arose, he wanted to be ready. Telling her to use the cushion under the seat as a flotation device just might be the beginning of a beautiful relationship.

Finally, the plane touched down in Brazil. Unfortunately for Tony, a young family with babies trying to gather all their things from the overhead bin prevented him from catching Miss Bright Smile before she exited the plane. Tony and G made their way to Baggage Claim and found their driver, a rather unenthusiastic man holding a small sign with their names on it. Grabbing their bags off the carousel, they stepped out of the doors onto the street in front of the terminal.

The Brazilian heat wrapped around them like a hot towel fresh out of a clothes dryer. G didn't mind the heat so much, primarily because one of his prescription medicines kept him cold all the time. Tony, on the other hand, who was impeccably dressed in a fitted shirt and tie, could have done without it. He knew he needed to get used to the heat since he would soon be spending an extended period of time in this place, or some place just like it, in the not-too-distant future. Would it be Brazil, or Argentina, or maybe Peru? Tomorrow's scheduled meeting with the Bureau of Commerce and International Trade in Brasilia might answer that question.

The next morning, after a short night's sleep, the two men got into their driver's car and headed to a distinguished-looking government building. The translator was waiting for them in the vestibule as promised. His pleasant demeanor helped put them at ease. Tony was filled with nervous energy, whereas G was as cool as a cucumber. G needed to be at ease. He could not expect the government of Brazil to get on board with his unusual proposal if he seemed unprepared or uncertain. Fortunately, G thrived in unusual situations such as these. He oozed quiet confidence and had an uncanny ability to make people believe.

While they waited in the hallway, the translator filled them in on some significant recent developments. The head of the Bureau of Commerce and International Trade, who was slated to head up this morning's meeting, had just been asked to step down by the President of Brazil. The second in command was being promoted to a prestigious position in the President's cabinet. Tony and G looked at each other. What will this mean for their project? Do they have a chance with this much upheaval in the agency? Will they even be given the time of day?

The two men were ushered into a room with ornate decorations and comfortable couches—not the austere office G had expected. When the meeting began, the head of the Bureau was extremely polite and professional; nevertheless, his inquiry seemed a bit lackluster. He did not ask many questions about the specific details of the project. G was ready with the answers. Surprisingly, the hard questions he had prepared for never came.

G did not expect an answer right away. The size and scope of their undertaking would certainly require review by any number of government agencies all across Brazil. The amount of paperwork required, including environmental impact statements, logistical plans, travel plans, flight plans, proof of visas, vaccinations, customs, waiver of government-provided health care, health insurance, liability insurance, and of course, the payment of hefty taxes and fees, was staggering. It had taken over a year for G's team to prepare and submit the required paperwork. Every time they thought they were done, the government informed them of a new requirement, each of which sounded suspiciously like it had been invented solely for the purpose of extracting more money.

There was a very real danger of a veto, notwithstanding the fact they had dotted every "i" and crossed every "t." G did not want to be told to start over or to try again next month or next year with a whole new set of fees. G knew that the bureaucrats before him would be tempted to explore every opportunity for upping his cost of doing business. He had already thought through that possibility. That was the reason why he submitted the same proposal to three countries—Argentina, Peru and Brazil. His countermeasures were already in place. *Let them bid against each other.* If one thought they could exploit his need for their approval, they would soon find out it would not work. He had already built in leverage for himself. He would shrug his shoulders and nonchalantly tell them, "Okay, no problem. Argentina's taxes and application fees are lower than yours anyway. My investors were worried about sinking so much of their money into Brazil. You are doing me a favor. I appreciate the confirmation. Good day, gentlemen."

Much to G's surprise, however, rather than the discussion resembling an inquisition by skeptical bureaucrats, it had more of a perfunctory feel to it—a mere formality. The officials did not come across as investigators doing international due diligence. The outgoing head of the Bureau was a short-timer whose attitude was, "*Why not? I've been fired. If it all goes bad, let the new guy deal with it.*" The second in command was buoyant, almost giddy, but his conversations were not directed to the Americans in the room. His mind was elsewhere. He was being promoted to the President's cabinet, which made him a short-timer, too. If somebody wanted to film a TV show in the rainforest, sure, go right ahead. Fine with him.

When their translator turned to them with a smile and said, "Congratulations and best of luck," it took G and Tony a little while to realize what was happening. They were in. Proposal accepted. They shook hands, said their goodbyes and walked out of the building. Tony looked at his watch and whistled. Thirty-eight minutes. That was how long their meeting had lasted. It was only 8:38 a.m., and they had already done a day's work.

G and Tony were shocked at the lightning-fast approval. As they walked around the block to find their driver, they tried to fathom the reasons why the men in that room had fast-tracked their project without the inquisition they had expected. They settled on two possible explanations. First possibility—when Brazil hosted the World Cup, it had drained much of the country's resources. Instead of being the economic boon they expected, the event had almost bankrupted Rio de Janeiro. Right when Brazil needed an infusion of cash, along came G laying down large amounts of money for a proposed project that would potentially net the government a mint in tax revenue. Second possibility—it was likely something much more basic. Neither of the two bureaucrats with the power to say yes or no really cared. One had just been fired. The other was being promoted. Neither one's future hinged upon how thoroughly they scrutinized an American television producer's request to spend a few weeks in the Amazon rainforest.

What did all of that mean for G and Tony? The stars had aligned. The timing was right. Cancel the flights to Argentina and Peru.

Tony and G both had a spring in their step as the realization hit them that they didn't have to spend the next two weeks wooing, and possibly bribing, the head honchos and powers that be in Argentina and Peru. Tony spotted the car parked on a side street. Their driver, who was sound asleep behind the wheel, was startled when Tony knocked on the driver's side window, which greatly entertained Tony. Even though it was still early in the day when they got back to their room, G and Tony agreed to pop a cork and raise a toast to their success.

Jungle Money had found a home.

Chapter Seven

Before the champagne bottle was empty, the two men heard an unexpected knock at the door. Curious to see who would want to speak to them, they both answered it. Standing before them was the soon-to-be-former head of the Bureau who they recognized from the meeting. His Portuguese was excellent; unfortunately, his English was not. Their translator had been relieved of his duties once they walked out of the government building, so they were on their own here. Their ability to understand this man without a translator was a bit of a struggle. He wanted them to hop in the waiting limousine which would take them to the airport. G was confused. They were not planning to leave Brazil for two more days. Why should they go to the airport?

At first, the official acted as though they were enjoying a private joke together. G's face did not have an "I'm joking" look about it. The official then looked as puzzled as G and Tony. He explained, in his best broken English, the plans for the rest of the day. A pilot was prepared to fly all of them to their chosen shooting location. The final step in the process from the Bureau's side was for this official to ride along, see the location from the air, drop a pin on a GPS to record the coordinates and return to the agency. At least that's what G and Tony gleaned from the official's halting English.

The official's revelation was met with blank stares. The smile faded from his face. He sensed that something was wrong. Something was indeed wrong. Tony felt panic rising in his throat. The Bureau was clearly assuming they had already chosen their shooting location. They hadn't. G did not intend to invest the time and effort required to choose one until they knew if they were in or out.

G had put together a carefully-chosen location scouting team made up of a top-notch ex-military logistics specialist, a professional tracker, a wildlife biologist and a botanist. He didn't yet have any Brazilian locals recruited for the scouting team whose knowledge and experience with the area could be extremely valuable. He thought he would have plenty of time to tie up that loose end before the time came. The problem was that the time had come much earlier than expected.

G had just talked to the professional tracker two days ago, who informed G that he was currently guiding some wealthy Arab clients on a Cape buffalo hunt in South Africa and would be out of pocket for the next two weeks. The rest of the scouting team members were each in their respective corners of the United States doing what they would normally do on any given weekday.

After G put the team together last year, he assured them they would receive at least two months' advance notice of the date for the scouting trip. The success of the venture rose and fell on finding just the right location. Location was everything. It would take all of their combined efforts and unique skill sets to bring this together. To say the absence of his team was a problem would be a gross understatement.

On the other hand, the approval of a foreign government to film a show of this magnitude was huge. Today had been nothing short of remarkable. By an unforeseen combination of factors, G had gotten his approval as soon as he came down to ask for it. All he had to do now was to show them the place. The outgoing head of the Bureau was prepared to stamp his approval on anywhere the group wanted to go.

The problem was that if the official realized they hadn't done the first thing towards picking out a location, he would report back to his superiors. The permission to shoot would immediately be withdrawn. G would have to begin the process anew with a newly-appointed bureaucrat. Who knew how long that could take? It was an almost certainty that the new as-yet-unnamed political appointee's review of the project would be much more thorough and exhaustive than the halfhearted inquiry of a man on his way out. Additionally, the cost of doing business in Brazil was, at least at this moment, significantly lower than Argentina. Funds were not unlimited. Losing Brazil's first-time approval guaranteed a significant delay and a serious outlay of money.

It was now or never for G. The choice was clear. Get in the waiting limousine, then jump in a plane and point out the spot, albeit without the input of his team, or risk losing the permission just granted and a big chunk of change as a result.

G had not gotten to where he was in life by playing it safe. He was not one to let opportunities pass him by. The look in the official's eyes let him know that there could be no hesitation. The government of Brazil did not offer free plane rides to just anyone. If now was the time that the host country was giving him to find and declare the shoot location for his television production, then by golly he would find and declare the shoot location.

Tony recognized the moment the change came over G. The initial hesitation and uncertainty disappeared. The man with the plan returned. G was excellent at reading people. He discerned that the official had been tasked with the job of flying with them, but he seemed reluctant as though he was looking for a way out. G put his hand on the official's shoulder.

"My good man, I am delighted to know you will accompany us on this flight. I insist that you sit next to my friend Tony here. Tony loves to fly in small planes, especially when they circle over areas for a better view. You might notice him holding an open bag in his lap, but don't worry. At least half the time he flies, the bag remains empty."

The official looked confused. G's flowery English did not mean anything to him. He shrugged his shoulders and asked for clarification.

"What do you mean?"

G pointed at Tony and pantomimed a man throwing up. Tony started to protest. Sure, he got air sick from time to time when riding in a plane, but he never threw up. G shot Tony a quick look. *Don't speak.* Tony remained quiet. They watched the official's face. He appeared to be on the fence.

After much hesitation, the official announced his decision. He declined the offer to ride along. He put his index finger to his lips—the universal sign language for "*Let's keep this a secret.*" He would trust them to fly to the location and, with the pilot's help, obtain the GPS coordinates for him. G nodded appreciatively, assuring him he would. Then G's face turned serious. He chose his words carefully, keeping it simple, so as to insure a clear understanding.

"Let me ask you about this pilot. Is he a good pilot?"

This time it was the official who put his hand on G's shoulder. He smiled and nodded.

"The pilot is professional pilot. Very good pilot. The best in all Brazil."

The official truly meant what he said. The pilot recruited to transport the visitors was a highly-decorated military veteran. Thousands of hours of flying time. Impeccable service record. Fluent in English, Spanish and Portuguese.

What the official didn't know was that the pilot he was describing would not be flying anyone that day. That particular pilot had been in a rather embarrassing car accident just the night before. Striking a parked police car while carrying two scantily-clad passengers, neither of whom was his wife, after enjoying a few too many libations, drew the ire of the local police chief. The pilot was sitting in jail. He was out of the picture.

Unbeknownst to the official standing in the doorway of G and Tony's hotel room, the Bureau was scrambling to find a last-minute replacement. The good news was that they found one. The bad news was that the substitute pilot did not have quite the same pedigree as the pilot originally chosen for the task. The second choice pilot was a skilled airman, to be sure, but his language skills did not match his flying skills. For all intents and purposes, he spoke no English at all.

Meanwhile, G, Tony and the official were blissfully ignorant of the predicament. They walked outside the hotel and found a waiting limousine. G jumped right in. Tony, however, didn't move. This was madness. They weren't ready to point out a location, not by a long shot.

G glared at him from inside the car and mouthed, "*Get in.*" Against his better judgment, Tony ducked his head and climbed in the back next to G. The official sat up in the front passenger seat. The driver resumed his place behind the steering wheel. Tony stared at G, incredulous that he would even contemplate doing what they were about to do. G felt the eyes upon him but ignored them. This was no time to go weak in the knees.

When they arrived at the airport, the car skipped right past the entrances for parking, ground transportation and ticketing. The driver pulled up to a gate manned by a single guard and after a brief exchange, pulled through and drove onto the tarmac. As they drove past passenger jet after passenger jet, Tony felt like they were cutting to the front of the line at Magic World. Finally the driver pulled up to a twin-engine Cessna. When they exited the car, the noise of a nearby plane made conversation difficult, so thank yous and goodbyes were communicated mostly by sign language.

The pilot of the waiting Cessna was a mustachioed man with aviator shades who made little effort to extend a warm greeting to the men walking up to his plane. He assisted the two Americans in boarding. He was puzzled when the official did not climb in behind Tony and G. It was clear that he was expecting a third passenger. The pilot stuck his head back in the plane and said something unintelligible. G pointed back and forth at himself and Tony and gave a relaxed nod, signaling that it was only going to be the two of them. *No worries. No worries at all.*

The pilot leaned out the door of the plane. The official stood rooted to his spot beside the limo and waved, as though he was a mom seeing her children off as they boarded a bus headed to school. The pilot shrugged his shoulders. He exited the plane to perform a final pre-flight check of his aircraft. After several minutes of circling the aircraft, he climbed back in the plane and closed the door. He removed his sunglasses and showed his passengers the beverages and the lavatory.

Getting down to the business at hand, the pilot pulled out a large electronic board affixed to a swinging plastic arm secured to the wall by the front passenger seats. The board displayed three interchangeable maps of Brazil, each overlaying the other. One map showed cities, major highways and bodies of water, with thin red lines delineating the main flight paths of air traffic. The second map showed the topography through use of elevation lines. The third map was a satellite image, a beautiful aerial view with startling detail which showed how green Brazil appeared to be from space.

The pilot tapped the screen. Tiny dots of light appeared. In some places on the map there were so many it looked like a flashlight was shining at them. In other places there were fewer dots. On most of the map there were no dots at all. When the passengers looked at him quizzically, the pilot pointed first at Tony, then at G and then himself, counting in Portuguese each time he pointed at a man. He then placed his finger on their location on the map and, once again in Portuguese, counted one, two, three. People. Population centers. The entire area surrounding his fingertip was lit up due to the dense population. He tapped the lower right hand corner of the map again and the lights disappeared. He showed them how to scroll through the different maps by tapping the screen, as well as how to zoom in and zoom out.

A squawk from his radio drew the pilot away momentarily to speak to someone. For some unknown reason, he reopened the door and exited the plane. Realizing they had at least a couple of minutes to themselves, G quietly spoke to Tony.

"Here's what I remember the scouting team saying about where to locate..."

Tony exploded, albeit in hushed tones.

"You didn't meet with the team for more than fifteen minutes, G, and you did most of the talking! What could you possibly remember about their method of selecting a good location? We need to stop right now, tell these guys we're not ready, contact the team and see if we can get everybody over here at the same time. I'll bet they'd drop everything to do it, but we need time to coordinate schedules. Maybe by the end of the month—maybe. You said our tracker guy, hunting guide, whatever he is, Bones, is out of pocket for the next two weeks. You told everyone we needed his input so we don't get eaten, remember? We are talking about the Amazon rainforest, G! It is monstrous big! There are places in there where no human has ever set foot! This is crazy!"

G's expression didn't change. He watched the vein in Tony's forehead protrude as he spoke. He heard him out. When Tony's rant stopped, however, G turned his attention back to the electronic board. Without a word, he overruled and dismissed Tony's objections, and Tony knew it. There were things Tony loved about G, but there were other things that scared him. G had no fear of failure. None. G was a big picture guy. Details annoyed him. He left details to other people like Tony, or Tamper, who was the logistics guy for this mission. Their past successes in previous joint ventures were in no small part due to Tony's painstaking attention to detail, inspired by G's unwavering belief in his vision. G did not see caution flags when starting a new adventure. Tony was waving the yellow flag as hard as he could. G saw him waving it but drove right past it and floored the accelerator.

The pilot reentered the plane. Sweat ran down his forehead, cheeks and nose from the heat of walking outside on the sunbaked tarmac.

"Eh. Eh. Um. We…fly…" He searched for the right word. "You see down."

The task was difficult enough without being compounded by a language barrier. At least someone had communicated to him the goal of the mission. This was a good sign. The pilot tried a new tack.

"I fly to…" At this he pointed to a spot on the map roughly three inches northeast of the airport. He said something else which sounded like a mixture of English and Portuguese, but neither G nor Tony caught it. They had no idea of the distance, but if there was a predetermined coordinate already discussed, this would greatly aid in the search. The two passengers nodded approvingly. G magnified the confirmation by giving the thumbs up sign.

It was at this point that a grave misunderstanding occurred. The pilot had just said, in his best broken English, that he would continue flying until they told him to stop and circle. The board had a tiny electronic plane showing his passengers exactly where they were on the journey. They had said yes and given him the thumbs up. They understood, he thought. Unfortunately, they didn't. His passengers thought the pilot was flying to their destination and would inform them when they arrived.

As Tony watched the pilot settle back into his seat, he found himself counting to three in Portuguese. He tried his best to mimic the pilot's accent. Even though he would probably never see Miss Bright Smile or Miss Universe again, he wanted to learn how to speak Portuguese just in case. Counting to three, if delivered in a suave and debonair way at just the right moment, could be the start of a beautiful relationship. You never know.

While Tony fantasized about the two lovely passengers from his last plane ride, he was oblivious to the presence of one additional passenger on the ride he was about to take. Unbeknownst to any of the men on the plane, there was a tiny stowaway on board. An Africanized honeybee had flown unnoticed through the open door, gotten trapped in the lavatory and hadn't figured out how to escape. Such a small creature, but in great numbers it could bring the largest land animals on earth to their knees.

The pilot taxied down the runway, lifted off and became airborne. Predictably, G went sound asleep shortly after takeoff. The man could not stay awake in an airplane. Most people had trouble resting comfortably in a plane, much less sleeping in one. G, on the other hand, reacted like a baby being rocked to sleep. His head was nestled up against the window. His eyes, hidden behind his sunglasses, were closed tight against the sun. From the pilot's seat, it looked as though he was studying everything passing three thousand feet below them.

Tony was fascinated by the little electronic plane on the board which moved ever so slightly every two or three minutes. He clicked through the various maps, his mind awhirl as he pondered the factors that would combine to make one location better than another. Away from population centers, but not so far as to be inaccessible by vehicle. Within a relatively short distance of the Amazon River, but not on land so low that a flash flood would wash their camp away. He was not quite sure how to read a topo map, but after clicking back and forth between the map and the satellite image he figured it out. Lines close together meant quick elevation changes. Lines spaced out meant more level areas.

Tony let his mind wander. Camping. Not high on his "favorite things to do" list. He thought of the one time he had slept in a tent. His buddies from college decided, out of the blue, to go camping one weekend. The destination? Blood Mountain, part of Georgia's stretch of the Appalachian Trail. Why

Blood Mountain, one might ask? Blood Mountain had not been chosen because it had breathtaking views or because of glowing recommendations from outdoor enthusiasts or because it was the site of a historic battle between the Creek and Cherokee Indians. Oh no. These were college guys. It was called "Blood Mountain," for crying out loud. What other reason did you need?

Long after the fire had gone out and everyone had crawled into their tents to get a few hours' sleep, Tony was still wide awake. He was uncomfortable lying on the hard ground. There were noises all around him. *Was that a footstep? It sounded like a footstep.* His ears strained to hear them. Someone was snoring. *Was that a cough or was it a bear's growl? Why do they call it "Blood Mountain?"* The whirring of millions of insect legs and wings was deafening. He had no idea how loud night in the forest could be. The sounds would not give him a moment's peace. He longed for a fan to provide some white noise, but they were fresh out of electrical outlets to plug one into. His mind would not shut off. After hours of tossing and turning, Tony finally drifted off to sleep.

Tony woke up to the highly unpleasant sensation of something walking across his forehead. After swiping his face in the dark, he felt something walking on his neck. He jumped up out of his sleeping bag and fell over the body of the friend lying next to him. He smacked the back of his neck, but just as he did so, he felt another something crawling over his ear. Tony screamed and began flailing his arms wildly, slapping every square inch of exposed skin. Flashlights came on in the other tents. Beams of light swung wildly around in the darkness and confusion. His tent mate found a flashlight and switched it on. Much to his horror, Tony saw that every wall of their tent was crawling with granddaddy long-legs spiders. Someone hadn't zipped the tent door zipper all the way shut. His sleeping bag was covered. Every surface was moving, alive with arachnids.

Tony freaked out. Preserving dignity was the least of his concerns. He tore through the flaps of the still-zippered tent with a loud rip and ran to his car. He spent the rest of the night sitting straight up in the driver's seat, wishing the sun would hurry up so he could see how to drive out of this godforsaken place.

An involuntary shudder went through his body at the memory. His friends never let him live it down. Tony smiled just a little as the memory played through his mind, but only a little. After his bad experience with tent camping in the tame foothills of Georgia, Tony had no intention of sleeping on the ground in a cheap tent in the Amazon rainforest. Tamper, the logistics specialist, promised him that he and the rest of the cast and crew would be housed in professional grade, state-of-the-art, African-safari style tents, complete with comfy cots, mattresses well off the ground and generator-powered air conditioning units. As for the contestants, well, their lodgings would be more akin to what college kids on Blood Mountain might construct than what high-dollar tourists on an African safari would expect.

Except the contestants wouldn't be given tents.

Chapter Eight

A little over an hour into the flight, Tony needed to relieve himself. He walked to the lavatory with a wide stance, arms outstretched for balance. When he opened the tiny door, he thought he heard a hum near his left ear. As quickly as he heard it, however, the sound dissipated and he thought no more of it.

He loosened his belt, dropped his pants and sat down on the plastic seat. Tony began to ponder one of the great mysteries of life, a question that all air travelers confront at some point in their lives. *When I push the flush button and hear the big whoosh, is all my poop and pee ejected out of the plane and into the atmosphere? Is there some unlucky person a few thousand feet below me that thinks it just rained, or worse, that he was just struck by a meteorite? There should be an informational placard posted on the wall of the lavatory answering these questions.*

After finishing his business, Tony flushed. As he washed his hands, he wondered if he had just ruined the hat of some poor Brazilian tourist. He looked for air freshener but found none. After deciding to keep the door cracked just a little so air could circulate, Tony began to walk back to his seat.

The plane hit an air pocket and lurched just as Tony prepared to sit down. He put his hand down quickly to steady himself. Just as his hand touched the fabric of the seat, it felt like someone injected it with rattlesnake venom. Tony cried out and recoiled in pain. Instinctively leaping away from the source of the pain, Tony accidentally struck the electronic board with his elbow. Losing his balance, he landed flat on his butt. The pilot began to shout in his native Portuguese. G, who had been rudely awakened, yanked off his sunglasses and blinked in the bright light, trying to comprehend what had just happened.

Pain shot through the edge of Tony's left palm. He examined his stricken hand while cradling it with the other. A bee's stinger protruded from his skin. Grimacing heavily, Tony pinched the tiny black dagger between his index finger and thumb and pulled it out. After a few seconds of examination, he flicked it into a corner. His eyes caught movement on the floor. A bee! Amber and black tiger stripes. Fuzzy upper torso. Tony bared his teeth, lifted his right foot and drove his Italian leather shoe into the floor of the plane, squashing the foul thing into nothingness. The pilot shouted again. Tony had no idea what he said. His hand hurt too bad to care. He hated bees. He hated spiders. He hated anything that had more legs than him. Right at this moment, he hated Brazil. What kind of bee was that? Why was he even here? The scouting team was supposed to be doing this, not him.

If their wildlife biologist had been there, as she was supposed to be, she could have explained it all to him. Back in the 1950s, some well-meaning person had embarked on an ill-advised venture to introduce Africanized bees to Brazil in order to boost honey production. The person thought he could contain the bees and control them. He was wrong. A few swarms accidentally escaped quarantine, and the results were catastrophic. Thus was born the killer bee. Though their stings were no more potent than other honeybees, their aggressiveness certainly was. Nature had neglected to instill in them any fear of having their intestines torn out when they pulled their bodies away from the stingers they left in their impaled victims. All their tiny brains were capable of thinking was either "Work, work, work," or "Kill, sting, kill." Tony's hand had come in on the "Kill, sting, kill" part. His mind could think of nothing other than stopping the pain.

Fortunately, the pilot had a medical kit on board for just such an emergency. G found it and brought it over to Tony, whose hand was already red and swelling. A few drops of topical benzocaine took the edge off the hurt, but only a little. G found a blister pack of pink pills that looked something like Benadryl, but the words were not in English. He studied the letters on the package to see if they might provide a clue as to the medicinal properties of its contents. After a few seconds, he found what he was looking for. He showed Tony. On the back of the box, he found a word that approximated "antihistamine." Tony eyed the pills suspiciously as he held his wounded hand.

G stepped up to the cockpit so the pilot could see the box. G asked him, "Is this Benadryl?" The pilot nodded vigorously. Tony eased himself down into his seat. G popped two pills out of the aluminum foil into the palm of Tony's good hand and found him a bottle of water. Tony swallowed the pills and washed them down. He wished he had some ice to cool the burning sensation but holding the cold water bottle helped a little.

Crisis over, the men settled back down into their seats. The flight began to regain some semblance of normalcy. Tony's eyes fell upon the electronic board. Watching the little digital plane fly across the map would provide a welcome distraction. Something was different, though. It didn't quite look like it had before. Looking more closely, he saw that the board was slightly askew. He must have accidentally hit it in all the excitement. Additionally, part of the screen was not lit up as brightly as before. He hoped the pilot wouldn't notice before they returned to the airport at the end of their time together. The pilot had plenty of screens and gauges to look at up in the cockpit. There was no need for him to look at this one. Besides, it was still lit up, mostly anyway, and showed both a map and an airplane. No harm, no foul.

Tony's pulse slowed as the excitement of the moment dissipated and the miles flew by. The pain of the sting transformed into more of a prolonged itch. His eyes began to grow heavy as the antihistamine took effect. The gentle bumping of the plane through mild turbulence, coupled with the medicine, had a hypnotic effect on Tony. For the first time in his young life, Tony went sound asleep while riding in a plane. If he had ever entertained any hopes of G remaining awake to monitor their location however, they were in vain. G didn't even attempt to stay awake. G didn't need any antihistamine to ferry him to dreamland. G could find it all by himself.

The pilot had a nagging feeling he couldn't shake. He was conflicted. On the one hand, he knew that the highest levels of the Brazilian government had bestowed their blessing upon his two passengers. He had been tasked with a very important mission—to fly these men wherever they wanted to go, no matter where, and to record the location so they could return on a future date. He had not been in on the initial discussions that had taken place between his boss and the original pilot who was even now sitting in jail. He knew surprisingly little about what the overarching purpose of their mission might be. No one had shared with him what the men were specifically looking for. He was a respectful man who had advanced through the ranks because he understood the concept of chain of command. He knew what "need to know basis" meant. If he needed to know, he trusted that these men would inform him. Since they hadn't informed him, he had to assume, at least for now, that he didn't need to know.

His fuel tank didn't operate on the same system as the pilot. The fuel tank called all the shots, and it didn't care whether you knew it or not. The pilot began to perform his mental calculations of time, distance, miles per gallon, and fuel remaining. He began replaying in his mind the brief orientation he had conducted for the passengers at the start of the trip. He had pointed to the most remote part of the Amazon rainforest when showing them how to operate the map. He had laughed and said, "You don't want to go there, do you?" He never imagined they would say yes. Much to his surprise, the older white man had held his thumb up and nodded in the affirmative.

The pilot didn't want to be disrespectful and question their judgment. He didn't want to show any reluctance to take these obviously important men where they wanted to go. It's just that planes like his didn't typically fly that route. For that matter, no planes typically flew that route. Ever. There was nowhere to go, nowhere to land, and nothing to see but impenetrable jungle. The distance involved would preclude them from being able to spend a lot of time circling at low altitudes once they got there, because he needed to make absolutely sure that he had plenty of fuel to make the long trip back safely. Running out of fuel before you land while carrying VIPs was not a good path to career advancement.

Still somewhere between sleep and wakefulness, Tony's eyelids fluttered. Disoriented, his brain still enshrouded in mist, Tony tried to remember where he was. Squinting against the bright light, he saw a blinding glare at the end of a short hallway. Glass. Amorphous blobs of fluffy white floated on a backdrop of blue. Almost like the sky. He remembered. Plane ride. Brazil. Location. Groggily, Tony leaned his head forward and opened his eyes despite the protests of his pupils to the rude intrusion of sunlight. He looked for and found the plane icon on the board. It hadn't moved at all. He must have only been asleep a couple of minutes. Satisfied, Tony dropped his eyelids again. Just a few minutes more. He returned to a blissful state of unconsciousness. He had no idea that his elbow had broken the board over three hours earlier. G didn't have any idea, either. He was asleep as well, still using the window as a headrest.

The pilot frowned as his internal conflict grew. He had tried twice, unsuccessfully, to get the attention of his passengers. He thought the younger one would wake up when he tossed a half-empty water bottle back at him and hit him in the knee. The man had barely stirred. He was clearly sound asleep, but at least the other man with the sunglasses was looking out the window. Nevertheless, he was no longer as comfortable in his assumption that his passengers would let him know what he needed to know when he needed to know it about their destination. This was new territory or new air for him. This was a part of Brazil that he had never flown over before. He could look at his instrument panel, of course, and tell exactly where he was in terms of altitude, direction, and air speed. He could look straight ahead and see exactly where he was in relation to the horizon. This wasn't his trip, however. He didn't know what he was supposed to be looking for.

He was keeping a close eye on his fuel gauge. If the fuel ran out, there was nowhere to park to walk to a gas station. He had no intention of having a search party find the remains of him and his plane scattered across miles of treetops because he allowed his passengers' plans, or lack thereof, to make him run out of gas. If the passengers weren't awake and interacting with him within the next ten minutes, he was going to breach protocol and take action. First, he would tip the wingtips enough to cause his passengers to wake up and grab their seats to avoid being thrown out. If by some unforeseen reason that didn't work, he might call it quits and head back. He was too far in and at too great a risk to worry about being polite. His superiors would have to handle any international relations problems.

He simply wanted to make it home to his wife tonight.

Chapter Nine

Dallas/Forth Worth International Airport, DFW had two distinct types of people—those in the midst of a mad dash to their gates and those already at their gates who were bored to tears, wondering if the clocks on the wall had dead batteries. For the latter group, aside from staring at their phones, people-watching was the only game in town. A teenage boy with a mouthful of braces, waiting on his flight to Atlanta, pulled his mother's sleeve and pointed.

"Look Mom, that's him. That's the guy. The one with all the tattoos. The Grunge. Right there."

Mom had long since given up on teaching her son Blake to use his inside voice. Having a son with Asperger's syndrome was always an adventure, she told her friends. She didn't know if he would ever develop a level of social awareness that would make him drop the volume on his own. Mom set her phone down and gazed across the aisle at the group of passengers waiting to board a plane to Charlotte. Her son saw where she was looking.

"No Mom, right here. Right in front of you. Him. The man with the tattoos on his fingers. That's the Grunge."

Terry Bishop, the object of Blake's attention, had a rather distinctive appearance that made him instantly recognizable. His head was…unique. He had a protruding brow that blocked the top half of his eyes, giving him the appearance of being perpetually angry. His cheeks bulged out from the sides of his face like half-inflated balloons that extended back behind his ears. He had sizeable rolls of flesh above and below the bump on the back of his head. Tattoos blanketed his neck which was noticeable because he had a lot of neck.

Terry stood no more than ten feet away. His eyes bored a hole in her son. A jolt of embarrassment washed over Mom. She quickly reached across her son's chest, as though she was seated next to him in a car, protecting him from an impending car wreck

"Son, we don't call people names. Tell the man, 'I'm sorry.' Sir, we're sorry."

As Mom studied the man's face to see if her apology worked, an older man a few seats away chimed in.

"No, don't apologize. Your boy is just stating facts. He is the Grunge."

The older man, whose black baseball cap said, "Korea War Veteran," leaned forward in his seat. His wife, seated next to him, desperately tried to shush him. He would not be shushed. To the contrary, he began to sing.

"Silent night. Holy night. All is calm. All is bright."

Blake didn't understand why the old man was singing "Silent Night" when it wasn't Christmas, but he was happy anyway. He loved Christmas. He knew the words and chimed in.

"Round yon virgin, mother and child. Holy infant, so…"

The man with the tattooed fingers, whose name was Terry Bishop, exploded. He set his bag down to free his hands and shot both of them a two-handed bird. He told them both what they could do to themselves and what they could kiss. He called Blake a retard. The teenager's feelings were instantly hurt. Terry stepped forward so that he was directly in front of the teenager.

"If you want to believe in fairy stories, that's your business, but don't make it mine. And that goes for you, too, old man."

The veteran wished he was fifty years younger so he could teach the Grunge a lesson. People all around stood up and craned their necks to see what the commotion was about. With that, Terry picked up his bag and walked to the other side of the waiting area by the windows. He looked out and saw baggage handlers throwing luggage into the cargo hold under the plane. He pulled out his phone and began scrolling furiously so he would have something to look at other than the people around him. It dawned on him that his seating assignment may put him near the teenager and the old man. *That would really suck*, he thought to himself.

"Mom, why does he hate Christmas?" asked Blake.

Mom looked at her son, shrugged and shook her head. Since Blake was a little boy, he had been obsessed with Christmas. It all began when her husband left a plate of cookies and a glass of milk on the fireplace for Santa. As is sometimes the case in children with Asperger's, her son would get missile lock on something and could not let it go. He thought about Santa and his mittens. How do you hold a glass of milk while wearing mittens? What if Santa spilled the milk? What if he dropped the cookies? How could he clean it up with mittens on? Would he have to take them off so he could clean it up? Would it make him late? Would Dad write a note telling Santa he would clean it up so he wouldn't be late? It was exhausting. Sweet, but exhausting.

This past December, her son's middle school was scheduled to sing Christmas carols for the patients at the local VA Hospital. The children had already sung the songs at the school Christmas concert. The music teacher's song list consisted of familiar tunes: "Santa Claus Is Coming To Town," "Rudolph The Red-Nosed Reindeer," "Away In A Manger," "Silent Night" and "We Wish You a Merry Christmas." Parents and children alike sang along. Anticipating that many of the VA patients would be older, the music teacher added a couple of classics to the playlist—one from the 1940s, "Let It Snow," and one from the 1950s, "Silver Bells." She assigned solos to the two best singers in the choir, both girls, who had surprisingly good voices despite their youth. There were many school activities that simply weren't right for Blake, but singing Christmas carols with the choir was right up his alley.

Ten days before their field trip, however, the visit to the hospital was canceled. A federal court judge granted an emergency injunction against the VA Hospital and a high school chorus at the request of the American Liberty Association. The plaintiff? Terry Bishop's father, a diabetic, who was convalescing at the VA Hospital following a foot amputation. He didn't like singing, period. It didn't matter what kind. Week after week he complained to Terry, telling him to make it stop. Terry told him somebody ought to get a lawyer and sue.

One day, Terry happened to be there when an elementary school was singing. As he listened to the words, Terry, a self-avowed atheist, hit upon an idea as to how he and his father could get a free lawyer. He called the A.L.A., explained the situation, and voilà, a lawsuit was filed. An injunction was granted in no time. Terry made the local newspapers. He was lauded by local TV reporters as a champion for those who opposed the imposition of state-sponsored religion under the guise of Christmas carols.

A Christian news network got wind of the story and sent a reporter out to the high school. As the reporter conducted an off-campus interview of two girls from the chorus, one girl's boyfriend leaned into the camera shot and yelled.

"Hey, tell the Grunge to go back to Mount Armpit! Let the Tykes in Toy Town play!"

The video clip of the unnamed boy scolding The Grunge caught fire and made national news. Terry Bishop became the poster child for everything that was wrong with America. Virtually no one could remember his real name, but then again, no one wanted to. "The Grunge" did just fine.

One of the local news stations sent a reporter to do a follow-up interview with one primary objective—ask him what he thinks of his nickname. When the reporter popped the question, Terry had the answer.

"Well, I'll be honest, I don't like being called Grunge very much. Both me and my dad believe in the separation of church and state. When we're getting forced to listen to religious songs, that ain't separation. It wasn't like he could go anywhere with his foot like it was. If people want to call me something, call me "Tattoo." That's what my friends call me."

Blake didn't see the post-Christmas interview. It wouldn't have mattered if he had. Like most of America, he had watched the video clip of the boy calling Terry Bishop "the Grunge" at least a dozen times. Terry Bishop would always and forever be "the Grunge." No matter how many times Mom explained it to him, Blake would soon be asking again.

"Why does the Grunge hate Christmas?"

The odds against Blake coming face-to-face with Terry Bishop were astronomical. Mom grimaced when the thought occurred to her that she and Blake may be sitting next to him. She wondered what it would cost to upgrade to first class. On the other side of the seats, Terry Bishop chanced a glance over at the three people who had already ruined his morning. Thankfully, none of them was looking his way. He hated the attention. He was glad to be getting away.

Terry still didn't understand how he had won a free trip to South America. He hadn't entered any sweepstakes that he could remember, but he really didn't care. Anywhere is better than here. Fortunately for all concerned, Terry ended up sitting close to the front of the plane while Blake, Blake's mom and the Korean War veteran were spaced out in the middle and rear of the plane. When Terry arrived in Atlanta, he made sure he was the first person off the plane.

Chapter Ten

DeShunta Jackson landed at Hartsfield-Jackson Atlanta International Airport early the same afternoon. She had never been to Atlanta, though she had long wanted to visit. The Atlanta airport was massive, filled with people of all stripes and colors. While the people all looked different, they all had one thing in common. They were all in a hurry, every single one of them.

There was no way DeShunta's legs could possibly move her body fast enough to keep up with the flow. As she walked down an impossibly long concourse trying to find Baggage Claim, she heard a beep, beep, beep coming up behind her. When she turned around, she saw a lady in uniform driving an old woman and a disabled man on an extended mobility scooter. She studied them as they went past. It sure would be nice to catch a ride on one of those scooters.

As DeShunta approached Gate A-13, a mobility scooter coming from the opposite direction was just dropping off an elderly woman with a quad cane. The voice of the airline employee at the gate came through the sound system.

"Paging passenger Ruth Duncan."

The elderly woman waved her hand and said, "Here I am!"

DeShunta saw her chance. She adjusted the speed of her walk so she could time her arrival to coincide with the moment the old lady got off. Right then, a grossly-overweight man no more than thirty years old, huffing and puffing as though he had just run a marathon, pushed past DeShunta.

"Hey, thank god you are here! Just in time. I need you to take me to Gate B-2. I've got a connecting flight to…"

Just as the sweaty man prepared to lift his considerable bulk onto the seat of the mobility scooter, DeShunta grabbed his shirt tail and yanked.

"Oh no you ain't! Can't you see a lady here? I been waiting patiently and you going to knock me down and jump ahead? I don't think so. You need to walk anyway. Look at yourself. Can't breathe and all you doing is walking."

With that, DeShunta hopped on. The man was dumbfounded, but he was not about to give up so easily. There was an empty seat on the other side of the mobility scooter. DeShunta watched his eyes. Just before he reached it, she swung her carry-on and plopped it in the empty seat.

"Taken," she announced with finality.

DeShunta enjoyed her solo ride to Baggage Claim. Finding her suitcase on the carousel was no easy task. Her black suitcase looked like every other suitcase, and every other suitcase was black. Every time she spied a suitcase that looked like hers, some tight-jeaned girl would step up and say, "There's mine," and some boy would happily snatch it off the belt for her. Finally she saw hers, grabbed the handle and pulled...but one side of the handle was broken. It wasn't like that when she gave it to the ticket taker back home. DeShunta screamed out in frustration. People throughout Baggage Claim jumped.

A heavily-muscled T.S.A. agent headed to Security stopped in his tracks. His Belgian Malinois, whose vest said, "Do Not Pet," snapped to attention. Knowing there was a situation, the agent fast-walked to DeShunta.

At least he meant to walk to DeShunta.

DeShunta had managed to extend the retractable handle and was just starting to pull her suitcase in the direction of Ground Transportation when she saw them coming. Already upset, the sight of a mean-looking policeman and his dog approaching her completely flipped her switch.

"Why you coming at me? Don't you bring that dog at me! Southland Airways going to snap off my suitcase handle and then you going to bring some rabies-having dog to bite me, too? You bring that dog over here and watch what happen! Come on! Bring it here!"

DeShunta threw down her small carry-on bag. She picked up her suitcase, lifted it up over her head and began to scream as she advanced on the T.S.A. agent. The service dog broke rank and jumped behind his handler, having never encountered anything like this in his training. The T.S.A. agent's arm was twisted behind him as the dog pulled on the leash with all his strength. The agent swiftly assessed the situation and decided on a plan.

Abort mission.

DeShunta expressed her feelings to anyone and everyone within earshot as she watched her antagonists walk away. She tried to calm herself down as she rode the escalator to Ground Transportation. There might be photographers wanting to take her picture. She didn't want to look mad for the public. When she got there, she didn't find any photographers waiting for her, but she did find a man holding a sign. She read the name on it, turned loose of her suitcase and put her hand on her hip.

"'Deshona' Jackson? 'Deshona?' Who told you 'Deshona?' That ain't my name. Ain't no 'Deshona' Jackson. It's 'DeShunta.' D, E, Capital S, H, U...You know what? Throw that sign down. And get this suitcase. Where's this southern hospitality everybody going on about?"

After a rocky start, the driver and his charge settled into his car and started the drive to DeShunta's destination. She pressed him for details about the television production, the participants, the location, the duration and the prizes, but he knew surprisingly little. He pulled off at an exit almost immediately after getting on the interstate in order to get gas. DeShunta looked at all the title loan businesses and liquor stores around the gas station. It looked like home. She did not fly all the way to Atlanta to see what she already saw everyday outside her own front door. She was glad when the gas pump clicked off with a loud thump indicating the tank was full.

The driver got back in the car and cranked it up. DeShunta told him he should have done that before he picked her up from the airport. He started to respond but decided against it. She was right. He turned on the radio. DeShunta informed him they didn't want to hear it. He sighed and turned it off.

After a brief time on the interstate, the driver exited again and headed south on a state highway. Vape shops and buy-here-pay-here used car lots gave way to green fields and golf courses. Houses were fewer and farther between. DeShunta had not expected to drive out into the country. Her vision of Atlanta was busy streets with trendy shops, historic theaters, horse-drawn carriages and people of all colors enjoying life in an urban setting. Her brows furrowed as she watched the A-T-L grow smaller and smaller, finally disappearing altogether, through the rear windshield.

A light rain began to fall. The driver set his windshield wipers to intermittent. When one of the wipers made a scrubbing sound, he quickly looked in his rearview mirror. He hoped the noise wouldn't evoke a response in his passenger, who had instilled no small amount of fear in him in the short amount of time he had known her. Before long, the rain subsided and sunlight broke through the clouds, giving everything a fresh, clean look. Rainbows formed on the suspended water droplets and then vanished as quickly as they came.

Thirty minutes later, on the right side of a long stretch of two-lane state highway, an estate of mammoth proportions took shape. A well-manicured lawn spread endlessly beyond majestic iron gates. A veritable castle, more akin to Buckingham Palace than Tara, materialized from out of the mist. Its original owner had been a world champion mixed martial arts fighter who succumbed to the temptation to buy more than he could afford, banking on the hope that big money from title fights would never stop rolling in. The champ reluctantly handed the keys over to a bankruptcy trustee less than five years after he built it.

Its present owner, Bert Redmond, had taken the original building and grounds to new heights of splendor. Bert was an outrageously successful comedian, who was starting a new comedy tour in Branson, Missouri later this month. Woe to all the senior citizens coming from all corners of the globe to pack out that venue. Bert's old people jokes were both ruthless and relentless. He knew his audience. His "How to Guide for Dating in the Nursing Home" had taken on a life of its own. Bert could not believe he got paid to have this much fun. His accountant couldn't believe how much people paid Bert to have this much fun.

Bert was in the process of ushering other invited guests into the entrance hall of his home when DeShunta's driver began to circle the fountain and slowed to a stop. When she stepped out of the car, Bert called her by name.

"You must be Ms. DeShunta Jackson! I am so glad you came! I'm Bert. Welcome to my home! Come on in!"

DeShunta was taken aback. Bert Redmond? The comedian? They hadn't told her she was being taken to Bert Redmond's house! And he knew her name! DeShunta smiled and thanked him. Bert's boyish good looks, smiling blue eyes and warm two-handed handshake made her feel very welcome indeed. She started to tell him she didn't find him funny, but he was drawn away to greet another new guest before she could.

Annaliese Parkman, the former Governor of Connecticut, had arrived. She, too, was taken aback when she realized whose home she was entering. Bert introduced himself, welcomed her and began to escort her inside when he noticed she had a companion.

"Hello. I don't think we've been introduced. I'm Bert. And you are…?"

"Hi, I'm Susan Hait-Parkman. I am Annaliese's life partner. Thank you for having us."

Bert told her she was quite welcome and opened the door for them, but he was slightly perplexed. Tony had told him only the contestants themselves were invited. By design, husbands, wives, girlfriends, boyfriends, family and friends were not invited. Maintaining privacy and secrecy were of the utmost importance at the outset of a production of this nature. Bert did not plan to play the bouncer however. Instead, he turned his attention to an energetic young man who was even now bounding up the cobblestone driveway. He was genuinely excited to meet this next guest.

"Could this be the one, the only, the man, the myth, the legend—Boedy Da? Better known around the world as the 'Spider Monkey'?"

Boedy's face lit up in amazement when he recognized the man calling out his name. He shook Bert's hand with vigor, his dreadlocks bouncing with each movement. Bert laughed when he saw Boedy's eyes travel up the front wall of the mansion.

"Hey, hey, hey, you look like you're scoping out your next climb!"

Now it was Boedy's turn to laugh. He couldn't help himself. It was as natural as breathing. Boedy promised Bert he would be a good boy and keep his feet on the ground. Bert smiled and patted the smaller man on the shoulder. As he started to turn away and find the next guest, Bert noticed that Boedy was hesitating, as though he had something more to say. Bert inquired as a good host would.

"You look like you were about to say something. Would you like a drink?"

Boedy smiled and thanked him for the offer.

"No, but I wondered if I could ask a favor. You see, my sister hitchhiked here with me. She's kind of, like, outside the gate back there. She really liked how your house looked from the road, at least as much as she could see. I was just wondering if she could, maybe, come in, like the gate? She doesn't have to come inside your house or anything. Would it be cool with you if she could just, like, stand here in front of it for a sec?"

Bert's eyes widened.

"Wait, she hitchhiked with you? Well, first, yes, of course she can come in. I'd love to meet her. But where is she going when she leaves here?"

Boedy smiled with quiet eyes.

"She'll hitchhike back home. She's used to it. She's a tough cookie."

Bert's face grew concerned.

"Boedy, there are parts of town between here and the airport that aren't safe. They aren't safe at all. I don't think that's such a good idea."

Boedy started to laugh.

"When you meet her, you'll see. She can fend for herself."

Bert, not at all convinced, watched as Boedy turned and bounded back the way he came. For a second, Bert imagined being a girl, seeing a car slowing down after the driver notices her thumb in the air, and then having to decide if the driver is trustworthy or if he is a serial killer who will make her body disappear without a trace. He shuddered at the thought. Tearing his mind away from the unpleasantness, he once again became the consummate host greeting star-struck guests.

Back inside the house, Celeste Schneiderman tried to find the hidden speakers which were playing the sweet refrain from a song that sounded most familiar. It dawned on her where she had heard it before. The movie about the wizard and elves. Yes, that's it. She noticed the sound grew louder and more distinct as they rounded a corner, and she soon saw why. There, in an antechamber off the main hallway, were three gentlemen and a lady dressed in garb reminiscent of the Renaissance lovingly playing a cello, two violins, and a flute. The lady with the flute gave a courteous bow in response to the surprised look on Celeste's face. Celeste smiled and gave a sort of bow in return.

Annaliese and Susan checked out the other people in the vestibule. Most looked to be unremarkably bourgeois, while some seemed downright uncouth. They recognized no one until they saw a bubbly woman sipping a drink and giggling as she listened to a young man telling a story.

"Sue, check her out. The lady busting out of her blouse over there. Why does she look familiar?"

Susan found the one Annaliese was talking about.

"Oh, yeah. Yeah, yeah. That's...I've seen her. That's the annoying wife on that show. Remember? She plays the dumb one, or she could really be dumb. I don't know which it is. I've seen her, but I can't think of her name. Sorry. No, wait. I've got it. Peaches. That's it. Peaches."

Annaliese smiled.

"Peaches! That's it. Thank you! I knew I'd seen her somewhere."

They looked around the room for a minute more. Satisfied there was nothing else exciting to see by the entrance, they embarked on a self-guided tour of the rest of the main level. Unlike those around her who were oohhing and ahhing as though they had never seen such opulence before, Annaliese actually had. Her residence at the Governor's mansion in Connecticut had been lavish, and the homes around it even more so. Annaliese's partner Susan quietly pointed out some missing grout in the stonework, as well as a burned-out light bulb in a chandelier that the help had overlooked.

DeShunta Jackson looked overhead in wonder. Beautiful stained glass windows caught her eye the second she walked in, at least before she spied the chocolate fountain. Although she had seen a chocolate fountain before at an all-you-can-eat buffet, she had never seen one that was two stories tall. As she thoughtfully chewed a strawberry covered in still-warm chocolate, she studied a life-sized painting of a pale, expressionless man wearing poofy sleeves and a poofy collar. *Who would want that? That's hideous. Rich man got poor taste*, she thought to herself.

DeShunta's brief moment of tranquility was suddenly interrupted by a bump from behind. Celeste Schneiderman was looking up at the stained glass windows and not watching where she was walking. She was considerably taller than DeShunta and did not catch her out of her peripheral vision. Celeste's elbow struck DeShunta squarely in the back at the same time she kicked DeShunta's right heel. DeShunta, who was not expecting a push, had to take a quick step forward to regain her balance. Celeste was mortified at what she had done.

"Oh god, I am so sorry! I was looking up and not paying attention. I am so very sorry!"

DeShunta turned to look at the person behind her, lifting her stricken right foot as she did so. Her eyes furrowed and her nostrils flared.

"What the hell wrong with you? Here we are, walking around this big place and you can't find somewhere to walk without stepping where my feet supposed to go?"

Celeste was stunned into silence not knowing what to say or do after her apology was not accepted. She silently prayed for a woman-to-woman reprieve. It didn't work. DeShunta put her right foot back on the ground and squared up to Celeste.

"Maybe if you get that hair out your eye, maybe you can see where you stepping. You got two feet; you need two eyes. You got one eye all covered up with that silly haircut—maybe that's why you stepping on my feet. Will somebody here help this woman to walk? Because she can't walk herself."

Celeste, shocked and embarrassed, mumbled another apology and hurried across the vestibule to the other side, as far away from the angry woman as she could get. DeShunta turned to the person nearest to her and began loudly recounting the story of the woman who couldn't walk, as though anyone could have missed it when it actually happened five seconds earlier. Thankfully, the uproar died down as quickly as it started, and everyone resumed gawking in wide wonder as before.

Chaz Pinoir-Sinclair's neck swiveled around like a CEO in an office chair as he tried to take in the sights and sounds of this magnificent place. He could not stop grinning at his great good fortune. A few months earlier, he thought he had ruined his life with the temper tantrum at the county dump. To the contrary, however, after he completed sixty days in jail, did eighty hours of community service and persuaded his mom to cough up $2,467.22 in restitution to repair the broken gate, his life had been on a joyous upswing.

Chaz had been featured on the homepage of the Green Peaks Club website. He met some very nice, high-ranking members of the Free Animal Passion Society. Well, maybe "very nice" was not the right description. They had been kind of nice, at least until he had declined to join them on their clandestine mission to free the koi from the pond in front of the Japanese steakhouse by the mall. He couldn't wrap his mind around how Lake Lancaster would be a better habitat for them. Sure, the lake would provide infinitely more room to swim around in, but then again, back home in their little koi pond there were no thirty-pound striped bass looking to add a little orange to their diet. The best and most exciting thing to happen to him, though, was being invited to this outrageous mansion in Georgia to try out for a new reality TV show. Chaz had absolutely no idea what the show was about, but he didn't care. He was all in.

Bert, distracted while talking with a dinner service employee wearing a white shirt, white gloves and black pants, almost closed the door on his last guest. Boedy had returned with his sister. Bert felt the bump, saw part of a person in the doorway and pulled the door back quickly.

"Oh my gosh, I am so sorry, ma'am! Please, forgive me! What a terrible host I am!"

The young lady gave a faint smile and tried to rub her bruised hip slowly, without being noticed, not wanting to make him feel worse. Bert desperately wanted to make her laugh. He leaned in with a conspiratorial grin.

"Well, to be honest, see, with all the fat people, we were running low on hors d'oeuvres, and I had to cut the line off somewhere."

Bert flashed his best smile at the young lady. Boedy thought it was great. His sister, however, looked almost penitent as she spoke.

"I'm sorry. I won't eat anything. I just wanted to see."

Bert instantly felt horrible.

"Oh, geez. Darling, you come in and eat as much as you like. I insist. Jeremy? Jeremy! Yes, would you please fix this young lady a plate? Get her one of everything. No, get her two of everything."

Bert looked down at Boedy's sister. She was the same height as her brother. She was slender but had a look of feminine strength about her. Her hair was a bit unkempt and her clothes had clearly seen better days. She didn't quite know what to do with her hands.

"Tell me your name, darling."

"Willow."

"Well, it is an honor to meet you, Miss Willow. My name is Bert. I am really glad you are here. So tell me, are you a climber like your brother?"

She shook her head.

"No. I leave the climbing to him."

Boedy liked her answer. He laughed easily. He knew his sister didn't like to talk about herself, so he decided to help her out.

"Willow likes outdoor living. Like a survivalist? She likes making fire and shelters and stuff. Getting her own food, fishing, hunting, woodcraft, bush craft, herbs, roots, berries. She can pretty much live in the woods forever if she wanted to."

Bert looked at her in wonder. How could such a young lady have those kinds of skills? Why would she want to have those skills? He was about to ask her when she spoke up.

"I was actually signed up to be on a survival show on TV a couple of years back, but I didn't get the paperwork in on time. Well, they said they sent it, but I didn't really have a mailbox at the time. I gave them the address of a friend of mine, but by the time she let me know it came, it was too late. They had already filled the slot."

Bert studied Willow's face. She had something none of the others had. With her skill set, she could survive, and maybe even thrive where they were going. No one in this room was better equipped to compete in Jungle Money than this last-minute walk-up who didn't even know what Bert was thinking about inviting her to do.

Bert was an equal one-third partner in this venture. G and Tony, both longtime friends, had invited him in and he had accepted almost immediately. The three men had a great chemistry. Their vision of what could be was clear. Each had their own separate and distinct role. Bert provided most of the start-up capital. They had left him behind in America to start the party while they flew to South America. As Bert watched Boedy talking to his sister, the thought of her being dropped off on Stewart Avenue or in West End and having to hitch from there made his mind up. He was inviting her onto the show. She would be safer in the jungle. He would deal with his partners later. *Easier to ask forgiveness than permission*, he thought to himself.

Before Bert could speak with her any further, though, a nearby scream of excitement startled him, causing him to spin around. Excited conversation on the backside of the vestibule garnered everyone's attention. Guests looking up the stairwell were struggling to catch their breath. An open-mouthed lady near the bottom step looked around to see if everyone was paying attention, as though royalty was entering the room. The legs of the person descending the stairs came into view first. Highly-polished leather shoes clicked down the stone steps. Perfectly hemmed slacks. As he continued down the stairs, there appeared an impeccably-tailored Berzins Brothers blazer over sleeves adorned with gold cufflinks. Pink Artyoms dress shirt. Powder blue bowtie.

Suddenly, a familiar face came into view, and the reason for the excitement became clear. Bobbing his head side to side ever so slightly, his famous salt and pepper coiffure on full display, former Senator Bradford Kingston, III descended into the midst of the throng. The Senator from the great state of Vermont grinned and waved. Out of instinct, he turned and reached for the hand of the nearest onlooker.

In this case, the nearest onlooker was DeShunta Jackson.

DeShunta did not recognize the esteemed former Senator. Much to the crowd's collective dismay, she did not take his extended hand. One of her hands remained securely on her handbag while the other maintained a tight grip on the wooden skewer piercing a chocolate-covered strawberry. In deference to the unknown VIP, however, she did stop chewing. The Senator laughed loudly as though they were old friends sharing a private joke and redirected his attention to the others desperately seeking his attention. DeShunta resumed chewing, only slightly annoyed at the interruption. The voices of excited people resonated off the high ceilings like it was an echo chamber. Bradford Kingston knew how to work a crowd.

Willow spied the chocolate fountain and grabbed her brother's shoulder. She pulled him by the shirt until they were standing right next to it. She stared in wonder, never having seen such a thing. Willow saw the skewer in DeShunta's hand and reached for one of her own. She stabbed a strawberry and held it under the falling chocolate until it was thoroughly covered. Willow turned to her brother and smiled a child's smile, which Boedy returned. They were close; it was easy to tell.

Boedy put his forehead against Willow's and they both bowed their heads and closed their eyes. DeShunta watched them closely. At first, she couldn't tell what they were doing, but then she figured it out. In the midst of all the chaos, they were asking a blessing. Praying. Before they could finish, a young man covered in tattoos leaned in with a disbelieving look on his face.

"Are you guys seriously praying over a chocolate-covered strawberry?"

"Uh huh," Willow nodded.

"Jesus," Tattoo scoffed.

Boedy's face lit up.

"Dude! You nailed it!" Boedy smiled.

Celeste watched the man covered in tattoos in fascination. She tried to read what the tattoos on his arms and hands said without getting caught looking. She couldn't read much without being too obvious, but the messages seemed to have a pretty fatalistic theme—God is dead, live it up, then you die. *Nice. I'll bet he's fun at parties.* Celeste found herself thinking about Mrs. Jankowicz. She had tattoos on her wrists that also carried a deadly meaning, but she didn't get them voluntarily. This guy in front of her, on the other hand, had done it to himself. *Craziness.*

After allowing the guests to mingle a bit longer, Bert looked at his watch. It was time. Bert held up his hand and cleared his throat.

"Everyone, if I could have your attention. Excuse me, may I have your attention?"

The noise level did not change a bit in response to Bert's announcement. It was clear to Clarence Humberton, who was standing roughly in the middle of the foyer, that the crowd was not ready to give Bert their attention. It was even clearer to Clarence that this polite southern boy had no idea how to manage a group of people. Clarence specialized in people management and decided to lend Bert a hand. He sucked in a double lungful of air and then expelled it at a volume equivalent to the launch of a space shuttle.

"Hey, shut up! The man is trying to talk here! Shut up and listen! Show some respect!"

Senator Kingston vaguely heard a man shouting across the room, but he hadn't finished his conversation with former Governor Annaliese Parkman. He was delighted to meet her. He knew, of course, that she was out of office and was certain it would fascinate her to know how he spent his days now that he was out of office. He continued explaining his theory on why it was better to drink water rather than coffee as the first drink of the day. The Senator did not notice anyone coming—at least not until Clarence had his mouth within inches of his ear.

"Hey, you! Yes, you! Are you deaf? Am I talking too softly? Then I will speak up. Shut up for a minute, would you? The man is trying to talk!"

A stunned silence came over the room. Senator Kingston, unaccustomed to such a rude public rebuke, dropped his smiling visage and replaced it with a cold stare. Clarence, completely unconcerned, turned to Bert and nodded. *Problem handled. Take it away, Bert.* Bert tried to suppress a smile but was unsuccessful. Satisfied he had everyone's attention, Bert addressed the crowd.

"Ladies and gentlemen, thank you for coming here today. You are all very special people from all walks of life who have been invited from all over our great country. You each have unique and distinct life experiences which have helped create who you are today. You may already know some of your fellow guests' stories—others you will learn as we go along. I know you are wondering exactly why you have been invited here. The rumor and speculation can finally end. I will not make you wait or keep you in suspense any longer. The time has come to reveal the reason why you are here."

Bert smiled broadly at his audience. The circle of people tightened around him. Excited faces stared eagerly at him from all over the room.

"But before I do, I first have an apology to deliver."

Groans arose from every corner of the vestibule. Even a short delay seemed unbearable. Bert laughed at the effect his delivery was having. His mischievous grin and obvious enjoyment of the moment kept the crowd at bay. His dimples showed when he laughed, which did not escape the notice of the ladies.

"George Commander and Anthony Longino, who go by 'G' and 'Tony,' and I personally chose you to be the recipients of the invitations you each received. You may or may not have heard of George, or G. Many years ago, he produced, directed and starred in a little show called "Rust Bucket Junkies. Anybody remember Rust Bucket Junkies?"

Bert studied their faces to see if he'd rung any bells. Clarence and Senator Kingston both recognized the name of the show and gave knowing nods. Bert continued.

"I personally loved the show. For some of you younger ones who may not have seen it, G was a classic car enthusiast. He loved searching through junkyards, looking for old, rusted-out car bodies. He struck a deal with General Motors where they would sell him the rolling chassis of a new non-unibody, limited-production Impala, the skeleton upon which he would mount the body of, say, an old '57 Chevy, or a '67 Chevelle, or whatever he found in the junkyard that week. He would get a grinder with a sanding wheel, remove all the rust, mount it and then paint it outrageous colors. They were beautiful! People starting buying them like hotcakes. When people saw a neighbor or cousin or somebody driving some sweet classic car, of course, they want to know where they bought it, right? Well, word got out and spread like wildfire. People started invading every junkyard in America trying to find old cars to bring to G. A television producer saw it and took a big gamble, betting that viewers would tune in just to see if today's junkyard would become tomorrow's gold mine. This was unlike anything that had ever aired before. No script. No makeup. No rehearsals. Just real life. People couldn't get enough of watching G and his junkyard treasure hunts. Thus was born the very first TV reality show—'Rust Bucket Junkies.'"

Chaz's face fell a little. *Is that where we're going? A junkyard?* Chaz didn't want to go back to a junkyard. Ever.

"So G, the original Rust Bucket Junkie, chose you and is offering you a wonderful opportunity. You could thank him yourself but, unfortunately, he is about forty-seven hundred miles south of here right now, getting ready to start you off on a grand adventure. He wanted me to apologize for him not being here to meet you in person."

Bert heard someone in the back of the room having their own conversation. The Senator again. One of the others tried to shush the talker, who was being rude to Bert by not paying attention, but they were unsuccessful. Bert saw what was going on. A twinkle appeared in the corner of his eye.

"So, we have a talker in the bunch, do we? I have at least one or two at my show every week. I love them! I like to make them part of the show. Let's see how long it takes him to realize we're talking about him. I don't want to name names, but I'll describe him to you. Picture a really old guy. Retired. Past his prime. One foot in the grave and the other one slipping. Wearing Dry-Blue undergarments with the Velcro straps. His biggest fear in life is leakage. Do you have the picture? He visits the memory-impaired unit in the assisted living facility just to cruise for chicks. The greeter says, "Sir, stop asking the hospice nurse what time she gets off work." A real piece of work. The kind of guy who tugs at his catheter in time with the music while he's riding in an elevator."

The real Bert Redmond had arrived. Peaches screamed in laughter. Clarence burst out laughing. Celeste wrinkled her nose in disgust at the unwanted mental image. Annaliese, who was the one trying to shush the rude one, heard what Bert said and couldn't hold it in. She pressed her face into Susan's shoulder and laughed. Bert grinned.

"But enough about Senator Kingston."

The Senator, who had been lost in conversation, noticed everyone smiling at him. He turned his head back to Bert and laughed, not wanting to appear as though he had missed something. Annaliese and Susan looked at each other and laughed again. Bert thanked the Senator for joining them. Prank over, Bert continued his monologue.

"Now for the other man who wants me to apologize for not being here with you. Tony Longino is an acclaimed actor turned producer. You might know him from the TV series "Mastermind," where he plays the role of Trick, tracking down... "

Bert could not finish his sentence due to DeShunta's sudden realization of who had invited her to this place.

"Oh lord! Are you telling me that fine-looking brother has invited me to be here? Child!"

DeShunta mock-swooned and fell backwards into the hands of a surprised, and almost-overwhelmed, young man in a purple shirt. The glass containing his drink miraculously survived the fall to the Italian marble floor, but its contents spilled all over his shoes. An attendant wearing a white uniform rushed to the scene and quietly cleaned up the liquid. Bert laughed.

"I can see that Tony needs no introduction. He would be humbled and flattered by your response. Unfortunately, Tony and G could not be with us today. They are even now scouting out a location for our project. They have asked me to extend their deepest, most sincere apologies for not being here to greet you in person today. So, it's time. Let me tell you why you have been invited here."

You could hear a pin drop in the silence of the room. Well, it was almost silent. Senator Kingston had a nose whistle. Everyone in the room could hear it but him. No one looked at him out of deference to his station in life. No one but DeShunta, that is. She glared at the Senator.

"You want to take care of that?"

Senator Kingston looked behind him, then to his side before realizing the woman was speaking to him.

"I'm sorry?"

"Your nose. It's whistling like the wind through the crack around the door to my apartment. I can't hear the man speak for all that wind whistling out your sinus."

The Senator mumbled an apology and began to root around in his pockets for a handkerchief. Unable to find one, he pinched his nose and did a few quick sniff-huffs until the sound subsided. DeShunta gave him a withering look. *You would think a man with a suit like that would be able to take care of his personal hygiene without needing to be told.* Satisfied that the irritating sound had stopped, DeShunta turned her attention back to Bert.

"You are being presented with a rare opportunity which, if you accept, will open up a whole new world to you. G and Tony would like for you to be a part of a televised reality show which will be filmed in a South American rainforest. The name of the show will be "Jungle Money." And when I say money, I mean big money."

A collective "oooh" emanated from the crowd. Their faces expressed excitement. The veil of secrecy was finally lifted. A reality show in an exotic location! Bert smiled at their reactions.

"Unlike other reality shows you might have seen in the past, however, this one will be different. You see, you will get to make the rules. Each day, one of you will be king or queen of the jungle. You get to tell everyone around you how it is going to be as you compete for big money. Did I mention there would be big money?"

Smiles flashed all across the room as the weight of his words settled in. Some could not fully comprehend his statement, or understand how that could work. Others excitedly pondered the possibilities. Former Governor Parkman felt a warm glow building within her. She liked making rules. Her hesitancy at participating in something that was way outside of her box was starting to evaporate. The world could stand to see a strong woman making the rules for a change.

"So, here is what we are about to do. You are about to watch a short film created just for you to show you what Jungle Money will look like and the parts you will play if you accept. You will be interviewed on video. Tony and G think each of you holds great promise, but they haven't fully made up their minds that you are right for the show. The interviews you give today will help them decide. Part of the interview will require you to agree to a waiver, release and hold harmless agreement, so that if there happen to be any mishaps along the way, you won't blame it on Tony or G or me. Last but not least, you will be asked on video how you would like your money to be paid out to you—one lump sum, monthly payments or what. That is something we need to cover now because one of the twelve guests in this room will be rich beyond their wildest dreams before the show is over. If you make the cut, the interview you give today will likely be shown on TV as a teaser trailer in the weeks leading up to the show. By the way, this show will be broadcast live to millions of viewers across this country, the good old US of A, as well as South America, Canada, and I don't even know where else."

Mouths opened. Nervous laughter filled the room. Some felt fear rising in their throats. Others remained wide-eyed and silent at the enormity of what they had just heard.

"We are dividing you up into two groups, men and women, just for the sole purpose of speeding up the filming of your interviews. Ladies, allow me to introduce you to my lovely wife, Beth. Say hi, Beth!"

A beautiful lady standing in the back, who had slipped in unnoticed, smiled warmly and waved.

"Hey y'all!"

The attendees replied, almost in unison, "Hey, Beth!"

She laughed at the reception she received. The sweet personality and fun she radiated made you want to know her better.

"Come on, ladies. Time's a-wasting. Let's go show the world what tigers or tigresses you are!"

Beth giggled and waved at the ladies to follow her. Bert rubbed his hands together excitedly and told the men to follow him. Smiles abounded as each person followed the designated host or hostess.

Beth walked slowly, knowing that the ladies who followed her were awed by the luxuriousness of the mansion they were exploring. Stunning marble. Italian frescos. Vaulted ceilings. Stained glass windows, each one more beautiful than the last. Oriental rugs that were almost too exquisite to be walked on. Candles that gave off an aromatic splendor that would make the walk beautiful even if taken blindfolded at midnight.

As the hallway transitioned from one section to another, they passed by ornate statues of elephants. Annaliese leaned close to the nearest elephant, horrified at the prospect that she could be looking at actual ivory. Noticing the sudden interest in the elegant carving, Beth answered the unspoken question.

"Don't worry. It's alabaster. Me and Bert just love elephants. We don't want to have their teeth as decorations. Speaking of which, can you imagine if some hunter took some of your teeth and decorated his house with them? Lord help, I sure would hope I'd flossed before they shot me!"

Beth had an infectious laugh. The former Governor sniffed and said she already knew it was alabaster. Bright light poured out of a room into the hallway just ahead. As they neared, they saw gigantic double doors, at least twelve feet high, adorned with medieval locks, door knockers, and intricate scrolled woodwork. When they entered, they could see it was a library which also served as a grand conference room. Looking overhead, Celeste wondered how anyone could get a book down from one of the top shelves. Her eyes fell upon a tiny but very tall spiral staircase in the corner. She looked at the bottom and saw that the base had wheels. *That is crazy. Somebody else might climb that thing but not me,* she thought.

A camera crew stood at the far end of the impossibly long conference room table. There were umbrellas illuminated with spotlights, screens, and video equipment coming at them from all sides. Their pupils, moments earlier adjusted to the pleasantly muted light of the hallways, rapidly contracted down to the size of pinpricks in defense against the harsh lights which seemed as bright as the sun. DeShunta held her hand up to shield her eyes.

"Y'all going to blind me."

The ladies giggled in part because of DeShunta's comment, but also because they had a burst of nervous energy when they saw the cameras pointed at them. Beth smiled and invited them to sit in the stately antique chairs that ringed the mahogany table. They all had difficulty pulling out the heavy chairs but managed to get seated. Everyone watched expectantly as Beth walked around to the head of the table.

"Ladies, here is where it all begins. It will come as no surprise to you that the path you are taking will require you to essentially live in front of cameras. Every moment, every activity will be recorded. Well, except for personal hygiene, of course. What kind of show do you think we're running here?"

Beth appreciated the laughter almost as much as the women appreciated getting the answer to one of their many questions.

"In order to participate in perhaps the most exciting adventure of your lives, you must become comfortable in front of cameras. Act as though they aren't there at all. We are going to have a video session in order to accustom you to life in front of cameras. We are going to talk about all kinds of things. Whatever comes to mind, ask me. One of the purposes of this exercise is for you to get to know one another. Once again, G and Tony extend their sincere apologies that they couldn't be here to interview you for the show, but in their absence, Bert and I will do our best to get you prepared. I've got to check in with Bert about something real quick, and then I'll be right back."

Celeste shyly raised her hand.

"So, you said we get to make the rules for this show?"

"Yes, you do."

Annaliese was not a hand-raiser.

"For the men, too?"

The ladies laughed as they considered the implications of being able to dictate to the men. None beside Annaliese had yet considered that possibility. Beth laughed.

"Well, to a certain degree, but remember, the men will have a say in the rules as well, especially if they get picked as king for the day."

The ladies groaned in unison, expressing mock disgust at the idea of a man telling them what to do. DeShunta spoke up next.

"Let me ask you this. Are we going to be mixed in with the men, or is it going to be man versus woman?"

Beth smiled.

"Excellent question. Mixed in as much as you want it to be. Men and women will hopefully work together, but you make the rules. If you don't want to be, and you are Queen for a Day, the men have to do what you say. "

"They better," DeShunta retorted.

"Well, I am going to go check with Bert about a couple of things, and then I will be back. Richard, go ahead and turn on the cameras. Have fun, ladies!"

With that, Beth gracefully exited the conference room door. The sound of her heels began to echo down the corridor. The videographers turned on even more lights than there had been before. The cameraman named Richard, who seemed to be in charge, spoke.

"Beginning Interview Tape One. The date is May 1st. We are on video."

Chapter Eleven

Tony and G were both dead asleep. The muted roar of the plane's engine provided the white noise, and the periodic air pockets provided the rocking. Sleeping pills and general anesthesia could not have done a better job of knocking them out. They didn't mean to be. They intended to be glued to the windows finding the perfect spot to carry out a multi-million-dollar reality TV event that would hopefully capture the imaginations of viewers in two continents.

A bump and a momentary drop in altitude shook G awake. *Must have dozed off for a couple of minutes*, he thought to himself. When he remembered where he was and what he was doing, he sat up quickly and looked at the monitor before him. It looked like the little digital plane hadn't moved far; as a matter of fact, it didn't look like it had moved at all. G breathed a sigh of relief.

Refreshed by his nap, G rubbed his eyes and stretched. Tony was still sound asleep. G smiled. His guard was down. He was defenseless. G felt it was his duty as a friend to take full advantage of the situation. He knew Tony would do the same if the roles were reversed. It's just what guys do. G looked around and spied a drinking straw still in the paper. He picked it up and extended his arm toward his companion. G expertly placed the end of the straw within an inch of Tony's left ear canal and slowly, ever so slowly, leaned to his right until the straw brushed up against the hairs on the outside of Tony's ear. Tony, still asleep, didn't move, but his easy breathing became quieter. It was time. G pushed the end of the straw into Tony's ear canal and spun it.

Tony sprang from his seat, his left hand flying up to swat his ear. An oath erupted from his mouth. His unfocused eyes sought in vain to find the killer bee that had invaded his sleep and crawled in his ear. Not finding one, and badly confused, he looked around the cabin to find G. When he saw G's shoulders going up and down and his face contorted, Tony stood and began beating G's right shoulder with a balled-up fist as hard as he could swing. G was helpless to stop the beating. Defending yourself is hard when you are incapacitated by laughter. When the punches started to hurt, G grabbed for his friend's arms to stop the pounding. His vengeance complete, Tony glared at G. He was 100 percent awake now. G's voice was sickeningly sweet, like a mentally-deranged mother in a horror flick.

"Did you have a nice nap, dear?"

G got no reply aside from an icy stare, which pleased him greatly. Initially startled by the sounds of a struggle, the pilot was relieved to see that his VIP passengers were finally awake. He had been staring at the fuel gauge for quite a while now. G spread his feet out wide for balance and carefully walked to the cockpit. The pilot said hello, one of the few English words he said well. G returned to the mindset of a steely-eyed executive. He saw a worn binoculars case by the seat, opened it, and found a pair of high quality Bushland binoculars inside. He and the pilot expressed their mutual admiration for the binoculars, which did not require anything more than smiles and nods. Putting them up to his eyes, G whistled at the clarity. A whole new world opened up to him. G looked down at the jungle below.

After an uneventful ten minutes or so, G suddenly pointed down and to the southwest. The pilot obediently changed the trajectory of the Cessna ever so slightly, already knowing what had drawn his passenger's attention. The Amazon River. As the pilot followed the break in the line of trees made by the river, an open area came into view. This piqued his interest as well. He dropped altitude and dipped his wing as they prepared to pass over it. G no longer needed binoculars, as his naked eyes were more than sufficient. He leaned forward until his nose almost touched the glass.

Suddenly, the most incredible sight appeared before them. A magnificent waterfall. The river widened above the falls and then dropped off into clouds of mist more beautiful than the mind of an artist could imagine. Both men involuntarily laughed at the sheer beauty of it. G pointed excitedly and yelled for Tony. A flyover of this waterfall, tracking the exact same route they were taking right now, would be the perfect promotional commercial. Talk about capturing the imagination. This was it. This was definitely it. Scouting done. Location located.

Tony shoved his way into the crowded cockpit after hearing G's shout. As soon as he saw the scene unfolding before him, Tony cried "Whoa!" and began shaking his head in disbelief. In all of his musings about the possibilities of what they might find in the way of shooting locations, he had never entertained the possibility of something this beautiful. It had never occurred to him that there might be waterfalls, although thinking about it now, he didn't know why. It was stunning. Simply stunning.

G was done. As far as he was concerned, the issue had been decided. After a ninety-second flyover of a Brazilian waterfall, his mind had been made up. G was a big picture guy. He needed nothing more. Tony, on the other hand, was a detail guy. He grabbed the binoculars from G and began scanning the surrounding terrain. He spied a relatively open area to the west and pointed. G and the pilot reluctantly tore their eyes away from the picture postcard view of the waterfall and sighted along Tony's finger. The pilot saw the opening and made for it.

The clearing was possibly a thousand yards long. The vegetation was not very high. After a couple of passes looking for fallen trees or rock formations and finding none, the pilot came to a preliminary conclusion. It was possible.

He could set the plane down if they wanted. He got the attention of his passengers, and with a questioning look on his face, pointed straight down. Understanding his meaning, G said an enthusiastic yes.

Tony, on the other hand, asked him to hold on and make another pass, so he could check for hazards himself. The pilot obliged. Tony was not quite filled with the same pioneer spirit possessed by the other two men. He felt inadequate. He tried to set aside his frustrations with G, but it was difficult. Why had they put together a highly-trained and specialized scouting team of military people and wildlife biologists if not to have them picking the place? He knew it was pointless to fret over things he couldn't change, but Tony couldn't get past it. Who knew what was down there waiting for them? Still reticent, but knowing he was outnumbered two to one, Tony nodded his approval. Having gotten the consent he needed, the pilot circled around for his approach.

Far beneath the noisy plane, in the dim light of the jungle floor, a beast moved. The large black head of a tapir lifted slightly. Its short trunk-like snout moved this way and that, anxiously tasting the air. Its hind-quarters shifted uneasily. As the foreign noise grew louder, the brutish animal turned and stepped into the shallow, sluggish, coffee-colored water.

She quickly realized this was not a safe escape route however. She could feel it in the water—an uncomfortable feeling she had experienced before and never wanted to feel again. The mother tapir understood why her striped baby had stopped mid-stream and wasn't following her. Even though it was young and inexperienced, it felt the same physical discomfort its mother was feeling. Despite their instinctual desire to leap out of the water to safety, they remained motionless.

Mere feet away, underneath the surface of the brackish water, lurked a brooding evil. It was a slimy, repugnant, water-breathing creature with little intelligence, unimpressive teeth, and slight musculature. It could sense that larger animals had just stepped into its abode, and it didn't like it at all. Five other water-breathers just like it held their place next to a submerged tree branch. Malevolent round eyes, the size and shape of pencil erasers, peered into the inky black water around them. None of them moved, save their mouths which opened and closed, opened and closed as they breathed the stagnant water. They would not yield their place. All who would enter their domain beware.

The baby tapir had the instinct of the young to freeze when threatened, which served it well right now. Though it could not see the electric eels that glided mere inches away from its legs, it knew instinctively to be afraid. The eel closest to the baby, a seven-footer, was giving off a warning charge. The water tingled. Because the baby had stopped moving however, the eel did not yet feel threatened enough to give off the full six hundred volts it was capable of delivering. The future for the baby hinged at that moment on two things—one, whether the eel swam up against the young tapir's body, and two, whether the young tapir moved before the eel glided away, scaring the eel. Compounding the problem was the fact that the mother tapir did not like the feeling in her lower legs, which was just as uncomfortable as the shock waves her baby was receiving. Her discomfort caused her to pick up her nearest foot and splash it back down to the bottom of the moss-covered streambed. The eel was not pleased. Her baby started to panic as the electrical charge ramped up in response.

At that moment, the deafening noise of a low-flying Cessna less than a hundred feet overhead assaulted the ears of the tapirs and caused them to forget all but the terrifying sound. The baby and its mother both leaped clear of the water and plunged blindly into the underbrush, seeking a place to hide far from the noise. The eels felt the vibration of the propellers and quickly snaked their way to the bottom of the deepest pool. Jungle creatures everywhere within sight and hearing dove for cover.

The pilot touched down on a grassy strip where no plane had ever landed before. When the plane finally stopped bumping and bouncing and came to rest, Tony clapped the pilot on the shoulder. The pilot grinned broadly. He enjoyed when people appreciated him for doing what he did best. Even he was amazed at what a smooth landing it was. How could this remote strip of jungle land be so free of bumps? When the propellers stopped spinning, the pilot opened the door and jumped out. His passengers, glad to be out of the cramped space, hit the ground and took a few stiff-legged steps while taking in the world around them.

The first thing they noticed was the sound of the jungle. Insects by the millions were rubbing their legs and wings together in the trees, the bushes, and on the ground. The smell of decaying vegetation, mold, water vapor and heat flooded their nostrils. Just as G realized he could hear the sound of the waterfall in the distance, he felt the pin prick of a mosquito bite. The pilot climbed back in the plane and came back with a spray bottle of insect repellant for all of them. Tony, already having been bitten several times within the first few minutes after touchdown, grabbed for the bottle and began squirting himself. When he finished, he tossed the bottle to G. As Tony looked around him, he made the mistake of licking his lips right after spraying his face. As if the awful taste wasn't bad enough, his tongue went numb. Not a great start. Tony wondered how long the effects would last.

G was ready to explore, even if his companion wasn't, and the pilot was ready to oblige. The clearing did not look that ominous to him. He wanted to go see the waterfall. G and the pilot started toward the edge of the clearing nearest the tributary stream and were soon lost from sight. Tony did not see them leave. He had gone back to the plane to find a bottle of water and a rag or paper towel. He wanted to wipe his tongue with a wet cloth. Who knew what kind of mutant children he might father one day after ingesting South American bug spray?

Tony, troubled at being left alone, sighed and shook his head. He didn't sign up to be on this search party. They had hand-picked a select team to handle this part of the process months ago. He looked down at his feet. His shoe tops were dirty and had plant life on them, even though he hadn't taken more than a dozen steps since they landed. A giant centipede, larger than anything Tony had ever seen, was crawling on one shoe. Tony quickly picked up that foot and shook it in the air. When that did not dislodge the creature, Tony took a few steps and kicked the side of the plane. The quick ride and sudden stop were more than the insect's many feet could withstand. It flew into the side of the plane with a thump, bounced off and dropped into the grass. Tony began a brisk walk away from the plane. He could buy a pair of new shoes. For now, he just wanted to be away from large crawling insects.

Walking in the trail of flattened grass left by the plane's wheels as it landed, Tony made his way down the clearing. He was unaccustomed to the sights, sounds and smells of the jungle. When the flat grass trail ended, Tony had a decision to make. There was still quite a bit of clearing in front of him before it ended at thick jungle. He could explore it if he wanted to. The sound of water, louder than the soft gurgle of the tributary near the plane, piqued his interest. The allure of the waterfall was overwhelming.

Chiding himself for his cowardice, Tony got his courage up and did the unthinkable. He took a step out of the flattened grass and into the high grass. Half expecting to feel another centipede crawling up his leg, Tony fought the urge to retreat to safer ground. Visions of snakes consumed him each time he contemplated taking another step. After a long pause, however, he took another step. He stood there for a few seconds. Emboldened by his success, Tony began high-stepping through the undergrowth toward the sound of rushing water. He realized that he hadn't breathed in well over a minute. He exhaled and found he was out of breath. Mentally calming himself, Tony attempted to regain control of his lungs. After less than a minute of regular breathing, Tony's lungs adjusted and walking became easier.

When he got to the end of the clearing, Tony's attention was drawn to the sound of water to his right. The stream he had walked alongside was met by another feeder stream, which created the noise he heard. Glancing at the thick-stemmed bamboo shoots that lined the stream, Tony knew he couldn't walk through them without a chainsaw. Sections of the riverbank were dark even in the light of day. What would they be like at night? He suddenly felt very alone. Where had G and the pilot gone?

Using only his eyes, Tony tried to find a passage down to the waterfall. How badly he wanted to go. Why had G taken off on him like that? Tony didn't want to walk in the chest-high grass anymore. Anything could be lurking in the tall grass, looking for a quick meal. A hungry jaguar could be right there, licking its lips like it was sitting in the jungle drive-through, waiting for a single black male with a side of fries. As he weighed the pros and cons of pressing ahead, a sudden rustling in the grass behind him startled him. Something had moved. Something he couldn't see. On high alert, Tony fairly fled the high grass. No one was here to see him, so he did not have to walk slowly in order to preserve his dignity.

As Tony sprinted back to the plane, he placed his feet in the line of grass flattened by the plane's right wheel. If he had chosen the path of the left wheel, however, he would have discovered the source of the rustling noise. A bushmaster, whose middle had been squashed by the weight of an airplane's tire rolling over it, was thrashing upside down in agony as its serpentine life ebbed away. Its jaw opened reflexively and then shut, over and over again, its inch-long fangs making a futile effort to inject venom into its unreachable killer before the eternal darkness took it.

Tony breathed a sigh of relief when he finally stood next to the plane again. He checked his leather shoes. Dirt, grass, grass seeds…and a crawling thing. Tony lifted his foot and whipped it, launching the tiny creature into the grass. He scanned the edge of the clearing where G and the pilot had entered the jungle. It was like they were never there. A thought occurred to him. What if they were lost and couldn't find their way out?

Tony was beginning to get creeped out. He decided to wait five minutes, but no more than five minutes, before calling out for them. The longer he stood there, the more certain he became that they were lost. How could they find their way back to the plane with all this impenetrable jungle around them? Then a thought occurred to him.

Do planes have horns? As Tony scrambled his way to the door to find out, a second distressing thought occurred to him. Do planes have locks? And did the pilot take the keys with him?

Wait until Tamper finds out what we're doing, Tony thought to himself. *Just wait. He is going to flip his lid.*

Chapter Twelve

Bert had just stepped out of the cavernous meeting hall set aside for the men when Beth rounded the corner and saw her husband. Their affection for one another was palpable, evident in every look and movement. Giddy from the excitement of the adventure they had just begun, Bert placed his hands behind her back and dipped her as though they were concluding a ballroom dance. He loved her laugh. She loved his spontaneity. He tried to kiss her, but she leaned back and pushed off on his chest.

"Later, big boy! Later! We've got important things to do right now."

Bert had given the men the same information and instructions in their room as Beth had given the ladies in the other room. Unlike Beth, however, Bert stayed to watch the instructional video narrated by Tony. Bert had numerous cameo appearances throughout the video, most of which involved him squatting in the woods with his pants around his ankles, reading a newspaper and swatting flies. Beth had already seen it and didn't feel the need to see it again, but Bert, who lived for laughter, wanted to watch the men's reaction. The men did not disappoint. They howled. Bert bragged to the men how his acting classes had really paid off. Once their laughter died down, he slipped out of the room to meet Beth as planned.

They stood quietly in the dim light of the hallway roughly ten paces from the door. Suddenly, a flood of bright light burst out of the doorway when the videographer flipped the switch. They paused for a moment to hear the conversation begin. Senator Bradford Kingston, III, having decided that he would preside over the discussions, cleared his throat and began an impromptu, yet professional-sounding introduction.

"Hello everyone, might I introduce myself? My name is Bradford Kingston, III, former Senator from the great state of Vermont. As part of this most distinguished and august body, I would suggest that, before we undertake the crafting of laws that will govern us as we embark on this endeavor, we might all benefit from…"

Clarence Humberton cut him off like a circular saw through a kneecap.

"Look, we all know who you are and what your pedigree is. But this ain't the Westchester Abbey Dog Show last time I checked. Ain't none of us better than anybody else. Let's get one thing straight. You ain't running the show out wherever in east Egypt they're sending us. Not by a long shot. So don't start talking like you are, 'cause you ain't.'"

The outburst by Clarence stunned the Senator into silence. He was used to deference from his audiences. In the early years of his political career, he used to have open events that welcomed all comers. They could be dicey, depending on who showed up. They could go well, or they could be disasters. As his popularity grew, and more people began filling the venues where he spoke, however, he could be more selective with his audiences. His staff began to prescreen those who would be admitted to make sure they were supporters, not detractors. The Senator grew fond of a certain few reporters who seem to report on his events with more fairness than others. Why put a damper on otherwise productive meetings by allowing rabble rousers to attend, when they were merely taking up seats that more agreeable listeners could be using? The Senator did not answer Clarence right away, instead turning his head toward the videographer.

"We can start the tape over, can't we? We should begin again. Yes, why don't we?"

All of the men in the room looked at Steve the videographer, who silently shook his head and continued filming. Having reached a dead end, the Senator reluctantly addressed Clarence.

"We are all in uncharted territory here, and I, for one, am rather uncertain as to the procedure we are to follow. I would suggest that someone track down our host and find out how he would like for us to proceed. Perhaps you there, young fellow?"

Chaz, who was the young fellow seated closest to the door, went into deer-in-headlights mode. His trademark forty-five degree head tilt, which kept the hair out of one eye, swiftly changed to the high noon position. Both eyes hid beneath the mop of hair that swung across his face. The mere thought of becoming an active participant in a fight between the two intimidating men terrified him. Overwhelmed by movie lights, Senators, comedians, mansions and angry men shouting, he froze. Chaz gave no indication that he either heard or comprehended. His instincts told him that if he didn't show movement they might go to somebody else, kind of like the reaction a spotted fawn has when a pack of coyotes is approaching. After an awkward pause, a new voice came from the corner of the table.

Aston spoke up. He was a thirty-something year-old man with immaculately-trimmed hair, expertly gelled and spiked with frosted tips. He wore a form-fitting purple shirt, buttoned low so as to show off his furry carpet of chest hair, along with a gold necklace and gold ring. He was not a fan of the Senator and was delighted to see someone knock the crown off the politician. Emboldened by Clarence's breach of protocol, which leveled the playing field between aristocrat and peasant, Aston spoke before he lost his nerve.

"Senator Kingston, while we are here waiting for all this to start, I need to say something. You have promised time after time to address the looming disaster of climate change. Every time an election rolls around, you make the same promise to do something, and you never do it. My significant other went to a fundraising event for you and asked you that very question. When are you going to act? We see all the glaciers disappearing year after year. We all see the temperatures getting hotter and hotter. We see the state of California on fire every year. Global warming is literally lighting our country on fire. We know the ozone layer is almost gone from greenhouse gases. Worst of all, we are seeing the extinction of endangered species happening right before our very eyes. Marine life, marine mammals, just gone, dying at an alarming rate. When are you going to do something about it?"

Chaz's neck muscles began to relax now that everyone had stopped staring at him. The topic had changed to something he was passionate about. He felt a kinship with Purple Shirt as soon as he started talking. He kind of looks familiar, Chaz thought to himself. He kind of sounds familiar, too. Then it hit Chaz who Purple Shirt was.

This was the whale harpoon guy.

Aston Mead was the man in the purple shirt. He was always a little different. From the time he was a baby, he was full to overflowing with life and laughter. As a small child, he preferred dress-up dolls to Army men. When his mom took him and his sisters to shop for Halloween costumes, Aston invariably picked the princess. Public school teachers thought Aston was cute—flamboyant but cute. His father, retired military, would have none of that. The boy needed strict discipline. The elder Mr. Mead put his son and daughters in a private Catholic school where they had uniforms in the classroom and paddles in the principal's office. Catholic school would straighten him out.

They tried. It didn't work.

Aston spent his days in Catholic school somewhere between nonconformity and outright rebellion. It was the dress code he had the most trouble with. If the headmaster required the boys to wear their school-issued ties, Aston would dutifully wear his tie...backwards, dangling down his back between his shoulder blades. The headmaster thought he handled the problem by sternly telling young master Mead to go to the bathroom, fix his tie and return to his classroom. Young master Mead did all those things, but he did one thing more. He took off his pants, spun them around, put them back on and walked crotch-behind all the way down the hallway, somehow making it back to his desk without the headmaster noticing. Aston held firm convictions, but the headmaster held a firm paddle. More than a few tears were shed in that office over the next few years. Nevertheless, against all odds, Aston made it to his senior year while still enrolled at the same school. It looked as though he might actually graduate.

Until picture day.

The headmaster made it clear to all students that he would suffer no foolishness when it came to pictures for the yearbook. He interrupted an English literature class to personally tell Aston that he would wear his coat and tie in prescribed fashion and made Aston promise, in front of his teacher and classmates, to do so without incident or complaint. Aston assured his nemesis that he would comply.

The photographer set up shop in the back of the library early the next morning. Portrait appointments were scheduled alphabetically by first names, so Aston was the first one of the day. When he walked into the quiet library straight from the parking lot, his shirt, tie, pants, shoes and blazer were all regulation, as promised. When the photographer looked up to see who had arrived, however, he saw Aston Mead sitting on the stool in front of the black backdrop wearing full makeup, complete with foundation, blush, eyeliner, eye shadow and lipstick. His older sister, who had graduated the year before and was therefore beyond the reach of the headmaster, had a glorious time making up her brother's face.

The photographer, uncertain as to what to do but having no one to ask at that early hour, took Aston's picture. Aston was hurrying to the restroom to wash his face before his first class when he came face-to-face with the headmaster. If looks could kill, he would have died on the spot. With his portrait a fait accompli, however, what could the headmaster do? Aston barely felt any pain from the all-too-familiar paddle. The aching in his butt cheeks felt like a red badge of courage as he exited the office unable to hide a smirk.

Like most students, Aston looked forward to the day the yearbooks came out. He was even more excited this year because now all would see his victory over the headmaster and his silly dress code. When the yearbooks finally came, Aston and his girlfriends, who knew what was coming, flipped through the pages as fast as their fingers would allow. Aston found the M's quickly enough, but as he looked for his picture, his smiling face became crestfallen. He had no picture. There was only a solid gray square above his name. Aston McIntire Mead—invisible.

Aston knew he shouldn't have done it, but he did. He strode down to the office, yearbook in hand, found the headmaster in a meeting, barged in and told him everything he thought about him. He held nothing back. Once he finished, he walked straight out of the school, down to the road, turned right and headed home as in home home. Nineteen miles and five hours later, Aston was lying on his bed staring at the ceiling and wondering what he had done.

To no one's surprise, Aston was expelled from school which marked a big turning point in his life. He left everyone and everything he knew and traveled to Burlington, Vermont, where he found like-minded people in the arts district which became his new home. He became an avid protester. Any civil unrest or conflict between government and citizens quickened his pulse because those felt like opportunities to get back at his old headmaster. After a time, however, spray painting buildings at night lost its luster. He wanted to make a difference. At first, he had trouble finding a cause he believed in.

That was when Aston discovered the barbaric practice of hunting whales.

For years, the world had banned whale hunting, at least until Norway decided to ignore the world and resume commercial whaling. Aston chanced upon a video on whale wars one day and was profoundly moved. He had found his cause. Aston Mead became an international eco-pirate, dedicated to the mission of ending whale hunting no matter the cost. Unfortunately for him, his dedication to whales cost him dearly.

Aston's newfound passion soon found him swimming to the side of a stricken minke whale in the North Atlantic as a reality TV film crew looked on. The war between commercial whalers and anti-whalers was always a messy affair, and this was no exception. Aston swam through blood-stained waters to place himself between the whaler and their prey with the fervent belief they would launch no more harpoons if a human was in the way. Aston guessed right—they didn't fire anymore. The problem, however, was the fact that the penthrite in the explosive whale grenade already embedded in the minke's body did not explode right away. It waited until Aston's legs, protected only by a wetsuit, were in the blast zone. Whether it was shrapnel from the grenade or flying bone from the whale didn't matter—the result was the same. Aston lost his left leg above the knee. He would have died if not for the swift action of one of his compatriots who was an ER trauma nurse in her everyday nine-to-five life.

Donations flowed in from all corners of the world after the TV show aired and people learned of Aston's sacrifice. When the wounds to his stump healed, he was fitted with the most advanced prosthetic leg available on the market. With the passage of time, his limp became barely noticeable. His impact on the Norwegian whaling industry, however, was anything but. The international outcry pressured Norway to ban the practice, at least for now, which was due in no small measure to the very public loss of Aston Mead's left leg. When he finally returned to the streets of Burlington, Vermont, he was hailed as a hero. It was this battle-scarred Aston, no longer intimidated by power or celebrity, that spoke to the former Senator.

"Senator, I'm trying to figure out what we, the people, got out of paying your salary. Your constituents, like me, told you time and again that we want climate change legislation passed, but where is it? I can tell you that I have seen climate change firsthand. I have seen, with my own eyes, green mountains where there used to be glaciers. I have swam in arctic waters and felt their warmth, a temperature that nature never intended. I have seen men slaughtering living, breathing, thinking, feeling mammals whose intellects rival our own."

Aston leaned back in his chair, lifted his left foot in the air and began to hike up his pants leg. The Senator cringed. Like Chaz, he too recognized Aston, although he couldn't recall his name. He knew what was coming. This was the whale wars guy. He was going to take off his artificial leg and show it to everybody. *He's probably going to blame me like I'm the one that fired the harpoon*, the Senator thought grimly to himself.

Sure enough, Aston pulled off his prosthetic and held it above his head. Once Aston had looked each person in the room in the eyes, he lowered his leg and returned his gaze to the Senator.

"I have done everything humanly possible to stop men from killing our planet. Can you say the same, Senator?"

Every head turned to the Senator to see what his answer would be. You could cut the tension with a knife. The Senator, under attack from all sides, unsheathed his oratorical sword and prepared to defend the realm.

"I can feel your frustration, good sir, and quite frankly I share in it, too. Not enough has been done to protect our precious Mother Earth from the excesses of mankind. If we continue to dawdle and dilly dally, we will be too late. I must remind you however, that I am no longer a Senator. I do not have the power you seem to think I have. I am now a constituent just like yourself."

Chaz glanced back at whale harpoon guy to see his reaction. The Senator had a point. If he was no longer in office, how could anyone expect him to do anything? He couldn't. So, how could whale harpoon guy be mad? Without waiting for a reply, the Senator, or ex-Senator to be precise, continued in his defense.

"Time and again my colleagues and I have been prepared to enact common sense legislation to reign in Big Oil, cap the emission of greenhouse gases, reduce our dependence on foreign oil at the expense of our environment and clean up our water. The Senate passed a bill mandating the production of car engines that would get fifty miles per gallon, but the other party in control of the House refused to enact it. I wanted to go further. I proposed a bill that would mandate production of cars that get no less than seventy miles per gallon. If the automakers thereafter chose not to spend their money so as to comply with the law, preferring profit over protection of the earth, I proposed that they pay a 10 percent penalty based on earnings received from the sale of non-compliant cars. The earth has a constitutional right to healthcare, and it should be paid for by the ones making her sick."

The Senator scanned the room to determine the effect his words were having. He breathed a tad easier when he saw Chaz nodding his approval. Aston's expression made it clear that he was not convinced. Before Aston could respond, Clarence injected himself back into the conversation.

"Wait a minute. You are saying that automakers should pay a 10 percent penalty if they can't figure out how to make a car go seventy miles to the gallon? Are you nuts? Look, I know a lot of guys who work in the auto industry. Good, salt-of-the-earth, dues-paying guys who just want to work hard and make an honest living. You are not suggesting that they be penalized and get less wages just because their employers don't give their employees the tools to bring this upgrade to pass, are you?"

The Senator was back on familiar ground now. He didn't know much, if anything, about car engines or reality shows. Political questions, on the other hand, were what he ate for breakfast, lunch and dinner. This one was easy.

"Absolutely not. The middle class has sacrificed enough already. It is time for the rich to pay their fair share for a change. The millionaires and billionaires need to give back a little of what they have earned off of the blood, sweat and tears of those very same workers you just described. I would propose an additional 50 percent income tax on the top 10 percent of Americans, the wealthy, the ones who have won life's lottery but who don't want to share the wealth. Only then will we have a ghost of a chance to save mankind from certain extinction."

Clarence liked that. He liked it a lot. He didn't care a bit about this Save The Whales and Hug A Tree stuff. If however, there was a new government mandate that produced contracts for autoworkers that kept workers working and dues coming in, he would be the first to step up and make it happen. Clarence could be as effective in the art of persuasion as the Senator, if not more so, although his skill set was less genteel and slightly more unpleasant for the one who needed persuading.

Back in the other conference room where the ladies were meeting, the room temperature was rising, but it wasn't due to the lighting. Mystic Origin was dominating the conversation, taking it in a direction neither Beth nor Bert anticipated.

"You can tell us. You won't get in trouble. We'll make sure of it. So, how much are you getting paid?"

The speaker was a small, older woman who, despite her age, wore dreadlocks in her hair. Not surprisingly, "Mystic Origin" was not her given name. She was born "Dierdre Brown," a rather ordinary name. Dierdre was nothing close to ordinary however. She did not fit any mold. When Dierdre turned twenty-one, she and her legal name parted ways. She chose a new name that she felt more accurately described her spirit. Mystic Origin. She did not like when people only called her by her first name, "Mystic." She felt it to be rude. She did not like when people called her "Miss Origin." She especially hated it when people tried to shorten her name to "Mys." Call her by her full name or she would ignore you and act as though you hadn't spoken at all.

Mystic Origin had entered the public eye when she appeared on a TV documentary as the leading proponent of "Freeganism." She and her male companion and sometimes partner Leaf (no last name, just Leaf), lived in the San Francisco area. They survived on rescued fruit and vegetables they found in dumpsters behind restaurants and grocery stores. On the documentary, she prickled when someone called her practice "dumpster diving." She preferred to call what she and Leaf did, "Freegan rescue missions." Her diet and lifestyle afforded her the ability to live without working, which made the current topic of conversation slightly puzzling.

"So, how much do they pay you compared to him?" Mystic Origin asked Summer, the young blonde-haired assistant videographer. Summer's cheeks flushed a bright pink. She had always been a quiet girl, more comfortable behind a camera than in front of it. She spoke through her camera lens and the moments she captured. This was Summer's first paying job that wasn't babysitting. She was beyond thrilled to have been given the chance to assist with the production of a real live television show. The experience she would gain from assisting with this project would be invaluable to her. The fact that she was being paid was icing on the cake since she was willing to do it for free.

Seeing that the girl had been rendered speechless by the question, and perceiving that there was an inequity of power between her and the man behind the camera, Mystic Origin redirected her inquiry to Richard, the forty-something year-old man operating the video equipment.

"Sir, I didn't catch your name earlier. Before I agree to participate in this venture, I need to know that those around me are being treated fairly, and that includes you and her. How much are you being paid? Certainly you believe in equal pay for equal work, don't you?"

Richard's face blanched. Like Summer, he thrived behind the camera lens not in front of it. He had been tasked with filming it all, the significant as well as the seemingly insignificant, the profound as well as the mundane. His was not to direct. None of this was scripted. One of the cardinal rules of being a good videographer in a production of this nature was to capture it all but do not become part of the event. The ability to disappear in a room, and to make those being filmed forget he was there, was one of the reasons Richard was so highly sought after.

DeShunta had been staring at Mystic Origin's face ever since they entered the room. What was that dark on her face? Did she not wash her face today? DeShunta leaned closer for a better look. She squinted for a few seconds and finally understood what her eyes were telling her. That was hair she was seeing on her face! Thick black hair. DeShunta's nose wrinkled. How long has she been growing those sideburns? How long has she had that mustache? Disgusted, DeShunta was on the verge of asking her when Mystic Origin started grilling the camera people. DeShunta, now caught up in the back and forth, decided to hold off and ask her later. This had gotten interesting.

Summer, who up until the moment she was thrust into the discussion, had been taking still shots of the contestants. Now, she was at a loss. She did not know what to say or how to respond. Should she respond at all? She stayed quiet, hoping the woman with dreads would grow tired of waiting for an answer and turn her attention elsewhere.

Mystic Origin had an infinite amount of patience however. She had spent the last three decades of her life waiting on stock boys and kitchen help to exit back alley doors with arms full of soon-to-be-reclaimed food before she could eat. She had been ticketed and hassled and arrested for ignoring unjust city ordinances prohibiting what she considered to be a religious calling. No one would outlast her. She asked the question twice more. Finally, she got what she had been waiting for. In a barely audible voice, Summer answered the question.

"Seven twenty-five an hour."

A knowing smile appeared on Mystic Origin's face. Armed with all of the information that she needed, she turned her attention back to the man.

"Minimum wage. The young lady is doing the exact same work as the man, and she is making minimum wage. Sir, I am willing to bet that your corporation is paying you more than minimum wage. Am I right? Sir, can you hear me? Are you able to sleep at night? Do you want to tell this room full of women why you feel like women are less valuable than men?"

Richard felt heat spreading up the back of his neck, but he was the veteran of many a tight situation. He had determined a long time ago that he would not become part of the production. That was his guiding principle. If the subject decided to spend her time in front of the camera verbally assaulting him, so be it. He would neither respond to it nor slow it down. He was Lights Camera. The Action was totally up to her.

DeShunta started to grow bored with all this talk of how much the camera girl got paid. DeShunta wanted to know how much DeShunta was going to get paid. She had just watched a video of Tony Longino telling her she could win millions of dollars if she came to stay with him in a rainforest in Brazil. Tony said he had invited twelve people, so she had a one-out-of-twelve chance of winning the money. DeShunta's mind started whirling. She had played scratch-offs, Mega-Billions, Power Drop and every other gas station lottery contest for as long as she could remember. She knew her chances were one in ten billion, or something like that, but she played anyway. *You can't win if you don't play*, she reasoned. If she won, she could move out of apartment building U and go far away from Cedrick the downstairs neighbor who broke her TV. That idea made her actually consider doing something as crazy as getting on a plane and playing games in the jungle with the people sitting around this gigantic table.

When the hippie woman started repeating herself, now demanding to know how much Richard the cameraman made, DeShunta grew impatient. She exhaled, giving a long, loud sigh designed to express to the hippie woman that her time for talking was about up.

Mystic Origin heard DeShunta's blast of air and recognized the intent behind it. Up until this point, Mystic Origin had kept her verbal onslaught directed at the meek and mild camera people. Everyone in this group needed to understand that gender inequality in the workplace was a problem everywhere and needed to be rooted out wherever it was found. This group clearly did not understand the importance of what Mystic Origin was trying to do. She locked eyes with DeShunta whose sigh needed addressing, at least in Mystic Origin's mind.

"You people don't understand the problem we are seeing here, right before our very eyes."

DeShunta did a double take and shook her head. Oh no, she didn't. DeShunta came alive.

"What you mean, 'you people?' You saying we ignorant? I know you ain't saying we ignorant! Look at you. Did you know that they sell tweezers that will pluck out them hairs growing between your nose and your upper lip? They do. They sell them at your neighborhood Buymart in the personal grooming aisle. They have greeters up front that will show you where they at. You going to have to ask because I can tell you ain't never been there before. And razors. Go on ahead and get you some disposable razors while you back there, and you can catch those sideburns while you at it."

Mystic Origin hesitated, not because she lacked a comeback, but because she knew she had just crossed into dangerous territory. A tense stand-off ensued, the two women glaring at each other, their brains racing to decide their next move.

Celeste had been listening to all of this harsh talk, which was very distressing to her. She was already not feeling well. She had felt a wee bit nauseous this morning and had not been able to shake it. She knew she needed to eat something, but she just didn't feel like it at the time. One thing was for certain. She had to get out of this place and get to a restroom quickly. It couldn't wait.

"I'm not feeling very well. Excuse me."

Celeste stood up and took two steps toward the door. Suddenly her vision narrowed to a black tunnel. The world went quiet and dark. Nothingness. Calm. Black. Silence. Soft, almost inaudible voices in the distance. Chairs scraping on the floor, perceived more from the vibration of the floorboards in contact with her face than through her ears. Rude shaking, annoying because she was comfortable. A loud voice close to her ear interrupted her dream.

"Hey! Are you all right? Call 911!"

Annaliese Parkman had taken charge. The former Governor directed Summer to find Beth. Summer sprinted out of the room, camera still in hand. Mystic Origin dropped to the floor beside Celeste, closed her eyes, and began to think positive thoughts of healing.

DeShunta hurried over to the fallen girl and pushed the hippie woman out of the way. DeShunta lowered herself to the floor and cradled the still-unconscious girl's head in her hands. She was pale as death. The mother in her taking over, DeShunta brushed the girl's hair off of her face and felt her forehead. Cold but clammy. DeShunta felt all over her head for signs of injury. The child had fallen hard and could not have survived the fall without a serious lump at the point of impact. The sound of running feet could be heard coming down the hallway. Beth and Summer burst into the room. Rushing over and kneeling beside them, Beth took one of Celeste's hands and patted it.

"How is she? How are you, baby? Can you hear me? Did she hit her head? Hey sweetie, we're here. We've got you. Can you talk to me?"

The women breathed a collective sigh of relief as movement returned to Celeste's face. Moaning slightly, her eyes fluttered open. Squinting up into the bright lights, she became aware of the throbbing pain in her head caused by the impact from the fall that she didn't remember. Celeste apologized, for what nobody knew. DeShunta shushed her. Beth asked if she needed a doctor. Celeste didn't answer right away, not at herself enough to make that call. DeShunta answered for her.

"Yes, we need a doctor. Don't you see this girl on the floor? We got all kinds of issues. We need a brain doctor, one that specialize in head bumps."

She paused.

"And head lice."

Mystic Origin saw red. There was no need whatsoever to go insulting this poor girl who had passed out cold in the floor. She rushed to her defense.

"That girl doesn't have head lice! Why would you say such a thing? She doesn't need that!"

DeShunta glared back at her.

"I wasn't talking about her."

Chapter Thirteen

Back in Hollywood, California, the team had assembled. They sat in stunned silence, staring at G, as they heard the unexpected news.

"So team, Brazil is where Jungle Money will happen. It has already been decided. Right beside a beautiful waterfall. Tony and I have walked it ourselves, and the Brazilian government has given its stamp of approval. You'll love it. You will absolutely love it. We took some pictures while we were out there. Let me pull them up on my phone…"

He stopped there, wanting to let the weight of his words settle in. They couldn't see his eyes because he was wearing sunglasses, as he often did. G looked as cool as ever, but he was holding his breath.

Professional tracker Bentley Barrington, IV, better known as Bones, had a shaggy mane of light brown hair, permanently suntanned skin and stubble on his face. His easygoing South African accent was the type that made you want to try to mimic it the next time you were out of other people's earshot. Nothing got under Bones' skin. Bones had just stepped off a plane following a twenty-two-hour flight from Kenya and driven straight here. He had been looking forward to the multi-national location scouting trips for the better part of a year. *Now we are not doing any trips at all?*

Bones broke the silence. He started laughing. Laughter is good, G thought to himself. Laughter is good. He didn't expect it to last, though.

It didn't. The shock waves caused by G's revelation that he and Tony had decided on the location without them or their input were measurable on the Richter scale.

Tamper didn't say a word. He threw the black binder he put together months ago for the scout team at the back wall of the war room as hard as he could. Just before impact, the cover opened. Paper exploded in a shower of fluttering white. G knew that Tamper wouldn't take the news well.

He didn't.

Tamper, ex-military, former Army Ranger, was the head of logistics for the entire project. He had a buzz-cut and a close shave. His wife-beater t-shirt revealed tattoos up and down his arms. If supplies got to the shoot location, it would be because Tamper made it happen. Helicopters. Off-road vehicles. Portable electrical generators. Medical supplies. Food for months. Fresh water supply. Video cameras and people to aim them. Future reality TV stars. None of these things happened if Tamper didn't get them there and, when the time came, get them back out again. He had the most challenging job of anyone on the entire project, which everyone freely acknowledged. Of all people who needed to be intimately involved in scouting out the location, it was Tamper. That was now out the window.

As if it wasn't bad enough that he hadn't been consulted or even made aware the site selection was taking place, G had picked a spot so deep in the Amazon rainforest that no road existed without a two-hour flight to find it. Tamper's master sergeant voice came out in full force.

"What were you thinking, G? We need roads, G! Roads! Are you out of your mind? This is impossible! This is insane! Why did you fly out there? You could have saved the trip. You could have thrown darts at a map right here and done just as well. Where are we right now? What is the name of this hotel we're in? Hand me that notepad on the desk. What does it say? The Landmark. I'll bet room service at The Landmark could pick a better location than you! Somebody hand me the phone right now and hit zero. I'm going to talk to the first maid that comes to the room, and I guarantee you she can do a better job of picking a place than you!"

Denise Milton, the team's wildlife biologist, didn't take orders as a general rule, but today was not the day to prove it. She dialed zero and handed the phone to Tamper. G started to interject, but Tamper cut him off, his index finger pointed at G's jugular. G decided to let him go. This had to happen. G needed the team to get this part over with. If he didn't let them vent, they would walk. If they walked, the show didn't happen.

Before the front desk had a chance to answer the phone, however, an unsuspecting Hispanic woman peeked her head in the door and said, "Housekeeping." Perfect timing. Just what Tamper needed. He popped the phone down on the receiver and turned his full attention to the newcomer in the room. Speaking as sweetly as his blood pressure would allow, Tamper asked her if she would help him with something. With no small amount of hesitation, but not sure that she had any choice, the woman nodded yes. Tamper took her upper arm in his hand and ushered her over to a gigantic monitor.

"Now ma'am, let me ask you, if you wanted to go to an exotic location where you could enjoy some time in the sun with your husband or boyfriend, or both, where would you choose? There are no wrong answers here. Where would you go?"

The housekeeping attendant looked very uncertain about what she was being asked to do. Elise LeFleur, the team botanist, was as perturbed as anyone, but she didn't want to see this poor woman made sport of, especially when the targets should be Tony and G.

"Let her go, Tamper. She has no idea what's happening here. Pick on somebody else, why don't you? Hey, I have an idea. It doesn't look like G is doing anything at the moment. Pick on him. Just a suggestion."

G, whose arms had been folded, began scratching the back of his neck, a sure sign of his rising anger. He was the director and producer. For all of their training, qualifications and titles, the people in this room were all his employees. At-will employees. They could be fired for any reason or no reason at all, without recourse or severance pay, and they all knew it. Clearly, however, today was not Bosses' Day. Tamper was nowhere near finished, and he was not to be dissuaded.

"Ma'am, I promise not to embarrass you. I just need your help. Look at this map, and tell me—if you were going on vacation, where would you go?"

The woman stepped back a few paces and looked at the touch screen, trying to orient herself. She muttered to herself in her native tongue, saying something about crazy gringos. After several seconds of study, the woman pointed at the Caribbean. Tamper was delighted.

"Ah, the Caribbean. Excellent choice. Blue water. Blue skies. Which island do you like?"

The woman studied the wall-sized monitor for a few moments longer. She began sounding out the names and finally pointed at one of the islands in particular. She smiled uncertainly, hoping she was done here.

"Wow, Jamaica! Beautiful island! Lots of open water for people to get there by boat, lots of runway for people to fly in and out by plane, lots of roads for people to ride in little tour buses to little chairs under palm trees where they can sit and sip fruity drinks while looking at all that beautiful blue water. Excellent choice, ma'am! Do you know, I think you would make an excellent television show producer. Have you ever thought about being a television show producer? See that guy over there? He's a television show producer, but he doesn't know about things like boats and planes and cars that will get people like you and me to those wonderful places where you sip little fruity drinks. I cannot thank you enough, ma'am. You have been a tremendous help to us today!"

With that, Tamper pulled out his wallet, shoved a few dollars into her hand, grabbed the housekeeper's face, pulled it close to his and kissed her square on the forehead. The woman, certain that the man was crazy, mumbled something close to "gracias" and ran out the door. When she was gone from sight, all eyes fell on G.

If they expected G to be shaken, however, they were wrong. This wasn't his first rodeo. He looked frighteningly calm. Although his face was frozen, his eyes betrayed a hint of the fire behind them.

"Feel better?"

Tamper didn't answer right away, trying to figure out his angle.

"If you've got some more theater to enthrall us with, Tamper, please, be my guest. I'm really enjoying it. I'm not sure the senorita did. She was just trying to make sure you had enough towels. But I can see now that I overestimated you. I thought you knew something about logistics in remote locations. Now, though, I see that we need to set you up a booth at the county fair selling cruises to school teachers and retirees with knee replacements, because you apparently only specialize in places where senior citizens can take a stroll without their walkers."

Tamper strode over to G and got in his face. The two men met nose to nose, but this time it was G's turn to bark.

"I have never heard so much whining in all my life! Does it come as a surprise to you that we are shooting a show about surviving in the jungle in…let's see, what do they call those things, trees everywhere, rivers, wild animals, no civilization…hey I've got it! Jungle! That's it. A jungle! We're shooting Jungle Money in a jungle! Golly gee willikers, who'd a thunk it? You know, when you dropped a résumé claiming to be a logistics expert in remote locations, I didn't expect you to wet your pants and bawl like a three-year-old when we picked a remote location!"

Tamper started to shout back, but G's volume went from loud to thunderous in an instant.

"Now, you listen to me! I've listened to you all I'm going to! It's time to decide. Are you going to do the job or not? If it's too big for you, let me know and I'll find somebody else! You are not the only game in town. There are others with your skill set, maybe even better than you, who will hear the kind of money I've offered you and jump at the chance. I can have you replaced inside of a week! So, if you're walking, walk! Maybe you can catch the senorita before she gets on the elevator, and you can ask her to change your diaper before you leave!"

Tamper knotted up his fists, clenched his teeth, and glowered at G. No one in the room breathed. This was a dangerous moment. Tamper had spent his military career giving orders, not taking them. He took enormous pride in his ability to get in and out of places that would make a mountain goat wait and take the bus. He wanted to do this. The challenge drew him like a magnet, but logistics men plan, and G had taken all the planning away from him.

When Tamper held his tongue, G knew he had a chance. Before he lost the best logistics man in the business, G dropped his tone and continued at a much lower volume.

"But if you are who I think you are, you will find a way to make it happen. You will take to heart the fact that I wanted you, of all people, to be there to help me choose the location. Of course I wanted you there. The show doesn't happen if we can't get there, which is why I reached out to the best in the business when I called you. The Brazilian government however, had a different idea, and they didn't put it up for a vote. When they told me to choose right then, I had to choose. I could have backed out and scrapped the whole idea, but I didn't. I trusted in my team and their abilities. We were dealt what we were dealt. Nobody ever said this would be easy. That's why I chose you. Somebody said you were the best, and I believed them. If you can pull this off, you will be legend in this industry. Now, can you do it? Can you make this happen?"

All eyes fixed on Tamper. He inhaled deeply, closed his eyes, and exhaled slowly. When Tamper's rigid shoulders loosened and dropped back to their normal anatomic position, G knew there was a glimmer of hope. Finally, it came. Tamper nodded. He would do it. The room breathed a collective sigh of relief. Before anyone had time to object or rethink, G pronounced it a victory.

"Well, all right then. The team has spoken. Pack your things, boys and girls. We're going to Brazil."

With that, G turned, strode over to the door and walked out without a glance behind him. The team looked around at each other, bewildered at what had just transpired. Bones wasn't bothered in the least. He put his broad-brimmed leather hat back on his head, slapped Tamper on his back and strode out the door himself. Bones didn't care how deep they were going. The deeper the better. That's where the wild things are.

Chapter Fourteen

The epic size of Bert Redmond's terrace level game room could not be explained—it had to be experienced. Though not quite as large as a Vegas casino, it was definitely bigger than a cruise ship casino. The flashing lights, the craps tables, the roulette wheels and the counters for buying chips—everything was there. The only things missing were the one-armed bandits. There were no slot machines. Thousands of people attending fundraisers at Bert and Beth's had walked into this room, and without fail, they all asked the same question. Where are the slot machines?

The answer was self-evident. There weren't any. Bert thought slot machines were boring. He enjoyed explaining his reasoning to those who asked.

"A chimpanzee can play a slot machine."

Instead of slot machines, Bert had something he considered to be far more entertaining. He had videogames. Row upon row of vintage arcade machines, straight out of the 1980s, lined the walls. Every video game that had ever made its way into the lobby of a small-town movie theater was there. Unlike the videogames in movie theaters however, Bert's spit out money if you won. Quarters, to be exact. At the bottom of each videogame there was a shiny gold pot, the envy of all leprechauns everywhere, waiting to catch the quarters if the player was lucky enough to win. The sound made by a thousand dollars' worth of quarters raining down into a solid gold pot was almost deafening. Black tie fundraisers could be dry, no matter how worthy the cause, but not at Bert's and Beth's house.

Tonight, three people had Bert's and Beth's game room all to themselves. They were not on a side wall playing just any old vintage game, though. Not these guys. They were playing the video game that Bert had personally designed and created himself with the help of a brilliant team of gamers from Georgia Tech. Bert Redmond fans all over the world knew who created the game without having to be told, just from hearing its name.

"Don't Put Me In The Nursing Home!"

The concept of Bert's game was simple. In the arcade version, players sit in wheelchairs beneath a movie screen which curves all the way around them. Each has a console in front of them with their controls. The game starts in a virtual house. The player's mission is to catch Grandpa, stuff him in a car and drive him to the nursing home. Grandpa however, has other plans. He is tricky. Despite the fact his character is old, wrinkly, barefoot, has a pointed bald head, bushy eyebrows, overlarge ears, bent spine, potbelly, and uses a walker, he is impossibly fast. In addition to his speed, Grandpa has an endless array of weapons at his disposal, including false teeth that will latch onto your leg, hemorrhoid cream that will make you slip, green fart clouds that will blind you, and fungus-covered toenails that he will clip at you like bullets from a machine gun. The wheelchairs spin independently of one another depending on which way the player points the controls. The surround sound system was worthy of any 4-D movie theater.

Bert, Tony and G were hot on Grandpa's tail while playing in three-player team mode. After twenty-five minutes of play, they finally popped the net over Grandpa and wrestled him into the car, which was a red convertible with the top down. As the driver, G had to navigate the convertible through tree-lined streets to the nursing home. Tony and Bert had the duty of fending off the attacks of Grandpa's angry old friends who threw walkers, rotary phones, pill bottles and purses to stop them. G had control of the accelerator and steering wheel. Tony and Bert each had control of the doors on their side of the car which they could fling open whenever they wanted to flatten an attacking pedestrian. When they finally made it inside the gates of the Sweet Dreams Nursing Home, World War II-era big band music began to play. G cheered. Tony massaged his aching forearms as they watched the virtual road pass by them on their way to the front door of the nursing home where the real battle would take place.

"Hey Bert!"

"Yeah, man?"

"Am I going to hell for playing this?"

Bert laughed.

"No, Tony, you are not going to hell for playing this. No old people were harmed in the making of this video game. Didn't you read the important notice and disclaimer that my patent attorney from Dewey, Cheatham & Howe made me put on the opening screen? I had to pay him a hundred thousand dollars just to write that important notice and disclaimer. A hundred thousand dollars! Next time we play, I am pausing it so you will see what a one hundred thousand dollar notice and disclaimer looks like."

"Yeah, but I'm pretty sure I just killed at least two hundred old ladies with a car door back there."

G chimed in.

"What are you worried about, Tony? Did you see how many I ran over in the crosswalk? They are terrifying! Bert, what did you use to make such a realistic squishing sound when I ran over them? I may need counseling after this!"

As badly as Bert wanted to explain the fun he had selecting sounds for the game, it would have to wait. He would tell them later. The nursing home door was about to open. The nurse that was about to appear was not a nurse at all. Grandpa in all his fury had escaped from the back seat and was about to kill them all.

Less than two minutes later, despite their best efforts, the game was over. Grandpa annihilated them. Bert blamed G for their defeat, while G blamed Tony. Computer-generated Grandpa cackled with delight as he heckled and insulted the losers. Tony shouted epithets at Grandpa until Bert had to remind him he wasn't real. The wheelchair seats automatically returned to their upright and locked positions.

Tony loved Bert's video game. The more irreverent and inappropriate, the more he liked it. Annihilating helpless senior citizens with cartoon car doors was right up his alley.

Tony's craving for entertainment at the expense of others had started at a young age. Right out of high school he had worked at a beach restaurant famous for the abuse heaped upon customers by the waiters. People waited two hours to be seated at a table where they would be insulted and paid exorbitant prices for the privilege. Tony excelled at his job. Heaven help the overweight customer who ended up at Tony's table. He would immediately cry out for "maintenance" to "bring the reinforced chairs." He made his ugliest diner (picked by him completely at random) wear a paper bag over their head, with only eye holes torn out, until the entrées were served. Premature removal by the customer meant that no one at the table got their meal until the offender came to the kitchen and washed at least one dirty dish. He was strict with his rules, too. One family whose bag-removing member refused to wash dishes never got their food.

Tony would loudly ask a young teenage girl sitting next to her father what her name was. When she would say it, Tony would yell her name to an old man sitting with his wife at an adjoining table. He would then explain to the girl and her father as loudly as he could that the man at the other table had been asking for her name all night. When you are oh-so-good at your job, as Tony was, when you have a killer smile, and when you have complete autonomy from a happy manager who is raking in the cash every night that you work, you can get away with murder. With his skill set, Tony was a food service serial killer. All these years later, Tony was the same guy—just a little older. He was even better now at his "craft" than he was back then.

G walked around to the back of the soda fountain and helped himself to a fountain cola. After taking orders from the others, he poured Bert a root beer and Tony a diet cola. Together, they walked through a door to a seating area just outside the game room. Looking up through the skylights, they could see the sun had set and the stars had come out. G took a swig from his fountain cola, swallowed it and gave a prolonged, "Ahhh." His companions sampled their drinks and nodded to indicate they passed the quality control test. G leaned back on the plush sofa, put his feet up and crossed one foot over the other.

"We have twelve contestants, gentlemen. Six men, six women. I thought we'd only have five women. The lady we invited, the one who pulled Cameron Hernandez's son from the burning car, she backed out. Man, she would have been great. Tony, I don't think you know this, but Beth went to see her. Bert, didn't she fly to the Augusta burn unit to meet with her?"

Bert nodded.

"She did. Beth said the lady was really honored to be asked, but she is too self-conscious about her burns. At first, she seemed to be leaning towards yes, but then she got cold feet. Actually, I shouldn't say that about someone who crawled into a burning car to save a stranger, should I? A stranger who turned out to be a major league baseball player's son at that. But Beth told her she totally understood. You know Beth. They are now best friends. Beth is having her come down for a weekend once the show is over."

"So, we thought we were just going to have eleven," G said, "but on meet-and-greet night, Bert said some girl showed up, completely out of the blue at the last minute, who claims to be a survival expert. Is that about right, Bert?"

Bert burped his agreement. He tried to burp more words but ran out of carbonation at word three. He coughed and then began speaking like a California surfer dude and a valley girl possessed by Bert Redmond.

"Yep, that's right. Here comes the Spider Monkey saying, 'Hey bruh, like, this is my sister. Do you mind if she, like, looks inside your house before she, like, hitchhikes back to her refrigerator box in California? She doesn't believe there's such a thing as indoor plumbing.' And so, I was, like, 'Yeah bruh, like, sure, you know?' And so, she was like, 'Hi Mr. Redmond. I like t-shirts with cats and bubble tea and living in the woods, and I can, like, kill a mastodon with a number two pencil.' And so, I was, like, 'Wow, that's very impressive. So, could you, like, clear your calendar for the next three months starting, like, day before yesterday, and live in the jungle with anacondas and Pygmies?' And she was, like, real serious and counting numbers in her head, you know? And then she says, like, 'M'kay, but I can't be gone longer than a year because, like, Soap Drop Stillwagon is playing Light Path Amphitheater next June, and I missed them last time.'"

Tony and G didn't make it through Bert's monologue before both were cracking up. Bert was a master of mimicry who created characters out of nothing and anything. No one ever knew if he was telling the truth or just making it up as fast as he could pull it out of his butt. There may be an element of truth in the nonsense he was spewing, but they wouldn't find it out tonight, that's for sure. They would have to wait to meet Bert's valley girl in Brazil.

After they stopped laughing, G shared with them the idea he had been turning over in his mind.

"So, why don't we make things interesting?"

"Define 'interesting,'" Bert said suspiciously.

"What if we placed a little wager on who wins this thing?" G suggested.

Tony leaned back as he contemplated the idea.

"You mean betting on our own game?" Tony asked. "Isn't that what kept Pete Rose out of the Hall of Fame?"

"G, you dog," Bert chuckled. "Dude, so let me think about this. The thought of taking some or all of your money and Tony's is delightful. You know I'm all in. But I'm back here in Georgia, so I can't influence the outcome. You're planning on being behind the scenes, at least that's what you've said, but you are there on location. Tony, on the other hand, who I don't trust any farther than I can throw, is right there in the midst of them running the games. That guy sitting right there would have his thumb on the scales the whole way! Look at his face! He knows it! He'd cheat his way right into your wallet and mine, G!"

Tony was unable to suppress a grin, even by faking a stretch that happened to include placing an arm in front of his mouth. Bert became more insistent.

"Man, what am I thinking? I may as well hand you two scoundrels my share of the TV revenue right now. How would you like it, G? Tens and twenties? I know how Tony wants his. He doesn't want cash. He wants gift certificates to Heart Throb magazine, so he can be the first to see his smoldering look on the cover under the headline, 'Man Hunk Tony reveals what he's looking for in a soulmate.'"

Bert pulled up his shirt and struck a cover boy pose, except instead of showing washboard abs, he showed dad bod fat rolls. Tony couldn't defend himself because he was laughing. G interrupted Bert's mock modeling gig.

"So, who you got, Bert?"

Bert plopped back down on a sofa and grabbed his chin as he thought.

"Okay, I know this bunch better than you guys because I got to hang with them while you guys were off playing National Geographic Explorer instead of being at my house where you were supposed to be. My money's on the Senator, the politician, for three reasons. One, he has been schmoozing and sliming and charming people out of their money his whole life, so he already has an advantage. Two, when the indictments come out and I am being led away in handcuffs on my way to federal prison for this, I at least want the headlines to read, "Bert Redmond caught betting on reality TV show—claims he was donating the money to nursing home for Senator Kingston." And three, old people are gold for Bert Redmond, baby. They never let me down. You know I got to bet on the silver senior!"

"I'm going with the Spider Monkey," Tony announced. "Boedy Da's going to run the table on these guys. Anybody who can climb a building without ropes can crush any challenge we can throw at him. Plus he's got the dreads of a winner. Spider Monkey. Final answer."

Bert looked at G and said, "You're up, dude. Put your money where your mouth is, o wise and all-knowing guru. Who you got?"

G didn't hesitate.

"I've got DeShunta."

"Whoa, coming in hot from left field here!" Bert exclaimed. "DeShunta? Why DeShunta?"

"I watched the videos taken during the meet-and-greet—not just the interviews, but also the hidden camera footage taken in your vestibule while you were welcoming everybody," G explained. "Did you see the way she put the Senator in his place when he was coming down the stairs like a princess at Prince Charming's ball? She does not get intimidated. And everybody in the world has seen her fight the bouncer when she got cheated by the sleazy pawn shop owner that sold her a broken TV. DeShunta don't play. Nobody is going to mess with her."

Tony had misgivings about inviting her from the start, even though it was his idea to call her in the first place.

"Yeah, but seriously, G, how is she going to do any of the physical challenges? And how long do you think she's going to put up with living in a hut in the heat with bugs and snakes and all that? She's going to tap out."

G pulled down his ever-present sunglasses and grinned.

"You disagree. Fine. Sounds like easy money for Tony."

Tony looked at him side-eyed, wondering what he was missing. G doesn't throw his money away on a whim. Tony just couldn't see how G's bet could possibly pay off. Hearing no objection, G announced the stakes.

"So, a hundred thousand dollars to the winner," G declared. "Deal?"

Tony looked at Bert. Bert looked at Tony. They thought about their choices and G's choice. How in the world could DeShunta win? Not possible. Tony was happy with his choice. Bert started second-guessing his choice. The Senator was in his late sixties or early seventies, but then again, he was in good shape for an old guy, fit and trim and used to making strangers love him. Bert and Tony spoke at the same time.

"Deal."

G smiled and put his hands behind his head.

"Well, alrighty then. Looks like we've got ourselves a bet."

Chapter Fifteen

G stood in the sweltering heat of the Brazilian jungle, having left his luxury condo in Beverly Hills far behind. He marveled at what his eyes were seeing. The elevated view overlooking the waterfall was breathtaking. He could almost touch the azure-blue sky overhead. Flocks of brightly-colored macaws sailed noisily through the foliage. Mist rose over the jungle down below. A rainbow appeared, shimmered and disappeared, as though wanting to see the opening ceremonies but too shy to withstand the attention. Richard, the videographer, was having one, and only one, problem with filming—he couldn't decide where to point the lens. Every angle was more beautiful than the last.

Two months had passed since G and Tamper had their showdown in The Landmark hotel. G had no idea how he did it, but Tamper had pulled it all together. He had faced down the impossible task and conquered it. Tamper had managed to transport everything necessary to film a reality show deep inside the world's largest rainforest. There were no roads to drive it in. No airports to fly it in. Endless river travel but no docks, marinas, or gas stations. Despite insurmountable obstacles and impossible odds, he did it. Somehow Tamper did it. When G called Tony yesterday on a satellite phone from a semi-cleared area on a mountaintop and said they were ready, Tony could not believe his ears.

The day had finally arrived. It was Go Time.

A small sound rose above the din. It was quiet, barely perceptible over the noise from the jungle below. G and Richard looked at each other, listening intently. Was that it? Was that them? Seconds ticked by.

Wup, wup, wup, wup, wup, wup.

Blades turned by the powerful rotors of UH-60 Black Hawk helicopters sliced through the air. The unmistakable sound was soft at first but rapidly grew in volume and intensity. Any minute now and they would see the source of the sound.

Suddenly, there they were. Three helicopters materialized over the jungle between two mountainsides, with the power and might of the US military behind every nut and bolt. The Brazilian Air Force had acquired these helicopters from the United States for a combat mission in the Amazon region in 2006. When put to their intended use, they were angels in the air to some and death from above to others. Somebody, meaning G, had pulled some serious strings with officials employed by the cash-strapped Brazilian government in order to create an entrance as grand as this. The sight and sound injected testosterone into all who bore witness to the pageantry of what was unfolding before them.

"Get ready for this," smiled G.

"Oh, I'm ready," replied Richard, who was hunkered down and in position behind his camera and tripod.

G placed his headphones on his head and yelled into the microphone.

"Tony! Hey Tony!"

A crackling voice sounded from G's earbuds.

"Yeah?"

"Can you hear me?"

"I can barely hear you, but yeah, I can hear you. Everybody is here, parachutes on and smiles all around!"

"Sweet! Hey, did Bert get you the signature pages for everybody's waivers and releases?"

"What?"

G yelled louder. "The waivers and releases! I don't have them! I haven't seen the signature pages! Tell me Bert got you the signature pages!"

Long pause. Longer pause. G wondered if he had lost the connection.

"Tony? Tony! The waivers! Do you have the waivers?"

The crackling voice of Tony returned.

"Um, about that…I've been meaning to tell you. Bert said their lawyers said no. Clarence got a union lawyer. They wouldn't sign. Is that a bad thing?"

G felt sick. Bile rose up in his throat. The only things that stood between him and losing every dollar he had ever worked for were twelve notarized signatures at the back of twelve Waiver, Release, Hold Harmless and Covenant Not To Sue agreements. G intended to be there at Bert's and have each contestant sign in front of a notary public on video so there could never be a question about whether those were indeed their signatures, but then Brazil happened. The legalities had been left up to a comedian. It had slipped his mind until 4:30 this morning when his subconscious shook him awake. He sat bolt upright in the bed when the realization hit him—he had never seen the signatures.

"Don't even screw around about that, Tony! Did Bert get them or not?"

"G man," Tony shouted, "I would love to find an ink pen and something to bear down on, but the helicopter is shaking too much. Can't they sign them after they jump? If they survive the fall, we don't really even need them, right?"

G spewed a string of blue words that, among other things, cast aspersions on Tony's intelligence and questioned whether his parents were ever married. G heard no verbal reply from Tony. All he could hear was Tony laughing.

G lifted the microphone away from his mouth and spit in the grass. Let somebody die during all of this and get a hundred million-dollar lawsuit slapped on his desk, and then we'll see how hilarious Tony thinks this all is. He felt somewhat reassured that Tony had the signed waivers, despite his denials, based upon what he could divine solely from his ability to interpret guy speak and guy laughter. Stupid Tony. What a jerk. G grinned in spite of himself. Tony really knew how to yank his chain.

A mile above the treetops, twelve people were bursting with nervous energy. Their anxiety levels were off the charts. G did not often display outward signs of nervousness, but signs of strain were evident today. He paced back and forth beside Richard's camera as he watched the lead helicopter approach. This could be an unparalleled success or an epic failure. He would know which it would be in minutes. As he began to make out the people inside the helicopter, a moment of doubt crossed his mind. G shook his head violently and immediately dismissed it. It was too late to back out now.

Jungle Money would begin exactly as planned—with a skydive into the Amazon rainforest.

Each contestant was securely harnessed in for a tandem jump with a professional. For all but two, this was a first-time experience. None besides Boedy and the Senator had ever been skydiving before. As they neared the drop zone, some of the contestants were laughing while others were crying. Some were boldly looking out the open door, while others were hiding their eyes. Celeste was making the sign of the cross, while Aston, who was next to her, began yelling, "We are all going to die!" By the third time he said it, Celeste finally had enough. She started beating his shoulder with her balled-up fist as hard as she could and screamed, "Shut up! Just shut up!"

Each contestant was outfitted with a Mini-Go camera to record their jump once they leaped out into space. Each helicopter had a ride-along videographer filming the contestants before they jumped. Even though Summer was not jumping, her heart was beating out of her chest. Her hands were shaking so badly that it was all she could do to hold the video camera. When they took off from the airstrip early this morning, she did not know that the group in her helicopter would be the first to jump. Despite her nerves, she was capturing it all. She had to. There would be no retakes or do-overs if she missed this. The quality of the video that would be played at the start of this reality TV show rested solely in her hands.

The lead helicopter headed for the clearing, while the other two helicopters remained a respectful distance away. Summer had her camera trained on the pilot and his gauges. After a moment's pause, Summer swung the camera back around to the door, and it was a good thing she did. If she had waited one second longer, she would have missed the first jump.

Chaz the eco-warrior, smiling so big that his helmet barely fit, gave the thumbs up to his jumpmaster and out the door they went—no hesitation, no fear. Their parachute exploded into full canopy, bringing cheers and wild applause from the observers on the ground. Adrenaline filled Chaz's veins with endorphins beyond anything he had ever experienced. The Mini-Go affixed to his helmet captured not only his flight but his shouts of joy as well.

Although Chaz's figure seemed small to those on the ground, there was no mistaking the sheer exhilaration from the frenetic movements of his arms and legs. G held his breath as they neared the ground. When Chaz and his companion touched down, they fell and were momentarily enveloped in the canopy. Chaz clawed his way out from under the parachute, stood up and raised a triumphant thumb in the air. G was beaming as the crew cheered. Elise LeFleur and Denise Milton jumped around in a little circle and clapped. When Elise turned in G's direction, he gave her a high-five.

One down.

Richard pondered what kind of adjustment he should make with his lens if the next jumper's angle of descent led into the relative darkness of the trees rather than a landing in the brightly-lit clearing. Before he could think it through, out popped parachute number two. A far less-animated figure began a gentle fall from atmosphere to terra firma. Those on the ground tried to guess the jumper. In contrast to the limb-flinging first jumper, the second appeared to be clinging tightly and trying not to move as though fearing even the slightest movement might cause them to slip from the harness. Someone guessed Annaliese Parkman, and the others agreed. That's who it had to be. When she had almost reached the ground, a gust of wind picked her up and lifted her back up in the air, but only for a second. She landed without incident. The crew waited for her to stand and give the thumbs up, but she was not as celebratory as Chaz. They could only assume that she had survived unscathed since she appeared to be walking normally.

Two down.

A scream from a bystander caused G to look up. He was horrified to see chopper number one listing heavily to the left. Someone tried to radio the pilot, but there was no answer. Suddenly a clump of people, bound together and tangled tight, fell out of the helicopter. No chute opened. They fell and they fell...and then a chute opened—only one. They were falling too fast. Then a second chute opened but only partially. The clump of people split into two, and the second chute opened all the way. The helicopter swung crazily. G screamed into his mike.

"What is happening?"

G grabbed for his binoculars and hurriedly put them to his eyes, praying no one was about to die. He could barely breathe as he watched the people land. Thank you god. They were on the ground and not tangled up in the trees. He saw movement. He saw...fighting. What was happening?

G pulled the binoculars away and looked back up in the sky. *What is chopper one doing up there?* It was listing heavily and spinning slowly. Just then, G heard a panicked voice come across the radio.

"I don't know what I'm doing!" Tony screamed. "I don't know how to fly! Sweet Jesus! Tell me what to do!"

G could not comprehend Tony's words.

"What are you saying, Tony? Surely you don't mean…"

"I'm flying the…help me, help me, help me!"

G heard shouting in Spanish; then the helicopter righted itself. Presently, he heard Tony again.

"Oh god! Oh god! Thank you, Jesus! Thank you, Jesus!"

What was going on? Tony came back on the radio.

"Oh, thank you, Jesus! Thank you, Jesus! I'm having a heart attack."

G yelled into the radio, spraying saliva everywhere.

"What just happened, Tony? Answer me!"

Instead of answering, Tony asked the question he was afraid to ask.

"Are they alive? Are they okay?"

G looked through his binoculars again.

"Yes! They are…I don't know what they are doing…fighting it looks like, but yes, four people are…well, that's got to be Clarence…he's bent over. He's hurt it looks like, but they are all moving. What happened up there?"

Tony breathed heavily into the radio. He couldn't speak. He closed his eyes and knelt on the floor of the helicopter, trying to catch his breath. G ranted and raved, not understanding why Tony wouldn't answer him. Finally, Tony calmed himself enough to speak.

"Okay. So, DeShunta decides today she's not jumping out of the helicopter. She was all in back at Bert's place when we first told everybody about the skydiving. "Yes, I'm in," she said. She was still in when we left the helipad this morning. "Yes, I'm in, stop asking me," she said, but then we got up in the air and the helicopter started swaying and she's out. Total one-eighty. 'I'm out,' she says. Well, okay. I wasn't going to make her jump. Nobody in their right mind would try to make her jump, right? I told her, 'It's okay, you don't have to jump.'"

Tony stopped to take a breath. His rapid breathing made him lightheaded.

"But Clarence, you know the big guy? What an idiot! He thought it would be funny to push her toward the door. Big mistake. Big mistake! DeShunta grabbed him by the nuts, like seriously by the nuts. He may need a doctor. So, Clarence is screaming, and DeShunta is pulling away from the door as hard as she can toward the cockpit. Somehow she gets a hold of the pilot's shirt collar with her other hand. The pilot starts getting choked, he grabs her wrist and the helicopter starts to tip. Clarence has got her arm, and she's pulling on the pilot, and there was no way the pilot could stay in his seat. The guys they are harnessed to are trying to pull them apart, but then the thing tips and they all fell out! They fell out, G! The rest of us are all holding on for dear life. I jump up and grab the controls, but then the pilot gets back to his seat. Thank God, he didn't fall out, too! If he had fallen out…man. We'd all be dead, G! He's flying it now. G, we almost died!"

G stooped over with his chest almost touching his knees. He felt nauseous. Their production, millions of dollars and thousands of man hours in the making, had almost ended right then and there. The spectacular entrance he had planned so carefully was ruined. Ruined! He flung his sunglasses to the ground and threw his clipboard across the clearing. G did not feel Richard's camera lens trained on him. Richard caught it all.

"All right, Tony," G declared. "We're done. We're done. No more jumping. We're pulling the plug. Tell the pilots to set them down, like right now. I want all the choppers on the ground. We're done."

Chopper number one obediently made its descent. All the observers on the ground turned their heads and shielded their eyes to defend themselves from the barrage of leaves, branches and dirt that sprayed them like a pressure washer. Summer was the next-to-last passenger to exit, followed by Tony, who was clearly shaken. Once they were clear, the pilot, whose feathers were ruffled by the skirmish with DeShunta, lifted off and headed for home, having no desire to stick around for goodbyes.

When the landing zone was clear again, chopper number two began its descent. Celeste didn't know why they were landing instead of jumping, but she was more than okay with it. Aston had pretended to be scared, but in truth, he was looking forward to jumping. He tried to ask the professional he was harnessed to why they were going down, but between the noise and the language barrier, he was not able to make himself understood. He looked at Tattoo, who simply shrugged his shoulders. He had no idea, and neither did Willow. As they neared the ground, the trees, bushes and vines ringing the small clearing whipped violently back and forth in the tornadic winds created by the rotors.

Chopper number three remained in a safe position a mile above the treetops, patiently waiting its turn. Stephen, the videographer assigned to the third helicopter, had his camera pointed at Mystic Origin, whose raised arms and quiet chants made it appear as though she was appealing to a higher power. She was sitting on the floor up against the wall when the pilot received the radio transmission. The jump was off. The pilot looked in his mirror at the passengers behind him. The pros and their novice partners hadn't even finished harnessing one to the other for their tandem jumps. They didn't have time. The pilot positioned his helicopter so his passengers could observe the other helicopter. Plans had obviously changed, though he didn't know why. Peaches, the Senator, and Mystic Origin saw the other helicopter depositing its passengers on the ground, and though disappointed, they resigned themselves to the fact that they were destined for a safer, gentler landing than the daredevil entrance G had originally planned for them. No jumping today.

Boedy Da saw the same thing they did. Boedy, though, had a different idea.

When Boedy heard the pilot tell Stephen, "We're not jumping. We have to land," his heart sank. That was not acceptable. Boedy was an adrenaline junkie, and the rush was right outside that open door. No one was taking this moment away from him. No one.

So, out the door he went.

Five thousand feet below, G had just placed his sunglasses back on his face when he heard voices crying out, "No! No, no, no, no, no!" Startled by the outcry and confused because nothing untoward seemed to be happening with chopper number two, which was on the ground, G followed their gaze to find the object of their uproar.

Just below chopper number three, a body was hurtling to earth. Clad in a gray and white speckled suit, with head down and arms tight, the body plunged like a stone. Suddenly the body's arms lifted. Black wings appeared between the flyer's arms and his sides. It was a wingsuit! G instantly knew who it was.

"Boedy!"

Spreading his wings changed his angle of descent almost immediately. Boedy made a decided swing forward, changing his trajectory from a vertical drop to a more horizontal flight. His dreadlocks streamed away from his beaming face. He laughed out of sheer exhilaration. He was flying over the Amazon rainforest! Boedy's leather necklace, sporting a silver cross, fluttered at the back of his sun-bronzed neck. He cried out in exultation as he soared beneath the Brazilian sun.

"Yeah, baby!"

A few thousand feet below him stood Boedy's sister, Willow. Unlike those around her who were screaming in terror, Willow cheered.

"You maniac! That's my brother! Go Boedy, go!"

Everyone on the ground held their breath. The boy in the wingsuit was obviously an experienced jumper, but that clearly did not translate into a wise jumper. Intoxicated by the allure of TV stardom, a potential audience of millions, an incredibly beautiful and exotic location, and a once-in-a-lifetime chance to jump where no one in history had ever jumped, Boedy had thrown caution to the wind. He was offering the ultimate sacrifice to the god of adrenaline. Icarus was flying much too close to the sun.

Boedy shot across the sky like a flying squirrel. He was knifing through the air at a ground speed of over a hundred miles an hour, and he was picking up speed. For a brief moment, his body was framed by the arc of a rainbow which materialized in front of a bank of storm clouds starting to form over the horizon. No one would notice the rainbow until the film was reviewed much later.

Boedy was able to pull off his unauthorized jump because he leaped before the professional skydivers had a chance to intercept him. To wait longer was to guarantee no flight. He made his impetuous decision to fly before the chopper was over the jump zone, however. He leaped out when the chopper was hovering over the chasm a considerable distance from the waterfall. By now, he was sailing over the treetops at close to two hundred miles an hour, and he was still picking up speed. Nothing under him even remotely resembled a safe place to land. He might look like a flying superhero, but he was anything but immortal. Boedy gauged his distance above the trees. He could see the plateau above the waterfall in the distance where a helicopter sat and people were on the ground. Could he make it? As soon as he asked the question, he knew the answer. He was dropping too low too fast. The witnesses had a glimmer of hope when he caught an updraft that lifted him almost level with the top of the distant waterfall, but that hope died when the air current normalized. He was losing altitude. He wasn't going to make it.

Boedy was not as close to the waterfall as he would have liked, but it would have to do. He couldn't wait any longer. Slamming into the world at three hundred miles an hour could hurt. It was time to pull the ripcord.

Out popped his chute.

Willow cheered when she saw her brother's parachute deploy. She stopped mid-cheer when she saw it did not balloon out into a puffy white marshmallow like it should. Some on the ground tried to mentally calculate where he would land with the thought of running there to help, but it was much too far. The jumpmaster back on chopper three could see that it wasn't good. The pilot came to the sick realization that if Boedy died, he might have to turn in his wings for allowing an international incident of this magnitude. G heard a voice in his ear.

"G?"

"Yeah, Tony."

"This is bad, G! He's not going to make it!"

"Tony, this is not bad."

G's voice was flat, toneless. Tony shouted into his mike.

"Why not? How can you possibly say that?"

"We're covered, Tony."

"What do you mean 'we're covered?'"

"He signed the waiver, Tony."

Tony's mouth opened. Leave it to G to see the end game. If the boy killed himself on camera chasing thrills, at least G had made sure they would win any lawsuit that his parents or his sister might try to file. He hoped so, anyway.

"Tony, no screwing around. You did get the signatures, right?"

"Yeah, I got them."

G sighed in relief. This time he knew Tony was telling the truth. Right then a new voice rose above the din, authoritative and commanding.

"Get moving! Move, move, move!"

Tamper's voice startled everyone. When the former Army Ranger barked his orders, his team snapped out of the fog they were in and flew into action. Tamper had not gotten through life by being stunned into inaction by the unexpected. You adapt, you improvise, you overcome.

"Get in! What are you waiting for? Let's go get him!"

Dr. Jane, the team's emergency medical doctor, found herself picked up bodily and dropped roughly in the front seat of Tamper's Paleo Growler UTV. Other team members leaped on the back and held onto the roll bar as Tamper took off like a shot. No, they wouldn't make it in time to catch Boedy before he fell to earth, but they would get to him as quickly as humanly possible and do whatever needed to be done to save his life or to retrieve his body if he couldn't be saved.

The Growler's engine was screaming. After plunging into the jungle on a very car-unfriendly trail, Tamper couldn't see what was happening in the air. He was running roughly parallel to the river at the top of the plateau and was headed to the treacherously steep trail leading down to the base of the waterfall. He couldn't operate the walkie-talkie, shift gears and steer all at the same time, so he shoved the walkie-talkie into Dr. Jane's hands and shouted. Dr. Jane, whose face had just been soundly slapped by the recoil of palm leaves being pulled back by the antenna passing by, had no idea what he said, but she had a good idea that she had just been told to call somebody. She found a button on the side of the device, squeezed it and yelled into it.

"Hey, this is Jane! What is happening? Where is he?"

Boedy knew he was screwed. The most amazing flight he would ever know was coming to an end, and it would end badly. His chute hadn't fully deployed yet, and it needed to be fully deployed to slow him down from the blazing speed he had attained in the wingsuit. He hoped he might somehow catch an updraft to make it up to the top of the waterfall. He was actually close to being high enough, but he was still going to be about twenty-five feet too low. So close. The roar of the water was growing louder by the second. The height was dizzying. When you are flying, the height is awesome. When you are landing, the height is terrifying. His senses were at a fever pitch. His will to survive innervated every nerve ending and fiber of his being with one goal.

Live.

The cascade of water resounded like never-ending thunder. The limitless hydraulic power generated by such a vast quantity of water, millions of gallons per second, could lift a mountain by the roots if such power could be harnessed. Far below him were two very bad options. There were gigantic slick-as-glass boulders that he could never stick to, even if he survived the impact. There was a churning maelstrom at the bottom of the waterfall that, for all intents and purposes, could be God's washing machine. Boedy felt like a leaf in a hurricane. He was overwhelmed by his insignificance. He didn't think he would make it, but he had to ask.

God, please save me. Please don't be through with me yet.

As he approached the nearest column of water to his left, he dropped his right shoulder and banked hard right. Looking in front of him, he saw an opening. A moss-covered outcropping of rock created a gap between two torrents of water. Was that a floor? There was no time for calm reflection. The bottom of the waterfall below was certain death. This opening before him offered at least a chance at life. Now or never. Boedy aimed for the opening, doing his best to create air brakes with his wings so as to slow the landing.

In the time it takes for a hummingbird to blink, Boedy pierced the wall of water and entered the sudden quiet of a cave underneath. That infinitesimally short moment of peace ended abruptly when he smacked the back wall of the cave at a speed no one could survive. The Mini-Go on his head exploded into a thousand pieces. His body crumpled to the floor and lay still as stone. No heartbeat. No breath. No signs of life. Had he been able to hear, Boedy would have heard a loud noise coming from the cave's opening, a thrumming that could be heard even over the sound of the falling water.

Wup, wup, wup, wup, wup.

Dr. Jane shouted over the radio.

"Repeat, this is Jane! We are almost at the bottom near the river! What is happening? Where is he? Somebody tell us!"

"This is G. We just lost sight of him. He is below the top of the waterfall. Chopper Three, do you see him?"

The pilot of the third Black Hawk helicopter didn't answer right away. It wasn't because he didn't hear the question, and it wasn't because of the screaming coming from his remaining passengers Peaches, Mystic Origin and the Senator. It was because he was not sure what he had just seen. G's screams reached a fever pitch.

"Answer me! What happened to Boedy?"

The white noise emanating from the speaker stopped, which meant someone had just pushed the Talk button. Everyone on that frequency held their breath, desperate to hear. Long seconds passed. G started to scream into the receiver again, but held his tongue, afraid he would miss it. After a long pause, the third pilot began to speak.

"Sir, the boy flew into the waterfall. That much I know for sure. I lost sight of him, but then ...what's your name, ma'am?"

G heard background talk but couldn't make it out. The pilot resumed.

"Miss Peaches screamed, 'There he is!' and pointed down. I didn't see him at first, but then I saw him. It was strange. He headed away from you, away from the waterfall, over the treetops. I had him in my sights for a second, but now I don't. He dropped below the tree line into the trees. I can't see him anymore."

Tamper stopped his UTV and shushed everyone so he could hear the crosstalk. He heard the pilot's words, but he didn't know what to make of it. While he was pondering his next move, the pilot's voice came on again.

"Sir, I moved to the west and just spotted him again, but it's weird. He saw me and aimed the other way like he was trying not to be seen or something. Maybe he knows how much trouble he is in. I don't know."

G could not think. This was madness.

It was not madness for the living being that flew out of the cave, though. She flew until she was almost completely out of earshot of the whirring helicopters. After a mile and a half, she slowed her flight and grabbed onto a tree limb with her knife-like talons, where she breathed and tried to still her racing heart.

The excitement of the falls was soon forgotten here in the quiet of the lush jungle. Sharp eyes that missed nothing caught movement. A newborn marsh deer fawn flicked its tail a hundred and fifty feet below. A few seconds later the baby deer's ears twitched.

The massive harpy eagle, adorned with white, gray, and black plumage, dropped from her perch and flew silently toward her mark. Her six-and-a-half foot wingspan was impressive, but the killing power resided in her feet. The fawn would not hear the gentle movement of air signaling the malevolent descent of the apex predator until it was too late. The back talons entered the unsuspecting fawn's neck and punctured the spine, rendering it immobile. Lift-off was slowed only for a moment as the eagle adjusted her grip on her prize. The eagle's mighty wings lifted both her and the tiny fawn into the air, leaving no evidence the encounter had ever occurred. She laid the young deer carefully across the fork of a tree at the top of the canopy and plunged her razor-sharp beak into the soft white underbelly to begin her meal.

If the fawn's life had not been taken, it would have been looking up into the curiously full, round face that distinguished the harpy from all other raptors on earth. Due to her size and the mask of feathers surrounding her head, she could be easily mistaken for something or someone else. The harpy knew who she was. She didn't care whether a television producer and his crew did or not. The hole in the waterfall had always been safe, which is why she had made her nest there. Now that it had been invaded, she would never return home. She would make a new one elsewhere.

G shook his head. Everything that could have gone wrong did go wrong. He checked in with his ground crew. Thank god that DeShunta had survived the fall from the helicopter and appeared to be relatively uninjured, aside from a few scrapes and bruises.

Clarence, on the other hand, was hurt. He had possibly dislocated his shoulder, but that wasn't his worst injury. He needed the help of a urologist on an emergency basis. His private parts were damaged, and quite frankly, in G's opinion, it served him right. G couldn't dwell on it. He had to act. The contract with the contestants obligated the show's producers to provide full, unlimited, world-class medical care for every possible need, no matter the cost. G never expected they would need a urologist out here, but they did now. He was fairly certain that Dr. Jane could secure the services of a board-certified professional from Rio de Janeiro. He would put her on that task when she made it back to camp.

Back at the plateau, G's voice whispered over the radio.

"Tony. Hey Tony, you there?"

"Yeah G, I'm here. What is it?"

"Do you know any good alcoholics anonymous programs around here?"

Tony scrunched up his face.

"Why you asking me that, G? You don't drink."

"Yeah I know, but I'm thinking about starting."

Chapter Sixteen

After the third helicopter was down on the ground with its passengers safely unloaded, G immediately set to work dealing with the two emergencies that faced him. He assigned Denise Milton the task of providing medical care for Clarence. She protested, reminding G she was a wildlife biologist, not a doctor. G took her aside and whispered harshly in her ear.

"He's the same size as one of your lowland gorillas, and he has the same IQ. Stop whining, be a team player and go help Clarence!"

Tamper and Dr. Jane had already taken off on a search-and-rescue mission to locate Boedy. G instructed Bones to join Tamper in the hunt. Who better to hunt than a South African hunter? The jump masters and the two remaining helicopter pilots, who had no further obligations now that the jumps were over, recognized the gravity of the situation. They volunteered their services to Bones, who gladly accepted.

Willow demanded that she be allowed to join in the search for her brother. The look on Bones' sun-bronzed face reflected his aversion to the idea. Fortunately for Bones, all the seats were taken in his Ozinaki Montana UTV. He promised, in his calm, reassuring voice, to bring her news as soon as they found him. It shouldn't take long, he assured her. Bones could tell by the look in her eyes that she was not satisfied with being on the sidelines, but his plan was not up for discussion.

G was not supposed to play the charismatic host today. He was not slated to deliver the big "Welcome to Jungle Money" speech to the group. That was Tony's job, but Tony had inexplicably walked off. He didn't head in the direction of the search party. He just walked off without a word to G as to where he was going.

The contestants needed direction. The cameras were rolling. This was the moment they had all been waiting for. Worry, indecisiveness and hesitation on his part would spoil the opening. *I can come up with an impromptu welcome speech*, he told himself. Feeling the eyes upon him, G stepped up on a large rock. Summoning all the warm and fuzzy feelings he could muster, G smiled and addressed the crowd.

"Good morning! Actually, I guess it's technically afternoon, isn't it? My name is George Commander. Welcome to Jungle Money!"

Chaz gave a war whoop, which sparked a flame and spread through the group like wildfire. Peaches, Celeste, Annaliese, the Senator, Tattoo, Mystic Origin and Aston joined in the celebration. Willow, who stood with her arms crossed, gave a quiet, unenthusiastic "Woo hoo." G was relieved to see that this part of the group, with the exception of Willow, was still excited about being here notwithstanding the train wreck of a morning they'd just had. Their enthusiasm injected some desperately-needed wind in his sails.

"On behalf of myself, Tony Longino and Bert Redmond, we'd like to express our sincere gratitude to you for doing perhaps the most outrageous thing you have probably ever done—accepting an invitation to fly to the Amazon rainforest for a contest unlike anything you have ever encountered before. You will be competing for a cash prize…"

Peaches burst in, her syrupy-sweet Southern accent expressing the excitement she felt.

"How much cash? Tell us! You didn't put that in your little letter we got. We noticed. I read it twice. We want details, Mr. George! How much?"

The onlookers laughed at her eagerness and looked at their host expectantly. G smiled conspiratorially.

"All in good time, Madam Peaches. All in good time."

Peaches scoffed in mock disgust, which echoed the sentiments of her fellow contestants perfectly. G could tell right away that she was well-liked by her compatriots.

"So, let me give you the lay of the land. This beautiful plateau…by the way, how do you like the view?"

The whistles of appreciation and expressions of wonderment at the incredible views all around them reinforced to G that he had made the right choice in a location. The depth of satisfaction their oohs and ahs gave him could scarcely be measured.

"I am so glad you like what you see. This plateau provided the clearest, safest and prettiest landing zone we could find. This is not where you will be staying for the duration of your time here in Jungle Money, however. Your camp, your home, and your contests will all be down below. I think you will really like the view of the waterfall you'll have from down there."

A string of obscenities in the distance assaulted their ears. They all turned and saw Dr. Jane and others trying to get Clarence into what appeared to be a golf car. A stone's throw from Clarence, two other team members were tending to DeShunta, who was still seated on the ground. After seeing the source of the yelling, they turned back to G.

"You may remember from the informational video you watched and from the conversations you had with Bert and Beth, every moment of every day will be videoed. You will be wearing Mini-Gos at all times. Your video feed will be monitored and received by our production team who will be putting together the best moments of each day for an audience that we hope will include North America, much of Canada and portions of South America."

The Senator's eyes widened. He thought the show would only be made available on certain local channels in the US.

"We'll need to be on our best behavior, won't we?"

G nodded.

"That would be wonderful, of course, but all we ask is that you act natural. Be yourselves. Now, there are some special people standing behind you. We have an incredible video production team that will help us capture the memorable and exciting moments. They are second to none. You may have already met some of them. We have Richard, Steven and Summer, as well as Jason and Wally."

The distant sound of DeShunta screaming at someone momentarily drew their attention away, but then they turned back to G.

"Other team members you will meet during the course of your time here will include Tamper who is our logistics man. Tamper is a former Army Ranger, which won't be hard for you to guess when you see his buzz-cut hair and dog-tag necklace. Bones is a professional hunting guide from South Africa. He's got long hair and a cool accent and will help you with some of our contests. Dr. Jane is an emergency room doctor. Come see her with any medical problems. Elise LeFleur is our botanist, who will help us know which plants, berries and fruit are edible and which are harmful. And…where is Miss Denise? There she is. She is over there helping Clarence. Denise Milton is our team's wildlife biologist. She has specialized knowledge, training and experience that will help us survive and even thrive in an environment where the animals rule the jungle. We are in their home—not vice versa. When you encounter animals, and you will encounter animals, Miss Denise is your resource. We want to coexist with them and keep the disturbance of their habitat to a minimum."

Celeste raised her hand.

"So, are there any people that live around here? Like any Native Americans? Or, I guess that's wrong…Native Brazilians? Am I making any sense?"

G nodded.

"I understand you completely, Celeste. No, there are no people. There are no cities for hundreds of miles. Tony and I flew over this entire region less than two months ago and expressly looked for any signs of civilization. Bones and Tamper have been all over this area. There are none. You are all alone out here--well, except for every kind of bird, snake, lizard, insect, mammal and fish you can possibly imagine."

Celeste felt an involuntary shiver run up her spine. The ladies standing by her saw it, and they shared a nervous laugh. G continued.

"So, what else? I'm trying to remember. Tony will be giving you directions all along the way. You will have lots of Tony time. He will lead you through a series of challenges that I think you will enjoy. Tony is, I believe, already down the mountain, which is where we all need to be. So, unless you have any other questions, I'd like for you to follow Miss Elise who will show you the way to the trail down to the base of the waterfall. Watch your step because it is very steep and narrow in certain places, and it is a long way down if you fall."

When DeShunta saw the group by the helicopter begin to break up, she knew she needed to move whether she felt like it or not. With assistance she was able to stand and begin to make her way gingerly towards the trailhead. When she got to the landing zone and walked between the two idle helicopters, she saw a portable set of three steps at the beginning of a long strip of red carpet laid out on the grass. Evidently, someone was supposed to step out of one of the helicopters like royalty—probably Tony, she guessed. If it happened, she missed it, and she was not pleased in the least.

Two small concrete columns had been placed on either side of the red carpet. Atop the columns were baskets containing ferns. Figurines with a jungle theme had been placed in the ferns by means of sharp sticks pressed down into the dirt. DeShunta liked figurines. She had a small collection back home. Most were made of fragile porcelain. She turned to the lady escorting her.

"What they going to do with these plants?"

The lady shrugged her shoulders.

"I have no idea. I know we are not coming back up here until the whole thing is over and we are ready to leave. The ferns will surely be dead long before then."

DeShunta nodded her understanding.

"I'm going to get me a party favor, then."

Looking at the various choices, her eyes fell upon a fat and happy frog. She liked frogs. They didn't bite people. They just chilled in the water, ate flies and croaked. She reached over to the fern basket, took hold of the frog and lifted the small stake clear of the dirt. She brushed the dirt off the stick and continued her slow walk to the trail that would lead her down to the bottom. As she walked, she got an itch at the back of her neck, no doubt from one of the innumerable mosquitoes that greeted her when she touched down in the grass. It hurt to use her right shoulder, so she reached up with her left and used the sharp end of her party favor frog to scratch where it itched. It hit the spot perfectly.

"Mm, hmm. I got me a good back scratcher," she said to no one in particular.

Thirty minutes later everyone, including DeShunta, had made it to the bottom of the treacherous trail. The sight that greeted their eyes was unlike any they had ever seen. A cataract of water thundered down into a pool—the very definition of a tropical paradise. A perpetual mist filtered the sun and provided natural air conditioning. They could scarcely take in all the flowers and blooms that surrounded the water accentuating its beauty. G left them alone to enjoy the gorgeous sights and sounds while he went to find Tony.

The medical tent was one of the last places G thought to look. He stuck his head inside, almost as an afterthought, but he was glad he did. There, lying on a cot with his forearm covering his eyes, was Tony.

"Hey man, what are you doing? Are you all right? I've been looking all over for you!"

Tony didn't respond right away. He slowly rolled his head side to side without lifting his arm.

"G man, I just need a minute. I just…I can't…I can't even begin to tell you how scared I was up there."

Tony slowly exhaled. He lifted one knee up, set it back down, lifted the other knee and set it back down.

"G, nobody was flying that helicopter but me. Do you know how sensitive those controls are? I wasn't even sitting in the seat. I was having to reach over. We tipped over, G. People were falling out! I don't know how they didn't die. All of us—I don't know how we all didn't die."

G stood quietly, not knowing what to say. He decided not to say anything. After a minute of silence, G responded uncharacteristically softly.

"But you didn't die, Tony. You did an amazing thing. You righted that helicopter and saved you and the pilot and…who else was in there? Summer—you saved Summer. And look, Clarence and DeShunta are all right. They are going to be okay. Nobody died, Tony. So take a minute, calm yourself, and let's get ready for the opening ceremony. You can do this. They are all still down at the waterfall, but they'll be walking down here in a few minutes. You can do this, Tony."

Tony pulled his arm away from his face and looked at G.

"So, you're saying DeShunta is okay? Clarence—I don't care about Clarence. What an oaf. Who thinks it's funny to pull somebody towards an open door thousands of feet above the trees? But I've got to ask the rest of them, G. I've got to ask them how they are feeling about all this—about going forward with all that's happened."

G didn't like the sound of this.

"Look, you say what you've got to say, but we are doing this thing, Tony. Gather yourself, collect your thoughts, and be the professional you know you are."

Tony laid his head back down and looked at the tent ceiling. He sighed a deep sigh and slowly shook his head.

"Man, I just can't do this. Not today. Tomorrow maybe, but today…"

G took a quick step forward and slapped Tony sharply across the face. The sudden and unexpected sting propelled Tony to jump up off the cot. He pushed G in the chest, knocking him across a folding chair and onto the floor. The angry glower on Tony's face was a stark contrast from the look he had when G entered the tent only minutes earlier—which was exactly what G was looking for. G stood up and got right back in Tony's face.

"Nobody died, Tony! Almost, nearly, coulda, shoulda, woulda, but nobody did. So suck it up, buttercup! Now, if you've finished having your pity party, we've got a wildly successful reality TV show to make happen out there. "Jungle Money." You may have heard of it. So, go put on your disco dancing outfit, let the music move you and slay the ladies just like you are supposed to. They're not all ready to wuss out like somebody else apparently is. Some of them even feel like dancing. So, go dance. We've got a schedule to keep, and by golly, we're going to keep it."

Tony's jaw was tight, his fists were clenched and his breathing was heavy. He stared G down like a prizefighter waiting to hear the bell. They had never had a cross word before, much less a physical altercation. Things had changed between them. It was a dangerous moment. G could not do this without Tony. Tony was the picture—G was just the frame. The future of the show hung in the balance.

Think, G. Think.

Without breaking his stare, G made a tiny move. He wiggled his hips ever so slightly, then he stopped. He allowed seconds to pass. He thrust his pelvis almost imperceptibly; then he stopped. Seconds passed. He did it again. Wiggle, wait. Thrust, wait. Wiggle, wait. Thrust, wait. His expression didn't change. G could keep a straight face no matter what was happening around him.

Tony's brain registered the undignified attempt at dance. G was one ugly dancer. Tony tried with all his might to keep a straight face…but he couldn't do it. The corner of his mouth turned up. G knew he had him. He began wiggling and thrusting in earnest, throwing down moves that would make Elvis Presley and James Brown roll over in their graves, all while never breaking eye contact. Tony started to laugh despite himself. G liked when Tony laughed. Good things happened when Tony laughed.

"All right. Go get changed and dance like the funk soul brother you are."

With that, G grabbed Tony's face, pulled it towards him and kissed him on the lips—or at least he tried to. Tony jerked his head sideways and wiped his face with his arm, all while spewing, sputtering, screaming in protest and questioning G's manhood.

"I knew you played for the other team! I knew it!"

G exploded into laughter. He turned on his heel and ran out of the tent. When he made it out into the bright sunshine, G breathed a sigh of relief. He knew before they ever started that this would not be easy, but the wheels had almost fallen off before they even touched the ground. Close calls make good TV, he reminded himself. Hopefully, that was as close a call as they would experience.

Glancing behind him, G saw his friend shaking his head and grinning as he exited the medical tent. That was the Tony he knew and loved. Having survived that crisis, G's elevated heart rate returned to normal by the time the contestants began to wander into the camp area a half hour later.

As the contestants arrived in camp, they gathered around the pergola and small set of benches Tamper had constructed for their meetings. They chatted about what had happened thus far and speculated about what was to come. As the conversation began to wind down, they began to look around for directions. Former Governor Annaliese Parkman was the first one to notice there were no tents. She called out to G, who was standing next to Richard the videographer.

"So, where are our tents? Where are we supposed to sleep?"

Rather than answer, G pointed behind her. She turned to see where he was pointing. A gasp was heard and then a second. A brutally handsome, bronze-skinned man wearing white-on-white strode confidently into their midst, rubbing his hands together like he couldn't wait to start. His million-dollar smile projected a sense of excitement and adventure, contagious to all who bore witness. More than one lady had trouble catching her breath as heart after heart skipped a beat.

Tony Longino, *the* Tony Longino, had arrived.

As he headed towards the dais near the pergola, Tony laughed at the wolf whistles and cheers. He opened his arms wide as though he was catching their praises in his hands. He had completely transformed himself since they last saw him at the landing zone up on the plateau. Gone was the man lying on a cot in the medical tent. Gone were the jangled nerves. Gone were the fears and doubts. In their place was a bona fide celebrity at the top of his game. No one could electrify a crowd like Tony Longino.

"Well, good afternoon ladies and gentlemen! I'm Tony Longino. Are you ready for some South American, Amazon rainforest-style Jungle Money?"

High-pitched squeals, cheers and ear-splitting screams erupted in response. If Richard had not been videoing, he would have stuck his fingers in his ears to protect his eardrums from bursting. Tony laughed at the reaction he received. The crowd's energy amped him up even more than he was before.

"I'm not sure, but I think somebody is a little bit excited to be here! That is awesome. I am glad you are here. We are going to have a fantastic time here in the jungles of Brazil. You are going to have the experience of a lifetime, and one or more of you will be walking out of the Amazon rainforest with an outrageously ridiculous amount of money!"

The contestants all shouted, save Willow, and some jumped for joy as though they had already won.

"The plan was for us to have all twelve of you parachute down into the drop zone on the plateau and then walk down to this stage together for a thrilling opening ceremony. Well, as you might have noticed, things did not go as planned."

"That's for sure," the Senator and Annaliese spoke in unison. Tony nodded gravely. He chose his next words carefully.

"I will speak plainly. What happened, quite frankly, was terrifying. Two of our contestants fell out of their helicopter. My helicopter, as a matter of fact. Because of the superb skills and lightning-fast reactions of the professional skydivers however, tragedy was narrowly averted. For a few brief moments, I found myself flying the helicopter, which is the most scared I have ever been in my life. Summer, I don't even like to think about what could have happened to us if our pilot hadn't made it back to the controls."

Summer looked around from behind her camera at Tony and nodded in agreement.

"Summer may be the youngest one here…I'm pretty sure she is, but she is braver than any grown man I know. Speaking of brave, look who is joining us!"

The group turned to see who Tony was talking about. Much to their surprise, DeShunta Jackson was walking up slowly but resolutely. Shock registered on multiple faces. No one expected her to feel like joining them after the fall she had taken.

"Wow, DeShunta my dear! Are you all right? How are you feeling?"

DeShunta had just experienced the fright of her life. She literally thought she was going to die. She hurt her right shoulder when she put her arm out to break her fall. Her back was aching. She had been given 800 milligrams of ibuprofen and had an icepack strapped to her right shoulder blade. Seeing Tony, however, was better than medicine. She rallied. She might have been banged up and bruised, but this is what she came for. She managed a smile and a nod for Tony.

"I'm alive. That's all I can say right now."

Tony was glad to hear her voice. Her words may have been few, but the smile she gave him, though brief, spoke volumes. He rewarded her with a smile of his own.

"I am delighted you are, my darling."

Tony started to talk about Clarence, but hesitated. DeShunta would blow up if he mentioned his name. After a moment's reflection, he decided to skip Clarence for the time being and talk about the person on everyone's minds.

"One of your fellow team members is missing. Boedy Da surprised us all with his wingsuit jump. Of all the things we discussed during our brainstorming sessions when we were trying to figure out the most exciting way to start the adventure, we never dreamed of doing what Boedy did. The truth, not sugarcoated, is this—we don't know exactly where he is right now. Tamper and Bones are even now leading two separate search parties to find him. Willow, I know you are very concerned about your brother. I would be, too. Don't worry—they will find him. As a matter of fact, they have probably already found him and are giving him a ride back to camp right now. He is an amazing young man. I'll bet you he is just fine."

"Or dead," DeShunta interjected. "I think he's dead."

Upon hearing DeShunta's insensitive declaration, Willow covered her eyes with her hands and began to cry. Others gasped. Peaches wrapped her arms around her and rocked her back and forth. Tony frowned.

"Well DeShunta, we just don't know, do we? What I do know is that we will find him. We have the best mobile medical care unit available outside of a major metropolitan hospital right here in our camp, and we have an incredible doctor and team of nurses trained in emergency field medicine to provide it."

Celeste was swatting her legs. Annaliese, who was next to her, was waving her hand in front of her face to combat the flying insects. Celeste suggested that their perfume might be attracting the bugs, but after today, they won't smell so sweet. Annaliese smiled in agreement. After the exchange, both of their faces reverted to the serious looks that they had before. Tony hesitated before saying what was on his mind, knowing the possible consequences, but he had to ask. It was only fair.

"I have a question to ask all of you, and I want you to give me your honest answer. Do you want to continue with this, or do you want to suspend it and try it again some other time? Honest answers."

G's heart stopped. What in the name of reason was Tony saying? Tony always had a spur of the moment, off the cuff side to him that gave a real, unrehearsed feel to his appearances. Putting the future of Jungle Money into the hands of the contestants however, was far too off-script for G to countenance. He held his breath. Postponement was clearly a thought none of them had entertained. Mystic Origin, the freegan, was the first to respond.

"When you say 'some other time,' do you mean tomorrow? Later this week?"

"No, I mean not this year. Possibly next year, possibly not at all."

Several people protested. Mystic Origin was one of them.

"Why would you call it off? We just got here!"

Aston, the harpoon guy said, "If you are worried about us, don't be, because we are ready for this. I say let's go."

"It was a scary start, but we made it. I'm in," said Annaliese.

Tony studied the faces surrounding him. It was not surprising that the ones who had made it safely, without injury, would still be gung ho. The real question was whether the others would agree—one in particular. Tony stepped over to DeShunta and looked deeply into her eyes.

"DeShunta, if anybody here has a good reason to call this thing off, it's you. There is no shame in bowing out under these circumstances. If you'd like to pass, everyone here will completely understand. I will get you on one of the two helicopters up on the plateau, and you can be in an airplane home by tomorrow. Just say the word."

DeShunta pondered her options. She didn't answer right away. As she thought, she reached up and gingerly massaged her sore right shoulder. She knew she would be even more sore tomorrow. Still, if she went back home without an adventure, without a TV appearance, none of her friends and neighbors would believe that she was even picked for the show, much less that she flew to Brazil, rode in a helicopter, fell out of the helicopter, and got to talk to Tony Longino. A long minute of silence passed with no one speaking out of respect for the traumatic event she had just been through.

"I be okay. Let's do this thing."

The group erupted into cheering and applause, overwhelmed with relief and flooded with the excitement of knowing that the adventure was truly about to begin. Tony's face changed from cloudy with a chance of thunderstorms to blue skies and a new sunrise. Seeing him smile made it worth it for DeShunta. *Lord have mercy, that man is beautiful.*

The Senator, who was standing nearby, quick-stepped over to DeShunta to applaud her for her brave decision. He clapped her on her back and said, "Let me be the first to…"

He didn't finish his sentence.

A wicked left back fist from a mad black woman smashed into the side of the Senator's jaw—the not-unexpected result of him having slapped the raw nerve endings in DeShunta's injured upper back. The blistering tirade that poured forth from DeShunta's mouth brought complete clarity as to what had just happened and why. No one blamed her, and in fact, once the shock had worn off, everyone, save the Senator, tried to quietly suppress grins.

Jungle Money Life Lesson number one: Don't ever, ever, ever clap DeShunta Jackson on the back after she has fallen out of a helicopter.

Chapter Seventeen

Once everyone realized that the Senator was going to survive with everything intact, aside from his wounded pride, they looked again at Tony. His face beaming, Tony made the announcement he had been waiting so very long to make.

"You heard the lady! Let's do this thing! Let the Jungle Money games begin!"

With Tony's pronouncement, the somber mood vanished. The sound of joyful music came from out of nowhere. It seemed to originate from somewhere behind the pergola, beyond a stand of trees.

They were drawn to the happy sound like moths to a flame. It was not just the ladies who began skipping toward the music—the men found musical springs in their steps as well. People who had only met each other briefly in a Georgia mansion a few weeks ago were now unashamedly holding hands and dancing down the path.

When they came out from behind the trees, they found themselves at the edge of a small, circular clearing. Situated inside the clearing was an outdoor theater, a small arena complete with a stage and backdrop smartly decorated in a rich jungle theme. Torches blazed from atop posts, and garlands of colorful flowers adorned the spaces in between. In the distance, above and behind the stage, the top of the waterfall could be seen. The view was breathtaking. A camera could never say it right.

Two lines of smiling South American men, adorned in flashy dance costumes, created a passageway for them to pass through. Their teeth were gleaming white, and their skin was darkened by a lifetime spent under the equatorial sun. Each man bore a colorful drum upon which they beat syncopated rhythms in perfect unison. Upon the stage there was a bevy of Brazilian beauties wearing giant feathered headdresses and revealing golden outfits which showed their shapely bronze legs to great advantage. They danced the samba, the highly favored traditional dance of Brazil. The dancers shook their hips in flawless rhythm at a blinding speed and with effortless elegance. Steel drums played by another group of men wearing a more primitive native type of garb provided the melody from the back of the stage. Their red headdresses flared and moved as they drummed.

Caught up in the moment, Aston the harpoon guy jumped up onstage and began to dance the samba alongside one of the ladies. Between his pearly white, perfectly-veneered teeth, the frosted tips in his gelled hair, and his fitted silk shirt, it was clear that Aston was ready to make an impression. He was good. He was very good. The smiles of approval that the dancers gave made it clear that he had their respect. Dance erased all barriers of language, culture, politics and party.

Aston's enthusiasm was contagious and lit a fire under the other contestants. Shyness was thrown out the window. Everyone jumped in, even the stodgy old Senator, although none were so brave as to jump up onstage with Aston. Laughter, music and movement reigned supreme.

One of the male performers, who wore a barely visible wireless mic by the side of his mouth, began to sing a contemporary Brazilian song more akin to rap than pop. The audience immediately began to clap along in time, swept up by the quality of his voice. Their enjoyment was not diminished in the least by their inability to understand his words. They laughed excitedly when he began playing a jew's harp in between verses. Even G found himself dancing in the back.

When DeShunta could contain her enthusiasm no longer, she raised her hands and began shaking them as she walked in a semi-circle, looking first to the sky, then back to the ground, then back to the sky again. Peaches liked it so much that she began to chant, "Go DeShunta! Go DeShunta! It's your birthday! It's your birthday!" No one knew if it was her birthday or not, but the chant caught on. The contestants ringed DeShunta and began cheering her on. They did not anticipate the reaction they would get.

DeShunta started twerking like a pole dancer at a gentlemen's club.

When she did, the howls went up, the roof came off and the house came down. Summer, the apprentice videographer, was laughing so hard and wiping so many tears that she was physically incapable of filming.

After several minutes of frenetic dancing, the sea of dancers began to part. From way in the back, a striking figure wearing all white bounded up a set of stairs and slid to a stop at the edge of the stage. Tony Longino! His very presence exuded energy and electricity.

Sidling up to the incredibly gorgeous woman dancing to his right, Tony began matching her step for step. His magnetic persona, coupled with her exotic sensuousness, captured the attention of everyone within sight or sound. Theirs was the kind of chemistry that transcended time and space, country and culture. Faces shimmering from sweat, Tony and his partner came together, parted, gyrated, swung away, twirled and returned, a flawless display of what dance could be. One after the other, the onlookers began to feel hints of fatigue, but the professionals danced tirelessly on and on.

The steel drummers suddenly stopped playing, laid down their drums and sprinted forward. Without slowing down, they leaped out into space with primal screams, startling their audience as was their intention. Aston, knowing his time for participation had come to an end, slipped off the stage and rejoined his group.

The men, who were wearing little more than headdresses and loincloths, landed on the ground in front of the stage and began doing a series of cartwheels and backflips. Peaches, Celeste and DeShunta screamed their appreciation for the chiseled abs and well-defined muscles on display before them. The performers began throwing choreographed kicks at one another at the end of each tumble and roll. Their observers couldn't decide if they were witnessing gymnastics, dance or martial arts. Chaz knew exactly what he was watching and excitedly called it by name.

"Capoeira!"

One of the performers stopped and gestured at the contestants, inviting any who wanted to join in. Chaz, who had taken two weeks of free capoeira classes at a strip mall near his house, badly wanted to step forward and try. He looked at the performers with his trademark forty-five degree head tilt which allowed him to see past his hair, but his introverted nature wouldn't allow him to do it.

The sweat-soaked performer saw Chaz's eagerness and knew he just needed a little push. He grabbed one of his fellow performers and together they ran to Chaz and lifted him bodily into the fray. Some of the men formed a human ladder while other performers locked their arms to form a safety net. At first Chaz was reluctant, but he quickly warmed to the idea of climbing the human ladder. When he neared the top, with the apparent approval of the uppermost ladder man, Chaz did a perfect backflip and landed in the flexed but flexible arms of the men down below. Everyone in attendance roared their approval at the completely unscripted moment.

The human ladder collapsed by design, and the human net broke apart as the performers fell back into their original positions. They formed a ring around Chaz and one other performer who faced off in the middle. The performer did a cartwheel and finished it by throwing a swing kick a safe distance away from Chaz's face. Chaz, whose every inhibition had vanished into the sweltering jungle air, executed a backflip followed by a forward roll toward his "opponent" which he finished off with an energetic kick of his own.

The performers shouted their approval and converged on Chaz, lifting him above their heads as though he were a float in a Carnival parade. They pounded him on the back when they returned him to earth. They bounded back up on stage and resumed their stations behind the female dancers, where they picked up their steel drums and began the melody anew.

Hearing their tune, Tony and his beautiful partner poured all their energy into the final samba of the show. As though on cue, the two were bathed in the light of a late afternoon sunbeam after the passing of a cloud overhead. Tony grabbed his partner bodily, hoisted her overhead, lowered her swiftly and flipped her head back as her torso bent backwards over his knee. He raised his hand in triumph as the last note sounded and the last drumbeat died away.

The audience burst into applause, punctuated by whistles and shouts. He helped the lovely lady to stand. The two hugged and laughed as they tried to catch their breath. By this point, the contestants were gathered in a large knot just in front of the stage, clapping with their hands over their heads. Now that the dance was over, a tiny microphone was brought to Tony, who hooked the earpiece into his ear and clipped the receiver onto his lapel. Breathing hard, he tried to calm himself so he could speak

"Ladies and gentlemen, once again, welcome to Jungle Money! Oh my. I'm still trying to catch my breath here. This is our Jungle Money arena and theater built just for you. As you begin your quest to win all of that wonderful jungle money, you will see what a magical place the Amazon rainforest truly is. Now get ready, because the jungle is about to come alive all around you!"

With that pronouncement, hidden doors made of bamboo opened from the floor of the stage. An explosion of tropical birds, impatiently waiting in cages underneath, made their break for freedom. Hundreds of toucans, parrots, and cockatoos in every size and color imaginable created a living rainbow of flight over the joyous ceremony. In an involuntary breach of standard operating procedure, Richard pulled his eyes away from his video camera to look up overhead. The little screen on his viewfinder wasn't quite big enough for him to take it all in. His lens was pointed up in the right direction. *Surely it will capture most of it*, he thought to himself. All eyes were looking up, and all mouths were hanging open at the scene unfolding before them. Tony's smile was as bright as the Amazonian sun.

Much to the delight of everyone, a cockatoo landed on Celeste's head extracting a squeal of surprise. To her credit, she did not panic and swat at her head to scare it away. Instead, she froze and did her best to keep her head level so that the bird would not have to dig its claws deeper into her hair in order to keep its balance.

Everyone laughed at the awkward situation she found herself in. Many reached for their cellphones out of habit in order to snap a picture, having forgotten that they had turned them in to Tony prior to boarding the helicopters. It was going to be exceedingly difficult for them to live without their electronic appendages for that length of time, but Tony had assured them that the photographers and videographers would capture every moment for posterity's sake.

When all the birds that wanted to fly had flown, everyone turned their attention back to Tony. He waited for the whooping and hollering to die down, but it wouldn't. He laughed and let it go on. After another minute or so, he addressed the contestants.

"So, how do you like the way Brazil says 'hello'?"

The contestants roared so loudly that Tony had to laugh. It was clear that they felt most welcome in this place.

"You have just experienced a taste of what this country and the people who call it home have to offer. I am hopeful that you will return the love, so that they feel the same way about you by the time you leave. Remember that you are not only representing yourselves, you are also ambassadors of the United States. Like it or not, the people who you come in contact with, who have never met an American before, will form their opinion of one from you. By the magic of television, that will soon include people from many places around the globe. Keep in mind the great cloud of witnesses, as we'll call them, watching you as you enjoy this glorious adventure."

Standing way in the back with crossed arms, G smiled despite himself. *We just might pull this off after all.*

The throaty sound of an all-terrain vehicle's engine could be heard coming from the other side of the trees. As the noise grew louder, it became clear that the ATV was going to be driven straight into the arena theater. The driver's face was unfamiliar, but the passenger's face was anything but. Tony stopped speaking rather than try to compete with the volume of the motor.

Clarence Humberton, with one icepack on his shoulder and another icepack between his legs, hove into view. He was loudly chastising his driver for failing to avoid a pothole in the path. Several of the Brazilian drummers and dancers, standing near the entrance, backed away quickly, startled by the loud angry and unfamiliar New York brogue.

Clarence's mood had soured even before he touched the ground in this place. He was enraged by what he considered to be criminal behavior on the part of his helicopter pilot in failing to secure his passengers so they wouldn't fall out and die. He was highly annoyed by what he considered to be the unwarranted overreaction of DeShunta Jackson to a little playful gesture on his part. He was incensed by the malpractice of Dr. Jane when she told him that his swollen and bruised reproductive organ did not warrant the prescription of a 90-day supply of narcotics. He was miffed that the snot-nosed kid driving him seemed to hit every bump and depression along the path just to spite him. Topping it all off though, was the unforgivable slight being perpetrated upon him even now.

They were having the opening ceremony without him.

Clarence was mad and wanted the whole world to know. The dancers and performers closest to him would be a good place to start.

"What are you looking at? Bunch of banana-eating stripper wannabes! And you, get that look off your face! Go play the drum in the jungle with the rest of your cannibal friends!"

The Brazilians could not understand the words, but they understood the intent perfectly. The tone of the big man's voice and the contempt in his eyes made his message clear. After having put the natives in their place, Clarence turned back to his driver, who had slowed to a stop well before reaching the stage.

"Well drive on up there, would you? What are you waiting for, a police escort and a trumpet?"

The young driver responded with a "No sir, sorry sir," and gently pressed the accelerator. When he reached the stage, the driver stopped and ran around to the passenger side in order to help Clarence stand to his feet. Clarence Humberton was not a patient man under the best of circumstances, and these were not the best of circumstances.

"Let's go, let's go, let's go! While we're still young!"

Tony, seeing his audience's attention had been diverted, smiled at the new arrival.

"Clarence, welcome back! I'm glad to see…"

Clarence cut him off as effectively as a power outage at a lamp store.

"I bet you are glad to see me. You should be. You tried to kill me! What kind of sandlot minor league team is running this show? You have earned yourself a lawsuit, buddy boy—a big fat lawsuit. I guarantee it. You are going to be hearing from my lawyer. You might want to write his name down. Benito Francisco Bonnano, Esquire. Never lost a case in twenty-five years. That's B-O-N-N-A-N-O. Hey, you're not writing! That's okay actually. He'll be writing you. When he gets through with you, I'm going to own those helicopters and that expensive zoot suit you're wearing, and you'll be walking home through the jungle in your skivvies. All the jungle money is going to be mine!"

This was not Tony's first day on the job. He had dealt with tough crowds before. This one was no different. All eyes turned to him, eager to see his reaction. When he began to speak, he remained as cool as a cucumber.

"I apologized to everyone else, and I need to extend the same courtesy to you, Clarence. I am sorry you decided to scare DeShunta by pushing her toward the door when neither of you were fully harnessed in. As it is, I am grateful…"

Clarence exploded.

"I didn't do one thing to that crazy woman! She is mentally unstable and needs to be hospitalized! Do you know what she did to me? Do you know what she did? She…"

When DeShunta's ears heard the disparaging remarks leaving Clarence's mouth, everything changed. Moments earlier she had been a happy woman enjoying music, song and dance. No longer. The sky began to darken. Tectonic plates began to shift. The earth began to shake. DeShunta erupted with a violence and fury that volcanoes could never hope to duplicate. The noise that blasted out of her lungs was ear-splitting. Even if the words were undecipherable, no one needed an interpreter to guess their meaning. Though she was too short for any but the closest to see, her physical presence was evident by the parting of the crowd around her. The hapless bystanders, who had the misfortune of standing between her and her antagonist, were knocked over like so many bowling pins. In the chaos that ensued, one thing was very clear.

Clarence Humberton was in mortal danger.

When Clarence caught a glimpse of DeShunta breaking free of the crowd, he recognized his peril. Moving with surprising speed for a big man with a groin injury, Clarence maneuvered himself behind a gaggle of dancers to a momentary position of safety. He was stunned at her reaction. This did not happen in his world. No one challenged him physically. Ever. Someone forgot to give the memo to DeShunta however. When she got to him, she was going to introduce him to a brand new world—a world of hurt.

Clarence tried to lose her in the crowd, but a trail of hastily-dropped ice-packs gave his position away. Several of the male performers, staff members and other contestants moved in to separate the combatants. DeShunta howled in frustration at her inability to lay hands on the union boss.

The Senator, clearly distressed at the melee, pleaded with Tony to step in and take control of the situation. Annaliese, disgusted with Tony's lack of leadership, joined in the Senator's request and added, "You are letting this get way out of hand!"

Tony's face betrayed no hint that he shared the Senator's or the Governor's sentiments. To the contrary, Tony looked as though he was anything but displeased.

"This is one lively group. If you think I am here to provide you with adult supervision though, think again. Every day is a day in the classroom if you are willing to learn. You are in a classroom unlike any you have ever experienced before. Understand this—I am neither teacher nor principal. For the next few weeks, this is your kingdom. You make the rules. You reign in this rainforest. So, make yourselves a home and enjoy the ride. This is Jungle Money!"

Clarence scanned the crowd to see if he could catch a glimpse of DeShunta. He was relieved to see that she had been intercepted before she reached him. He realized that he had been holding his cupped hands protectively over the front of his trousers, instinctively guarding against a repeat injury. He released his grip, relaxed his arms, and turned his attention back to Tony.

The conflict successfully deescalated, at least by all appearances, Tony couldn't help but grin in anticipation of the news he was about to share.

"I would like for all my contestants to come up on the stage here with me. Come right on up. We have steps on each side there. Come on up. Come right on up. Gather around."

The contestants made their way up onto the stage and formed a semicircle around Tony. Once they were assembled, he glanced at the faces around him with a twinkle in his eyes.

"Each day will begin with a coronation of royalty. One of you will be King for a Day or Queen for a Day. What you say goes. Your rule rules, no matter what."

Clarence liked what he was hearing. King for a Day sounded good. When they got a little taste of Clarence, they would appoint him King for Life. While Clarence pondered the possibilities, Mystic Origin asked the question on her mind.

"You and the guy back in the mansion, I forget his name, both said we get to make the rules, but how do you pick who gets to be Queen for a Day? Or King? Is it a vote? Do we draw straws?"

Tony rubbed his hands together and smiled.

"Good question, Mystic Origin. So, are you ready to find out how it will be decided who is King or Queen for a Day?"

A resounding "yes" brought a smile to Tony's face.

"Excellent. We have a very special guest who will be making that selection every morning at the start of each day. She is not a native Brazilian, but she is very much at home in this rainforest. She has taken to it quite nicely. I think you will like her a lot. Without further ado, let me introduce you to....Mother Nature!"

Tony turned and backed away from the center of the stage. Denise Milton, the team's wildlife biologist, appeared from the back and made her way through the dancers. The contestants had met her briefly up on the plateau and made the logical assumption that Mother Nature must be her nickname. At least, they did until they saw the small person holding her hand and walking beside her.

Only it wasn't a person. DeShunta placed her hand over her mouth and shouted in surprise.

"Oh, my god!"

Shuffling along next to the beaming Denise Milton was a full-grown female orangutan. Bottom lip stuck out. Calm expression. Overlarge belly. Impossibly long arms. Reddish hair sticking straight up from her head. The simian held the hand of her human companion while her other arm swung by her side. When Denise stopped, her small friend stopped as well. The audience could not contain themselves. The sweet expression on her face was as adorable as it was intelligent. She locked eyes with Aston, and he laughed with unbridled joy.

"Hello, Mother Nature!"

She maintained her peaceful demeanor in the midst of all the excitement as though she couldn't see what all the fuss was about. Tony kneeled and stretched out his arms. Mother Nature let go of Denise's hand and ambled over to him. Without hesitation she gave him a hug. After a few seconds, she released him, turned, and looked at the crowd. For some reason, she pointed at

Mystic Origin and rolled back her lips, who pointed back at her. The contestants laughed at the sight, which was unlike anything they had imagined when they were invited onto the show.

Tony turned to the back of the stage, and his lovely dance partner made her way toward him. She carried a velvet pillow, supported by both of her hands. Balanced on that pillow was a crown which sparkled in the sunlight. She walked like a runway model to the end of the stage and held it aloft for all to see. After allowing a few moments for the contestants to gaze upon the regal headpiece, Tony gingerly lifted the crown off of the pillow and thanked its lovely bearer.

The sides were covered with fabric of the deepest purple, the color of royalty. The band was made of the finest silver. The crown was adorned with an intricate pattern of jewels and precious stones, the most numerous of which were shiny diamonds. Peaches' voice rose above the din.

"Where on earth did you get the crown? It is magnificent!"

Tony was pleased.

"I'm so glad you like it. This crown is believed to have belonged to John VI, monarch of the United Kingdom of Portugal, Brazil and the Algarves, who ruled here from 1816 to 1825. He had exquisite taste in headwear, didn't he?"

Annaliese was incredulous.

"But how did you get it? Why isn't it safely stored in a display case in a climate-controlled museum somewhere?"

Tony nodded in appreciation of her question.

"So, here is the story. When Napoleon invaded Portugal, King John VI fled and traveled roughly 4,500 miles to Brazil. Unfortunately for him, his family didn't like him very much. His wife conspired against him, and his sons did their best to remove their father from the throne. Poor King John's death was rumored to have been caused by arsenic poisoning. This crown was nothing but trouble to him until the day he died."

Annaliese persisted.

"But seriously, how did *you* end up with it?"

Tony smiled.

"When G and I first flew to Brazil to scout out a location, we met with a number of government officials and gave them an outline of the show, including King and Queen for a Day. Before we flew back home, one of the ministry officials tracked us down and told us he had just the thing for us. He drove us to a man's house, which was a mansion, really. It was incredibly beautiful on the outside, but oddly enough, it was practically empty on the inside. It looked like the owner had maybe fallen on hard times and sold everything or had it repossessed. Anyway, the owner took us to a vault roughly…ten feet by ten feet. He opened it up and lo and behold, there was the most beautiful crown you have ever seen. How he got it, I have no idea."

Annaliese asked, “So, did you buy it from him?”

Tony laughed.

“Not exactly. We tried. Oh, we tried. The price he wanted us to pay was way, way more than we wanted to spend. He was certain he could convince us his price was fair, but we failed to come to terms. Then G hit upon an idea. “How much would it cost us to rent it and return it to you at the end of the show?” I thought G was nuts. There’s no way this guy is going to let us borrow his crown and take it to a remote place like this. But G can read people. The guy was clearly strapped for cash and wanted to make a deal very badly, so he dropped his price a ton and let us rent it. That is how it came to be that I am standing here before you holding the crown of John VI, monarch of Portugal and Brazil.”

Every mouth formed a “wow” as they gazed upon the rare and beautiful antiquity in Tony’s hands. As they were taking in the sight, Tony did something no one expected.

Tony handed the crown to Mother Nature.

Amid the gasps of the stunned onlookers, the orangutan took the crown with barely a glance and began to shuffle toward the contestants. Tony began to speak in singsong fashion.

“Mother Nature decides
who will wear the crown,
who will make the rules
until the sun goes down.”

People strained to see as the simian made her way to the men and women before her. Was she really going to choose someone? Without hesitation, Mother Nature made her way to Terry Bishop, the young man who was different from all the rest—the one with every square inch of exposed skin, save his face, covered in tattoos. When she stopped before him, the young man’s smile widened. Those around him grabbed his shoulders in excitement. The orangutan stood quietly in front of him, as though waiting. Not quite knowing what to do, Tattoo looked to Tony for help. Tony offered a suggestion.

“Kneel down. Kneel.”

Tattoo knelt, placing his left kneecap down on the stage and bowed his head before the creature. Mother Nature calmly placed the crown upon his head. Having done so, she turned and walked back to Tony without a backward glance. Having been thus adorned, Tattoo rose, careful to keep his head level. When he stood up to his full height, applause came from every corner. Tony congratulated him and declared him to be the duly anointed King for a Day.

Back in the production room approximately a quarter of a mile away, two men in a climate-controlled environment viewed the proceedings on a bank of monitors. Wally, whose film-making talents had been honed in the making of dozens of wildlife documentaries from locations around the globe, grabbed video clips from first one camera and then the next. He was putting together the first-cut day one video that he and Jason would present to Tony and G. Soon, they would create the pilot show from the hours upon hours of raw footage being shot that day. Jason was creating a backstory video for each contestant from the electronic library they had created months earlier.

"Jason, what we got on Tattoo?"

Jason, who had been eagerly awaiting this moment ever since Wally invited him to join him the previous year, was already clicking away on his computer.

"Let's see here, what do we have on Mr. Tattoo? Pulling it up, pulling it up, hourglass spinning. Okay, here we go. Tattoo Interview Clip One, Tattoo Interview Clip Two, Three, Four…looks like we've got a total of sixteen clips from the mansion."

Wally and Jason had been there at Bert Redmond's mansion months earlier for the first meeting of the contestants. Every word uttered by every person there had been captured, labeled, catalogued, and archived for later use. Jason opened Clip One, and an image of Tattoo materialized, frozen in position. He clicked on the big sideways triangle in the center of the box. Frozen Tattoo came to life and began to move and speak.

"The letters on the back of my fingers? Nah, I don't mind you asking. It spells 'Infidel.' I-N-F-I-D-E-L."

Tattoo lifted each finger as he read off the letter inscribed on it.

"My other fingers just have scrollwork on them. Why? Well, I'm not a Muslim, so according to the Koran I'm an infidel. I'm not a Christian or a Jew either, so everybody considers me to be an infidel."

An unidentified person out of view of the camera asked, "So, what are you?"

"I'm an atheist. I don't believe in God. If I can't see it or hear it, and nobody else can show it to me, there's nothing to believe in. It doesn't exist. Kind of like Bigfoot."

Someone else off-camera could be heard chuckling. Tattoo's face remained serious.

"I don't mean to offend you. If you believe, that's fine. I don't care. Santa Claus, the Easter Bunny, the Tooth Fairy, chupacabras, whatever. If people's lives are happier believing in things that aren't there, then power to them. I just can't believe that a god would allow so many bad things to happen to good people, unless he's sick or sadistic. If he does, I don't want to have nothing to do with him anyway. I've got no use for him. It's a crutch. I'm stronger than that and don't need it."

A few seconds passed with no one speaking. Tattoo looked off-camera and then returned his eyes to front and center.

"Look, you asked, so I told you. If you didn't want to know…"

Jason clicked the double lines and paused the video clip. He glanced over at Wally, who slowly shook his head.

"Sad, man. Just sad."

Jason nodded. Scrolling down through the files, he chose Interview Clip Eight at random. Play.

"Oh okay, we're back to religion again, huh? Well, like the one lady in the…you know, the one with the dreads was saying. I just don't think it ought to be all out in public, you know? Freedom from religion, which some people call freedom *of* religion, is one of our most basic rights. That's why America was founded in the first place, because people didn't want to be forced to practice a particular religion by the King of England. I just don't want to have to look at it, and I shouldn't be forced to. Nobody is saying you can't be all religious in your home or your church, but if I'm not in one of those two places, I shouldn't be forced to watch it. There needs to be limits, especially when you go out in public."

When the next question was asked, both Wally and Jason recognized the questioner as Bert Redmond.

"So, let's assume you are out in public, maybe at an outdoor concert, or a 10K race, or a Fourth of July parade or something. What should happen if someone is praying or singing a religious song, or holding up signs with a religious message or something like that?"

Tattoo leaned back, inhaled a double lungful of air while looking at the ceiling, blew it out with his cheeks puffed out, and then leaned forward with a "Let me explain it to you again" look on his face.

"Well, I don't care about praying, because that doesn't impact me. If somebody wants to talk to their selves, okay by me. But the other stuff now, like I was saying, the government started this mess with the whole King of England thing. It's their job to make sure that it doesn't happen again."

"So, the government should, what, intervene?" Bert asked.

Tattoo nodded.

"Yeah, they should. They need to be doing something to earn all that tax money we give them."

Jason hit Pause. Tattoo's face froze right as he began to blink. His eyes were not quite completely covered by his eyelids. Wally locked his fingers behind his head, straightened his legs, and pushed his rolling chair back from the table filled with monitors. He exhaled, stood up, and popped the top on a cola. Schiiick. Bubbles fizzed. He slurped it quickly to keep it from spilling over. Must have shaken it while grabbing the can.

Jason pondered a question out loud as he began to unwrap a candy bar.

"Okay, so what does Tattoo's kid get if she loses a tooth just before midnight on December 24th? Anything? Nothing?"

Wally's foot flew up almost instantaneously. He meant to deliver a swift kick to Jason's butt as retribution for the dumb question he just asked, but his accuracy was off. He didn't mean to catch Jason's elbow and launch his candy bar into space. He was nevertheless delighted that it did. Laughing uproariously, Wally ran out the door before Jason could give chase, trying his best not to spill his drink while he ran. Jason, running with murderous intent, pounded after him, determined to empty Wally's drink all over Wally's head.

Chapter Eighteen

Trayton smiled to himself as he drove down Ponce de Leon toward Decatur. It was ten 'til ten, and he was almost to the parking lot. The oak tree-lined road had many early-morning joggers pounding the pavement before the heat of the day set in. Saturday mornings were the perfect time to get in a sweat. You could be done, get a shower, and still have almost all day to play. He wasn't a huge fan of hot yoga, but his girlfriend Celeste loved it. She said it cleansed her mind while it cleansed her pores. As a result, he had started doing something he never thought he would do. Yoga. Once he started, though, he had learned that he actually enjoyed it, as much as you can enjoy sweating in a sauna while holding stretches for unbearable lengths of time.

When Trayton learned that Celeste was taking off on a Brazilian adventure, of which he knew very little, he had initially thought that was the end of hot yoga for him. That had changed when he met Karena. While serving the breakfast crowd at NeedaCup, she had been the one to recognize him from class. Karena had big, bouncy blonde hair and striking green eyes that made you want to continue the conversation just to look into them a while longer. Karena had asked him where his girlfriend was. He didn't really know why he did it, but he did. Without stopping to think, he responded instantaneously.

"Oh, we're not together right now."

Technically, it was a true statement. She was off somewhere in Brazil for who knows how long. But he kept having these nagging, and annoying, pangs of conscience. Celeste was, of course, coming back. Her absence was only temporary. But what if Celeste ended up liking Brazil? That wouldn't be so bad. After all, they weren't married or anything. They hadn't really been getting along all that great before she left anyway. Actually, if he broke it off now, that might be the best option for all concerned. It would not be a fun conversation. Although it might seem a little rude, it might be best to do this over the phone while she was over there. It would give her time to cool off. Maybe he could just text her? No. He dismissed the idea as soon as it popped into his head. He would have to talk to her. The unpleasant thought made the smile disappear from his face.

The parking lot across from the yoga studio was almost full, but Trayton lucked out by pulling in just as someone was backing out to leave. He heard Karena's lyrical voice as soon as he got out of the car.

"I guess I will have a partner this morning after all!"

Trayton quickly gave her a once-over, and gave her the dimpled smile that she said was so cute. Karena was the reason that yoga pants had been invented; he was sure of it. He had nothing planned for the rest of the day. The glow radiating from her face made him hope that she didn't either. This was shaping up to be a fine day. A fine day, indeed.

Chapter Nineteen

A sumptuous meal had been prepared for the contestants, and what a tropical feast it was. There were fresh fruits galore, like mangoes, bananas, pineapples, guava and kiwi. A pig wrapped in banana leaves had been buried in a pit dug in the ground and roasted. The steaming hot pork it produced smelled divine. Salad made with the freshest greens possible filled bowls to overflowing. There was a selection of grilled fish straight from the river, wild caught by Bones and several of the male performers during the days leading up to the arrival of their special guests. Wild honeycomb provided the dessert. It was everything they ever imagined a jungle buffet could be. As people rushed to get in line, Peaches spoke up.

"Before we eat, someone should ask the blessing. You know, ask to keep us safe, bless the food and all."

Several people clasped their hands in front and began to bow their heads. Tony glanced at Tattoo, who interpreted Tony's look as a sign that he was to make a ruling. He cleared his throat.

"Look, I'm the King for a Day. You got to respect my rules and I'll do the same when it's your turn. But we ain't having no prayers. No God today. You can do it on yours."

At that, Tattoo walked past the silenced crowd and began to fill his plate. Peaches looked stunned. People didn't do that where she was from. They may live like hell on Monday, but they were in church on Sunday.

Everyone ate until they were full. Some weren't able to eat as much as they would've liked due to the heat. As the guests slowed down and the line thinned, Clarence's return trips became the only thing to watch. Annoyed by the looks of those seated at the tables near the buffet, Clarence felt the need to justify himself.

"Who knows when we'll get to eat again?"

Eventually, even Clarence had his fill. As he lounged in his chair, he felt a movement deep within his belly, hidden beneath his belt. Clarence had a food baby baking in the oven. By all signs, he could tell he would need to break out the quilted oven mitts and deliver it in no more than an hour. He began to cast his eyes around the tables. It would be wise to know in advance where to find the porta-pots.

One by one, faces began to turn towards Tony. They were excited to hear him explain the first event. He appeared to be waiting on something. They noticed Tony looking past them, his eyes fixed on the edge of the clearing. As the minutes continued to pass, some grew impatient. What was he waiting for?

DeShunta, who was ready to get the show on the road, followed his gaze. He was watching Mystic Origin. She had picked up an elephant ear tree leaf that had fallen to the ground and was carefully placing it at the base of the tree, as though she was returning a baby to its mother. She began to talk to the tree, lovingly, and then patted the trunk. When DeShunta heard her say, "Here's your baby, mom," DeShunta had heard all she could stand.

"Oh, we ain't having none of that! Get yourself over here and quit playing like plants is people!"

Startled, Mystic Origin turned and saw that everyone was watching her. She scurried over, careful to stop on the side away from DeShunta. Tony had an amused look on his face as he watched her rejoin the group.

"Are you ready for the first event?"

"Yes!"

"Look behind me."

A leather-skinned Brazilian man, flanked by two younger men, both of them burly and rather intimidating-looking, stood before what appeared to be a covered table. He lifted the cloth that concealed a large object, revealing an ornately-carved chest with a giant lock. Without waiting to be asked, the contestants evacuated their seats at the tables and formed a semi-circle around the chest. Tony reached in his shirt and produced a gold key.

"Tattoo, Your Majesty, would you like to do the honors?"

The man wearing the crown looked at Tony with a wry look. "Tattoo" was the name reserved for his friends to use. His real name was Terry Bishop, and Tony knew it. Good manners required one of two things before calling him by his nickname—friendship or permission. Tony had neither. Terry's smile disappeared. Tony, amused at the stand-off he had created, held his confident smile without breaking eye contact. Feeling the cameras on him, Terry weighed his options. Tony was the label maker. If he wanted, he could assign a nickname to anyone and everyone. Terry realized he had a worse nickname than Tattoo. "The Grunge." Terry really, really didn't like "The Grunge." When he considered his options, Terry realized that there were worse names than "Tattoo."

What the heck, he thought. *Why not? I can live with it.*

Stepping forward, Tattoo took the key from Tony's hands. He inserted it into the lock, turned it, and after a squeaky complaint from the rusted components, the lock popped open. Holding the lock with one hand, Tattoo tried to lift the lid of the chest with the other. Due to the weight of the lid, however, he discovered it would require two hands. Straining more than he thought he would've had to, Tattoo opened the lid, which groaned in protest.

There before them lay a fortune in gold bars, silver coins, paper money, diamonds and jewels. Celeste gasped. Clarence shouted an oath. Willow uttered a phrase that would make a sailor blush, causing some to laugh and others to raise their eyebrows. Tony gave them time to take it all in. Without asking permission first, Annaliese boldly reached in and grabbed a gold bar. Due to the weight, it almost slipped out of her hand. The Brazilian keeper of the chest and his henchmen looked sharply at Tony but couldn't detect any cues to stop her. Once the others saw that Annaliese was not being chastised for touching, they began to reach in as well. Tony was clearly enjoying their reactions.

"Take a minute to look. I don't need to tell you about the gold and jewels, but the appearance of the money may be unfamiliar to you. That is because the coins you see were minted a long, long time ago. You may be wondering how much is in here. I will put it this way. To the best of our knowledge, only a handful of Brazilian cities exchange this much money in a single year. You have heard the words "small fortune" before? Take out the word "small." This, ladies and gentlemen, is what you are playing to win."

The Senator, who was no stranger to large sums of money, gave out a long, slow whistle. Aston laughed. Chaz smiled and excitedly rubbed his hands together. Annaliese slowly shook her head, thinking about the terrible financial choices these young kids would make if they got their hands on that kind of money. They didn't know how to put it to good use like she did. After allowing the size of the prize to sink in for a few moments, Tony broke the trance.

"So you will know, we have six contests planned out for you. Not all of them can be completed in a day, although it may be theoretically possible. Only one person will take home the grand prize—the treasure chest and all the riches inside, but all is not lost for the rest of you. There are exciting possibilities along the way. Each person who wins one of the first five contests gets to go in the treasure chest and grab one handful of treasure—as much as you can hold in one hand. You can't help with the other hand. It's like the game at the arcade called "The Claw," except instead of getting a stuffed animal, you get a Lamborghini. You have all kinds of extremely valuable things to choose from—gold bars, gold coins, silver coins, diamonds, rubies, emeralds, sapphires and who knows what else. Jungle money galore! Whatever strikes your fancy, it is yours to keep, even if you don't..."

The Senator interrupted Tony, unable to hold his question any longer.

"You've got to tell us the story behind this fabulous treasure. Was this in the guy's safe, too?"

"No, no, no," Tony answered. "The guy with the crown would not have been selling off everything he owned if all this was his."

Clarence, who was running his fingers over the surface of a sea of coins, let fly with a sarcastic guess.

"So, are you going to tell us you found it at the end of a rainbow somewhere? Had to fight off a pack of leprechauns to get it, did you?"

Tony appreciated his humor.

"Not quite. You'll like the true story even better, Clarence. Check this out."

Clarence had just started to fold his arms when DeShunta barked at him.

"Hey, hey, hey! Uh, uh! I seen what you did! Put that back!"

Clarence's face quickly changed from life-of-the-party to hand-in-the-cookie-jar. Although people were crowded around and it was hard to see, a distinct metallic "clink" sounded, as though someone had just tossed something back in the chest. Clarence shrugged his shoulders and showed his empty hands. DeShunta narrowed her eyelids down to slits.

"I'm watching you."

Tony cut his eyes over to Richard, who winked at him. He got it on camera. Tony continued with his story.

"My man G has a lot of varied interests. He is an avid scuba diver, snorkeler and deep sea fisherman. He sails those little boats with the two canoe things side by side which have the little platform between them tying them together. Do you know what I mean? Schooners? Not schooners. I forget. I'll have to ask him. Anyway, he does kite surfing, wind surfing, you name it. He's all about that salt life."

Celeste picked up a blue diamond and held it up to the light. The vivid, sparkling blue matched the color of her eyes. She was careful to put it back in the center, not wanting to get on DeShunta's bad side. She turned her attention back to Tony.

"G has always been fascinated with shipwrecks, diving down and swimming around inside them. Several years ago, he got together with a group of guys and they started searching for old, undiscovered shipwrecks. We're talking like Christopher Columbus, Ponce de Leon, Blackbeard the pirate kind of stuff. They never found anything, which is bad because it costs a ton to look. Well, that all changed when he found the wreck of the Merchant Royal, also known as the El Dorado of the Seas, two years ago near the British Isles. People have been trying to find that ship ever since it went down in 1641. That's right—1641. Celeste, you know that big piece of ice you were just admiring there? Somebody dropped that in that chest there four centuries ago. Four centuries!"

Chaz and Aston both grabbed coins out of the chest and brought them close to their faces, blocking out the sunlight and squinting hard, straining to find any writing that would give a clue as to the date. When the others saw what they were doing, they reached for their own coins to examine.

"The coins you are holding are sovereigns and various denominations of shillings, both silver and gold of varying degrees of purity, depending upon who was king or queen at the time they were struck."

"Tony, help me understand here," said the open-mouthed Senator, scarcely able to take it all in. "Why in the name of humanity would G be offering us this priceless treasure, which has got to be worth who knows how many millions, after all he went through to find it on the ocean floor?"

Tony nodded in understanding.

"Two reasons, Senator. Number one—because this was only a small part of what they found on the El Dorado. Don't you worry about G, not even a little bit. I promise you, G's going to make it just fine. But it was when he found the lost ship and saw what it was carrying that he got the idea for "Jungle Money." He decided to use part of it as an investment into something that could bring much, much more. The second reason why you are standing in front of this treasure chest is you and the television ad revenue and money he expects to receive from streaming this show. Who wouldn't want to tune in or click on a show where people such as yourselves are competing in the jungle to win a priceless treasure? If I was you, I wouldn't worry about the "why" as much as I would the "what do I have to do!"

Tony flashed his million-dollar smile at Celeste, who could not suppress a shy smile of her own. She felt a flush and a warm rush but immediately chastised herself. She needed to be thinking about what this could mean for her future with Trayton. She quickly looked down at the contents of the treasure chest and tried to decide what she would pick out if she won the first contest. Peaches closed her eyes and turned her face to the sky.

"Oh Lord baby Jesus, please let me win that treasure chest. I will give you a big old donation in the offering plate if you will. Amen."

Tattoo cut his eyes at Peaches. He had hesitated before but now he understood the power of the crown.

"Oh, no ma'am. We're not having none of that. I already told you."

Peaches, who had a naturally warm and sunny disposition toward everyone she met, looked at Tattoo in disbelief. He was going to monitor her speech and tell her what she could say and what she couldn't say? Seriously?

Tony nodded to the men standing by the treasure chest. At his signal, the two big men pushed forward, jostling people as they came, and inserted themselves between the contestants and the chest. They closed the lid and snapped the lock back into place. Tony thanked them and looked at the eager crowd.

"So, are you ready to begin?"

He laughed at the shouts of yes, some of which were imbued with frustration from having been asked so many times.

"Okay. Animals are obviously a huge part of the Amazon rainforest. This is their world. The tribes and people groups that inhabit various places in the rainforest worship some of these animals as gods. The jaguar, for example, is commonly viewed as a god and worshipped by many. Animism is common here, which is the belief that rocks and trees and places have souls and spirits, just like they believe animals do. They believe the natural world around them is supernaturally ordered."

Mystic Origin nodded her head vigorously. This comported perfectly with her belief system.

"The first contest is simple. We call it, "Treasure Hunt." Our team has hidden carved statues or totems, each of a different animal, within a one-mile radius of the arena theater. Your goal is to find and bring back those totems. If you are the first to bring back a totem, you get to open the treasure chest and grab yourself a handful of treasure. What if somebody else comes in after them with a totem of their own? Then, in order to get some treasure like the first person, the second person has to bring back a real animal to go with their totem. If you bring back a totem and a real animal, boom, into the treasure chest you go. If you are paying attention to me, you will notice that multiple people can reach into the treasure chest and get themselves some treasure this first game. It's just that the treasure becomes harder and harder to win the longer the game goes on."

Annaliese raised her hand.

"So, do you mean like, if someone has already brought in a statue right before we do, we can just go catch a bug or something and that counts?"

Tony grinned a mischievous grin.

"The real animal you bring in must be bigger than the totem you bring. Bigger, taller, longer, wider or heavier. In some way it's got to be bigger. So no, a little bug won't do it."

Peaches waved her hands dismissively. She didn't see herself dragging some large animal into camp. Tony had one more thing to say.

"One important thing you need to know. The jaguar god trumps everything. Whoever brings back the jaguar god is the automatic winner of the hunt. Two handfuls of treasure to the winner who bags and tags the jaguar god, plus the game is over. So for the rest of you, whatever you do, you better do it before the jaguar appears because the jaguar is king. It doesn't matter if you are in the middle of bringing in a whole herd of deer or an entire flock of birds to go with your totem. It doesn't count if you don't beat the jaguar back to camp. Regardless, the first contest is over by the evening of the second day, even if no one finds the jaguar god."

Tattoo raised his hand.

"Okay, so two questions. Number one, will you hold onto my crown for me?"

"Of course," Tony answered.

"Number two, where will we find these animal statues?"

"It's a good question that our king asks. Every adventure begins with a single step, but you've got to know where to step. When you are in an unfamiliar place, a map can mean the difference between success and disaster.

Your cell phones are gone, which is okay because there are no cell towers or chargers in the jungle anyway. An old-fashioned paper map is what you need in this place. So, everyone step right on up, and I will hand you one. Come right on up and get your map."

Annaliese took hers and started to walk away but stopped when she looked at it closer.

"Mine is torn. Where is the rest of it?"

"You are correct, Governor," Tony responded. "Your map is torn. Each of you is holding in your hands a part of a complete map of all the land and rivers and streams within a one-mile radius around the arena theater. Everyone's piece of map is torn from someone else's. The complete map is here in my hands."

Tony produced a rolled-up parchment, which he carefully unfurled like a flag.

"The map has been prepared by two men on our team who are experts in map-reading, mapmaking and orienteering. Our professional tracker Bones and our logistics man Tamper, formerly an Army Ranger, have covered every square inch of this place and have prepared two excellent hand-drawn maps. The complete map, which is just like yours but with all the pieces still together, will remain here with me. Before you take off into the jungle, you are welcome to look at the big map in its entirety for sixty seconds each, not a second more, but once you leave, you can't look at the big map again. You can only take the piece of map that has been handed out to you. No one here has any more map than anyone else—they simply have different pieces of it. Your map will have one of two things on it. Either it will have a drawing of the location of the god, or the totem rather, or it will have an arrow pointing to the nearest totem."

The Senator turned his piece of the map upside down, studied it for a minute, and then flipped it back to the way he was holding it before.

"I need one of those 'You Are Here' markers. I can't tell what I am looking at, except here's the river."

Aston leaned over to look at Celeste's piece of the map.

"Is that the waterfall you have there? Yes, it is. I have the arena theater on mine. Our maps connect."

Celeste held the left side of her map up against the right side of Aston's and exclaimed, "Hey, they fit together! And there is a picture of a..."

Aston shushed her. Celeste giggled. Clearly, Aston's map piece contained a picture of an animal totem. Tony smiled.

"You can choose to work alone, and win a piece of treasure all for yourself, or you can work in pairs or even larger groups. The larger the group, the more adjoining pieces of the map you have, the higher your chances for success...but there's a catch. Regardless of how many people helped find a totem, only one person from your group can stick his or her hand into the treasure chest. You will have to figure out amongst yourselves how to split it."

Tattoo looked at his piece of the map. There were parallel lines running everywhere. A topographical map. There weren't any animals drawn on it, but there was an arrow pointing to one side. As he was studying his map, Mystic Origin had a question.

"What is her name?"

Tony, who was clearly puzzled, asked, "Whose name?"

"The jaguar goddess."

"Okay, I see what you are asking," Tony replied. "Her" is actually a "him." In Portuguese, jaguar is "onca," O-N-C-A, with a soft "c" sound, but we have named ours "Pantera," which as you might have guessed is Portuguese for "panther."

"If it's not a "her," then it's not a goddess, and therefore has no power over any of us," said Mystic Origin with disgust, dropping her map on the ground.

The rest of the group watched with bewilderment and disbelief as Mystic Origin walked away. More than one person concluded she suffered from mental illness. *She did know that it was just a statue, right?* Tattoo wondered. *That is one weird chick*, he thought to himself. He looked around to see if anyone was going to do anything with her map. No one moved, so he picked it up off the ground and looked at it. A path ran right through the middle of it starting at what appeared to be the clearing near the pergola. At the top of the map there was a drawing of a little jaguar head. Tattoo quickly folded his map and pushed it into his pants pocket. He looked around to see if anyone might have seen, but everyone seemed to be too engrossed in their own map to have noticed his.

Tony tried to think of how to respond to Mystic Origin, but DeShunta spoke up before he could.

"There are only six statues, but there are way more than six of us, plus ain't no picture of a statue on my map, just an arrow. That mean we don't all have a equal chance. Some of us ain't gonna get a statue, and that ain't right. If we all work hard and try, we should all get some of the treasure. Equal pay for equal work. Ain't that right?"

DeShunta looked to the Senator for approval. The Senator gave a hesitant, halfhearted head shake/nod that conveyed no clear meaning. Annaliese, Celeste, Chaz and Aston wanted to agree with her, since they had all said similar things before, but this was different. Jungle Money was on the line. Everyone was very conscious of the fact that cameras were rolling. No one said anything or even nodded. What if they ended up with the prize but lost some or all of it because they were caught on video nodding their head in agreement with DeShunta?

Tony turned to Tattoo.

"What about it, King Tattoo? DeShunta says everyone should get a share of the treasure even if they don't find a statue...sorry, totem, as long as they tried hard. Equal pay for equal work. You are wearing the crown, which means you are the rule maker today. What says Your Majesty?"

Tattoo chewed on his lip. Mystic Origin, who had been standing on the periphery of the group listening, spoke up.

"You know, if we all shared it, everyone would win. If we don't share, think how disappointed you will be if you don't win."

About that time, DeShunta cried out and slapped her leg. A horsefly had just bitten a chunk out of her calf. Sweat was running down her face and everyone else's face, too. The Amazon heat was stifling. DeShunta was tired of waiting.

"Come on and decide something! I am wringing wet with perspiration standing out here in this sun waiting on you, and now I just got bit by some bee. Hurry up!"

Tattoo didn't do well under time pressure, especially when he was mad. He didn't answer right away. DeShunta took a couple of steps towards him and pointed at his inked-up forearm.

"Why don't you read your arm right there and maybe you can find where it say, 'Make a decision.' Here it is, right here. Look here, by your elbow. I found it for you. It's right above where it say, 'Hurry yourself up.'"

Tattoo felt his face and neck flushing red. He didn't want to split it with anybody if he won. He was holding two pieces of the map, one of which had the location of the jaguar. He could do this all by himself. He felt peer pressure, though. Everyone was saying equal pay for equal work. What was he going to do, say no to the women and be called a greedy, male chauvinist sexist? But what was wrong with keeping what you earned? Unfortunately for Tattoo, every second he deliberated was another second he was making DeShunta mad.

"Do you mean to tell me you can't read your arm? What kind of man go in a store and get another man with a needle to write words on his arm and can't read what it say? You can read, can't you? Or maybe not. Oh, I'm sorry. I didn't know you can't read. I couldn't tell, although now I can see it around your eyes a little..."

Tattoo found his voice.

"No, we're not sharing it. The winner gets the treasure. Period."

DeShunta, chin jutted out, took a step toward him and announced, "I knew that was what you were going to say. Why didn't you just say it? I sure wasn't going to share it with you if I got it."

Tattoo felt his blood pressure skyrocket. For a moment, he had actually considered giving her and everybody else money just for trying. He was done with that. No more crazy talk. Game on.

Tony clapped his hands together once and looked around.

"Well, the king has spoken. Ladies and gentlemen, you know the rules. Good luck and be safe. Remember, it's a jungle out there."

Chapter Twenty

Trayton sat in his swivel chair, quietly staring at the computer monitor, transfixed by the article he was reading. A sigh and a soft rustling of the sheets from the adjoining room reached his ears. He half-closed his eyes and smiled ever so slightly. Karena had been all he could have ever dreamed of and more. He leaned forward so he could see into the bedroom from the office. "Office" was perhaps an overly-ambitious description of the large walk-in closet where he had placed a small table, a lamp, and a laptop computer. It was actually big enough to be quite functional, with the sole exception of the thick cord from the power strip that made closing the door a thing of the past. That was a small price to pay for having a bit of privacy when surfing the net. There are things a man likes to see that his girlfriend just wouldn't understand. A little harmless flirting online never hurt anybody.

Trayton pushed back on his chair so he could lean his head out of the door. He had to catch his breath when he looked at her still-sleeping form. Karena's hair flowed across her pillow like an ocean wave captured on an artist's canvas. She was breathing easily, completely unaware of how beautiful she was. His chair squeaked when he leaned a little too far. He silently cursed, not wanting to disturb the dreaming goddess he had captured and won.

Aurora padded into the closet office, almost looking confused, although it was hard to tell with the hair that perpetually covered her eyes. Trayton petted her little head and neck with both hands.

"It's okay, girl," he whispered. "It's okay."

Trayton had a small problem that he had to confront, and he was not looking forward to it. It had seemed like such a good idea last night. An innocent cup of coffee with Karena had led to an invitation to dinner, which had included a bottle of wine they couldn't finish at the restaurant, which had progressed to a little kissing in the parking lot. When he buried his face into Karena's sweet-smelling hair, she began pressing her body into his arms and into his hands. When she pushed against his oh-so-inconvenient blue jeans, his course was set. There may have been a fleeting thought of Celeste that made him hit the brakes, but the wine made his brake fluid leak. It was no longer a question of whether; it was simply a question of where. Under the cover of moonlight, his house had been the perfect spot for a midnight rendezvous.

Unfortunately for Trayton, they had both fallen asleep and had slept hard until late the next morning. The sound of a thrown newspaper slapping down on the wooden front porch jarred him into wakefulness. It was a bright, sunny, neighbors-walking, runners-jogging, prying-eyes-everywhere kind of morning.

Dilemma.

Celeste's driveway, his driveway, wasn't more than ten steps from Mrs. Jankowicz's driveway. *Maybe she's not there*, he thought, biting his bottom lip. *C'mon, don't be there, don't be there.* He held his breath as he lifted up the plantation shutters an inch or two.

Nope. No such luck. There she was, Mrs. Jankowicz, sitting on her front porch drinking her coffee, just like every other morning. What was worse, he could see that she hadn't gotten her newspaper from where the paperboy had thrown it on the sidewalk. Anytime she saw Trayton walk out of his house, Mrs. Jankowicz would call out a good morning and ask if he would mind bringing her the newspaper. Of course, the answer was always yes. No was not a possibility. Once he brought it to her, she would trap him on the front porch for at least fifteen or twenty minutes while she talked about deadly-dull, old people stuff.

Trayton's shoulders slumped. He dropped his chin to his chest. His car could not be more visible if it had been on a TV game show in the showcase showdown, and the game show host had just screamed, "And now behind Door Number Two…a new car!"

Trayton began imagining the repercussions if any of the neighbors, especially Mrs. Jankowicz, saw him escorting a young lady out of his house. A number of scenes played out in his mind's eye, and none of them ended well. How could he explain it? What explanation could he give? *Think man, think.* As he searched for an answer, his gaze traveled up the wall with no particular destination. He first looked at Jimi Hendrix, hoping for some inspiration, but all he found was "Foxy Lady," and then much to his distress, "All Along the Watchtower." That's exactly where all his neighbors were right at this moment—watching his house.

He found himself looking at a picture of him and Celeste at the Piedmont Park Festival. She was laughing and he was, too. He genuinely cared for Celeste. It was just that she wasn't here and Karena was. It was as simple as that. *It's not like we're married*, he thought.

Wearied with unpleasant thoughts, and in no hurry to rush the inevitable conflict, Trayton turned his attention back to the computer. He started to click on justflirt.com to see if the hot Ukrainian girl he had been talking to had replied to yesterday morning's message, but a sleepy girlish voice stopped him cold in his tracks.

"Hey."

Ukrainian girl could wait. Trayton clicked the X in the top right corner of his screen. The beginnings of a smile formed at the corners of his mouth. He leaned back in his chair so he could see into the bedroom.

"Hey yourself."

Karena smiled and stretched, just as naked as she was last night. She was not a shy girl. This was going to be a good day, he thought. A very good day indeed.

Chapter Twenty-One

High on the side of a lush green jungle mountain, Tattoo fought for air. His thigh muscles were on fire. His lungs screamed. He silently cursed every cigarette he had ever smoked. He cursed the nameless, faceless CEO of the tobacco company that had danced a jig the day Tattoo bought his first pack of cancer sticks. He cursed the migrant workers that had carried tobacco leaves from some godforsaken field in North Carolina or Virginia and dropped them into a chopping machine so that he could smoke them. He cursed the truck driver that had driven them to the convenience store where he usually bought two packs every three or four days. He cursed the store clerk…no, wait. He missed one. He cursed the stock boy that had opened the box with a box cutter and put them on the shelf. Now, he could curse the store clerk behind the bulletproof glass counter that had sold each pack to him.

Pausing to wipe the river of sweat streaming down his face, Tattoo went back up and down the list. Had he missed anyone? He did not want to miss anyone. He wanted to give a flying finger to everyone involved in making his thighs burn and lungs scream. Maybe it hadn't been such a hot idea to set out for the highest point in the entire Amazon jungle after all. Actually, it had been a hot idea. Too hot. Miserably hot. Life-threatening kind of hot. And he hadn't brought any water. Stupid. Stupid, stupid, stupid. Tattoo cursed anything and everything, including himself.

But then he remembered. The treasure chest. Only he had felt the weight of the lid. He had been the closest to the fortune inside. He thought about the smell of the money. There had been a kind of metallic smell to the coins. He should have smelled the jewels, or better yet, the gold bars. They would have probably smelled like the coins, but he couldn't be sure.

Tattoo stopped and stared up the seemingly endless trail rising higher and higher in front of him. It was never going to end. He screamed a swear word and plopped down on the trail, exhausted. He laid flat on the jungle path, using the back of his arm to block the light from his eyes. *I'm just going to lay here a couple of minutes*, he thought, *just long enough to catch my breath.* When his arm touched the Mini-Go camera on his forehead, it made him think of all the things he had said out loud over the last several minutes. He had offended pretty much every race and nationality in his breathless tirade. *Whoops. They'll get over it,* he thought.

The feeling of something small worming its way across his leg made Tattoo bolt upright and struggle up off the forest floor. After brushing off his leg and finding nothing, he looked up the mountain. This was one narrow path. It was straight enough, but the elevation was a killer. He was certain that few had ever found it. As far as he could tell, not one of the others had even attempted it. They were all scurrying around on more level ground far below him where the path was broad, and the way was easy.

But he had the map. Two pieces of it. He knew where the jaguar god was—they didn't. Well, maybe they didn't. Actually, as he thought about it, they could be looking at the big map right now and seeing exactly where it was hidden. The thought of someone running past him and beating him to the jaguar god made him pick up his pace. All he had to do was get the jaguar god off of this blasted mountain, show it to the world and voilà—a rich man he would be.

Every step was a battle. It was impossible to go more than seven or eight steps without stopping to rest. Holding onto trees helped him not to slide down and lose his progress. They also helped him pull up. They weren't spaced evenly enough, though. Why couldn't they be spaced more evenly? Whoever had planted this jungle had done a poor job, in his estimation.

Tattoo pulled off his Mini-Go for the one hundredth time and ran his fingers down the headband. Something pricked the skin on his forehead every time he put it on. It had to be a remnant of the tiny sliver of plastic that had once secured the price tag to the headband. When the tag was pulled off, a sharp, pokey little piece remained. He knew that for sure because of the sore spot that it had irritated into his forehead. No matter how many times he felt for it, however, he couldn't find it. Exasperated, he jammed the Mini-Go into his pants pocket. He would insist on a different headband when he returned to camp.

As the minutes turned into hours, Tattoo's worry grew. He should have brought water. Why hadn't he thought of it? He wasn't one of these nylon-wearing prissy men who always had their little plastic bottles and timer watches handy. It wasn't second nature for him to pack for a walk like it was for these fitness nuts. He stopped and looked at his elbow while holding onto a tree. Droplets of sweat dripped one after the other onto the ground from his elbow. How much water had he lost? How much water did he still have in him? He badly needed a drink. Could you seriously die from needing to drink? What if his quest for the jaguar god killed him and he died alone on this mountainside?

Worried, Tattoo stopped his climb. He should really go back down. He should hustle down the mountain, which would be loads easier than climbing up it, find a water bottle, and then try again. He had two days. There was no need to rush. He needed food, too, although he wasn't overly hungry at the moment. If anyone asked him where he was going, or what was on his map, he wouldn't tell them. It was none of their business.

But he had come so far already. He had made so much progress. Thinking of walking all the way down, then starting over again made him sick. He just didn't think he could do it. He wasn't made for this. His body was weary, but even so, his mind was motivated. He was willing to do whatever it took. That meant he had to shut his mouth, stop whining like a little baby, and get his fat self up the mountain. There was no Plan B.

Time had long since lost all meaning when Tattoo crested the summit. Surrounded by dense foliage, he didn't realize it was the summit until it dawned on him that everywhere he stepped was down. Despite his dehydration and overtaxed heart, Tattoo flashed a smile. Jamming his shaking hand into his pocket, he searched for the pieces of the map. It didn't have the exact detail of a highway road map, but as best he could tell, he should be right on top of the god.

Tattoo didn't realize that he had walked over three miles, a full two miles past where Tamper and Bones had found a suitable location to hide the jaguar two days before his arrival. After forty-five minutes of wandering around the top, anger began to bubble up from deep within his soul. *What exactly am I looking for*? he wondered. *A totem pole? Is it buried underground? Did that smug TV star Tony play a cruel trick on me? Am I reading this map wrong?* Self-doubt began to creep into Tattoo's mind. *What if this is the wrong mountain?* No, that couldn't be it. There was some kind of marker at the bottom of the trail where he started up, and there it was on the map.

A half hour later, after still finding nothing, Tattoo's smoldering anger burst into flames. He grabbed a fallen branch and hurled it into the nearest tree. He saw a fluttering moth settle on a leaf on the ground and stomped the life out it with his shoe. There is nothing up here! Cursing his very existence and very aware of his need for a serious infusion of water, he pointed his toes downhill and began a furious descent.

Stumbling down the mountain, spewing oaths with every step, Tattoo planned his revenge. The first thing he was going to do was drop kick that butt-scratching monkey Mother Nature for putting a crown on his head. The second thing he was going to do was grab Tony by the collar, yank his head down and knee him right in those pearly white teeth. The third thing he was going to do was...he wasn't sure yet. Something terrible. His mouth felt like it was full of cotton. He couldn't unstick his dry tongue from the roof of his mouth.

Tattoo caught something other than green out of the corner of his eye. He squinted in an effort to make sense of what he was seeing. Taking a few more cautious steps to remove the trees that were blocking his line of sight, Tattoo realized what had caught his eye. There before him stood the ruins of an ancient temple. It had been hidden from his eyes by the foliage while he was climbing up but visible while descending from on high. In the center of the space, there was a table or platform of sorts. Breathing too hard to be stealthy, Tattoo stomped noisily into the center of the enclosure. He stumbled towards the platform, which appeared to be a pedestal. Beneath the leaf litter and orb spider webs, a dark round object lay. He brushed the dirt and debris off of it so he could see. When he finally had it cleared off, he was so shaken he had to hold onto the pedestal to steady himself.

Tattoo had found the black panther god.

The teeth of a big cat were unmistakable. The eyes and ears were fairly well-defined, but they were seriously worn away on the edges. He had envisioned a yellowish golden cat with black spots like the picture on the map, but this all-black one was cool looking. *How did they make it look so old? And how did they construct this old temple? They couldn't have built this for the show—this is the real deal, isn't it?* But it couldn't be. Nobody lived out here. Tony and G said so. Tattoo wanted to continue this train of thought, but he was too tired to think. He grabbed a vine wrapped around a stone column to help himself stay upright. There was only one thought that mattered. He had found it. By god, he had found it. The jaguar god was his. *Now, how do I pick this thing up?*

Right then, Tattoo felt the unpleasant sensation of tiny legs on the back of his hand. Another bug. So what? By this point, he had felt a thousand bugs. Flying bugs, crawling bugs, you name it, they had all been on him at some point while he had been in this jungle. He didn't even bother to brush this one off. *It will get tired of me at some point*, he thought.

Big mistake. Big mistake.

A bullet ant is the nuclear warhead of the insect world. The venom contained in the abdomen is so potent that everyone who has had the misfortune of being stung by one agrees—it is quite literally the worst pain in the world. The sting of a bullet ant is like someone stuck the barrel of a gun up against your exposed limb and fired a bullet at point blank range. Some say the name reflects the immediate desire of the victim to stop the pain, no matter the cost.

The tiny stinger of the vile creature pierced Tattoo's knuckle between the N and the F in Infidel. The reaction was instantaneous. A horrifying scream echoed through the jungle. His face contorted in a way nature never intended. He did not stop screaming until his lungs were completely emptied of air. He gulped a fresh supply of oxygen and screamed again. Gripping his wounded arm with the opposite hand, he instinctively applied vice-like pressure to prevent the poison from traveling through his blood vessels to his heart. His mind ceased to function. There was only pain. Screaming at it was his only defense. The death grip he had on his wrist pinched nerves, bruised muscles and pulled skin to the point of tearing but it didn't help. Pain burned like lava from a volcano. Pain enveloped his hand and swallowed it like a tidal wave. Pain was all-consuming. If there had been a cliff nearby, he would have jumped. His hand cried out for release. If he had brought a machete, he would have cut off his own arm to make it stop. The closest thing to a rational thought cried out to him. *Run down the mountain to camp. There has to be a doctor.*

Tattoo fled the ruins and began to sprint downhill, screaming as he ran. Distracted, dehydrated and deprived of rational thought by the pain, Tattoo took his eyes off the path. Caught in the throes of a madness born of misery, he looked at his afflicted hand while he ran, causing him to veer.

Tattoo ran headlong into a tree at full speed.

The thud of skull on tree trunk was sickening, but he never heard it. In its own harsh way, the jungle had just bestowed a great kindness upon him. Although violent, the black silence of unconsciousness at least stifled the screams.

A light rain began to fall high above on the jungle canopy. The raindrops had to navigate the pungent maze of leaves, flowers and vines, but eventually they fell upon the still form of Tattoo lying awkwardly on the soft earth below. Drops landed on his face. The drops turned into trickles, and the trickles turned into waterfalls. Harder and harder they fell, soaking his skin. Torrents of water flooded across his ever-reddening arm, but he didn't know it. Water ran into his ears, his nostrils, and his mouth. His throat began to fill. The sudden lack of oxygen triggered an alert system in his brain. Drowning. Sputtering, choking, spewing and coughing, he rolled over and gasped for air. When consciousness came, the penalty for living began anew. Pain. Fortunately for Tattoo, it was short-lived. The shock to his nervous system brought merciful relief. He lost consciousness again.

Meanwhile, the tiny creature that had inflicted the grievous wound writhed on the forest floor. Completely by accident, Tattoo had stepped on its head. In moments, its tiny body lay still in the mud, soon to be erased from existence.

At the base of the mountain, those who weren't within earshot of the noisy waterfall stopped what they were doing and became as still as statues. A ghastly, other-worldly cry came from far away. Was that a scream? Imaginations ran wild. Annaliese shuddered and rubbed her arms. DeShunta heard it, too. Her eyes grew wide. Someone or something had clearly met a bad end. Tony heard it, but tried to forget it. He really hated the woods, which was ironic given what he was doing. It was probably just an animal. He set about the task of intentionally forgetting what he had just heard.

The clouds eventually parted. The broiling sun continued its slow march toward the horizon as steam rose from the humid world beneath it. Brightly-colored birds painted the green landscape with all of the colors of the rainbow as they darted in and out of the branches. Far below the surface of the soil, the roots of a million trees drank deeply from the life-giving water that had fallen from the heavens. Time had not changed this Garden of Eden since its creation eons ago.

Tattoo's eyes fluttered open. With conscious thought came an instant awareness of his hand. Pain seared his nerve endings as he looked reluctantly to see its condition. The swelling shocked him, as did the redness. Gingerly touching it with the fingers of his other hand, he felt the heat. He needed immediate medical attention, but even if he could call 911, no ambulance would ever make it up here. Like it or not, if he wanted help, he would have to take himself to it.

Wet clothes, throbbing headache, dry mouth, and a hand on fire made Tattoo grit his teeth. Head swirling and mind unclear, he stumbled to his feet and took a few uncertain steps down the path. Then it hit him. The jaguar god. How could he forget the entire reason for the nightmare he was experiencing? He must bring it with him. No matter the cost, he had to bring it down with him.

Tattoo entered the ruins much more carefully than he had the first time. Anxiously, he scrutinized the stone pedestal and vines encircling it with great care, looking for any sign of ants. Seeing none, he looked for a branch to brush away the leaf litter that covered much of the god head. Using only his uninjured hand, he swept the branch back and forth across the top of the stone. At long last, the entire head was exposed. Despite the burning pain that wouldn't go away, Tattoo managed a half-smile.

The jaguar god was his.

He put his good hand on top of the jaguar, gripped it, and tried to rock it. It didn't move. Worried, he adjusted his feet and used his body weight to push. After a tense moment or two, the stone base of the jaguar head lifted clear of the moss that held it fast to the pedestal. It was heavy. He could do it, but there was no denying the fact that it was heavy. He had assumed that the trip down the mountain would be much easier than the trip up. Now he wasn't so sure, especially since he only had one functioning arm.

Tattoo thought of the fortune waiting for him in the chest at the bottom of the mountain. That was the motivation he needed. Pain was temporary, but the things he was about to buy would last forever. *A Ferrari, a mansion built on a huge estate like Bert Redmond's house, a swimming pool surrounded by TVs and girls coming out my ears,* he thought. *I've just got to show the jaguar god to Tony and G and wham bam thank you ma'am, I am rich and chilling like a villain. Worship me, haters.*

It took several tries for Tattoo to successfully lift the god to his shoulder and balance it, but as consumed as he was with thoughts of the reward waiting for him far below, quitting never entered his mind. He grunted. He blew out air. He sweated, even though he didn't know how his body could still have any water left in it. He never stopped moaning from the searing pain in his hand, not even for one moment. But he was determined. Nothing could stop him from showing his god to the world.

Tattoo spread his feet wide as he walked, doing his best to balance on the uneven terrain down the mountain. He had to keep his eyes on the ground in front of him to watch for hazards so he wouldn't trip. He tried to shift the heavy head to a more comfortable position. He stopped and wrestled with it. Having found a suitable carry position, he looked up to find his bearings again. When he did, something was in his path that hadn't been there moments earlier.

Standing in front of him in a line, as still as statues, were several small native men barring his path down the mountain. They were almost completely naked. Each held a primitive bow with an arrow nocked, drawn and pointed at his chest.

Tattoo had no god to call upon in his hour of need, but in that dark moment he wished he did. He dropped the jaguar god and dropped to his knees. It was the only thing he could think of to do to persuade them not to send a dozen sharp, stone-tipped arrows to pierce his body in a dozen places.

Chapter Twenty-Two

Dr. Jane brushed a sweat-soaked strand of blonde hair out of her eyes. She studied Tamper as he walked back to the UTV where she sat in the front passenger seat. His face betrayed his deep dejection. His crestfallen visage stemmed from the fact that they were returning to camp empty-handed. The search-and-rescue mission was all search and no rescue. Boedy Da was nowhere to be found. Tamper, who told her that "No man left behind" was his creed when he was fighting ISIS and Al-Qaeda, had failed.

A fallen tree blocked the trail. Dr. Jane watched as Tamper hacked through the underbrush on the side of the path with his machete and cleared a way around it. She read the words on his sleeveless t-shirt. Wounded Warriors. As he swung the blade, she could not help but notice the strength in his arms. After chopping a way through the vegetation, he jumped back in, turned the ignition key and the engine roared to life. A small plume of smoke jetted from the exhaust as Tamper shifted it into gear. Grabbing onto the UTV's roll bar with tired hands, Dr. Jane prepared to be bounced, battered and bruised for the hundredth time. They rode without speaking, preferring the sound of crunching tires to conversation.

Jungle expeditions were not Dr. Jane's forte. Her natural habitat was the city, an urban jungle filled with honking cars and shady bars. She was a medical doctor from Detroit, specializing in emergency medicine. Despite her youthful appearance, she had seen it all and treated it all. Gunshot wounds. Knife wounds. Burn victims. Drug overdoses. Bodies mangled in motor vehicle collisions. Heart attacks. Strokes. Frostbite. She had saved more than she had lost, but she had seen more death in her young life than most military personnel will see in their career.

Early in her residency, they lost a child to a stray bullet one awful Saturday night. The tragedy so rattled her that she actually considered leaving the medical profession. A wise old charge nurse had interceded, however. The nurse had taken Dr. Jane down the corridor, around a corner and down another hallway, where she could no longer hear the anguished cries of the inconsolable mother. She had gently taken Dr. Jane's pale white hands into her warm brown hands, looked over her reading glasses into Dr. Jane's eyes, and said something the young doctor would never forget.

"Proverbs 139, verses 13 and 14, says this: 'For you created my inmost being. You knit me together in my mother's womb. I praise you because I am fearfully and wonderfully made.' Do you know what that means, child?"

Dr. Jane, who was unable to speak, shook her head no.

"It means this. God is in the knitting business. When a baby is brought into this world, His work is perfect. The world is hard, though. Sometimes his little children get torn and unraveled. But if we are real lucky, we can be one of the ones who knit them back together. That makes God happy. You want to make God happy, don't you?"

Dr. Jane nodded.

"Then get back down that hallway and see if He won't give you another chance to knit one of His babies back together again."

The charge nurse retired not long after that event. Dr. Jane couldn't remember her name, but she would never forget her words. She carried them with her in her heart. They gave her meaning and purpose when life in the emergency room made no sense and her efforts seemed pointless. God was in the knitting business. So was she.

A tremendous lurch which almost ejected her from the UTV snapped Dr. Jane back into the moment. When they slid to a stop despite a clear path ahead of them, she looked questionably at Tamper. He didn't look at her. His gaze was fixed on something above and beyond her. He nodded as though pointing with his head.

Dr. Jane turned to look but saw nothing. She swiveled her head back to Tamper. His eyes were still locked on whatever it was.

"What are you looking at?" she asked.

"Look at that tree branch above your right shoulder."

She looked, but saw nothing of interest. A green tree branch. Big whoop. What was she missing? Wait. It was moving. The tree branch moved.

Dr. Jane screamed and leaped into Tamper's lap. She beat the steering wheel and cried, "Go, go, go, go, go!" Tamper cut the steering wheel sharply to the left and moved the vehicle forward away from the "branch."

"Emerald tree boa," he said flatly. "They're all over down here. Beautiful snake. Bones started pointing them out to me about as soon as we first got here, and I've been seeing them ever since. Bones said he had one as a pet for a while."

Dr. Jane was not impressed with his show and tell.

"Go! I don't care! It's a snake! Don't stop anymore! Drop me off by the waterfall—somewhere where I can be safe!"

Clearly annoyed, Tamper hit the gas and sped down the path. His passenger looked at him in complete bewilderment. *What is wrong with him? Why would he stop next to a snake? And what is wrong with Bones? Who keeps something like that as a pet?*

Several minutes later, just as she began to ask when they were going to reach the river, Dr. Jane began to recognize her surroundings. She heard the roar of the waterfall over the sound of the engine. Moments later they entered the clearing, and the river and waterfall came into view. It was breathtaking.

The beauty of the sight made her temporarily forget the disappointment of not finding Boedy Da. She wished there was a way to take this waterfall back to Detroit so that she could see it every day when she looked out her window. She hit Tamper's arm and motioned for him to stop. He looked at her quizzically.

"I want to get out right here."

He brought the UTV to a gradual stop. Without a goodbye, she jumped out and headed toward the falls. He shrugged. She was a big girl, and it was less than a fifteen-minute walk to camp.

Dr. Jane could feel her blood pressure start to normalize when Tamper was gone from sight and the sound of his motor could no longer be heard. The only sound was the sound of hundreds of thousands of gallons of water pouring into the river every second. Finally, she was somewhere safe. A swim would cool her off and calm her nerves. A swim was just what the doctor ordered.

As she neared the riverbank, she looked for a big rock or fallen log to sit on while she stripped off her clothes. She was mindful of the fact that she was a shapely young lady and did not want to be within view of any onlookers. After looking unsuccessfully for a jungle changing room, she stopped herself. She looked down at the pants legs of her shorts. Filthy. Covered in dirt. She pulled on the front of her shirt. The same as her pants. Sweaty and dirty with bits of leaves and even a crawling beetle which she quickly flicked off. Her clothes needed a bath as much as she did.

"Why not?"

With that, Dr. Jane marched right into the deep green waters of the nameless river below the nameless falls and plunged beneath the surface, clothes, shoes and all. She swam underwater until she ran out of air, not caring how far she had gone from the bank. When she came to the surface, she changed her course to face the waterfall. She swam against the gentle current just hard enough to stay in the same spot in the river.

The water instantly cooled her body, and the river began to purify her soul. She used her hands to wipe the dirt and grime off of her face and arms. Running her hands over her legs under the water almost completely stopped the itching that she had been trying to ignore. She stopped washing and rested her eyes on the waterfall. The sight and sound was almost hypnotic. There was nothing like this back in Detroit, she mused.

As she relaxed, she remembered that she had needed to pee for quite a while. She hadn't wanted to ask Tamper to stop and make her venture off alone after the snake episode. Now however, she was alone, and the fullness of her bladder could no longer be ignored.

Dr. Jane swam back toward the shoreline so that she could get out and find a place to drop her pants and squat. As soon as her feet touched and she could stand on the river bottom, she started to unbutton her pants, but then thought better of it. *Why not just go? Who knows how many fish have peed in this river just this morning?* The pee would be washed out of her pants by the current within minutes. She laughed inwardly at her city girl ways. Getting out to pee would have never crossed a country girl's mind. She bent her knees, spread them slightly, and felt warm relief as she released her urine. She felt clever, having figured out how to relieve herself without the unwanted intrusion of prying eyes.

What she didn't realize however, is that she was not alone.

Dr. Jane's decision to relieve herself in the river drew the attention of a tiny unseen fish swimming placidly a few feet downstream from her. A one-inch-long candiru instantly reacted when the first drops of warm discharge reached his whisker-like barbels. The translucent, eel-like catfish swam directly to the source of the warm stream. His tiny brain had a singular parasitic mission—to swim into the soft, unprotected urethra of whatever creature was eliminating urine, wedge himself in by fanning out his spiny fins, and drain blood from the surrounding tissue until he was full. He cared naught about the discomfort of the host.

Dr. Jane's tranquil bathroom break was rudely interrupted. Much to her great distress, she felt something spiny touch her upper thigh and slip inside the leg of her shorts. Before she could even react, whatever it was tried to wriggle inside her panties. Yelling out in shock and surprise, she violently contracted her muscles, jammed her hand into her pants and dug out the alien invader, causing her to scream anew at the detestable sensation of having a spiky wiggling creature touch her hand.

"Oh my god, get out of there! What are you? Get out! Get out!"

When she finally slapped the vile thing out of her pants leg, she lifted her arms out of the water and high-stepped to the shore.

"Gross! What was that? Was that a fish? Oh my god, I'm not even safe in the water!"

Dr. Jane reached the shore as fast as she could. With a strong pull on a slender tree limb overhanging the water, she was standing on dry land again. *Thank god I didn't skinny dip*, she thought. *Thank god.* When she thought about what could have happened, she shuddered. No longer wanting to swim, she found her way to the trail that Tamper had taken and double-timed it back to camp.

Chapter Twenty-Three

Day One was rapidly drawing to a close. The tropical sun dropped lower and lower in the sky until it disappeared completely behind the trees. The first star became visible in the still-illuminated but slowly-darkening sky. The contestants began to make their way back to the arena theater. Each person yelled out the all-important question as soon as they came in sight. Did anybody find an animal totem? Each was relieved to find out that no one had. They still had a chance.

The way they walked betrayed their fatigue. They were dragging. They were hot, tired and hungry. They smelled so bad that they could smell themselves. Everyone was fighting a losing battle against a never-ending assault of biting insects. Despite their many differences, everyone's needs were the same—cold drink, hot meal, soothing shower, and a good night's sleep, hopefully on a soft mattress in a quiet, air-conditioned room. No one really expected the air conditioning, but then again no one had said there wouldn't be.

Nobody seemed to be in charge. Tony was not there to direct them. A suggestion was made to try to find him back at the tents in the distance, but no one wanted to do it. The light was fading. Nobody had built a fire, and none of them had flashlights. No one wanted to be walking around in the jungle in the dark, so they stayed together as a group, milling about, waiting for someone to direct them. As Chaz scratched the bites on his legs, he looked around with his head tilted at forty-five degrees. He spotted movement underneath the stage area. Curious, he made his way to the stage. As others noticed, they followed him to see what had drawn his attention.

When he reached the stage, Chaz could tell that it looked differently than it had only a few hours earlier. The area underneath had been enclosed somehow. He walked the perimeter of the stage and finally came to an opening that appeared to be a window. Peering in, he saw movement even though it was dark under there.

"Hey, is anybody home?"

A girl's voice answered, "Who wants to know?"

She sounded almost playful. Without answering or asking for permission, Chaz dove inside the opening just beyond the window. He was followed by a couple of others, all eager to see inside.

A different voice bellowed from underneath the stage. This one was anything but playful.

"Hey, hey, hey, what y'all doing? Who invited you in? You ain't asked nobody permission to come in here. Out. I'm serious. Out."

Pause.

"Out! Get yourself out of my house!"

Chaz hustled out from under the stage and stood a healthy distance away, watching to see if he was going to be pursued. The other unwelcome visitors came out as well, bewildered, wondering what they had done to offend. The last one out was DeShunta Jackson, clearly the owner of the makeshift abode. Rising to her full height of five feet five inches, DeShunta placed her hands on her hips, glared at the onlookers and set them all straight.

"This here mine and Celeste house. This ain't your house. She going to have a baby. I don't mind helping her. She can't be doing nothing strenuous, but y'all can. You can go find your own house."

The listeners gasped when they heard the news, wondering why they hadn't been told. Celeste was pregnant? Celeste was mortified at DeShunta's words and shook her head. She wasn't pregnant! At least she didn't think she was. She hadn't had a pregnancy test. She regretted telling DeShunta about not having had a visit from her dreaded Aunt Flo recently. Clearly uncomfortable, Celeste bit her fingernail and stared at DeShunta in shock, wondering where that had come from. She did not want to challenge DeShunta however, because quite frankly, she was a little afraid of her, but she couldn't let this false statement go unchallenged.

"No, I am not pregnant," she flatly declared.

Their newfound friendship had sprung to life only a few hours earlier. Celeste was ready to start her trek into the jungle. As she prepared to set out, DeShunta remarked that her back and shoulders hurt from the fall out of the helicopter, and she was getting more and more sore by the minute. Celeste watched the others begin running through the woods looking for statues and animals, but her sympathetic nature made her pause. She suggested going to look for Tony or one of the staff people to see if they had an aspirin, but she didn't know where to look. Everyone had gone. DeShunta said she wanted to lay down out of the sun somewhere cool, but there were no chairs or furniture of any kind.

Celeste half-jokingly said the best place might be under the stage. To her surprise, DeShunta agreed. Celeste was glad DeShunta thought her suggestion was useful and turned to go. DeShunta evidently didn't think it was time for Celeste to go however. She told Celeste that now was the best time for "us" to make "our" place and "it won't take no time to do it." Celeste didn't respond because she wasn't sure what was happening. Was DeShunta directing Celeste to build a little house under the stage? Was DeShunta declaring Celeste to be her roommate? Did Celeste have a say in any of this? Celeste was at best passive/aggressive, but when she was around strong personalities, she was completely passive. DeShunta was a strong personality.

So that's how it was that Celeste found herself building a screened-in porch under the elevated stage for her and DeShunta after flying all the way to Brazil to compete for millions of dollars in priceless treasure.

The flooring above them, almost head high, at least for DeShunta, made a fine roof. The soft sandy earth underneath was easily shaped into a seat. The stage faced west, making DeShunta have to look directly into the setting sun as she eased herself down into her earthen seat. Celeste and DeShunta gathered and placed palm branches and elephant ear leaves to build a front wall. Although it was not anything Celeste ever intended to do with her afternoon, it was quite a nice space they created.

As Celeste prepared to run, DeShunta reached up to massage her aching shoulder and upper back and said, "This right here just need some thumbs dug into it. You got some strength in your hands. Here, right here. Dig your thumbs into it."

Celeste didn't know what to do. She could tell that the other woman was hurting, and her pain was legitimate, but there was a contest going on and she was missing it. She hesitated. That was all the time DeShunta needed. She grabbed Celeste by the wrist and placed her hand on her shoulder.

"Now, dig your thumbs."

Celeste figured that the quicker she started the quicker she would finish. The unwilling masseuse began to knead the muscles in DeShunta's injured shoulder with her hands. DeShunta winced in pain. Celeste apologized and worked her thumbs a little less vigorously. After several minutes of massage, DeShunta told her, "That was good. That helped. Thank you."

Celeste asked if she was going to hunt for her totem. DeShunta told her she was, but she planned to wait until after she could ask Tony or the doctor lady for some pain reliever. At that point, DeShunta produced her portion of the map.

"Here. Take this with you. If you find it, we'll split it."

Celeste looked at DeShunta's map. There was a drawing of a parrot's head in the center of the paper. She started to ask DeShunta if she was sure, but by then DeShunta had crawled underneath the stage and was settling herself down into the sandy seat they had made. Celeste trotted away toward the base of the waterfall where her piece of the map told her a statue of a monkey was waiting for her. She still wasn't quite sure what had just happened, but somehow she didn't feel like it was wasted time.

Fast forward four hours. Evening had come and everyone was gathering where they had last been given instructions. Someone noticed that Tattoo had not yet arrived. Chaz conjectured that he may have already won the prize and was digging around in the treasure chest right now. Annaliese dismissed the idea and declared that Tattoo was simply late and would be joining them soon.

They were standing around waiting for directions when Chaz had inadvertently invaded DeShunta's home under the stage under the mistaken belief it belonged solely to Celeste. DeShunta made it abundantly clear that she was not planning on sharing her prime real estate with anyone else.

"I don't know if you noticed, but they ain't no hotel room vacancy for rent sign posted here. Do you see one? Because I don't see one. That mean you got to find your own. Where you going to stay? I'll tell you where. Somewhere else. Because it sure ain't here."

She raised a good question. Where were they going to sleep? Looks of realization swept across the faces before her. There were certainly no hotels. There were a few tents in the distance where the performers and staff were apparently staying, but they appeared to be too small to accommodate all of the contestants. The question had never occurred to them. They just assumed they would be given a place to sleep. But looking around, no such place seemed apparent.

Chaz, still stinging from his unpleasant encounter with DeShunta, thought about her question. Where was he going to stay? He thought about the animals and birds he had seen today. He hadn't seen any snakes, but he knew they were out there. Chaz hated snakes. So did his mother. He thought about his home. His mom would have turned down the covers for him by now. She did that every night even after he started high school. She promised him that she would turn his bed back at home every night while he was gone. It made her feel a little closer to him. He would never say this out loud, but he wished he was home.

After pondering the question for a bit, Aston ran his hands through his frosted tips, cleared his throat and expressed his thoughts.

"Surely they have tents or hammocks with mosquito netting somewhere for us, don't you guess? Or maybe some sleeping bags we can use to sleep on the stage?"

He searched the nearest faces for signs of agreement and affirmation.

Chaz answered, "Yes, the stage would be good," but then he made the mistake of glancing back at DeShunta. He was shocked to see that she had come out from underneath the stage and was standing not more than ten feet away from him. She shot dual laser beams at him with her eyes. Chaz tried to casually stroll away from her at a calm, measured pace so as not to look scared, but he couldn't do it. The tension was too thick. His body was overloaded with nerves. He took a few bounding leaps to put some quick distance between them. Much to his delight, someone made the announcement he had been waiting to hear. Tony was coming.

"Hey, hey, hey!" Tony called out cheerfully. "How is everybody?"

The smile. Tony's smile was brilliant even in low lights at the end of a long, hot day. The electricity from Tony's smile could jump start a car. With teeth that white, you just knew that his breath smelled like a peppermint smoothie splashed over wintergreen ice. As he approached, DeShunta, Celeste, Peaches and Mystic Origin watched how he moved—strong, confident and relaxed, like a big cat. Tony reached up overhead to give a two-handed wave to everyone, which caused his shirt to momentarily ride up and reveal his stomach. The chisel that had carved those abs had clearly belonged to Michelangelo. Each lady filed the mental image away. Tony's abs would have to be discussed at some point. DeShunta wanted to applaud and would have but for the fact that she was still irritated by the unwanted intruders in her newly-constructed home.

"I said, how is everybody?" Tony demanded with a smile.

Mystic Origin cut right to the chase.

"We are hot, we are tired, we are hungry, we are thirsty, and we don't know where we are going to sleep. What is the game plan here?"

Tony turned to speak to Richard. Mystic Origin did not like being ignored. She repeated her question, except this time she spoke more slowly, with more volume, punctuating each word with an audible exclamation mark.

"Tony, if you want to know, we are hot. We have not been fed. We have not been shown to our rooms, or tents, or wherever we are supposed to sleep."

Tony gave a wry smile.

"Well, at the beginning of the day, I told all of you to make yourselves a home. Remember?"

Chaz stared, not comprehending. Annaliese squinted her eyes and cocked her head, sure that she must have misheard. The Senator's face clearly showed he was confused. Aston cursed under his breath but loud enough to be heard. It was Clarence Humberton who broke the silence.

"Wait a minute. Don't get cute with us. You said to make ourselves *at* home, not make ourselves *a* home!"

Tony's expression made it clear he had been waiting for this moment all day.

"Richard and Summer, our contestants need a little refresher course on the instructions given to them earlier. Can you turn on your monitor there and hit Play?"

The cameraman and his assistant clambered up onto the stage. After a few moments of electronic adjustments, which seemed very out of place in the darkening jungle, a blue light appeared and grew. Suddenly, there before them, Tony's pre-recorded face filled the mobile screen, speaking familiar words from his opening speech.

"For the next few weeks, this is your kingdom. You make the rules. You reign in this rainforest. So make yourselves a home and enjoy the ride. This is 'Jungle Money!'"

Mystic Origin's face turned sour as she heard the replay. Was he really saying to make yourself *a* home as opposed to *at* home? Annaliese spat like a baseball player standing in the on-deck circle as she debated the same question. Without warning, the replay turned into a remix of one line set to a backbeat.

"So make yourselves a home—make yourselves a home—make yourselves a—make yourselves a—make yourselves a home."

The monitor showed close ups of the contestants' faces at the exact instant they were hearing Tony's words in the arena theater. The pre-recorded Senator took the same step backwards and forwards as the video played and replayed his moment. Everyone laughed but him. He was too hungry for mirth by this point. Peaches' hand brushed the same fly away five times, which made her and those around her laugh and try to duplicate the move.

When the video replay mercifully ended, and the screen went to black, sullen eyes returned to their host. Tony was having a glorious time all by himself, dancing and singing.

"So make yourselves a home! Make yourselves a home! Make a little, make a little, make a little home!"

He danced his way over to DeShunta and flashed his pearly whites.

"And some of us paid attention and have already made ourselves a home, haven't we Miss DeShunta?"

DeShunta felt the pride of unforeseen accomplishment. Putting her hands on her hips, she nodded a slow, knowing nod. She looked around at the crowd with a self-satisfied look. *None of these people ready for this challenge*, she thought to herself. *Pitiful.*

"None of you really expected to have a maid and a butler at your beck and call out here, did you?" Tony asked. "Because they are not here. I hope you didn't think we would have a buffet spread out before you again tonight like we did earlier today. This is Jungle Money not Buffet Money. You can feed yourself. You are surrounded by fruit-bearing trees, and unless your name is Adam or Eve, you can eat from them all as far as I'm concerned. There are nuts, there are all kinds of edible plants and roots and greens, not to mention animals and fish of all kinds."

Mystic Origin, who was holding a chameleon in her hand, erupted.

"Killing the innocent and spilling their blood is wrong! It's barbaric! It's senseless murder! Fish have feelings, too! If you start filming the killing of fish and animals, I will make sure P.E.T.A. finds out!"

Tony cocked his head. "Are you a member of P.E.T.A.?"

Mystic Origin did not hesitate. "Yes sir, I most certainly am."

"Me, too!" Tony grinned. "People Eating Tasty Animals! I am a life member. Thank you for your support. With your help, we are making a difference, one barbecue at a time."

Mystic Origin, horrified by his words, turned her body to shield the chameleon. Tony smiled and continued.

"You are in luck, ladies and gentlemen. There are two mango trees behind the stage. As you can tell, you are about to lose your daylight. If you hurry, though, you will have just enough time to go back there and gather a few pieces of fruit for dinner and maybe even have enough left over for breakfast. Tomorrow, our botanist Elise LeFleur will give you a class on which berries are safe to eat and which aren't. Eat all the mangoes you want. Sleep where you want or where you can. You can start the hunt for the totems again in the morning. The treasure chest still has every bit of the jungle money in it since no one has won it yet. Sleep well, and remember—make yourself a home!"

No one but Tony found humor in his words. Their grumbling only heightened the experience for Tony. He wrapped one arm around Richard, the other arm around Summer, and pulled them toward the staff compound.

"Day one is done, Lady Summer and Gentleman Richard! Let's go see what Chef Raymondo has in store for us tonight!"

The stunned contestants came to the grim realization that Tony was serious about there being no dinner other than mangoes. Someone made a break for it, and the rest followed in a mad dash to the trees behind the stage. The light was fading so quickly that they didn't have time to deliberate.

None of them had a clue what to do about a place to sleep. It wasn't until they began to feel their way back to the stage that someone remembered they still hadn't seen Tattoo come in.

Willow wasn't worried about Tattoo. She was only concerned about her missing brother.

Chapter Twenty-Four

Early the next morning, just before sunrise, Tony sipped his coffee to see if he had added enough French vanilla creamer. Satisfied he had the right mixture, he sipped a little more so it wouldn't spill as he walked from his comfortable tent to the arena theater. He was eager to see where the stars of the show had decided to spend the night. He smiled to himself as he imagined the unkind comments he was sure to receive. He wondered who would be the grumpiest. His money was on Clarence, although Mystic Origin might rise to the occasion.

Tony debated as to whether to ask Denise to get Mother Nature and come with him. The beloved orangutan's presence might redirect the contestants' focus away from their stiff muscles and onto the excitement planned for the day. As he stepped out of his tent however, he decided against it. It was still a little early and a little too dark for the coronation of today's king or queen.

As he poked his head out of the opening of his tent, he saw Summer standing there, camera gear in hand.

"Ready for day two, young lady?"

"Yes, sir," Summer smiled.

Tony and Summer enjoyed their quiet walk. Tony learned that Summer was not a coffee drinker, but she was a sodaholic. She told him about her plan to try to go cold turkey and break her soft drink addiction while she was in Brazil. With all the heat, she needed to be drinking water instead of sugar. He agreed that was a wise plan. He gained a lot of weight his first year of college until he figured out it was caused by a steady intake of soda pop. He quit the soft drinks, lost his belly and rediscovered his abs. His start in showbiz would have never happened if he had remained a fatty. Before she could stop herself, Summer told him he looked really good and was definitely not a fatty. As soon as she said it, she regretted it. She did not want to come across as a teenaged groupie throwing herself at him. Tony smiled and complimented her on her excellent eyesight, which made her laugh. He was just on the right side of cocky to be funny.

All was quiet except for the sounds of birds flying down from their perches ready to start their day. When they walked by the pergola, Tony looked to see if anyone had made their bed there, but it was empty. As they neared the entrance to the arena theater, Tony could see the shapes of bodies lying still on the stage. A couple of the bodies started moving when they saw him approaching.

Suddenly, the stillness of the morning was interrupted by the sound of someone yelling. Tony jerked his head to the left and saw Aston running towards him from the general direction of the mountain path. What in the world? When Aston reached them, he was breathing like a horse. He held one finger up, letting Tony know he would speak as soon as he was able. For now, he could only say one word.

"Tattoo!"

Tony looked past Aston but saw nothing. Aston held his finger up again, still struggling to get enough oxygen in his lungs.

"I went for a run and saw somebody coming down the mountain. Scared me to death. It's Tattoo! Tattoo came back!"

Tony looked puzzled, then a sick thought occurred to him. Had Tattoo been gone all night? Wasn't he there last night when he told them to make themselves a home? His heart sank when he realized he had never done a head count. He just assumed everyone was there, although it had been a little dark when he left. When Tony didn't respond right away, Aston's voice expressed his frustration.

"You know, Tattoo? Something's wrong with him! Bad wrong. I think he might die. You need to come quick!"

Tony threw out his coffee and began running. He yelled at Summer over his shoulder to fetch Dr. Jane. He had no idea what he was going to find but it sounded medical related. Summer said okay and ran back towards the tents.

Tony ran behind Aston, who led him to the base of the mountain. When they got there, sure enough, there was Tattoo. He was stumbling out of the entrance to the mountain path. Something was very wrong. Tattoo was yelling incoherently and not walking steadily at all. He was flailing one arm wildly, while holding a red package tightly to his chest with the other. He looked horrible.

"What in the world?" Tony exclaimed. "What happened to you, man?"

As Tony got closer, he realized that Tattoo was not carrying a red package after all. That was his arm. Tattoo's words came fast and jumbled. It was clear something terrible had happened.

"Need a doctor! Ant bite. Water. I need water! They have my god. Need water! Please. Water!"

With that, Tattoo's eyes rolled back in his head and he collapsed. Tony didn't know what to do. He didn't have any water to give him. He had thrown out his coffee. He knelt down beside Tattoo as did Aston. They looked at his arm. Aston wondered aloud if he had been bitten by a snake. They were afraid to touch his arm, so they leaned all around trying to see if they could find any fang marks. They couldn't find any. Aston noticed the raised red area between Tattoo's knuckles that seemed to be the most swollen and angry place on his arm. They debated as to whether an ant could inflict such damage. Neither one had ever heard of such a thing and so they dismissed the idea. They concluded it must have been some type of deadly spider bite.

Tamper drove up with Dr. Jane less than two minutes later. She quickly assessed Tattoo as having an anaphylactic reaction to an insect sting, which was life-threatening based upon his obvious symptoms of distress. She told them she needed to stick him with an EpiPen as soon as possible. The men loaded Tattoo up into the UTV, which was no small task due to his size. Tamper turned the vehicle around and headed back to the medical tent. Dr. Jane's mind raced as she tried to keep her and Tattoo from falling out of the bouncing machine. They had already lost somebody on day one, and they were about to lose another on day two. They needed to shut this thing down. Jungle Money was a great idea on paper, but it was turning out to be a complete and total disaster.

Since Tony and Aston were on foot, it took them a full fifteen minutes to walk from the mountain path to the medical tent even with the quick pace they were setting. When they arrived, Summer was waiting outside. She confirmed for Tony that Tattoo was inside. Tony and Aston quietly ducked inside the medical tent to see how Tattoo was doing. Ever conscious of the need for film footage, Tony waved at Summer to come in with them. Dr. Jane glanced up to see who had entered, shushed the new arrivals, and then turned back to her patient.

Tattoo lay quietly on his back on a gurney next to a loud oscillating floor fan that pushed cool air across his body. A cold wet towel covered his eyes and forehead. His t-shirt was dripping wet from the water bottle Dr. Jane had emptied on him. She helped him hold up his head while he drank from a water bottle. He dropped it on the floor as soon as he finished it. The nurse handed him a second water bottle, which he began drinking without even pausing to take a breath. Dr. Jane took it from him after a few swallows and told him to lay his head back.

"Honey, I'm going to insert an IV in your good arm. You might feel a little pinch, but only for a sec."

Tattoo didn't flinch. Compared to what he had been through over the last twelve hours the needle felt like a backrub and a kiss goodnight.

"We're going to put a cold washcloth on your hand and your arm, okay, honey? It will cool off your hand and arm and make you feel better, okay?"

Tattoo gave a quick nod but continued his rapid breathing pattern. Tony looked at his arm. It looked bad. His skin was swollen to the point of bursting. It was angry red, which looked even worse next to the white towels. Dr. Jane pushed the towel down into a basin filled with cold water and gently wrung out most of the water. She carefully placed it on Tattoo's hand and arm.

Dr. Jane looked up, caught Tony's eyes, and then looked down at Tattoo's arm. Tony saw what she was pointing at. His hand was trembling. It had been difficult for her to figure out which to treat first—the life-threatening dehydration or the life-threatening allergic reaction to the insect bite. With little time for deliberation, she had chosen to cool his body temperature and hydrate him as swiftly as possible and then deal with the bite.

For a second, the room got brighter. Tony turned and saw that Annaliese and the Senator had come through the opening of the medical tent to see what was happening. Annaliese placed her finger to her lips in a sign to Tony not to announce their presence. Aston felt like the room had gotten too crowded, so he excused himself and slipped outside.

After Dr. Jane started the IV, she searched for and found an EpiPen, hydrocortisone cream and antihistamine tablets. After placing them on a table next to the gurney, she felt the side of Tattoo's neck. Still hot but cooler than before. She took the cold wet towel off of his forehead and wiped it across his cheeks and mouth and then his ears and neck. Tattoo blinked and squinted his eyes. Dr. Jane leaned over so Tattoo could see her face.

"Okay honey, have you ever used an EpiPen?"

Tattoo shook his head. He struggled to speak, sounding as though his tongue was too thick for his mouth.

"What ith an EpiPen?"

"It's basically a shot that will keep you from going into anaphylactic shock. You are having an allergic reaction to the venom from whatever stung you. Your eyes are shutting, you are having trouble breathing and your voice sounds funny to me. Does it feel like your tongue is swelling?"

Tattoo nodded.

"I thought so. Okay, you're going to feel another pinch, but this one will be on your leg."

Tony saw her prepare to jab Tattoo's thigh. He knew there was a long needle in the plastic tube she was holding, and he did not want to see it. Before she stuck him, he wanted to be gone, but before he left he felt like he needed to say something.

"Well Tattoo, it looks like the good doctor is taking good care of you. I hope you get to feeling better. Get some rest. I'll be back to check on you later today."

Tattoo had not seen or heard Tony enter the tent. He had been resting easy until then. When he heard Tony's voice however, he raised himself up from the gurney and turned his head in Tony's direction as far as he could.

"They took my god! They took the jaguar god! I killed mythelf to get it, but before I could thow it to anybody they took it! They had bowth and arrowth and made me give it to them!"

Tony had no idea what he was saying. He looked at Summer for help, but she didn't know either. Dr. Jane took charge.

"Honey, you have got to lay down. You are dangerously dehydrated and about to go into shock if I don't get this medicine in you right now. Tony, you need to leave right now."

Dr. Jane turned to look at Tony and was surprised to see four people standing behind her, including Annaliese Parkman and Bradford Kingston, III. They all needed to go. Part of her was terrified to order a TV star, a Governor and a U.S. Senator out of the tent. The other part of her was terrified not to. Tattoo was in serious condition, and there was no doctor around but her to take control of the situation. If his tongue swelled even a tiny bit more…

Annaliese, confident that she was seeing the big picture, stepped in.

"I can understand your frustration, Tattoo. It is important to you to bring whatever you found on the mountain…"

"It wath the jaguar god!"

"Okay, a jaguar god. It was important to you to bring the jaguar god down to show us."

Tattoo nodded furiously.

"That god ith worth a fortune, but thoth thtupid Indianths…"

Annaliese interrupted him. She knew that there were no Indians and that Tattoo was probably hallucinating, but she decided to play along with him. She knew some of his views from having seen him on TV back when he was making news headlines about his stand against Christmas.

"However, it is obviously vital to the Indians that the jaguar god not be displayed. And when it is so deeply offensive to a group of people for another person to make a public display of their god, we need to honor and respect their wishes and keep our religious displays private."

Tattoo exploded up off the table, blowing out air like a blue whale. He swung his legs down and tried to get his feet under him. His intent was clear. Annaliese protested and backed away. The Senator stepped between them and held his hands out.

"Whoa, whoa, whoa! Let's don't get crazy here! Look, there are many ways to handle this. You say you found a god. Good for you. We can take a vote. Everybody who believes you found a god can vote, and if…"

Tattoo drove the palm of his good hand directly into the center of the Senator's chest, knocking the breath out of him while sending him reeling.

"Nobody ith going to vote whether I can thow the god! I don't care whoth offended or not!"

Dr. Jane jumped to the side to keep from stabbing herself or someone else with the needle. She tried to grab Tattoo's good arm and steer him back to the table. He would not be steered.

"To hell with all of you!" he cried.

Annaliese, who had backed up near the entrance to the tent, interjected.

"Hey, there's no need for that! After all, it's only money!"

Upon hearing those words, Tattoo went completely berserk. Before he could get to the former Governor however, his foot slipped on a wet spot on the floor. He went down hard, landing with his full weight on his swollen arm. Tattoo screamed in pain, and then his eyes rolled back in his head. He lay still as a stone, unconscious. Dr. Jane, no longer intimidated by the VIPs surrounding her, took charge.

"Get out! Now! All of you! Get out!"

She grabbed Tony roughly by his upper arm and shoved him toward the entrance. The Senator started to give her a suggestion on how to treat the patient. She spun the Senator around and shoved him toward the door. Dr. Jane then glared at Annaliese and pointed. Annaliese held up her hands and made her way to the door.

"I'm going, I'm going!"

Rushed outside, their retinas recoiling from the bright light, the four unwelcome visitors shaded their eyes, trying their best to walk while sun-blind. The Senator placed his hand on Tony's shoulder to steady himself. While it did help him to walk straight to some degree, touching Tony was something he wanted to do anyway. This gave him a good excuse. The Senator loved to rub shoulders with Hollywood, and Tony was as Hollywood as Hollywood could be.

As she followed the men out into the blinding sunlight, Annaliese closed her eyes for a moment, raised her face to the heat of the sun, and gave a contented sigh. She relived the moment and replayed her words in her mind. It felt good to put God and religion in their place. Religion divided people. Public displays of religion in the name of God always generated controversy. There was only one way to handle it. Stop it. It was 100 percent effective.

Annaliese stopped, opened her eyes, and took in a deep breath. She let it out slowly. Raising her arm in a victory gesture, seen by no one but her and Summer who was following behind her with the camera, she celebrated the moment. She wasn't sure if Tattoo was telling the truth or not when he said there were Indians pointing bows and arrows at him. He seemed like he was delirious and was probably just talking out of his head. No matter. Either way, no indigenous peoples would be offended on her watch. No, sir.

Besides, she thought, *if they kept him from bringing the jaguar god down to camp, these natives, real or imaginary, just kept my chances of winning alive.*

Chapter Twenty-Five

G was just coming out of the video tent where he had been meeting with Jason and Wally when the two Brazilian helicopter pilots walked up. He grabbed the nearest one's hand and shook it for a long minute thanking him profusely for staying the night to continue the search for Boedy.

"I cannot thank you two enough for what you are doing. You didn't have to stay. So, I heard you went out again this morning. Did you and Bones find any sign of Boedy? Please tell me you did."

The pilot shook his head.

"No. We look yesterday seven, eight hour. This morning we look maybe two hour. We see nothing. Look everywhere. Sad for man. Sad for sister."

Dismayed, G crossed his arms and shook his head.

"Where could he be? I mean seriously, how far could he have gone? Maybe he's lost and can't find his way to us…or maybe he's injured and can't tell us where he is. And of course, there's the possibility he's dead. How far did you guys go?"

The pilot tried to think of how to explain it, but his fluency in English had its limits. He pointed to the waterfall and drew a big circle in the air with his finger.

G was at a loss for words. Not finding Boedy was an option he had never considered. Of course they would find Boedy. How could you not find him? Over forty people saw him jump out of the helicopter. They saw where he was flying. They saw him flying towards the waterfall. G didn't personally see him after that point, but Peaches and the pilot did. They said Boedy did a U-turn and flew away from the waterfall. They started hunting for him within minutes, maybe ten minutes of when he jumped. These weren't novice hunters either. This was Bones, world-renowned big game hunting guide from South Africa. This was Tamper, an Army Ranger who made a career of going into hell holes on the other side of the world to find bad people and kill them and bring his wounded battle buddies back home again. Who better to track Boedy down than those two? G just could not understand it.

"Well gentlemen, I am indebted to you for going way above and beyond the call of duty. I know you have to get back to your families. I have already spoken to your captain and told him I am paying for an extra two days for your services and for the use of your helicopters, and I have included what I hope you will find to be a generous tip for your troubles."

The two men both whistled. They knew what the price was for a three-hour flight in a Blackhawk helicopter. The cost to reserve two helicopters for three full days, plus the first helicopter that left on day one, was astronomical.

G nodded. He knew exactly how much he had just agreed to pay. These were extraordinary circumstances however.

While G was saying his goodbyes to the pilots, he was turning over in his mind what he was going to say to Willow about her brother. He knew he would see her within the hour. At this moment, he had no idea what to say or how to say it.

Meanwhile, a few hundred yards away, Tony was gathering the contestants for the selection of the king or queen of the day. The show must go on. Tony expected to get shelled with complaints when he greeted the group this morning. They had discovered last night, too late to do anything about it, that they had to build their own shelters. They learned they had to gather their own food, and the only thing readily accessible was mangoes. Aside from the two as-yet-unidentified people he could see moving around underneath the stage, everyone slept on a hard, wooden floor with no pillows or blankets.

Despite the physical hardships however, everyone was surprisingly chipper. It could have been the presence of the videographers that kept them from saying everything they wanted to say. It could have been the exciting possibility of being the first to find a totem animal and grabbing a handful of priceless treasure from the treasure chest. Whatever it was, Tony was pleasantly surprised at the warm reception he received from everyone.

Everyone except Clarence Humberton, that is.

Clarence appeared to be in abject misery. He had started off Jungle Money by receiving an injury to his genitals at the hands of DeShunta after his helicopter prank went awry. Every fiber of his being was crying out for a cigarette. He told Tony that he was going to add a count to his lawsuit for damages from intentional infliction of emotional distress because it was inhuman not to supply him with cigarettes. He would not have come to this godforsaken jungle if he had known they were not going to provide the basic necessities of life, such as cigarettes.

Now, to top it all off, he was suffering from a world-class case of crotch rot. Clarence had not bathed the day they flew into Rio de Janeiro because he was running late to the airport. He had not bathed the next morning because he knew they were flying into the heat of the Amazon rainforest where he would be sweating, so a shower would be useless. He did not feel like making the long trek to the river for a river bath last night because he was injured and wanted to keep ice on his groin and keep movement to a minimum. As a result, Clarence ended up wearing the same sweaty underwear for three days.

Tinea cruris fungus loves men like Clarence who wear the same underwear every day in the heat and humidity. The skin around his groin was red, raw and oozing. Clarence's healing protocol, which consisted of scratching every hour on the hour until symptoms improved, hadn't worked as well as he hoped. Walking was an excruciating ordeal. He walked with his feet spread as far apart as possible, sort of like a cowboy, although one that would likely never find a horse strong enough to carry him. He was perfecting that walk on the way from the arena theater to Dr. Jane's medical tent that morning when Tony and Denise brought out Mother Nature.

Clarence didn't like much about his current circumstances. He didn't like hot. He didn't like hungry. He didn't like nicotine withdrawal. He sure didn't like jungle rot. But the orangutan, that he liked. First of all, the monkey walked funny. Secondly, the monkey was ugly as sin. It would flip its upper lip up and bend it back, showing its god-awful teeth, which delighted Clarence to no end. But most fascinating of all to Clarence was that the monkey had absolute power. It could anoint anyone King or Queen for a Day. Tony did not influence it or direct it in any way. The beast just chose. Surely, Mother Nature could not have known what she was doing or the significance placed upon the first person she crowned each morning. But it was almost like she knew.

All the contestants stood in a circle around Mother Nature. Clarence would not have done so but for the fact he was walking to Dr. Jane's medical tent, which took him right by the group. Tony handed the crown to the orangutan as he recited the coronation chant.

"Mother Nature decides
who will wear the crown,
who will make the rules
until the sun goes down."

All eyes were on Mother Nature as she turned her attention to the circle of onlookers. Clarence caught her eye because he was still walking up to the circle. He walked bow-legged, rocking left and right as he approached so as to keep his thighs from touching his jungle rot. He was walking like her. She liked the way he walked. Mother Nature carried the crown in one hand while swinging the other and walked up to the human who captured her attention.

Mother Nature crowned Clarence Humberton King for a Day.

Everyone cringed when they realized what had just happened. Clarence was easily the most disagreeable of the bunch. He was loud, boorish, rude, overbearing, demanding, hypercritical, and downright unpleasant. DeShunta was a force, but she had fleeting moments of kindness and happiness, most of which involved Tony and Celeste. Clarence, on the other hand, had no tender moments. If he had any redeeming qualities, they had not yet surfaced.

Clarence was not expecting to be coronated that morning. He had not thought about the possibilities of making rules, but he planned to be a quick study. He was not going to let this opportunity pass. His eyes turned bright as he thought of a way to test the boundaries of his authority. Tony's answer to his first question was highly disappointing.

"No Clarence, I'm sorry. You cannot declare that any money won is automatically yours."

Clarence did not care if the video cameras were on. He told Tony that he had just earned three more counts in his lawsuit—fraud, intentional misrepresentation and false pretenses. He did not like Tony's reaction. Laughing was a sign that Tony wasn't taking him seriously. Clarence told Tony that he wouldn't be laughing when his attorney Benito Francisco Bonnano, Esquire got through with him. Benito hasn't lost a case in twenty-five years. Tony's laughter infuriated Clarence. *Just wait, Mr. Hollywood. Just wait.*

Clarence thought about alternatives. There weren't many. He was definitely not going to win any prize money today. He was not going out into the jungle with red, raw, oozing skin on either side of his privates. He was not planning to leave the medical tent if he could help it. The cot in Dr. Jane's tent was more comfortable than where he slept last night, and she kept a fan blowing. The fan was heaven. He was not going to leave heaven today, even if it gave him a shot at some priceless gold or jewels in the chest. Winning was out of reach today. Besides, the Senator, Chaz and Aston were rumored to have put their maps together and were on the verge of finding a totem and bringing home the prize. It was just a matter of time.

Clarence detested the Senator. He was a pandering blowhard. Clarence had nothing but disgust for Chaz. Chaz was a long-haired hippie, a mama's boy who had never worked a day in his life. He hadn't paid any dues to an employer or to society at large.

Aston, however, was in a whole different category of hate.

From their first meeting in Atlanta at Bert Redmond's mansion, Clarence pegged Aston as a fancy pants know-it-all who cared more about global warming than keeping America working. His dislike catapulted into outright hatred this morning when people started waking up and moving around. Clarence had suggested that they build one large hut for all to sleep in rather than eleven or twelve different huts. Actually, "suggested" may be too mild of a term. Clarence had simply decreed that they would build one large hut for all to sleep in. It was not up for discussion. It had been decided, at least in Clarence's mind. The words "get busy" may have also been part of Clarence's instructions. As he saw it, someone needed to be in charge and it may as well be him.

As Clarence was walking toward the grove of mango trees to find some breakfast this morning, he heard Aston pop off to one of the others. He couldn't hear it distinctly because Aston said it in hushed tones, but he heard enough. Aston said something and then said, "the big fat lard and his big fat mouth." Clarence had wheeled and shouted, "What did you just say?" Aston didn't answer, but his guilty face made it plain that Clarence had heard right. Just because Clarence hadn't yet started building his hut and Aston had almost completed his at the time he made his suggestion had nothing to do with work ethic. It was about efficient organization of labor. Aston was too stupid to recognize leadership when it was standing right in front of him.

From that very moment, Clarence loathed Aston and his spiked-up hair. If they were back in New York and not on camera, Clarence would have meted out swift and sure retribution. He couldn't do it that way here. He could do nothing but sit, stew and swallow his seething anger. Or could he?

All eyes were upon Clarence and his crown. Think, think, think. He watched the orangutan as he thought. Mother Nature picked something out of the fur on her belly, examined it, smelled it and then ate it. She looked up at Clarence as though she was waiting to hear the king's rule for the day. Then it hit him.

A global warming tax. Yes!

Aston had nagged the Senator about climate change from the moment they first met. Clarence enjoyed listening to the conflict to an extent because he loved watching politicians squirm. He loved to watch anybody squirm as long as it wasn't himself. This morning, however, Aston had embarrassed and insulted Clarence by talking about him behind his back. *Alright, hot shot, you want to play rough? I'll play rough. I may not be able to run into the jungle and beat you to one of your little animal statues,* Clarence thought to himself, *but I can notch a win nonetheless. If the rumors are correct, and you are the winner, let's see you put your money where your mouth is, big boy.* Clarence cleared his throat, pulled his shorts away from his crotch where the cloth had stuck to his ooze, and made his announcement.

"As King for a Day, I hereby declare that there shall be a 50 percent tax on any winnings paid out today. The tax money shall be paid to the United Nations to combat climate change."

Silence. Everyone stared at him to see if he was serious. He was. Deadly serious.

"Look, I get no personal gain from it. The money is going to a worthy cause, right, because according to our friend Aston here, cooling down the planet is a matter of life and death. So, there it is. A 50 percent global warming tax on all winnings. So says Clarence Humberton, King for a Day, having been crowned by an ugly orange ape with its hair sticking straight up and missing some teeth."

The contestants, unsure as to Clarence's game, all looked to Tony for guidance. Was this legal? Could he do this? Presently, Tony nodded.

"He is not directing the winnings to him or anyone who will directly benefit him, and the winners still get money. A climate change tax it is."

Mystic Origin cheered and clapped. She liked it. The planet was sick and needed a doctor, and doctors cost money. She grabbed Aston by the arm and squeezed it, knowing he had to be delighted. She did a dance reminiscent of a fairy queen like the one she had performed in a grove of trees at the Medieval Festival the previous spring. Flitting here and there, she hummed a tune to express her joy at the forthcoming healing that was about to occur. All eyes looked to Aston to see his reaction. His face was expressionless.

Pleased with himself, Clarence adjusted the crown on his head and continued his waddle walk to the medical tent. He would have liked to watch Aston chew on today's rule for a while, but his crotch was burning and needed attention.

After an unpleasant walk, Clarence made it to the medical tent. He showed Dr. Jane his ailment. She produced a yellow container of medicated powder and explained to him how to apply it. Clarence gruffly asked why she wasn't going to apply it.

"You're a doctor, ain't you? You are getting paid to make patients well, ain't you?"

Dr. Jane didn't bat an eye. He was a big boy. He could do this job himself. She gave him a clean sheet to drape over himself as he prepared to pour some powder into his hand and then she walked out. She didn't want to watch. She was pretty confident Clarence would make a show of it. She had no interest in being there when he did it, medical degree or no medical degree.

Clarence covered his crotch in powder and gingerly worked it in. The drying and cooling effect was immediate. The bite happened a few seconds later. There was medicine in there after all. It was not a bad sting, but it was noticeable. Thankfully, it subsided in less than a minute.

When Dr. Jane returned a few minutes later, she found an uncovered Clarence lying on the cot, legs wide apart, with the fan pointed directly at something that looked like a baby bird that had fallen out of its nest. She barked at him to cover up. As brash and uncaring as Clarence was, Dr. Jane's voice was so authoritative that he quickly obeyed. She was not amused, not even a little bit.

Back in the arena theater, Tony gave the contestants their instructions for day two.

"So, here is the schedule for Jungle Money day two. As I think you may have already figured out, you need a place to live! I see some looks on your faces that tell me I'm right. I love being right! It happens more often than you'd think. We here at Jungle Money want you to have the best deluxe accommodations that the rainforest can provide. So here is what we have done just for you."

"Oh boy, I can't wait to hear this," Peaches said sarcastically.

"If you will remember, back at the pergola there was a stack of cut-down trees, saplings, tree limbs, branches and elephant ear leaves. Guess what? Those are your houses! Some assembly required! Tamper and Bones cut those down and gathered them up when they were building the arena theater, then put them in a nice, neat stack for you. You will also notice a big stack of vines, just like the ones that Tarzan swings on. They gathered those up at the same time. You can use those like ropes or cord to bind your tree limbs together and voilà! Jungle Money huts for everyone! You get a hut! You get a hut! And you get a hut!"

Chaz, with his head tilted at forty-five degrees, looked in the direction of the pergola. He thought it was very cool that he was going to get to build an eco-friendly house. DeShunta and Celeste looked at each other for a few seconds…then shook their heads no. They were not going to build a hut. They were happy with their home under the stage. Tony continued.

"So no one has a time advantage over the other, we are all going to take the morning to build huts. You have the next two hours to pick out your spot, gather the building materials and build your house. I see Annaliese enjoying a mango over there. If you are interested, I will show you where there are some banana trees between here and the river. There is nothing like a good banana. You may want to gather some fruit and store it in your hut for later today. I will leave that up to you."

Willow raised her hand. "Where is my brother?"

A serious look came over Tony's face.

"Willow, I saw Tamper, Bones and the helicopter pilots leaving out to go look early this morning. They ran out of daylight yesterday, which is why they got up early as soon as it started getting light out. They will find him this morning, I guarantee it."

Willow seemed less than satisfied with his answer. She was clearly anxious and uneasy. Tony did not know how G planned to handle the Boedy/Willow situation. Quite frankly, he couldn't believe she wasn't raising more of a fuss than she was. He would find G and come up with a game plan. Meanwhile, he needed to get these contestants started.

"So, you have two hours. It is right now 7:55 a.m."

"It's too early to be awake," Celeste yawned.

"Early? I am usually walking into the studio for Wake Up America at 5:15 a.m., bright-eyed and bushy-tailed. Two hours, ladies and gentlemen. Stack some wood, store some food, and get ready for a treasure hunt! Let's meet right back here at 10 a.m. and see who wants some Jungle Money! Got it?"

"Got it," DeShunta replied with a smile, which Tony returned in brilliant-white, gleaming teeth fashion.

Tony led a procession of people to the banana trees. People grabbed armloads of bananas and carried them back to camp. They laid them near where they chose a home site and went to work.

DeShunta and Celeste were in the midst of the crowd, but instead of continuing to the pile of lumber, they peeled off and headed into the arena theater with their haul of fruit. They put their bananas under the stage, out of the sun, in the soft sand. Next they walked to the mango trees, loaded up mangoes and brought armloads back to their home. Having taken care of their food needs, the two unlikely companions were done with grocery shopping.

As the morning dragged on, Celeste found a shady seat by the pergola. The heat enveloped her as she watched everyone but her and DeShunta work. She closed her eyes and drifted off to sleep. She began to dream the sweetest dream. She was back home, walking across the parking lot of her father's jewelry store, carrying her little dog Aurora in her arms, except Aurora was still a puppy. She was going to surprise her father with a visit. As she neared the door, she could see him behind the counter talking to a customer. She was about to push open the door. She could not wait to see his look of happy recognition and the daddy smile that would immediately follow. She reached for the door…

Before she could reach it, she was awakened by a touch. With consciousness came realization—it was only a dream. Celeste was distraught. For a few brief seconds, her daddy had been alive again. Now, she had lost the dream. The door had disappeared. With sadness in her sleepy blue eyes, she blinked to see who had awakened her.

DeShunta Jackson was the owner of the hands that touched her. She was sitting directly behind Celeste holding a double handful of her hair. Celeste, who was startled and confused, asked what was happening. DeShunta told her to turn around and hold still. Too disoriented to do otherwise, Celeste did as she was told.

DeShunta began braiding Celeste's hair into perfectly symmetrical corn rows. Once she realized what was happening, Celeste's heart rate returned to normal. The gentle pulling of her hair over and over again relaxed her and put her back into a warm, sleepy state of mind. She drifted into a semi-conscious twilight where she revisited pleasant memories of her father. For the next hour, DeShunta worked on her hair. Celeste periodically reached up to touch her hair, using her fingers to "see" what DeShunta was doing. Though she didn't have a mirror, Celeste could pat her head and feel the artistry. Seeing the young girl's reaction to having her hair braided for the first time in her life pleased DeShunta.

"How it feel to be a beautiful black woman?"

Celeste laughed.

"It's wonderful! Thank you!"

Celeste didn't realize how much she needed a reassuring touch. Finished with the arduous task, DeShunta began the difficult process of pushing herself off the ground and standing to her feet. Celeste, who was much more nimble, popped up off the ground. While DeShunta was still struggling to get up, Celeste reached down and hugged DeShunta in a spontaneous expression of gratitude. As she squeezed, she started to say "thank you," but didn't get the words out.

A swift slap from DeShunta's open hand to the side of Celeste's head abruptly ended the tender embrace. The sudden impact generated a shower of stars, knocking Celeste off balance. She pressed her hand against the side of her face to stop the sting. The look of hurt on her face said it all.

Why?

DeShunta barked, "You know my shoulder and back hurt! Why don't you fall out a helicopter and land on your back and see how much hugging you want to do!"

With that, DeShunta finished battling gravity and stood to her feet. Celeste stared at her in bewilderment. She had flipped like a light switch, completely without warning. Celeste walked away, confused, hurt and uncertain as to what to do next. Maybe she should build her own private hut after all.

Chapter Twenty-Six

While the contestants were all off running through the jungle, G walked with Tony as he prepared to join the other performers for rehearsal. The second show would take place the night someone found the jaguar god, which would almost certainly be tonight. The show would be capped off by the opening of the treasure chest for the winner. It would be an exciting night, and the performers wanted their routines to be precision perfect, Tony included. He was looking forward to rehearsal for multiple reasons. As they walked, Tony asked G the question that had dominated his thinking ever since Tattoo came stumbling out of the jungle earlier this morning.

"So, Tattoo says there were natives with spears and bows and arrows that took the jaguar god away from him. Do you believe him? Is there any chance that could be true?"

G shook his head.

"No. I had the same question, so I sent Tamper to check. He drove up the mountain path, made sure none of the contestants were around to see and then hiked up to where he had hidden the totem. He said it was still exactly where it was when he hid it last Saturday, hanging down from a vine, easy as pie to see with all the bright painted colors. It's not far up the path either, not even a mile, so there's no way it would take Tattoo all day and night to bring it back to camp."

"What did Richard say about the trail camera?"

"I asked Richard as soon as I heard about what Tattoo said. He rewound the video and scanned through it from the time Tattoo hit the woods yesterday until he came back this morning. Nothing. Well, he said a troop of monkeys and a toucan triggered the motion sensor during the course of the day but no people. Plus, he had it rigged so it would trigger a booby trap when they pulled on the vine. It's supposed to make a big green and black Jungle Money flag fly up as well as set off a smoke bomb. The trap was still set when Tamper got there. There were no natives with weapons."

Tony breathed a sigh of relief.

"Okay, phew. I was starting to get concerned. He sounded so believable. I figured he was just delirious from getting bitten by ants. Denise said she was 99 percent sure it was a bullet ant. Between that and the dehydration—he was just talking out of his head."

G nodded in agreement, then his face turned serious. He lowered his voice as he spoke.

"Okay, we have a bigger problem. Boedy. They still can't find him."

Tony's eyes grew wide.

"How? How can that be?"

"I don't know," G said, shaking his head slowly, "but Bones and Tamper are losing their minds. Bones has combed through every square inch of jungle within a two mile radius of the waterfall. You know how thick it is around there. Bones has been through all of it. He got bit by a snake of some kind, thank god not venomous, while he was bear crawling through a thicket. He came across a carcass of some half-eaten animal—I forget what kind he said it was. Nothing. He is confident Boedy is not on land, so now he is diving at the base of the waterfall to see if he drowned. When Tamper got back from checking to make sure the jaguar god was still there, he joined Bones. They are going to drag the bottom to see if they can find his body. It's got to be there. There's nowhere else he could be."

They walked thoughtfully in silence until they reached the performers. Tony watched the leading lady with interest as she danced by herself while everyone was gathering.

"So, what do we do with Willow?" Tony asked. "She's out looking for a totem right now, if you can believe it, I think with Peaches, but she is obviously worried and for good reason. She's going to shut down or freak out or something when she comes back into camp today and her brother is not sitting here eating a mango."

G shrugged his shoulders.

"I have thought of nothing but that all night. I don't have an answer. I don't know. We should have never brought relatives to Brazil for multiple reasons. I know Bert is spontaneous and thought it would be a cool plot twist, and she would fill the vacancy left when the burned-face lady backed out. He had good intentions, but man, we've got a mess on our hands now."

Tony sighed.

"Tell me about it. I was betting on Boedy to win the whole thing. My guy never even made it into camp! My only hope now is that DeShunta and…who did Bert have?"

"Bert has the Senator. He says he's going to cheat his way to victory, so the Senator is sure money. That's what Bert thinks."

"That's right," Tony chuckled. "My only hope is that DeShunta and the Senator get stung by bullet ants, too, so somebody else wins and not you two. Well, we better think of something to do with Willow when Bones and Tamper pull Boedy's body off the bottom of the riverbed. Hey, I just remembered—we have stationary cameras set up at the base of the waterfall, don't we? Richard and Steven set one up there. Are they going to film them bringing a body out of the water? Because that would not be good!"

G's lips were tight, nothing but a thin, straight line.

"We're going to stick with the original plan, which is to film it all. When Boedy's family files a ten billion-dollar lawsuit, we're going to have the video to show that we did everything possible to find him as quickly as we could and render aid. I don't know what else to do right now. Be thinking. We need to be ready tonight because everybody, not just Willow, will be asking."

"All right, G man," Tony nodded gravely. "You'll come up with something. You always do."

As Tony walked towards the dancers, who were just starting practice, G rubbed his forehead with his hand. *What to do, what to do, what to do?*

Chapter Twenty-Seven

Everyone had long since plunged into the jungle and disappeared. When they left, a hush came over the camp. With the exception of a beautiful serenade from countless tropical birds, silence reigned. It was amazing how this spot could go from a buzz of voices, peals of laughter and frenetic activity to quiet with everyone gone.

Well, almost everyone.

Mystic Origin stayed in camp while the rest explored the jungle. She had tossed her piece of map yesterday. She had an inkling that Tattoo took it, but she had not seen him today. It was no big deal, though. Tony must have been distracted yesterday because he had laid the big map down on the side of the stage in the arena theater, all rolled up, and no one else had noticed. She could look at it whenever she wanted. She planned to do that very thing, but she wanted to finish building her hut first.

The A-frame had gone up quickly enough, but it was taking a little more time because of the building material she wanted to use to cover the walls—banana leaves. Her hut was going to look way different from the others. She was already getting compliments on its cool appearance before everyone took off. The only difficulty was that the banana trees were at the end of a long walk to the river, and then she had to climb to get the big leaves she wanted. It took her almost three hours to complete construction, but the end result was nothing short of amazing. Mystic Origin's hut would be the envy of camp. No one could match it.

Now that the structure was up, she needed to create a comfortable place to sleep. She badly wanted to start weaving the thicker vines into a hammock but recognized it would take her the rest of the day to complete. Building a home out of things she could find without having to purchase them had always been one of her favorite pastimes. Nevertheless, she did want to find an animal statue and earn the right to raid the treasure chest. She decided to take up the task of hammock making this evening.

Mystic Origin began walking to the arena theater to look at the big map. She was an hour behind the others, so she moved rather briskly. As she walked, the tropical sun beat down on her mercilessly. She lifted her hand up to shield her eyes and look at the sky. It seemed like the sun was bigger down here in Brazil, like it was closer to the earth than in her home in sunny California. If it was this hot this morning, how hot would it be this afternoon? As urban outdoorsmen, she and her partner Leaf were used to tolerating temperature swings that people who lived air-conditioned lives would never appreciate. You can still live your best life outdoors as long as you take countermeasures to protect yourself. But what could she do to protect herself from the heat of the rainforest, which was far more intense than any heat she had ever known? After a moment of quiet reflection, a thought occurred to her.

I can make myself a sun bonnet.

Mystic Origin was a crafty person who loved making things with her hands. The idea of making a hat made her happy, but she was torn. Part of her wanted to hurry to the big map, get her bearings and take off into the jungle to find a totem. That was the whole reason she came here, wasn't it? *Go win a million dollars, dummy!* The other part of her wanted to gather an armload of broad-leafed grass blades, sit down in the shade and weave a big, floppy hat. Making a sun bonnet in the shade sounded way more fun than running through the jungle in the heat. *Go make a bonnet! You'll be a better treasure hunter if your eyes are shaded and your head is cool!* She knew she would never accomplish either goal if she allowed her indecision to keep her immobilized, and right now she was rooted to the spot. She knew she had to decide.

After much deliberation, she reached a compromise with the other side of herself. She would gather the grass now and place it inside her hut but wait until this evening to sit and weave a sun bonnet. Both sides of her liked the plan. *Can you live with it? Yes. Can you? I guess so. Yes.* Having settled the matter without too much of an argument, she headed to the clearing between the arena theater and the river where the grass grew the tallest, eager to find the right materials to make an Amazon rainforest hat.

When she reached the clearing, Mystic Origin saw one section of grass that seemed to be the tallest and greenest. She grabbed the base of one plant and pulled, but it didn't break loose. She got a better grip, using two hands this time, and pulled with all her might. Nothing. The stalk of grass was thick and pulpy, not like the Bermuda grass that was so prevalent back home. She pulled on a few more but had very little success.

She lost her grip on the last one, causing her hands to slide up the blades. Feeling a sting, she turned loose and looked at her hand. A thin red line appeared on one of her fingers. She had received a small cut. She stuck her injured finger in her mouth and sucked the blood, tasting the saltiness as she thought about what to try next.

She needed a knife, or something sharp to cut with, but where could she find one? She stood and looked around. There looked to be a few large rocks sticking out of the ground along the tree line. Maybe she could find a sharp-edged rock there. She began walking slowly, head down, examining the rocks between her bare feet. She thought she found one, but when she felt the edge with her thumb it was too smooth to be useful. She tossed the stone aside and continued her search. Something else caught her eye, causing her to kneel and take a better look.

It was a…something made of woven grass.

It was hard to tell what it was. It almost looked like a sleeve or maybe a container of some kind. She picked it up. It was woven grass stuffed with more grass to give it shape. As she turned it over, she noticed it had four small protrusions and a smaller woven grass pouch attached at one end, also stuffed with grass. Suddenly, it hit her what she held in her hands.

This was a doll! Those were arms and legs. Definitely arms and legs. And that was a head. This was not clothing or a container—this was a doll! A handmade doll! Someone skilled in native handcrafts had made this.

As far as she knew, none of the other ladies in camp had ventured in this direction. Slowly, it dawned on her what this might mean. Mystic Origin stood up and scanned the area around her, turning in a complete circle. She peered into the trees. She raised her hand to shield her eyes from the sun so as to better see into the shadows. Fear and trepidation began to creep into the recesses of her mind. She suddenly felt very alone and vulnerable.

Movement caught her eye. It was much closer than she expected or desired. A tiny, brown-skinned child, wearing only a string around his waist, took a hesitant step forward from the shadows.

Startled, Mystic Origin's eyes went wide as she sucked in air to replace the breath that had been taken away. The little boy stared in wonder at her, transfixed by what he saw. Both were mesmerized by the sight of the other. Suddenly, Mystic Origin saw a tiny woman, not much taller than the child, grab for the boy and pull him back into the shadows.

All was quiet.

Though she could no longer see them, Mystic Origin's ears told her they had not run. She didn't know what to do. Her mind was racing almost as fast as her heart. Uncertain as to the best course of action, she decided to speak. It took her two tries to get words out because her throat had gone bone dry, but she finally managed to speak.

"I won't hurt you."

Mystic Origin was not a big person herself, standing five feet two inches tall, but she was pretty sure she was taller than the woman. She knelt so as to make herself not appear so physically imposing and waited. After a considerable amount of time had passed, she began to give up on the idea that she would see them again. They must have quietly slipped back into the jungle. She felt an overwhelming sadness. She did not want this encounter to end so soon. The innocence in the child's eyes was so pure. The mother's protective love for her baby was so evident and sweet.

On a whim, she changed tactics. She resumed gathering grass, trying her best to look relaxed and natural. After she had all the grass she could hold in two hands, she sat down in the clearing and began weaving a hat. Though it was exceedingly difficult, she turned her eyes away from the wood line so her visitors wouldn't feel threatened. She sang softly to herself. It was a freestyle, made-up-on-the-spot song of praise to Mother Earth.

"From the sky to the air to the trees to the earth to the roots to the springs to the rocks, you display your goodness..."

A sound came from behind her. A tiny sound. Slowly, she turned around. There he was, right behind her. The little boy had come back. Mystic Origin smiled. She slowly held out the doll that she had found, keeping her eyes on her hands.

The child reached out and took the doll from her. He did not run. He stood, bare feet planted, and stared. His calm little black eyes studied her. After a bit he made the tiny sound again. Mystic Origin smiled and mimicked him, making the exact same sound he did. With that, the little boy turned and ran back into the cover of shadows under the trees.

Mystic Origin hoped against hope that they would reappear. She resumed weaving grass to make a hat. She sang quietly. She used every tactic she could think of to coax them back out. After the better part of a half hour, when she could stand it no longer, she stood and eased over to the clear space between the two trees where she had last seen them. Just as her eyes began to adjust to the change in light from sun to shadows, she heard quick footsteps deep in the jungle. They were few in number, and then they were gone. Crestfallen, Mystic Origin turned and reentered the clearing. She picked up the beginnings of her sun bonnet and returned to camp.

As she walked, a question occurred to her. *Should I mention this wondrous encounter to the others? They would want to know.* If she did, there would be a mad rush to the clearing by those hoping to catch a glimpse. The mother and child would be pushed deep into the jungle, never to return. Worse yet, the Army man Tamper and his professional animal-killer friend with the long hair and big hat might try to capture them, though for what purpose she could not imagine. *They might put them in cages and sell them to a zoo.* Then where would they be? The beautiful Amazon innocents would have their idyllic lives ruined all because of her. She could never forgive herself. *What do we do? O Mother Earth, please guide us.*

After thinking it through, her mind was made up. Mystic Origin would keep this a secret. When she had an opportunity to sneak away, she would return to this clearing, alone, and try to renew acquaintances. Until then, no one would be any the wiser. She returned to the camp with a double armful of grass and crafted a homemade jungle-grass hat. When she finished, she debated about heading out into the jungle. By that point, it was early afternoon, it was hot and no one had brought home a single animal statue. She hadn't planned on spending the day in camp, but then again, how often does one get to interact with indigenous natives that have never seen the outside world before? They would be living here for weeks, she reasoned, so she would have plenty of opportunities to win the right to open the treasure chest. A good night's sleep would give her the energy to win the contests to come, and there was no better way to sleep soundly than on a comfy hammock. She marched over to the lumber pile, grabbed all the vines she could carry and dragged them back to her hut. She began to string a hammock, singing her Mother Earth song over and over again, adding lines to it as she went.

Chapter Twenty-Eight

On day one, everyone had started the hunt solo. Nobody had a wing man. They all headed into the jungle alone, convinced they could find an animal totem by themselves, thereby winning the prize without having to share. After many fruitless hours of searching however, the competitors realized this would not be the jungle equivalent of an Easter egg hunt on the White House lawn. The totems were well-hidden. This was hard and was going to continue to be hard. Their hopes for quick success on day one having been dashed, everyone went to bed rethinking their game plans.

On day two, strategies began to change. Three ladies changed the dynamic of the group. After examining each other's pieces of the map and finding they held pieces that fit together, Peaches, Celeste and Willow formed a team of three. Willow told them she intended to search for her brother until he was found, but she may as well look where the totems were supposed to be since he wasn't near the waterfall. As their competition watched them head out, others began to follow suit. Partnerships began to spring up. A renewed sense of hope replaced the exasperation that had hung over camp the night before. Surely, someone would find an animal statue before the day ended.

As the afternoon wore on and the shadows began to lengthen, the contestants began to return to home base. The buzz was that someone had located a god and was bringing it back to camp. Some thought it was Tattoo because he already knew where the jaguar god was located. Speculation, conjecture and rumor were on everyone's lips. As it turned out, the rumors were false. When Clarence heard them talking, he assured them it was not Tattoo. He was still in Dr. Jane's tent when Clarence left. It couldn't be him.

When Peaches' team returned to camp, they reported that the Senator, Aston and Chaz had formed a team. The men told the ladies they were sure they knew where a god was, but when their paths crossed again later in the day, they still hadn't found it. Richard, who was videoing the contestants as they came back to camp, quietly radioed Tony to inform him of their lack of progress. Tony thought for sure they would have a winner by now. Without a winner, a celebratory dance show in the arena theater tonight would be kind of awkward.

Annaliese strode back into camp without speaking to anyone. Grumpy from the bugs and the heat, she just wanted to lie down in her makeshift lean-to and be away from everyone for a while. She knew she would feel much better if she took a swim in the river below the waterfall, but first she needed some nourishment. A couple of mangoes from the stash she had amassed were just what the doctor ordered. She ducked into her primitive abode and reached for the fruit hidden away under the blanket.

Except there was no fruit.

Annaliese swore silently. It's here somewhere. She picked up the blanket, shook it out and threw it behind her. Nothing. She moved her hands along the ground underneath her tree-branch bed. Still nothing. It dawned on her that her blanket had been evenly spread out when she left that morning, but it was rumpled when she reentered her hut. She heard someone laughing outside, which angered her. What could possibly be funny? It was hot and buggy. Now, she had no food. She was miserable already, and yet things had just managed to get worse. She swiftly backed out of her shelter and faced the gathering outside.

"Who stole my mangoes? Someone stole my mangoes! I had them hidden and now they're gone!"

She glared around the group. Formerly smiling faces immediately lost all signs of mirth. No one fessed up.

"I said, who stole my mangoes? Obviously it was someone here who was too lazy to gather their own. Now who did it?"

DeShunta climbed out from her home under the stage so she could watch. If there was going to be a showdown, she wanted to see it. Annaliese went straight into cross-examination mode.

"DeShunta, you stayed in camp all day, didn't you? Didn't you?"

DeShunta squared up to Annaliese and placed her hands on her hips.

"No, I did not stay in camp all day. I walked up to the plateau above the waterfall. It was hot as hell. As a matter of fact, why don't you go there? That would be a good place for you. Hell, I mean. They might even elect you Governor again."

DeShunta's nostrils flared. She began breathing hard and talking to herself about what she was going to do if her provocateur said one more thing. Annaliese was seething, but she was not suicidal. She decided not to press her luck any further with DeShunta. Someone must have stayed in camp, though.

"Has anyone seen…what's her name? Somebody help me."

No one helped. Annaliese remembered on her own.

"Mystic, whatever she calls herself. Mystic Origin. Has anybody seen Mystic Origin?"

The dreadlocked owner of the name stepped out of her hut and replied, "Who is asking? And why do you want to know?"

"Did you stay in camp while everyone else went on the hunt?" Annaliese demanded.

"I chose my place in the cosmos, if that's what you're asking."

Annaliese knew a tacit admission when she heard one. No verbal denial equals a silent yes. So, Mystic Origin was the one who stayed in camp and helped herself to the fruits of Annaliese's labor, was she? Annaliese strode toward her quarry. Walking straight past Mystic Origin, she barged right into her hut and began a search. Mystic Origin exploded.

"Whoa! What do you think you are doing? Get out of my house! You have no right to be in here! This is an unlawful entry! I have constitutional rights against search and seizure without a warrant!"

Annaliese didn't have patience enough to tell her the obvious. They weren't in America anymore. There was no Sixth Amendment in the jungles of Brazil. Annaliese found a pile of banana leaves in the back corner of Mystic Origin's hut. She pulled them back in one swift motion…and there they were. A big pile of delicious, straight-from-the-tree mangoes. *That lying hippie!*

"Aha! What do you call that?"

"What do I call what?"

Annaliese glared at her and unleashed her fury.

"Look, Miss Dumpster-diver, you know exactly what I am talking about! This is not a big chain restaurant I'm living in—this is my house! This is my food! Mine! You can go and get your own food. Stay out of my hut! My god, you would think that out in the jungle you wouldn't have to guard your things like back home. What am I going to have to do? Build a fence to keep the burglars and thieves out?"

DeShunta, who was greatly enjoying being a spectator at a girl fight, said, "Oooooh" and started belly-laughing. Mystic Origin began to protest, but Annaliese wasn't finished.

"Don't even try to deny it! You were the only one here, so close your mouth!"

Mystic Origin clenched and unclenched her fists as tears of anger welled up in her eyes.

"I did not steal your fruit! I have not been inside your hut! I know what you are doing here, and it's not going to work!"

Annaliese shouted, "I'm just trying to eat the fruit that I gathered for me without having some freeloader steal it from me! What do you think I'm trying to do?"

Mystic Origin's face turned beet red as she launched her assault.

"You are attacking women of color, trying to keep us down! Well, we have voices! We won't be silenced any longer!"

Annaliese's eyes narrowed, and her nose crinkled up to express her incredulity.

"That's the dumbest thing I've ever heard! First of all, you're not a woman of color. Secondly…"

"Oh yes, I am! Don't act like you are colorblind. You hate me because of my skin! Women of color have been enslaved and worked to death and killed by politicians like you when their usefulness ended since the founding of America. Well, I refuse to be your slave and supply you with fruit!"

"You are white!" Annaliese exploded. "Look at you! You are as white as me! You just have a tan! You have…green eyes for crying out loud! Stop trying to turn this into a race thing!"

Mystic Origin's voice shook, but her anger gave her the courage to speak her mind.

"That's what the greedy and powerful always say! They got where they are on the backs of others and want to keep it all for themselves. That's exactly who you are!"

Annaliese had had all she could stand.

"Shut up! Just shut up! I'm not listening to you anymore! I picked fruit! You didn't! You stole it, and yet you are talking like you think you are entitled to it! Your legs aren't broken. You aren't in a wheelchair. Stop being lazy! Go get your own food, and stay out of mine!"

With that, Annaliese grabbed an armload of Mystic Origin's mangoes, turned on her heels and stomped back to her hut. She glared at Mystic Origin as she stormed past her. Daggers flew from both women's eyes. Mystic Origin stuck one index finger in the air. Annaliese stopped in her tracks.

"What is that supposed to mean? Are you flipping me off?"

"No. If I wanted to do that I'd use my middle finger."

Annaliese's jaw muscles were visibly tightened. She waited, certain an explanation would come. After several long seconds, Mystic Origin spat out the answer.

"One percenter! The top 1 percent have 99 percent of the wealth, and yet that's still not enough for them! That's you!"

Annaliese shook her head and resumed her mission. Mystic Origin stomped inside her hut and came out with an armload of fruit, but of a different kind.

"Look here, one percenter! Bananas! Bunches and bunches of bananas! You don't have any bananas, I'll bet, not that I would know because I haven't been inside your ugly old hut. But I don't need your mangoes! I have more fruit than I can eat! It…was…not…me!"

Annaliese was not listening. She didn't care what the crazy lady had to say. She had spent a long time last night gathering what she thought was a sufficient amount of fruit to last her a couple of days only to have it taken from her. Her mind began to work on the problem of how to secure her food so as to keep it out of the reach of thieves. She was determined not to lose one more piece of fruit.

Meanwhile out in the jungle, Aston, Chaz and the Senator had been racking their brains all day trying to decipher the landmarks on their maps. The map was clear as a bell at the start of the journey. It told them to follow the main path to the river. They took the river path and then veered off to the right at the fork just the way it was drawn on the map. The problem was that it dead ended right there, whereas the map showed that the path continued straight and then crossed a small stream. They retraced their steps and tried it again. Nope. Dead end. Again.

The Senator wanted to find Tony and tell him off for giving them a poorly-drawn map. An argument ensued about the best course of action. Aston became frustrated. Every suggestion that came out of the Senator's mouth involved running back to camp to complain to "someone in charge." Aston did not want to go back to camp. The animal totems were out here in the jungle where they were. Camp was the wrong way. The argument got heated to the point where Chaz began to shut down. He put his hands over his ears to block out the yelling by the other two men and began to pace back and forth. The fragile alliance was about to break apart.

Aston was certain the answer had to be right in front of them. He demanded the other two men give him their pieces of the map so he could study them. Chaz, who was open to trying anything, handed his over, but Senator Kingston wasn't willing to turn his piece loose. He wanted to hold it. "No way, no how will I turn loose of this map!" At this point, Aston began a harangue that could be heard all over the jungle. When he hit the ten-minute mark, the Senator finally broke down and handed his piece over, although with much protest. When Aston took all three pieces of the map and put them together himself, he realized their mistake. The Senator had been holding his piece upside down. Every time they put them together, the Senator's piece was flipped. No wonder they ran into a dead end!

When Aston unraveled the mystery and announced the breakthrough, the three men took off with renewed vigor. This time they took the left fork instead of the right. After a long trek through the jungle, they came to the edge of a shallow, sandy-bottomed stream as picturesque as anything they had seen in the rainforest thus far. They waded out into the water to cool themselves off. After a short respite, they started to climb out and resume the search when something way downstream caught the Senator's eye. He strained his vision to the limit, trying to make sense of what he was seeing. When he realized what he was looking at, he shouted for joy. There in the distance, suspended over the stream, was the snake god, just like it said on the map!

The three men made a mad dash through the water. Chaz, who got there first, climbed an overhanging tree branch to reach the precious totem. When he pulled on the carved image of the snake, a black and green flag flew up and a smoke bomb went off, scaring him so badly he turned loose of both branch and snake and fell into the water below. His teammates howled with laughter. Once Chaz came out of the water, he joined in laughing as well. They all cheered and celebrated in wild exultation underneath the Jungle Money flag.

They each took turns holding the painted wooden snake high over their heads. They didn't know where the cameras were hidden, but they wanted to give the producers plenty of memorable shots to choose from when they were putting together the show.

Three very happy men began hopping and skipping their way back to camp, laughing and talking along the way. The treasure chest's lid would soon be open! A handful of gold and jewels would soon be theirs! Aston demanded they stop and compare hands. Who had the biggest mitts? They compared palm width and finger length. They gripped hands and compared grip strength. They stopped at the side of another stream and took turns reaching down to grab handfuls of small river stones to see who could come up with the most. The Senator clearly had the biggest hands, so they agreed he should be the one to reach in the treasure chest. They debated whether he should grab a gold bar or go for the biggest handful of diamonds and jewels he could manage. Which would be the most valuable? After doing some mental calculations, the Senator announced that the average handful of treasure from that chest would be worth seven million dollars.

Aston and the Senator were so engrossed in their discussion of the value of gold per ounce and the television commercials for diamond stores that they failed to notice Chaz was no longer with them. When Aston finally noticed, he turned around in bewilderment. *Where is Chaz?* He asked the Senator, who looked around thoroughly confused as to how this could have happened.

"What do we do?" Aston asked. "I have no idea where we lost him."

The Senator swiftly weighed their options about how to go about finding their missing comrade. He felt the smooth edges of the wooden snake god and swiftly came up with the best plan.

"This is not good; not good at all," said the Senator. "After we get back to camp and show them the snake god, we should immediately tell someone in charge."

Momentarily stunned at what he was hearing, Aston began excoriating the Senator for his unbelievable selfishness. The Senator became defensive, protesting that it made no sense for them all to become lost and declaring they could search much faster and more efficiently if they left the snake god, which was quite heavy, back in camp with Tony or G or someone in charge. Then they could begin the search in earnest, unimpeded by the weight of the statue. Aston, who was no longer concerned about being in the Senator's good graces, turned heel and started back the way they just came, telling the Senator he hoped he got eaten by a jaguar, who preferred leaping on men walking through the jungle alone.

Aston only had to backtrack about a hundred yards before spotting Chaz. He was bent over looking at something on the edge of the trail. His body posture looked as though he was prepared to break and run at any moment.

"What are you looking at?" called Aston.

Without taking his eyes off of whatever it was, Chaz waved in Aston's direction as though he was trying to quiet him down. Aston hurried over to Chaz but stopped when he was still a healthy distance away. Chaz turned and looked at Aston very briefly, putting an index finger to his lips. He then pointed to the edge of the trail.

His voice so quiet it was barely audible, Aston whispered, "What are you looking at?" Before Chaz could answer, Aston spied something coiled up next to the path. It was a snake! Talk about a lucky break! Now they had a snake to go with the snake god! Aston was ecstatic, but he kept it all inside. That was potentially a million-dollar snake. If he made the wrong move and scared the snake, it would slither away and they would likely never see it again. Chaz and Aston stood side by side, scarcely moving. They were getting bitten by mosquitoes all over, but they were far too excited to care.

Their incredibly awesome day, which they didn't think could get any better, was getting better.

Together they stared, transfixed by what they saw. It was a snake, but the word "snake" didn't do it justice. Neither one had seen anything like it in their lives. They could tell—this one was special. Mesmerized, Chaz spoke in almost reverential tones.

"It shimmers. Look at it! Look at the colors! It changes color depending on where you stand," Chaz whispered with wonder in his voice. "Stand over here and look at the part where the sunlight hits it. Move your head back and forth. You won't believe this!"

Aston took a step, and the snake's head moved with him. Its tongue flicked out and tasted the air. It was primarily orange with black circles, but when he moved and changed the angle, blue, purple and green appeared and disappeared like an aura.

"How have we not heard of this kind of snake before?" Aston asked. "I don't even know if this is real. It can't be! We can't be seeing what we are seeing!"

Neither of the two young men wanted to see any snakes on this trip, but here they were on day two, gazing upon a Brazilian rainbow boa. It was like seeing the northern lights, the aurora borealis, but on a snake's skin.

"Hey, and guess what?" Aston exclaimed in whispered tones. "It's hard to tell with it being all coiled up, but I think the snake is going to be longer than the statue is tall. If so, it will meet Tony's qualifications. We are going to be elbow deep in that treasure chest, baby!"

Chaz beamed with happiness. Then a question occurred to him.

"Where's Senator Kingston?"

Aston gave him a withering look and answered, "He's not far."

A faint voice came to them, as though from a distance, and said, "Hey, I'm down here!"

Chaz and Aston looked down the path. They could make out a figure approximately fifty yards away, peeking out from behind a clump of trees.

"What are you doing down there?" Chaz asked in hushed tones.

"I'm standing guard over the snake god!" the Senator answered. "I don't want anything to happen to it!"

Chaz had an uneasy feeling wash over him. There was something unsettling about the Senator's tone. He felt a sense of urgency about catching the snake and getting back to camp as quickly as possible. He did not want the Senator to carry the snake god back to camp without them there to make sure everyone knew it was a team effort, not a solo accomplishment.

As Aston gazed at the remarkable snake, a problem came to mind.

"So, how are we going to catch him?" he asked.

"We'll kill it," Chaz answered. "That way it won't bite us, and it sure won't get away."

Aston placed his hand over his mouth and gasped. Chaz remembered who he was talking to. This was the whale harpoon guy! Aston was willing to lose body parts to keep animals alive and here Chaz was talking about killing one! *What was I thinking*? The blood drained from his face. He tried to backtrack and rewind the tape, but Aston cut him off with a sharp rebuke. Chaz's face and neck turned beet red from embarrassment.

The two men stood silently, thinking. Chaz shook off his embarrassment and focused on the mission at hand. What were the chances anyone else had found a god? Peaches, Willow and Celeste didn't have one when they ran across them earlier today. Tattoo was out of commission from the ant bite. Clarence was walking funny this morning and may not have even gone out to look. Boedy...poor Boedy. That just left Annaliese, DeShunta and Mystic Origin. If the men were the first to return to camp with an animal totem, they got treasure regardless. Maybe they didn't even need an animal.

Never taking their eyes off the snake, Aston and Chaz discussed their options.

But what if Annaliese had found the jaguar god and was on her way back to camp with it? Even though they were holding the snake god, the equivalent of a Jungle Money golden ticket, they wouldn't get a dime if they didn't get back to camp before her. The jaguar god trumped everything and everybody. If somebody had already found one of the other totems and beat them back to camp, they wouldn't get anything unless they also had an animal to go with it. When Chaz thought about all the riches in that treasure chest, and all the ways he could lose it, he was suddenly less concerned about appeasing Aston. He was pondering all these things when suddenly Aston screamed.

"It's moving! It's getting away! What do we do?"

Filled with adrenaline and desperation, Chaz grabbed a fallen tree branch lying on the ground. With a war cry worthy of a Sioux Indian at Custer's Last Stand, Chaz rushed the snake and began to pound it like a man possessed. Dirt, wood chips, sweat and snake began flying everywhere. Aston, temporarily abandoning his principles, cried out in excitement.

"Get it, get it, get it!"

Swinging wildly, Chaz hit the ground more often than he hit the snake. Finally he struck it close to the end of the tail. The snake halted its forward progress and curled back toward its attacker. Chaz jumped back and screamed. Emboldened by the thought of the prize awaiting him however, he leaped back into the fray, pounding the snake with renewed vigor. Aston screamed with joy.

"Yes! You got him! You got him!"

The snake, mortally wounded, lay twisting, writhing, coiling and uncoiling but went nowhere. Its movements slowed down. Chaz breathed like he had run a marathon. He turned to look at Aston, who was doing an Irish river dance, high-stepping and swapping his feet while shouting to the world.

"We're rich! We're rich! We're rich, we're rich, we're rich!"

Chaz's brows furrowed. *What happened to the whale harpoon guy? Isn't this the same guy who was giving me up the river two minutes ago for even thinking about killing the snake?* Chaz decided to let it go. It didn't matter. He didn't care. It was done.

The snake was dead—at least it seemed to be. Chaz threw away the big tree limb and found a smaller stick. He put the stick under the snake's body and tried to lift it but it fell off. He tried a second time. It fell off again. The balance-it-on-a-stick method of carrying the snake was not working. He needed a Plan B. Chaz studied the snake, poking it with the stick, trying to determine if it was really dead. The neck was partially severed just behind the head and the tongue was out. He was pretty sure it was dead.

"Just pick it up with your hand," Aston suggested.

"You pick it up!" Chaz retorted. "It may still be alive. What if it's like a zombie and it keeps biting after it is dead?"

"Come on, sissy," Aston jeered. "Be a man."

Chaz looked sharply at Aston, but the goofy look on Aston's face made it clear he was only joking. Chaz had been this close to letting him have it. Aston defused the situation just in time. His irritation gone, but his adrenaline and nerves still very much present, Chaz worked up the courage to pick up the snake. He stepped behind it, as far away from the head as possible. He bent over and slowly reached for the tail, like he was reaching for a live trip wire. Just as Chaz's fingers reached it, Aston shouted at the top of his lungs.

"Snake!"

Chaz jumped backwards and landed flat on his butt. Aston doubled over laughing. Spewing a string of dirty blue words, Chaz sprinted to Aston and shoved him as hard as he could. Aston fell to the trail and rolled to his side, still laughing. Propelled by an overdose of adrenaline, Chaz grabbed the snake by the tail and swung it like a pendulum, releasing his grip at just the right moment. The dead Brazilian rainbow boa landed perfectly across the side of Aston's neck and face with an audible "splat."

Aston's scream of terror so startled the Senator, even from half a football field away, that he took off in a dead run. The Senator sprinted to two large trees growing closely together and hid behind them peeking out from the gap in between. Certain that one of the boys had been bitten and was soon to die a horrible death, the Senator grieved the loss of life.

As he was grieving, he calculated what seven million dollars divided by two was.

When the Senator heard laughter and loud talking, he was thoroughly confused. He cautiously stepped out from his hiding place to see what was happening. He was greeted by the most wonderful sight he could imagine. Chaz was carrying a snake, his arm locked out straight so it was dangling as far away from his body as possible. Walking beside him was Aston, who was wiping something off the side of his face. The Senator cheered. They were going to be rich! Very rich!

"So, you said you think a handful of treasure is worth $7 million?" Chaz asked. "Divided by three, that's...what?"

They tried to do the math in their heads but simply couldn't do it. Aston stopped when they reached a sandy spot on the path. He grabbed a little pointed stick and scratched out the division problem in the sand. The answer to the equation was most pleasing. Aston had never had so much fun playing in the sand in his life.

"$2,333,333.33!" Aston screamed with delight.

"Gadzooks!" Chaz cried. "I'm going to buy an island! And a Dodge Viper! And I shall declare there is no speed limit!"

The three men, whose feet barely touched the ground, arrived back at camp thirty minutes later. Their fellow competitors were lounging around the campfire. Aston cupped his hands to his mouth and inhaled deeply. He gave a loud bugle call suitable for announcing a twelfth-century king returning from a crusade. The people around the campfire stood up. Others began to emerge from their shelters. The Senator held the snake totem over his head like a hockey player hoisting the Stanley Cup. As the men drew closer, people could tell that something was dangling from Chaz's hand—something long and serpentine. DeShunta pointed her finger at him and shouted.

"Don't you be bringing no snake around me!"

Of all the things that Chaz planned to do that night, *not* incurring the wrath of DeShunta Jackson was high on his to-do list. There was no danger whatsoever of him bringing the snake near her—primarily because that would require *him* to be near her in order to bring it, and Chaz was deathly afraid of DeShunta Jackson.

Word traveled fast. Everyone rushed to see what had just been brought into camp. Some were genuinely excited for the victorious trio. Others seemed jealous and sullen. As Clarence lay on a cot all by himself in the medical tent, having decided to take another nap in front of the fan, he was awakened by all the commotion up the hill. The ooh's and ah's and clapping and cheering made it clear somebody had just brought home a prize-winning animal god. Clarence grunted as he tried to lean up. His stomach made it difficult to sit straight up. It took him a couple of tries but he made it. As Clarence swung his legs over the side of the cot and stuck his feet into his oversized flip flops, he heard someone cry out, "You guys are rich!"

Keeping his thighs spread wide so as not to rub them together, Clarence cowboy-walked up the path to camp. When he got close and saw that the winners were Chaz, Aston and the Senator, Clarence cackled with delight. He was certain they had forgotten the rule of the day. He could not wait to remind the nancy boy, the hippie and the blowhard as to the destination of 50 percent of their winnings. He wanted to personally thank them for their selfless sacrifice which would surely save the planet from burning up.

Chapter Twenty-Nine

Earlier in the afternoon, G walked the perimeter of the staff tents to see if anyone was around. He didn't want anyone within ear shot when he called Bert. Satisfied that he was alone, he ducked inside his tent and reached for the satellite phone. Praying his phone truly had the earth as its calling area as advertised, he made the call and listened to it ring.

"Hello?"

"Bert, it's G."

"What's up, G? How's the rainforest treating you? Hey, has my main man Senator Kingston fleeced everyone's wallets and emptied the treasure chest yet?"

"No."

"Aw, man. Well, give him time. Big Brad Kingston knows how to get those campaign contributions flowing in his direction. So, how's Tony doing? Is he doing his rock star thing? Got all the ladies swooning down there?"

"Yeah, pretty much. Listen Bert, things have not gone as planned. We need to move up the pilot show. We need to get this show on the air as soon as possible."

"Why? I mean, I'm all in favor of airing the show, obviously, because that's when the ad revenue starts rolling in. What are you thinking? Try to put it together and have it ready to air in ninety days after you get back instead of a hundred and twenty?"

"No, sooner."

"How soon are you talking, G?"

"I'm talking this coming Monday."

Bert laughed. G heard him pull the phone away from his ear and yell to Beth, "Hey baby, I know you're all into the Hallmark Channel there, but G says Jungle Money's on the air in five, so tell your man in the flannel shirt under the mistletoe to hurry up and look at the girl right in front of him so they can swap slobber and box tonsils and run the credits so we can change channels and watch it."

G knew how to get Bert to dial in and get serious.

"Bert, Boedy might be dead."

"Do what?" Bert shouted. "What do you mean he might be dead?"

"He jumped out of the helicopter in a wingsuit yesterday morning, and we can't find his body."

"Holy guacamole, are you being serious right now?"

G heard Beth in the background frantically asking Bert who was dead. Bert immediately asked about Willow.

"What about his sister? Willow? How is she handling it?"

G exhaled as the weight of the crisis sat on his chest like an anvil.

"Willow is still in the game, believe it or not. She's obviously asking a lot of questions but so far not freaking out. Bert, we're dragging the river. Tamper and Bones are swimming directly in front of a stationary camera dragging the river bottom even as we speak. When they pull Boedy off the bottom, as they think they will, if the piranhas haven't gotten him yet, Richard and Steven's video cameras are going to be catching every minute of it. It's going to be horrific."

Bert shushed Beth, whose rapid-fire questions made it hard for Bert to listen or talk. G could hear by the tone in Beth's voice that she was hurt by her husband's rebuke, but at least they could talk now. Bert rejoined the conversation.

"G, we can't air this show, not with somebody dead! Not with somebody's body being pulled out of the water. That's gruesome! Nobody's going to watch that. Nobody's going to let us air that. At least I don't think they would. No TV channels. Maybe streaming, but even then…"

"Bert, I've thought every single one of those thoughts you just mentioned. The same things have been running through my mind. But think about it, Bert. Do you know how much money the three of us have sunk into this venture? Do you remember stroking that check? I do. I remember you stroking that check. I was there. It almost made you sick filling it out. But the return on that investment will make your initial investment seem like chump change. Do you know how much the treasure chest is worth? I pulled it out of a shipwreck at the bottom of the ocean and made a capital investment in this show with it. Do you know how much I paid just to get that guy in Rio to rent me the king of Portugal's crown? And the helicopters, do you know what it cost me to rent three Blackhawk helicopters for three days? Bert, I am not throwing all that investment away. We are going to get that ad revenue, come hell or high water. We just have to figure out how."

Bert started to speak, but G cut him off.

"Look, it's just us out here running the show," G said. "No one from the Brazilian government is here monitoring us. I don't think any of the dancers or performers have sat phones, at least I don't think so. But if word gets out that someone died and we get shut down, there is no "Jungle Money." All the salaries of our team members that you paid—poof. Gone. All the tents, all the supplies, all the transports, all the helicopter drops you paid for…"

"I get it, G!" Bert replied. "I get it! I don't want to lose all that money, either. What do you suggest? How do we air on Monday? How can we even do this? We don't have anything to show! The video production team is just now starting to shoot! There's no show to show! It will take three months at least for them to splice together even a halfway decent TV show, but they can't start until they have all the raw footage to splice. It can't be done! It's silly to even talk about it."

G was ready with the answer.

"Bert, hear me out. No, don't talk, just listen. They are all wearing Mini-Gos, right? We've got the stationary cameras set up at all the hotspots—the waterfall, the camp, the arena theater, the hiding places for the animal statues, and they are all sending the video straight to the production room. I've seen Wally and Jason looking at it. They are already putting it together, Bert. They were showing me this morning. They have a collection of video clips and shots you wouldn't believe. They had the clips from the first meeting at your house done a month ago. I'm telling you, between Richard, Steven, Wally and Jason, they can pull it off. They can be ready to air this coming Monday. But then we'd have to do something pretty different."

"Okay G, I'm listening. I'm panicking, but I'm trying to keep an open mind here."

"Good. That's good," G said, "because this next idea may stretch you. When we run out of prepackaged, spliced and diced magic from the production team, we're going to go Apollo 11 on them, Bert. Just like the moon shot."

Pause.

"G, I have absolutely no idea what you just said. Are you on crack? Because if you're on crack, I am not letting my kids watch the show. We have to set an example here."

"Shut up, Bert. I'm talking about going live. Right after I turned six years old, the astronauts landed on the moon. Apollo 11. They had a camera mounted on the side of their ship and had it pointed right at Neil Armstrong when he became the first man to set foot on the moon. "One small step for man, one giant leap for mankind." And NASA broadcast it live from the moon. From the moon, Bert! 1969. It was the biggest live TV event of the twentieth century. If they could do it then, we can certainly do it now. Are you in?"

"G, I'd love to but I can't. I get motion sick every time I'm on a spaceship. I get claustrophobic wearing the helmet, plus I let my passport expire. Big problem. Hey, is there a weight limit?"

"Shut up, Bert."

"Now I'm not saying I'll do it, but for the space suit, I'll need a 38 in the waist. And Windex. Lots of Windex. My face shield tends to fog up when I'm excited."

"Bert, you idiot, shut up! We can do this. I know, it would be risky. If we're beaming a particular contestant's video feed, we won't know ahead of time if he is going to be picking mangoes for the next half hour or swimming in the river or getting stung by a swarm of bees. The video team has I don't know how many monitors in their tent so they can see who has something interesting going on and switch back and forth. The problem is that they might miss something important that one of the contestants has happening to them. But I've got an idea that might just revolutionize the live reality TV genre."

"Oh, I can't wait to hear this," Bert said.

"Bert, we could have a separate channel for each contestant. Viewers could choose which contestant to roll with, so to speak. They will see their favorite contestant through the lens of the nearest videographer on the ground with them or from the nearest fixed stationary camera. If neither of those views are available, then they switch to that contestant's Mini-Go. If they want to see what's happening with another contestant, they just hit the channel changer or click on the other link to video and voilà, there they are."

"And where are all these channels supposed to come from?" Bert scoffed.

"That's where you come in, Mr. King of Cable TV. You know all those high channels you scroll through when you hit Guide on your remote and they say, "Off The Air" one after the other? Find us eleven of those, one for each contestant. I would say twelve, but Boedy… Anyway, you are always name-dropping about the big-name film and TV celebrities that come to your shows and want you to come meet their aunts and uncles and perform at their kids' birthday parties. Call in some favors. Ask. It doesn't hurt to ask."

There was a long pause, then Bert spoke.

"So, where does the ad revenue come in, G? That's why we're doing all this. These off-the-air channels can't sell advertising slots in that short a time, even if they would give us a channel on such short notice. I could more easily get us streaming live on the internet, but then what do we give MBC to show four months from now when time comes for us to live up to our contract to deliver a slick, professionally-done series called "Jungle Money?"

"We deliver exactly what we promised," G explained. "The live video feeds will be the teasers, the trailers that get viewers talking and buzzing. Then four months from now, our pro video team will have had time to put all that raw footage together to create one spectacular, unbelievably beautiful, drama-filled reality TV show, "Jungle Money," just like we promised MBC. The second time we'll bring the by-now-addicted viewers back for a totally different production, maybe including post-contest commentary by the contestants."

"Man, I don't know, G."

"Bert, it's either that or risk losing our entire investment because it never got shown at all."

"So, where does Tony stand on all this? He's the game show host in front of all the cameras. What's his take on it?"

"Well, I can't find him right this minute. He's around here somewhere. But right now, Bert, I need to know where you are on this. Go live or not?"

"Would there be a ten-second delay in case of bad language, wirty dirds?" Bert asked.

"It's whatever the station manager says it will be, but my suggestion is to have no delay at all. Let that be one of the tantalizing draws of the first run of the show. Raw, uncut, uncensored "Jungle Money," straight from the jungle to Joe Blow's living room in Topeka, Kansas. Unfiltered and in real time. What do you think, Bert?"

Bert sighed.

"I think you persuaded me when you reminded me of all the investments I have made in this thing. Let's do it. "Jungle Money Live," baby."

G stood up from his chair in the tent and pumped his fist in the air.

"That's the spirit, Bert! "Jungle Money Live"!"

Chapter Thirty

No one could find Tony. The staff was searching for him everywhere, high and low. He was not in the crew's dining tent. He was not in the arena theater. He was not at the waterfall. He was not by the medical tent or the huts. He was not dragging the river with Tamper and Bones. He was definitely not with the contestants celebrating the success of Aston, Chaz and the Senator returning to camp with a snake god and a snake snake. He was nowhere to be found. There was a reason why he could not be found.

Tony had made a friend.

Her name was Hyacinth de Sousa, but that's not what Tony called her. They met in a dance studio in Sao Paulo when the choreographer brought in the professionals who would perform with Tony as Jungle Money dancers. Tony was polite to the group of star-struck dancers, all Latin Americans, as they filed in. Each in turn said hello to the handsome celebrity in their midst. If first impressions carried any weight, Tony anticipated a fun time learning the dance routines with this group.

Then Hyacinth entered the room, and his whole world changed.

She was stunning. Her smiling eyes flashed like sunlight off a mirror. Her lashes were long. Her nose was delicate and exquisitely made. Her dimpled cheeks begged to be kissed. Her skin was a beautiful shade of bronze, perfectly smooth, the kind of skin you wanted to touch. She had long dark flowing hair, bunched up in a ponytail that reached the center of her slender back. The lines of her body were drawn by a master artist. She was feminine yet athletic, powerful yet soft and tender. She was graceful, elegant, confident and sure all at the same time.

When Hyacinth and Tony locked eyes, the look on his face was unmistakable. She smiled a shy smile, flattered at his unashamed attention, yet embarrassed since everyone was watching.

When Tony was just a boy growing up in Georgia, his Aunt Marilyn was by far his favorite. She was a fun and expressive woman. She had sayings for every occasion. At Thanksgiving, when someone asked her if Grandmother's pound cake tasted good, Marilyn would not answer with a yes or no. She would take a bite, close her eyes, smile and say "Honey, hush!" When her cousin married an extremely successful real estate developer and the family drove to see his mansion, Marilyn looked out the car window and exclaimed, "Honey, hush!" When she told the story of meeting the tall, dark and handsome man wearing dress blues at a military ball who later became her husband, her response when he asked her to dance was trademark Marilyn. She did not say,

"Yes, I'd love to"—at least, not in those words. She turned to look at her girlfriend beside her, and with a big smile she whispered, "Honey, hush!"

With those fond memories deeply engrained in his brain, it was no surprise what words sprang from Tony's lips when he first laid eyes on Hyacinth de Sousa.

"Honey, hush!"

Hyacinth was surprised. Did this man know her name already? He had mispronounced it, although the room was loud so she might have misheard him. When he said it again, however, she was certain of it. She needed to correct him.

"No. Hyacinth. Hy-a-cinth."

Tony did not understand what she said, but he loved the way she said it. He smiled his best Hollywood smile. She smiled back, treating him to the parting of ruby red lips which revealed perfect, pearly white teeth. Though she was enjoying the moment, she felt the eyes of her fellow dancers upon her and became self-conscious at the attention she was receiving. As she turned to see the choreographer, her neck and face were flushed and her heart was skipping. She did her best to even her breathing and calm herself. As the choreographer gave his instructions, she could not help but cut her eyes back to Tony to see if he was still looking. He was. She smiled a shy smile and turned back to the choreographer. It was going to take all of her willpower to concentrate on the task at hand. She was about to learn the dances that would captivate and entertain all of America.

Thus began the love affair of Tony and Honey Hush.

It had now been three months since their wonderful first meeting. Today was the second day of Jungle Money. After Mother Nature crowned Clarence Humberton as King for a Day, Tony had a few hours of free time ahead of him. The contestants had plenty to do to occupy their time between working on their shelters and gathering food, not to mention scouring the surrounding jungle for gods and animals that would yield them a small fortune. They could fend for themselves for a while. It was Tony's favorite time of day.

It was Honey Hush time.

Tony did not walk straight to his destination. He could not be obvious. He did not want them to be found out. There was an anti-fraternization/no-dating clause in the dancers' contracts. Tony probably had a similar provision in his contract, but he had never read it, so he didn't know for sure. Either way, their love was forbidden, which was most inconvenient for both of them.

Tony had discovered that if he carried the satellite phone and talked as though he could only get reception in far-flung corners of camp, he could go anywhere without being interrupted. "I'm sorry, I can't hear you. You are breaking up. Let me try over here. Hold on." He would look to the sky as though he was looking for a plane. If someone approached him, he wouldn't look at them—he would hold up one index finger to them as though he was in the middle of an important conversation and could barely hear. They always said "sorry" and quietly walked away. It worked every time. Somehow, the only place where he could get reception for these convincingly realistic, yet completely make-believe discussions was within sight of the tent of the very lovely Miss Honey Hush.

This morning, no one was around the staff tents. Tony walked quickly to her tent, opened the door flaps and ducked inside. There she was acting shocked to see him like this had never happened before. *Oh my god*, Tony thought. She took his breath away. Every single time, she took it right out of his lungs. Her ability to speak English could not compare to her native Portuguese, but it was good enough. The accent and the endearing grammar mistakes drove Tony wild. She greeted him with wide eyes and feigned surprise.

"You who invited?"

Tony stopped in his tracks. He gazed at the Brazilian beauty standing before him and in a low, smoldering voice said, "Honey, hush."

Hyacinth still did not fully understand her new name. She understood "honey." "Querida." A term of endearment. But "hush?" She had read every translation on the internet. It meant be quiet. Don't talk. Stop talking. Why would he say this to her? It was a mystery, but one that she felt no urgency to solve. She may not comprehend what he said, but she loved what he did when he said it.

Without another word, Tony walked over to her and took her in his arms. Their lips touched, a delightfully slow beginning to what would become a long, passionate kiss. His left hand held the small of her back while the fingers of his right hand traveled up and into her luxurious hair. He buried his face in her neck and breathed deeply. Her scent was intoxicating. She leaned back, secure in his arms. She reached both of her hands up to encircle the back of his neck, but only after her fingers lingered on his chest and broad shoulders along the way.

Tony's hands could not help but wander. Honey, eyes closed, placed her small hands on his big hands, although she did not hurry. His hands continued to roam, as she knew they would. She lovingly tightened her grip and guided his hands away, never stopping the kiss. Tony's breathing gave away his excitement. He smiled as he whispered in her ear.

"No ma'am. You need to keep your hands up here."

Tony took her by the wrists and lifted her hands back up to his neck. She pulled him close. He tasted her lips again. Never had he enjoyed kissing a girl like he did Honey. He was good for a minute. A minute was all he could manage. Tony resumed caressing her and began to push against her. She smiled and playfully wagged her finger in front of his face, touching his nose each time.

"No, no, no, bad boy."

Tony was tortured. He did not want their embrace to end. Ever.

"Honey, why not?"

She understood his desire, which greatly pleased her.

"My love, husband for to have save."

"But I need you now."

She wanted him to know she wanted him as badly as he wanted her, but she had a moral compass that guided her steps. What she believed was hard enough to explain in Portuguese, much less in English. Nouns and verbs she could do. It was all the other parts of speech that bedeviled her.

Tony smiled and pulled her close again. He took her face in his hands ever so tenderly and lifted it so they were looking into each other's eyes. She had the face of an angel. The rest of the world did not exist. Tony smiled his movie star smile.

This was the critical moment. She might lose him right now. She had lost other suitors over this very thing. She would be devastated if it happened, but she had one she wanted to please more. She silently prayed that she would speak the right words. She gathered herself and spoke.

"God Honey love. God Honey watch. God Honey, number one. Honey love love very."

She looked at his face, studying every expression he made, however slight, to gauge whether she had effectively explained what was in her heart. She thought of another way. She pointed at her heart.

"Tony here."

Tony smiled. Honey next put her finger on the left side of Tony's muscular chest and tapped.

"Honey here?"

Tony pulled her close for another kiss, deftly avoiding the question. Honey kissed him and smiled. She took Tony's left hand in hers, then traced a circle around his ring finger.

"Honey here?"

Tony laughed, a little nervously, shaking his head at how quickly the conversation had turned serious.

"Whoa, whoa, hold on now!" Tony pleaded. "We need to take things slow. Maybe?"

Her eyes showed a mixture of satisfaction that her point had been made but with a hint of sadness. She had laid her heart bare for him trying to answer his question as best she could. Tony saw the sadness and didn't like it. He never wanted to see her sad. Ever. He pointed at his heart.

"Honey here."

He smiled warmly and touched his nose to her nose, looking deeply into her eyes. When he did, the clouds lifted from her eyes. She smiled, and the sun came back out.

"Things take slow. But Portuguese! My English! You Portuguese!"

He laughed, grabbed her and pulled her close. He had promised her in Sao Paulo to learn Portuguese, but she was working way harder at learning English than he was at learning Portuguese. When did he have time? This sealed it, though. He needed to learn. He wanted to know what she was thinking and feeling. He loved the way she thought and felt. He wanted to know her better. *Man up Tony*, he thought to himself. *She is worth the effort. My god, she is worth the effort.*

Honey was glad that she had, at least based upon appearances, navigated the storm successfully. She released her grip on his wrists. He made a showing of good faith by caressing her with his hands going north of her shoulders rather than south. He reached around the back of her slender neck and slid the fingers of both hands up and into her full-bodied hair, then pulled her lips to his.

At that moment, they heard a voice outside. A woman was singing to herself, and her voice was getting louder. She was coming to Honey's tent! Panic struck them both. Honey's eyes flew wide. She put her finger to her lips in a desperate bid to keep Tony quiet. They could not be found out.

Tony looked around wildly. The back door to the tent was blocked by an ironing board covered with costumes, casual clothes and bathing suits. It would take far too long to move it. Tony spied the open window flap on the back wall. He did not hesitate. He ran silently on the balls of his feet and dove through the opening. His athleticism allowed him to leap out of the open window, hit the ground and roll out of sight, all in less than four seconds. Honey intended to grab a magazine off the bed and try to appear as if she was reading, but she couldn't reach it in time.

Rosa Pantalones, Honey's tent mate, opened the front door flap and entered the tent. She was clad in a bikini, having just returned from a cool dip in the river. When she saw Honey, she stopped in her tracks. Something was odd. Honey was standing in the middle of the room, eyes wide, breathing quickly, frozen in position as stiff as a board. She had a funny look on her face. Rosa's words came out fast, laced with suspicion.

"Hyacinth, what are you doing?"

Honey's heart was racing. Had she seen Tony going out the window? She had to have heard two people talking. *What should I say? Think, Honey, think!* Nothing came to mind. Not a word came from her lips. When Hyacinth didn't answer, Rosa spoke up.

"Was it a bee? It was a bee, wasn't it?"

Honey nodded quickly. *Sure. Yes, it was a bee.* Rosa shook her head in disgust.

"These tents are terrible. They don't keep out the heat. They don't keep out the bees. They don't keep out the spiders. It would not surprise me to come home tomorrow and have a monkey sitting on my bed!"

Honey nodded again. Rosa threw her towel across a chair and headed for the enclosed changing room. When she was out of sight, Honey closed her eyes, pointed her face heavenward and breathed for the first time since Tony made his break for the window. Her heart was beating out of her chest. *That was too close. If Tony was even one second slower! How did we not get caught?*

Honey covered her face with her hands and laughed silently to herself. She felt just like when she was thirteen and a boy from school snuck out of his house one night and knocked on her bedroom window. Her mother had heard the banging and asked who was there. Honey told her nobody. They hadn't kissed or anything. She didn't have time to open the window even if she had wanted to. She and the boy just laughed, then he had run away undetected. Nothing happened except for the thrill of not getting caught, which at age thirteen was delightful. She thought of nothing but that boy all the next week.

Tony's caper, however, was a hundred times better.

Chapter Thirty-One

Tamper laid on the ground, exhausted, looking at the sky. On Tamper's chest, a tattooed airborne Ranger clung to a tattooed parachute underneath the words, "Rangers Lead The Way." Bones sat in the UTV, staring at nothing in particular. If Bones hadn't been wearing a shirt, the long scar on his back, inflicted by a charging Cape buffalo, would have been visible. Bones' long hair was still wet from diving in the river over and over again. As they rested, they listened to the river, the birds and the barks from monkeys fighting over food, mates and respect for the pecking order. Tamper's frustration was evident in his voice.

"Bones, I just don't get it. Boedy's not on the river bottom. He's not in the jungle. He's not in the camp. He's not in a helicopter. He's not on any of the cameras. Where. Is. He?"

Bones quietly chewed on a twig as he studied a lizard sunning itself on the roll cage. His temperament was the polar opposite of Tamper's. Pressure rolled off him like water on a duck's back—a good trait for a big game hunting guide. He had stared down dangerous animals in dangerous situations for so many years that nothing seemed to faze him. The search for Boedy's body was no different. His words, flavored with a South African accent that was pleasing to the ear, came out measured and smooth.

"Your guess beats mine, man. It's like he just disappeared. Straight into thin air. Poof, like that. Gone."

"We can't spend the entire show off in the jungle by ourselves. We've got to run the next contest. Tony and G are wigging out that we're not there. Obviously, they want us to find him, but they need us back at camp with them."

Bones ran his fingers through his wet hair and replaced the hat that rarely left his head.

"Sucks, man. So, what's the play? Your call. I'm with you either way."

Right then, the sound of static emanated from the radio. Bones reached up to the front of the UTV and grabbed it. After listening for a few seconds, he turned back to Tamper.

"Sounds like we have a winner. They are rounding up Tony and bringing the treasure chest."

Tamper stood up and brushed wet mud off the back of his still-dripping pants.

"I don't want to miss this," Tamper said. "Boedy, wherever you are, sorry buddy. We've done all we can do today. We'll pick up the search again when we can. Let's go, Bones."

Bones turned the key in the ignition as Tamper jumped in. Ten minutes later, the two of them rode back into camp and found the contestants gathered in the arena theater. As Bones drove through the gate, they were greeted by the Senator proudly holding up the wooden snake god. Bones shouted, "Well done, man!" Tamper gave a big thumbs up. When Bones saw Chaz lift up a snake, he hit the brakes, switched off the motor, jumped out and trotted over for a closer look. Without hesitation, he grabbed the snake right behind the head with one hand while lifting the tail with the other. His eyes went wide.

"You found a rainbow boa? I don't believe this! You found a rainbow! I have always wanted to see one of these guys. Man, that is one beautiful snake!"

Clarence lumbered into view. He watched as Bones examined the snake. After a minute, something on the UTV caught his eye. He bent down and peered at the front tire.

"Well, lookie what we have here. It must be reptile day at the zoo."

Celeste stepped over to see what had captured Clarence's attention. When she saw, she wrinkled up her nose. Tamper had run over a large frog as he was driving alongside the river. The flattened frog was lodged in the tread of the all-terrain tire. Clarence grabbed it by its webbed feet and peeled it off of the tire. He held it up for all to see, then looked around for one contestant in particular.

"Hey DeShunta, I've got a little present for you—a peace offering if you will. I heard you wanted to add a little protein to your diet, so I ordered you a little takeout."

With that, he tossed the frog underhanded and watched it flip end over end and land at DeShunta's feet. She took two quick steps backwards and then looked him dead in the eyes.

"I will stab you."

The leering union boss's malicious grin disappeared as he pondered the unpleasant possibility. She might be serious. As Clarence and DeShunta each waited for the other's next move, they heard the sound of another approaching UTV.

Tony was chauffeuring three men, one of whom was a well-dressed fellow they had not seen before. Joining him were the keepers of the treasure. Excitement began to build as the realization hit the contestants. It was time to open the treasure chest for real. Richard, Steven and Summer were eagerly waiting with their cameras, ready to capture this moment from every possible angle. Tony pulled up close and jumped out, sporting a natty blue blazer and designer jeans.

"What is this I hear? Might we have a winner?"

Aston, Chaz and the Senator shouted, "Yes!" as loudly as they could. Aston and Chaz rubbed their hands together eagerly as they watched the keepers of the treasure struggle to lift the chest onto an ornate table. Tony invited the three men to come and stand beside him. None of them needed to be asked twice. They rushed forward, jockeying for position, each trying to be the one to stand closest to Tony. When the Senator leaned his shoulder into Aston to push him aside and squeeze in, Tony chuckled in amusement. When Aston retaliated with an elbow to the Senator's ribcage, Tony laughed out loud.

"Children, children! We're in the Amazon rainforest. We have 2.3 million square miles to work with here. I haven't done the math, so don't quote me on this, but I think there is enough room for all of us."

The other contestants laughed at the awkward wrestling match taking place in front of them. Tony winked at Richard, who winked back and nodded. Yes, he was catching it all on film.

"So, let's find out who won contest number one, the hunt for the gods. First of all, did anyone bring back the jaguar god?"

The contestants shook their heads.

"Okay, wow, so no one found the jaguar god; however, I understand that Aston, Chaz and Senator Kingston found the snake god. Congratulations, men! I know for a fact that it wasn't easy to find. But the snake god is not all they found. I believe you have brought something else in addition to the snake god. Bones, can you tell us what they have there?"

"Sure," Bones replied. "These guys have brought us a Brazilian rainbow boa. It's one of the most beautiful snakes in the world. They have beautiful iridescent skin as you can see. This one is a nice-sized male. The females get even bigger. He has tiny ridges on his scales which act like prisms to refract light and create a holographic rainbow effect. He's a beaut, man. Really remarkable. Hats off, guys. Well done."

Everyone clapped for the winners. Mystic Origin was the sole exception. Disgusted, she muttered, "senseless killing" and walked several paces away, talking to herself as she went. She did not go far however, as she wanted to see the treasure. Tony turned to the men he had brought with him in the UTV and nodded. They took their places by the treasure chest. Tony reached in his blazer, withdrew his hand and produced an old antique key.

"To the victors go the spoils. Aston, Bradford, Chaz, you are the victors. Alphabetically, Aston comes before Bradford and Chaz, so Aston, I will hand you the key."

Everyone packed in tight to watch Aston insert the key into the keyhole and turn it. The old locking mechanism turned inside, and the latch sprang loose. Together, Aston and the Senator lifted the lid. When sunlight hit the contents, involuntary gasps came from all around. They had already seen it once, but the sight of that much gold and jewels hit them like it was the very first time. Tony asked the men a question.

"As I told you yesterday, you are now permitted to grab one handful of treasure. There are three of you. Have you decided who will be the grabber?"

"We have," announced the Senator. "We compared hands and mine are the biggest. I will be the one to grab the treasure."

Tony gave the Senator the nod to go ahead. He smiled ruefully to himself as he thought of his secret bet with Bert and G. *Bert is going to be so happy when he finds out the Senator is elbow deep in the treasure chest.* Surprisingly, at least to Tony, the Senator grabbed a gold bar. He was unable to lift it one-handed on his first attempt, so he tried again. Aston and Chaz encouraged him to try harder. The Senator grabbed it again, squeezed with all his might and tried to lift it again.

He failed.

The 400-ounce gold bar weighed twenty-seven pounds. The Senator only knew it was very heavy and nearly impossible to pick up with one hand. By this point, Aston and Chaz were second-guessing themselves for choosing the Senator. Was he too old and weak to pull out the choicest treasure? They began to scream at the Senator like he was going for a personal record deadlift at a powerlifting meet. The Senator started growling like a bear. He gritted his teeth, dug under the bar in order to get a better grip and screamed. This time he did it.

The gold bar was theirs!

Aston and Chaz cheered as the Senator shouted in exultation. Tony leaned in to take a closer look and whistled at what he saw. Aston did a happy little river dance. When he stopped, he asked Tony a question.

"Is there any way to find out what this gold bar is worth?"

"As a matter of fact, there is," Tony said. "Let me introduce you to Miguel de Cortinas. He is a certified gemologist appraiser from Rio, who also deals in gold, silver and jewels. He is eminently qualified to answer your question. Mr. de Cortinas, can you help us out?"

The elderly Mr. de Cortinas lifted the gold bar, although it took two hands for him to do it, and peered at it through the jeweler's magnifying glass he wore on his spectacles. He turned it this way and that, straining to hold the beautiful, shiny yellow metal up to the light. He had a precision scale which he used to weigh it. Everyone held their breath as they waited to hear. Presently, he set the heavy gold bar down and flipped the magnifying glass out of his line of sight. He cleared his throat, and in a thick Portuguese accent, announced his verdict.

"This gold bar—exceptional. Size—obvious. Weight--12.24 kilograms. Opinion? Seven hundred thousand dollars U.S."

Aston, Chaz and the Senator whooped and hollered, their shouts penetrating deep into the surrounding jungle as they celebrated their once-in-a-thousand-lifetimes prize. The three men hugged and high-fived one another again and again, unable to believe the enormity of it all. After a moment however, Chaz stopped celebrating.

"Wait, hold on. Did you say seven hundred thousand?"

Mr. de Cortinas nodded. A worried look crossed Chaz's face.

"Senator? Excuse me. Senator? What happened to seven million? You said a gold bar would be more valuable than the diamonds and jewels. The man here says it's only worth seven hundred thousand."

The Senator's initial euphoria had passed. He unwrapped his arms from around Aston and thought about what he had just heard. *Didn't the gentleman say seven million something? Surely he didn't say seven hundred, did he?*

Clarence Humberton, who had retrieved his crown and was proudly wearing it on his head, cocked forward for style points, cackled with delight.

"Which one of you three stooges decided to take a bar of gold when you could have grabbed an entire handful of diamonds worth ten times that? Do you see the size of those things? What morons!"

Peaches, who had been saying the same thing to the ladies, nodded and laughed loudly along with Clarence. He looked at her, made a twisted face and said, "Duh!" She dropped her jaw, rolled her eyes heavenward and starting spinning an index finger around her ear. Their laughter infected the rest of the onlookers, although most tried to contain their smiles so as not to appear rude to the three men. Clarence then cleared his throat dramatically.

"Ahem! I said, ahem! Might I have your attention, please? This is your king speaking. His majesty, King Clarence the fourteenth, demands that you lend him your ear."

The noise from the celebration quickly became muted.

"As you will recall, I am your duly-elected king, having been appointed by the naked ape. Being a benevolent king, I enacted a rule that would benefit one, Mother Nature, two, Mother Earth, and three, those three mothers over there."

Clarence, who wore an evil grin on his face, pointed at the winners with glee.

"The Senator, Aston and Chaz have all said that global warming is a planetary emergency. Every four years, when the Senator runs for reelection, that's all we hear from him. We don't want the planet to be scorched, do we Senator? So, in order to give these guys their heart's desire, I selflessly decreed that 50 percent of the winnings from the first contest, right off the top, would go to stop climate change. And that's where it's going, right Tony? Right. Gentlemen, I want to be the first person to officially thank you for saving the world. I know you want to thank me, but you can't find the words. I get it. So the 50 percent that is left goes to you guys. Mr. de Cortinas, you are a numbers guy. What is 50 percent of $700,000?"

Mr. de Cortinas looked at Tony, who nodded, indicating it was okay for him to answer.

"Fifty percent of $700,000 is $350,000."

"Okay, so divide that into three equal shares for three equal guys and what do you got?"

"$116,666.66 U.S.," he answered.

People began to cut their eyes over to the winners to gauge their reactions. Clarence continued with his questioning of the Brazilian gemologist-turned-accountant.

"Thank you for that figuring, my good sir. But wait. I imagine that like in America, Brazil has some kind of income tax. Am I right? You know taxes, don't you?"

"Yes," Mr. de Cortinas answered. "Nonresident foreign nationals, temporary visas, stay in Brazil less than six months. Tax 25 percent at top."

"So, you knock out 25 percent for the President of Brazil to keep his grass mowed and his stogies lit, eh? Then on top of that," Clarence proclaimed, "good old Uncle Sam wants his cut. I know this from personal experience from doing a bit of online gaming. Uncle Sam takes 30 percent of your winnings even if it's from an offshore casino. Thirty percent! Can you believe that? I think it's highway robbery myself, but nobody is asking me."

Clarence then asked the question he so badly wanted to ask.

"Would you do a favor for the three amigos here and tell them what is left of their '$116,666.66 U.S.' after Brazil gets their 25 percent, Uncle Sam gets his 30 percent, and the greenhouse gases and the ozone layer get their 50 percent of the gross right off the top?"

The elderly man hesitated, knowing the answer would not be to the liking of the three men who seemed to be the center of attention. Nevertheless, he had been asked to do it, so he ran the numbers as requested. Mr. de Cortinas pecked on the screen of his phone for several agonizing minutes. He raised his eyebrows and paused. He appeared to go through the calculations again. Presently, he looked up.

"Hmm," Mr. de Cortinas mused, "Is no deduction for voluntary climate change donation. Brazil and U.S.—no tax treaty. Brazil tax…equals…minus U.S. tax…equals…hmm, okay. Three men each have, after taxes, roughly… $75,000."

An audible groan came from the Senator's throat, which instantly amplified the smug look on Clarence's face. Chaz looked at Aston and Aston looked at Chaz.

The elderly man nodded gravely and said, "There may be state tax, too. U.S. states maybe, I don't know..."

Clarence, who was beaming like he had just won the Miss America pageant, said, "I am pretty sure you have to pay a duty, a hefty tax to Customs before you can bring more than $10,000 in gold into the U.S., although you couldn't get it through the metal detector to get on the plane anyway. And don't they make you pay an extra baggage fee if your suitcase weighs more than thirty pounds?"

Clarence knew he was making up rules that didn't exist, but he didn't care. He could tell his words were having the desired effect, which pleased him greatly. Aston screamed a familiar word. It was a word known throughout much of the world, even among those who did not speak English. Clarence looked at Aston with mock sympathy.

"But just think of how much cooler it will be this time next year," Clarence said, his words dripping with sarcasm, "and we'll have you to thank!"

Aston screamed the word again, causing Clarence to laugh a black-hearted laugh. Aston screamed the word yet again. Clarence said, "Yes!" Every time Aston screamed the word, Clarence said, "Yes!" Scream. "Yes!" Scream. "Yes!"

The Senator was gasping, desperately looking at every face for a sign that this was a sick joke. He thought he knew the current price of gold per ounce, but he must have done the math wrong. He would begin a sentence, cut it off mid-thought, and then start a new one. He looked to Tony for help. No help came. Celeste said she was sorry, though she bore no guilt in the matter whatsoever.

Chaz was neither moving nor speaking. He was seething. His fists were clinched. His nostrils were flared. He was breathing quickly. His eyes were slits. They were fixed on the gloating face of Clarence Humberton. Clarence was beaming, pleased with himself beyond measure. Clarence was so focused on Aston's anguished cries that he never saw Chaz coming.

Chaz grabbed a piece of firewood, silently sprinted the ten or so steps between him and Clarence and leaped like a panther. He split Clarence's forehead open in a shower of blood and never slowed the blows. He smote Clarence with all the power and fury of an unmedicated psychopath.

Too shocked to move, the others stood immobile. The sound of the struggle reached the tents of the cast and dancers, but they did not leave their area to investigate. They were under strict orders not to interact or interfere in any way. Things would happen during the filming of Jungle Money, some unexpected, some even terrible. The cameras needed to capture them. The video could not be ruined by the presence of non-contestants. Those raw, unscripted moments could not be duplicated. They could not be redone. There were no "do-overs." There were no "Cut, Take 2's." As concerned as they were about what they were hearing, the cast dared not intervene.

Surprisingly, the first one to intervene was Willow. The diminutive girl charged into Chaz, who was growling like an enraged animal and knocked him away from his victim. He quickly threw her off and resumed his attack.

Tony looked around frantically for Bones and Tamper, who had left no more than a minute earlier when they lost interest when the subject turned to calculating taxes. Fortunately, they were still within earshot. Tamper and Bones roared back into the arena theater, jumped out and leaped into the fray. Together they tackled Chaz and pinned him to the ground. Chaz bit someone's arm. Tamper secured an elbow lock and began torquing the joint. Chaz's cries changed from howls of rage to high-pitched screams of pain.

Tony turned in the direction of the medical tent and screamed for Dr. Jane. Clarence was dazed and had blood running down his face. The Senator was still in shock, pacing, hands pressed against either side of his head, asking, "How can this be? How can this be?"

Aston, fighting panic, looked to the Senator. He frantically searched the Senator's face, hoping to see a sign that such a powerful man could reverse the financial travesty that was happening. When he saw the helplessness in the Senator's eyes, he turned to look at Tony. He found no comfort or hope there. Tony gave no sign that Clarence's pronouncement of the destination of the winnings was inaccurate in any way. The realization set in that Aston was truly going to lose almost all of his winnings to taxes.

Bones stood to his feet, satisfied that Tamper's joint lock on Chaz's elbow had the wild man under control for the moment. Chaz was still growling and trying to get at Clarence. Bones had no intention of allowing him to re-enter the ring. In a menacing tone, Bones barked, "No! Don't even think about it. Get hold of yourself, man."

Dr. Jane arrived and began tending to Clarence. The white towel she pressed to his forehead was quickly stained a bright red. She cradled Clarence's head in her lap. He began to revive. His eyes fluttered open. His foggy brain tried to make sense of the chaos around him. He sat up with the help of Dr. Jane.

Aston watched as Dr. Jane brought a cup of cold water to Clarence's lips. Clarence became strangled and coughed violently. Aston silently wished Clarence would die but then felt instant remorse for his evil thought. He was not a violent man by nature. Despite Clarence's rude and crude Yankee ways, he looked rather pitiful with a split and bleeding forehead trying not to drown from a drink of water.

For a split second, Aston felt a smidgen of empathy for the older man. Their eyes met. Holding his anger in check, Aston tried to demonstrate his humanity. Surely he had the ability to demonstrate compassion in the midst of conflict and strife.

"So, are you going to make it?"

Clarence's eyes instantly changed from unfocused and watery to crystal clear and ice cold.

"I don't know, nancy. You paid your taxes yet?"

At that, Aston went quite mad. He screamed in fury and charged. Clarence remained on the ground but drew back his fist, determined not to go down without a fight. Dr. Jane screamed as Aston descended upon them both. Bones rushed in from the side and thrust his shoulder into Aston's ribcage, forcing all the air out of Aston's lungs in one violent whoosh. Bones wrapped his arms around Aston's middle, lifted him and continued driving his legs. Bones' momentum carried them away from Aston's intended target. Aston kicked, causing Bones to trip and fall. They went down hard and began rolling.

Off to the side of the fray, Tony turned to Richard. For the moment, Richard was completely focused on capturing the drama unfolding before him. Tony tapped Richard's shoulder to get his attention. Richard looked up. Tony made a questioning thumbs up sign. In response, Richard nodded. He was capturing the action—all of it. The corner of Tony's mouth curled up ever so slightly. He knew this was TV gold.

Glancing around and seeing that his attackers had been neutralized, Clarence began to regain his composure. He stood shakily to his feet.

"Wow Tony, can you believe how some people react to paying their taxes? None of us like it, but jeez. But I can fix it. I'm still the king, right? As king, I hereby declare that there shall be no more global warming taxes. Aston and Chaz and the Senator have saved the world, so the rest of us can breathe easy. From here on out, winner takes all."

Clarence's pronouncement lifting the onerous tax surprised no one. He had missed competing in the first contest due to a combination of a groin injury and crotch fungus. After a day of recuperation, however, Clarence was off the injured reserve list. Barring disability from a brain injury, Clarence intended to win whatever the second contest might be. Realizing that he had lost his crown, Clarence began to look around to see where it had landed. Peaches, who had grabbed it off the ground before it could be damaged, handed the crown back to today's king. Clarence placed it back on his head and adjusted the fit. He reached for the white cloth held by Dr. Jane and dabbed his forehead. Seeing fresh blood, he started to tell her to meet him at the tent when a familiar voice stopped him.

"Hey king, look here."

Clarence turned to see DeShunta, who had an uncharacteristic smile on her face. She stood in front of the stage with what appeared to be a stick in her hand. Satisfied she had Clarence's attention, she began to walk unhurriedly toward an object on the ground. Leaning down with no small degree of difficulty, DeShunta took her stick and jabbed it into the object. Standing erect, she held it out for all to see.

"This here is a dead frog."

At the end of her stick there was indeed a skewered, tire-flattened frog. DeShunta adjusted her grip on the stick, holding it in the middle and turning it so the other end of the stick could be seen. This was no random stick. This was the carved wooden stick topped with a carved wooden frog that had been stuck in the dirt of the potted fern placed alongside the red carpet at the helicopter landing, which DeShunta had been using as a back scratcher for the last day and a half.

"This here is a frog god."

The others around her, including Clarence, all stepped forward to get a better look. Sure enough, there at the end of the stick was a small frog carved into the wood. The dead frog dangling from the other end was decidedly larger than the carved frog on the opposite end of the stick that held it aloft.

"I could have had the jaguar or the snake where they stuck in them plants, but I wanted the frog. I like frogs. They don't bite nobody. They just chill in the water, eat flies and croak."

Eyes began to widen and jaws began to drop as a possibility dawned on them. Tattoo, who had slipped in unnoticed, asked the question on everyone's mind.

"That's not a god, is it? It's too little."

All eyes turned to Tony for the answer. He was taken aback by this turn of events. Before he could answer, DeShunta made out her case.

"You tell me why it ain't a god. Everybody knows there's a big map right over here and what's it got drawn on it? A jaguar, a snake, and…"

She paused for effect.

"…a frog."

Tony did not respond. Determined not to lose her momentum, DeShunta walked over to the big map and unrolled it. Tapping a point on the map, she lifted up the corner and displayed it to Tony.

"Look right here up at the top. A carved frog. Look right here in my hand. Carved frog. Look right here at the end of my stick. Flat frog. Look like we got ourselves a winner."

Without waiting for permission or approval, DeShunta walked to the treasure chest. Stunned into silence, the others watched open-mouthed as she strode up to Mr. de Cortinas.

"Who told you to close that treasure chest? You better get that thing back open."

Mr. de Cortinas looked at Tony. Everyone stood with bated breath, waiting for his answer. Tony shrugged his shoulders…and then nodded. DeShunta smiled as the man reopened the chest. She raked her hands across the surface of the treasure, dragging coins and jewels close to her. She sorted through the mound of shiny gold and glittering diamonds until she found one she liked. She grabbed it along with a handful of others and walked over to the elderly man to show him what she had.

"How much this pink one worth?"

Mr. de Cortinas flipped down his magnifying glass and examined the diamond. He looked back at DeShunta and nodded appreciatively. After a minute or two of study, he announced his verdict.

"Fifteen carat pink diamond. Exceptionally rare. Clarity good. Color magnificent—very rare. At auction, bidding would start…"

DeShunta cocked her head sideways so that her ear was facing him. She wanted the soundwaves from his vocal cords to hit her eardrum as soon as possible.

"…five million U.S."

DeShunta shrieked and threw her hands in the air. The other ladies clapped and laughed with glee. She asked Mr. de Cortinas a question but stared at Clarence while she asked it.

"And how much is 100 percent of five million dollars?"

Before he could answer, Clarence butted in.

"Okay smarty pants, but you've still got to pay a 25 percent tax to Brazil and a 30 percent tax to Uncle Sam."

DeShunta didn't miss a beat.

"Hey Mr. de Cortinas, how much one of them shady tax lawyers in Rio that get you out of paying taxes—how much an hour?"

"About twenty-five hundred Brazil real per hour, which is maybe five hundred U.S."

DeShunta clenched her fists and did a choo choo train dance, which brought laughter from all save Clarence. Peaches could barely contain herself. She walked over and high-fived DeShunta, who was only too happy to oblige her. After the celebration ended, DeShunta once again turned to Clarence, who stood with a sour look on his face.

"Thanks for the frog, fat boy," she said with relish.

With that, DeShunta turned her face to the sky and laughed like a villain in a cartoon who had just taken over the world.

Tony shook his head and chuckled, amazed at the turn of events. As he turned to walk out of the arena theater, he almost walked straight into G. The mastermind of Jungle Money was standing right behind him, arms folded, grinning like a Cheshire cat. G began slapping one palm against the other, sliding it off the side after each slap. Tony knew what that motion meant. G was gloating. He had bet on DeShunta. His girl DeShunta was $5 million to the good, and then some, giving G a huge head start towards winning the bet with Tony and Bert. G was rifling through a fat stack of imaginary Benjamins—Tony and Bert's Benjamins to be precise.

Chapter Thirty-Two

The contestants hoped there would be a dinner show featuring a lavish banquet to celebrate the end of contest number one, and they were not disappointed. The austere living conditions, including the requirement that they hunt and gather their own food, were apparently lifted when someone won a contest. The performance in the arena theater that night was nothing short of spectacular. Everything was on fire. Torches blazed around the perimeter. The dancers danced inside rings of fire. The male performers twirled batons lit on fire. One of the men was a fire-eater. Another held flammable liquid in his mouth and spewed it out through a torch, transforming himself into a human flamethrower.

The lead female performer, introduced to them as Hyacinth de Sousa, was stunning. Tony needed no introductions. He knew she was stunning long before this show. He could not keep his eyes off of Honey Hush's impossibly small waist and curvy hips. Her silver ankle bracelets and toe rings sparkled against the background of her smooth bronze skin. She knew Tony was looking and loved the attention. When the dancers came down from the stage, Honey grabbed Tony and together they formed the beginning of a conga line. One of the other female performers danced up to Clarence with a seductive smile, pointed at him and curled her index finger to the sky. Clarence was only too happy to follow her. Everyone got out of their seats with a joyous shout and hopped in line. Even the stodgy old Senator and uptight Annaliese joined in.

As the musicians and drummers played their frenzied dance music, the conga line made two circles around the arena theater. On the second go-round, Honey Hush led them to a pathway of smoldering embers. She smiled mischievously as she watched Tony's face register what they were about to do—fire walking. She knelt down to remove his shoes from his sockless feet but Tony danced away, unashamedly terrified at the thought of stepping on fire. Honey placed her hands on her hips and laughed at his cowardice. When Tony bailed out, so did the rest of the competitors. The male performers, who were already barefoot, quick-stepped across the hot coals and continued the dance when they reached the end without ever missing a beat.

Celeste slipped out of the conga line before it made the second loop. She didn't feel well at all. The lighter fluid and smoke wafting through the air reminded her of the odious smell of gasoline—not one of her favorite smells. As she made her way back to the table, the scent of half-eaten fish wafted through the steamy jungle air and invaded her nostrils against her will. She was suddenly hot. Nausea began to creep uninvited into the back of her throat. She tried to imagine she was lying on her back on an iced-over Canadian lake wearing only her underwear with a cold north wind blowing across her body. She closed her eyes and plugged her fingers in her ears to block out all sight and sound and focus on the mental image of the frozen lake. Not today, nausea, she thought to herself. Not today.

She was winning the battle of wills—but then she felt a hand resting unbidden on the back of her right shoulder. The hand was huge, and the hand was hot. Another hand, equally large, planted itself on the back of her left shoulder—also hot. The beautiful imaginary frozen lake began to vanish. Clarence Humberton's hot breath, reeking of fish, entered her left ear with his request that she slow dance with him. His hot fish breath filled her nasal cavities before she could pinch her nose to keep it out. Her stomach churned and bile rose in her throat. Nausea overwhelmed her. She jumped out of her chair and ran a few steps but couldn't hold it in.

Celeste vomited up everything she had ever eaten, all to the beat of the Jungle Money band. If there was any bright side to it at all, a few chunks splattered on the top of Clarence's nearest foot. She prayed that the cameras were trained on the dancers and not on her.

DeShunta noticed and rushed over to help. She was surprised to see Celeste down on her knees, moaning softly. She couldn't tell if she was hurt or sick.

"Hey baby, what's wrong? What's wrong, huh? You not feeling good? Tell me what's wrong."

Tony caught movement out of the corner of his eye. Someone had collapsed on the ground, but he couldn't see who it was. He sprinted over and dropped to a knee, sliding to a stop next to her. Tony could tell by the color of her face that she was nauseous. Sure enough, she vomited again. Tony leaped out of range with catlike quickness before anything could splatter on him. DeShunta held her hair back while she puked.

"Go on, get it out. That make you feel a little better, baby?"

Celeste spit out the bad taste in her mouth. After a couple of spits, she nodded. DeShunta, still holding her hair, looked up at Tony.

"She need a doctor. She dehydrated. She need to be seen. Probably need a ultrasound."

Celeste was quietly moaning as she stared at the ground. As if puking in public on camera wasn't bad enough, why did she have to deal with DeShunta insinuating that she was pregnant? Why did she keep saying that?

Dr. Jane was summoned. She helped Celeste into a chair and took her temperature. No fever. None of her vital signs were abnormal. Her stomach didn't hurt when pushed and poked and prodded. She was a little dehydrated. Dr. Jane debated hooking her up to an IV and giving her some fluids. As she pondered the possibilities, food poisoning came to mind. That seemed unlikely, however, since no one else was sick and Celeste hadn't eaten much to begin with.

DeShunta looked at Dr. Jane and made a curved hand gesture in front of her belly, tracing an imaginary baby bump. Dr. Jane looked at Celeste. Celeste quickly shook her head no. *I'm not pregnant.*

Dr. Jane thought about the inventory of medical supplies she had in her tent. She had not packed any early pregnancy tests. She never thought there might be a need for such a thing. Pregnancy was a possibility worth checking out however. Unfortunately, there was no pharmacy or drug store around the corner where she could procure one. The only way to get to one required climbing aboard a helicopter.

Celeste pushed off the chair and, with Dr. Jane and DeShunta steadying her, stood to her feet. Dr. Jane radioed for Tamper to bring the UTV so she could take her to the medical tent, get her rehydrated and observe her for an hour or so. By this point the dance party had come to an end. The drummers stopped drumming when they saw the medical emergency. No one wanted to dance near Celeste's table for obvious reasons. The contestants grabbed their torches and began to make their way back to the huts.

G stepped up to Tony and grabbed his arm to get his attention.

"Tony, I talked to Tamper. He's calling off the search for Boedy. Says he's looked everywhere he knows to look. He and Bones are supposed to run tomorrow's contest. He can't keep looking, and we can't spare him anymore. We need to talk to Willow."

Tony agreed, but he wasn't sure what to say or how to say it. G spied Willow as she was about to exit the arena theater. He called her name. She turned to watch the two men coming towards her. The somber look on her face indicated that she was desperate for news about her brother, but she feared the worst. G tenderly placed a hand on her shoulder.

"Willow, I hate to say it, but we can't find your brother. We have looked everywhere—land, water, trees, river bottom, and everywhere in between. Tamper and Bones have spent two days looking. Nothing. Boedy has vanished without a trace. We don't know where else to look."

G held his breath, knowing the waterworks were about to start. Much to his surprise, however, Willow did not cry. Her eyes were sad, but he didn't see any tears.

"I understand, Mr. G. I do. My brother has been doing things like this his whole life—going off where nobody can find him. That's the way he likes it. That's why every time we say goodbye to each other, I hug him and say, 'Just in case.' He's not a hugger, but just in case it's the last time I ever see him, I want a hug. So he'll say, 'Just in case,' and let me hug him. He can take care of himself. He always does. But if not, he did it his way all the way to the end."

G and Tony studied Willow's face to see if there was more, but she was finished. There must have been many times when she didn't know if or when she would see Boedy again. She had been preparing for this eventuality her entire life. She turned and walked away. The two men watched in wonder as she made her way back to the huts. She didn't ask whether they would keep on looking, ask to be flown home, or ask any questions at all. G was prepared to talk with her about the possibility of trying to find hunting dogs or search-and-rescue dogs and flying them in, but she didn't wait around. She was done.

After she was gone, Tony wiped his hand across his forehead and said, "Phew. That was fun."

"Yeah, wasn't it?" G replied. "She'll want to talk again tomorrow, especially when she sees Tamper and Bones doing Jungle Money things."

"Probably so," Tony agreed. "Well, I'm beat, G man. Time to head back to my four-star canvas palace. My cot awaits. Let's do it again tomorrow."

G watched Tony hurry through the darkness to catch up to a dancer carrying a torch. She seemed all too happy to share her torchlight with him. G was about to turn and go when he noticed their faces appeared to touch. G strained his eyes to see, but the distance and the dark prevented it. It must have been the smoke from the torch that created the illusion. He slapped at the mosquitoes that had taken up formation by his right ear and headed back to his tent.

Meanwhile, a mile away from the arena theater, the river flowed endlessly underneath the darkening sky. The water above the falls was quiet, a mere murmur which gave no hint of the maelstrom below. The quiet ended when the water fell. Hundreds of thousands of gallons of dark water plunged over the sheer drop every minute. Though it was too dark to see, a perpetual mist hung in the air, rising up into the atmosphere from the roiling waters beneath.

The roar of the waterfall sounded throughout the cave hidden behind the cascade, but no one heard it. The still form of Boedy Da lay exactly where it had crash-landed yesterday. Flies had feasted at will all day, and with the night came the mosquitoes. They were the only ones who knew where he was, and they weren't talking.

No one would ever find Boedy's body in the cave behind the waterfall.

Chapter Thirty-Three

Although it was far too dark to see, Tony opened his eyes in the inky blackness of his canvas bedroom and stared at the ceiling. He reached for the watch on the nightstand. Upon finding it, he felt for the stem and squeezed. A tiny green light told him it was 2:05 a.m.

Tony had been laying in his cot for over three hours, but sleep had eluded him. It wasn't the heat that kept him awake. The electric fan blew enough cool air across his legs to make the heat bearable, and the generator that powered it was as quiet as a refrigerator. It wasn't the infernal mosquitoes that made it through the gauntlet of tent flaps, screens and zippers, although they certainly didn't help.

He was worried about Celeste. She was on her hands and knees retching when he had last seen her. Tony didn't do vomit. No actual smell was required to disable him—he gagged just thinking about vomit. Dr. Jane told him she would take care of her. She said she probably just ate something that didn't agree with her. She escorted Celeste to the medical tent and gave her some pink liquid antacid. Just after midnight, Dr. Jane poked her head in Tony's tent as he had instructed her to do. She had convinced Celeste to eat a saltine cracker. That was the good news. The bad news was that Celeste asked the doctor if she had a jar of cold pickles. Dr. Jane didn't think it was bad news, but it was bad news to Tony.

After getting the report from Dr. Jane, Tony found his satellite phone and called Bert not caring what time of night it was. Bert's incoherent speech made it clear he was fast asleep. Tony begrudgingly told Bert that he had bet on the right horse because Senator Kingston was the first one out of the starting gate to win some treasure. Bert cackled with glee. When Tony recounted DeShunta's unorthodox victory and how she won at least five million dollars simply by stabbing a dead frog that Clarence threw at her with a wooden froggy party favor, Bert could not believe it. He accused G of orchestrating her victory and demanded a congressional investigation into G's shenanigans.

Tony then explained the dilemma he faced with Celeste getting violently ill in the arena theater and his desire to get the girl checked out more thoroughly than they could do in the jungle. The story about Celeste's nausea jogged Bert's memory.

"You know, come to think of it, Celeste blacked out at my house during the meet-and-greet. Hit the floor and everything. She passed it off by saying she just stood up too fast."

Bert's reply alarmed Tony, who had not heard that story before. Tony hung up with Bert and began to pace around his tent. Should he be worried, or should he simply chalk it up to a girl with a sensitive stomach who would be fine in the morning?

Tony wanted a second opinion and knew where to go to get it. He slipped through the darkness with the help of a pen light to Honey Hush's tent. It was difficult to get Honey's attention without waking her roommate, but he managed to get her outside undetected. He told her about the stomach medicine and the saltine. Honey told him not to worry—Celeste just ate something bad. She would be perfectly fine in the morning.

As they sat there in the dark, Tony gave Honey the backstory on Celeste including the murder of her father. The language barrier made parts of the story difficult to communicate, but she got most of it. Celeste's story tugged at Honey's heart strings. They sat quietly and stared into the night serenaded by the scratchy legs and wings of a hundred million insects. Honey began to yawn. She leaned her head against Tony's shoulder and closed her eyes. Tony felt her body relax and her breathing slow. She was sound asleep against his arm.

Almost as an afterthought, Tony casually mentioned the girl's odd request for a snack. As soon as Honey heard the word "pickles," she snapped out of her dream and startled awake. Pickles changed everything. Honey did an immediate 360 on her opinion. Celeste needed a pregnancy test—no question about it, as well as an ultrasound if the test turned out to be positive.

That was what DeShunta had said—an ultrasound. Tony felt a little inner voice telling him to follow her recommendation. Celeste wasn't supposed to be pregnant. The medical exam on file said she wasn't, although that was patient history as opposed to a clinical test. But what if she was? Celeste may have signed an airtight waiver, release and covenant not to sue, but her fetus, if indeed there was one, had not. That was a problem.

Tony returned to his tent, but sleep eluded him. When the eastern sky showed the first hint of light, Tony got up and stood outside the door to his tent. All was quiet except for the earliest of birds and the last of the late-night crickets. After a fitful night's sleep, Tony had made up his mind. He was willing to get Celeste a pregnancy test and even an ultrasound if she needed it, but he was stumped as to how to do it. The logistical problems associated with getting Celeste from the middle of the Amazon rainforest to a medical facility with an ultrasound machine were daunting. He needed to seek the advice of someone who excelled at logistics.

Tamper might still be in the mess hall if he hurried.

When Tony stepped inside the mess hall tent, the aroma of fresh coffee called out to his olfactory nerves like a lover after too much time away. He was glad to see Tamper standing there holding a paper cup filled with steaming hot coffee, blowing on the surface to make it cool enough to drink. He was wearing a backpack covered in carabiner clips and paracord with a hatchet and a saw strapped to the back. He wore a belt with a machete strapped to one side and a pig-sticking knife, a multi-tool and a radio secured to the other side. Tony shook his head and grinned as he approached.

"Hey Tamper, just for fun, let's you and me head to the airport real quick, roll up to the security checkpoint metal detector and see what happens if you run through it. I'll stream it live on social media. Bet you get a bunch of likes. 'Hey y'all, Tamper dot com! Like and subscribe!'"

Tamper chuckled despite the early hour.

"Sure, let's do it," Tamper replied. "I can see the headlines now: 'Retired Army Ranger shot ninety-seven times at Rio de Janeiro International Airport because Hollywood heartthrob Tony Longino wanted to see what would happen. In what doctors call a medical miracle, the deceased lived long enough to shove every tool and weapon he owned up Tony's…'"

Tony cut him off.

"Hey, hey, hey! No need to get violent! I'm a lover, not a fighter. Plus I'm not fifty, so it's way too early in my life for a colonoscopy, but thanks for offering."

After a couple of more minutes of good-natured bantering back and forth, Tony brought Tamper up to speed on the Celeste dilemma. Tamper excelled at solving logistical problems. He listened quietly to Tony's story. When Tony finished, Tamper told him to eat breakfast and let him worry about it. Tamper walked out of the tent and disappeared.

Before Tony could finish his eggs and bacon and throw his Styrofoam plate away, Tamper tapped him on the shoulder. He had spent the last half hour on the satellite phone. Using his vast array of contacts, Tamper had made arrangements that no one outside of the Pentagon could have made in such a short amount of time. He had a bird on the way and a doctor in Rio de Janeiro for Celeste to see. Tamper then asked who was going with her.

Who is going with her? Good question, Tony thought to himself. Celeste was nauseous again this morning, or so he had been told. She felt lightheaded. Ideally, she should be accompanied on the helicopter ride by a doctor. The problem was that Dr. Jane was the only doctor in camp. She could not leave everyone else unattended while she escorted one lone contestant to a doctor's office. There was at least one medical emergency a day. Just yesterday, Dr. Jane had stitched up Clarence's forehead from his hairline to his left eyebrow. Clarence was a terrible patient who disregarded every piece of medical advice she gave him. Dr. Jane needed to be there to tend to him if nobody else.

So, who could go with Celeste? Even if Tony was a medical doctor, he couldn't go with her. He was the one running the show. Tamper couldn't go. So who did that leave? Tony mulled over the possibilities. Then the answer dawned on him.

Honey.

While they were getting to know one another during rehearsals in Sao Paulo, Tony and Honey discovered an app on their phones which translated English to Portuguese and Portuguese to English. Tony asked her what she did when she wasn't dancing. Honey said she worked somewhere medical related. A doctor's office maybe or a dentist's office. Or could it have been a drug store? Tony couldn't remember. He had tried to listen, but he was distracted. Every time he was around her, he had trouble thinking clearly. She was too beautiful. Honey was frequently annoyed with his questions. She would remind him they had talked about that very thing just the day before. It wasn't Tony's fault. Any mere mortal man would have trouble listening and retaining when talking to Honey Hush.

After a moment's pause, Tony told Tamper he knew just the person to accompany Celeste on the helicopter. Hyacinth De Sousa. Tamper looked at him funny. The dancer? Tony explained that Hyacinth was a certified nursing assistant who, at one time, worked at a radiology facility specializing in ultrasounds.

Tony might have fibbed a little.

Tamper looked at Tony without speaking or reacting, just studying his face. Tony realized he was being watched for signs he was lying. Tony often pulled things out of the lamp when he wanted to make something happen, and the truth was inconvenient. Tony had learned a survival technique long ago. If you don't know what you are talking about, but you must say something, say it fast, say it with authority, don't break eye contact and don't back down. Repeat it again if necessary. Most importantly, never ever back down.

Tamper's eyes had a missile lock on Tony's. It was as though he was reading his soul. Tony held his confident stare as long as he could. Finally, Tony broke the staring contest and turned his eyes away. Tamper knew Tony was feeding him bologna and calling it filet mignon, but was there really a down side to Tony's proposal? Did it really matter who flew with her? Tamper thought it through beginning to end, just as he thought all things through. There was a relatively small chance that Celeste would need medical care during the helicopter flight to the medical facility in Rio. Tamper's skills in emergency field medicine were considerable so he could fill in for Dr. Jane to a limited degree, but he would much rather have her here. After weighing the options, Tamper nodded. He was okay with it. Tony seemed relieved. He told Tamper he was going to notify Hyacinth that her medical skills were needed.

Chapter Thirty-Four

Although Tony and the rest of the staff were already in high gear, morning had not yet made its presence known at the quiet campsite where the contestants were still sleeping. Night was not ready to leave. Day was not yet welcome. Morning was still resting comfortably under a blanket of dew, serenaded by crickets who preferred to perform when the house lights were low. Dawn had broken, but the sun would not make its appearance for another hour or so.

The competitors had needed a good night's sleep, and fortunately they got it. Although the fighting and name-calling of the day before would not soon be forgotten, everything always seemed a little brighter in the morning. The first contest was over. Today the contestants would find out what the second contest would be. Pleasant dreams of the treasure chest had sailed through the brain waves of more than one sleepy head that night.

Mystic Origin and DeShunta were the first to arise. Both had bladders too full for their owners to ignore. As DeShunta crawled out from under the stage, she saw a head full of dreads coming out of a hut at the opposite end of camp. Her nose wrinkled when she saw who it was.

Ugh. Head lice hippy.

DeShunta didn't like anything about Mystic Origin. She didn't bathe, she didn't participate, and she didn't make a lick of sense when she opened her mouth. Yesterday, DeShunta learned that Mystic Origin ate out of dumpsters on a weekly basis, not because she had to, but because she liked it. Now DeShunta had another reason not to like her.

Mystic Origin was about to beat her to the one-seater privy.

DeShunta could tell that Mystic Origin quickened her steps when she saw they were headed to the same destination. *Oh no you don't! Rude!* Her nostrils flared. It was too early for niceties. DeShunta had to pee, and she didn't intend to wait.

"Hey, hey, hey. Where you going? You seen me walking this way first. I know you ain't about to cut."

Mystic Origin, never breaking stride, cut her eyes at the slower woman.

"You can wait your turn."

Mystic Origin slipped inside the door to the privy, turned around, dropped her pants, seated herself and began to pee. She stared at her bare feet. Her toenails were getting a bit long even for her. Suddenly, a shadow fell across her feet.

"I done told you. You ain't about to cut."

DeShunta cuffed the right side of Mystic Origin's head with an open-handed slap. To her credit, she didn't swing with full power. She wasn't trying to hurt—it was more of an attention-getter. Mystic Origin, who had not seen the blow coming, was knocked over onto her left side. When she looked up and saw her attacker, she screamed with rage.

"You stupid! Why did you do that? What is wrong with you? Now my pants are wet!"

"Why you peeing all over the seat?" DeShunta demanded. "Stop it! That is rude and unclean. Haven't your mama never taught you about using the bathroom?"

With that, DeShunta pushed her the rest of the way off the seat. She then backed up to the seat herself, never taking her eyes off of Mystic Origin, and dropped her pants. There was a whole lot of DeShunta, none of which Mystic Origin wanted to see. She paralyzed Mystic Origin with a ferocious glare. *Say something*, her eyes said. *See what happens.*

Initially stunned into immobility, Mystic Origin broke free of the spell that DeShunta cast on her. She was normally a devout pacifist, but not today, not after this rude awakening. Facing DeShunta, she stomped her foot out wide, like a sumo wrestler at the start of a match. Once in position, she squatted and peed right there on the dirt floor of the privy, staring at DeShunta all the while. DeShunta had not anticipated that reaction. Her raised eyebrows evidenced her surprise.

At that moment, from outside the privy, came Peaches' syrupy-sweet Southern drawl. She was blissfully unaware of the chaos within.

"Is anyone in there?"

The angry combatants within the privy shouted their answer in exasperated unison.

"Yes!"

Peaches recoiled as though she had been shot.

"Good lord, somebody sure is grumpy this morning! Are there two of y'all in there?"

"Yes!" they screamed, with even more volume and irritation than before.

"I was just asking, sheesh! You don't have to yell at me! It ain't like there's two potties around here. Y'all finish what you're doing. I believe I'll just wait."

Her sensibilities wounded, Peaches walked back up the path toward her hut. She could hold it another few minutes if she had to. As she neared the campsite she heard someone cough. Tattoo emerged from his hut. He took one step and almost fell. His foot was hooked on his blanket. He kicked it back inside the doorway and started down the path to the privy. Peaches looked at his arm as they neared one another.

"How's your arm? Is it still hurting?"

Tattoo showed her his hand. It was still slightly swollen and the skin was redder than the rest of his arm, but it was clearly better than the day before.

"No, it don't hurt no more. It just itches."

Peaches shook her head sympathetically. She thought about where he was most likely headed.

"If you are going to pee, be careful down there. It's a bit crowded. Some people woke up on the wrong side of the bed. You might want to go in the woods."

Tattoo scoffed at her advice. He wasn't about to bare his backside and go number two in a mosquito-infested jungle when he had a perfectly good privy to use.

"I ain't scared. I'll get them moving down there."

Peaches smiled a wry smile as she continued up the path. *Sure you will, buddy. Good luck with that.* About that time, from the other direction she heard somebody yelling. It was Tony. He was coming at a fast jog from the direction of the staff tents.

"Hey, has anybody seen the orangutan? Mother Nature is missing! Hey, everybody, help me look! Mother Nature? Where are you? Has anybody seen her? Hey, I need everyone to look! Mother Nature?"

Sleepy voices began to emanate from still-darkened huts. A few were grumbling at Tony's SOS, but most were genuinely concerned and willing to help. They might have petty differences with each other, but everyone loved Mother Nature. Aston and Chaz emerged from their huts already dressed and ready for the day. One trotted off in one direction and one went the other, hoping she had not ventured out into the jungle. If she had, they would never find her.

Several voices began calling her name. Suddenly, there was a scream followed by cursing. It was Annaliese.

"Get out of my house! Out! Shoo! Shoo! Out! Out I said! Leave!"

Tony ran towards Annaliese's hut. Much to his relief, he was greeted by the sight of a rapidly-exiting orangutan. She had a half-eaten mango in one hand and a bejeweled crown in the other. He laughed loudly.

"You little scoundrel! You scared me to death! Come here, you!"

Mother Nature had other ideas. She was frightened by the outburst from the woman in the hut. She would not risk having the man take her mango. Blocked on one side by Aston, blocked on the other side by Chaz, and chased from behind by Tony, she took the only escape route available. She headed to the privy. Her bow-legged retreat was surprisingly fast. Her pursuers lost sight of her as she rounded a bend in the path. Looking back and seeing no one, Mother Nature waddled behind a tree just off the path.

Just then, Mystic Origin came into view. Physically and emotionally drained from her experience in the privy, she trudged slowly up the path. Mother Nature eyed her closely. The small woman's pace was slow compared to the other humans. As Mystic Origin neared, Mother Nature smelled a familiar smell. Pee. Like most orangutans, Mother Nature drank her own urine at times. This woman was clearly a kindred spirit. Mother Nature needed a comforting hug. She had found the perfect person to give her one. She dropped her partially-eaten mango, stepped out from behind the tree and climbed up into the arms of a very surprised Mystic Origin.

Just then, Tony and his search party came into view. Alarmed, the simian looked back at her pursuers with apprehension. She needed to have both hands free to hold tight to her rescuer, which was not possible as long as she held the crown. Mother Nature plopped the crown on Mystic Origin's head and wrapped both her arms around her neck.

Thus was Mystic Origin crowned Queen for a Day.

Tony, recognizing the import of the moment, began to clap and cheer. "Long live the queen!" he cried out. Mystic Origin's shock at having been accosted by an ape almost as big as her was compounded when the too-large crown slipped down over her eyes. Her plight sparked immediate, uproarious laughter in her onlookers.

All except for one Annaliese Parkman. She was onlooking but was most definitely not laughing. To the contrary, she was beside herself with fury.

"Okay, now look here, Tony! This business of everybody coming into my hut and helping themselves to my food needs to stop right here and now! You need to lay down the law. You are in charge, or at least I thought you were. There needs to be some rules and some punishment for breaking them or else people are going to start taking matters into their own hands. Now, are you going to insure people have personal space and safety and security or not?"

DeShunta stepped out of the privy and made her way up to the group. She was listening to everything being said. When she reached the assembly, she gave a wide berth to the orangutan. She couldn't trust it. If that monkey ever tried to bite her, it would live to regret it. She shifted her gaze to Tony. That man sure was pretty, especially when he was looking all serious and everything. Annaliese continued her rant.

"I've been meaning to say this, but I've held back. We need walls! Gates, fences, something! There is an absence of trust here and for good reason. You need to get your staff out of their tents and out of the waterfall swimming pool and put them to work building us some walls and some decent doors that lock. We're surrounded by wild animals. We are living with strangers with different backgrounds and different values. We. Need. A. Safe. Place. To. Live!"

Annaliese turned her head in dramatic fashion to look directly at Mystic Origin and Mother Nature. Satisfied that her point had been made, she returned her eyes to Tony. She bit her lip for a moment as she decided whether to vocalize the last thought in her head. The bee in her bonnet cast the deciding vote. *Say it.* She cut her eyes back at Mystic Origin.

"And it doesn't shock me that when the orangutan got caught stealing my fruit, she ran to her mentor for comfort. They learn by example, you know."

Everyone in the group cringed. That will leave a mark. Mystic Origin's mouth dropped. Her eyes narrowed to slits. Before she could formulate a sufficiently scathing reply, Tony interjected.

"Annaliese, if you believe I am in charge here, you haven't been paying attention. By design, I am not. Yesterday, Clarence was. Today, Mystic Origin is. Who will be in charge tomorrow? I don't know. Ask Mother Nature. If you want a wall, build you a wall. If you want a door that locks, build you a door that locks. Nobody is stopping you."

Clarence listened to the entirety of the heated exchange. Hearing Annaliese's words brought to mind a memory of one of the key parts of her prior campaigns. Even though she had been the Governor of another state, one he didn't care about, it stuck in his mind because he thought it was so stupid. He could not resist getting in a dig of his own. A devilish grin appeared on his face.

"But Governor Parkman, I thought you and the good people of Connecticut didn't like walls. I thought they were 'immoral.' Didn't you say that at a press conference a year or two ago?"

Annaliese was dumbfounded. She could not believe he had just uttered those words.

"Are you kidding me right now? Are you seriously equating our situation here with a border wall between the U.S. and Mexico? Because there is no comparison! This is our home we're talking about! This is our safety and security! This is where we live, not some imaginary line between countries out in the desert somewhere!"

Clarence gave an exaggerated nod of understanding, dripping with insincerity, as though she had just enlightened him to a great truth. Before this newest conflict could escalate any further, Tony got the group back on track.

"Ladies and gentlemen! We have in our midst the Queen for a Day. She wears the crown of authority on her head. What's more, at least for the moment, she is holding the kingmaker or queenmaker in her very arms. It is time for our queen to tell us. Your Majesty, what is the rule for today?"

Tony's pivot back to the point of the exercise was deft. He was the perfect host because he was able to strike the perfect balance between diplomatic moderator and mischievous instigator. As Mystic Origin pondered Tony's question, Peaches offered a mango to Mother Nature, who hesitated before taking it, then handled it carefully as though it was a live grenade. Mystic Origin would have preferred to take the time necessary to come up with the best rule possible, but the muscles in her arms, exhausted from holding the large simian that would not release her, silently screamed for their owner to hurry up. Finally, after a withering look at Annaliese, she spoke.

"My rules are these—no walls, but sanctuary instead. No greed, but food to the homeless and helpless instead."

The Senator was puzzled.

"So, what does that mean in practice, exactly?"

"It means that goodness, kindness and compassion shall be the rule here, and we will model it for the world to see," she replied. "Personal space divides; open space unites. Hoarding food divides; sharing food unites. If we all have the same privilege to share our food with those in need, there will be no need. It may take some getting used to for those used to hoarding, but the love they will see blooming around them will bring their hearts around."

The Senator, being a man of words, wanted clarification.

"When you say we will all have the same "privilege" to share, does that mean it's mandatory or voluntary?"

Mystic Origin saw the Senator's question as an attempt to mar the beautiful new world she had just created. A scowl crossed her face.

"It is our duty as members of the human race and shall be our duty for the duration of our time in Brazil."

The group stared at Mystic Origin, trying and failing to comprehend her meaning. Tony, equally as confused but completely unperturbed by it, flashed a bright smile and nodded.

"The Queen has spoken, and so it shall be!"

Annaliese blew out a blast of air, put her hands on her hips and looked at the sky. She began to count to ten in her mind. Ten arrived too quickly. She needed to make it twenty. She cursed the timing of her outburst about needing walls to keep trespassers out. If she had been thinking, she would have waited to speak her mind until after Mystic Origin had decided upon her stupid rule of the day. She didn't regret saying it. It needed to be said, but in hindsight her timing was poor. Now however, Mystic Origin had enacted a counterproductive, completely unhelpful rule out of pure spite. Annaliese tried to keep her mouth closed and move on, but she just couldn't leave it alone.

"Fine! Just fine! You're not the one who is having to deal with break-ins and thieves! But who cares, right? Don't worry about me!"

With that, Annaliese stomped off back to her hut. *I may not get a wall built, but no one said anything about doors. I'll find a way to build a lockable door. You can bet your sweet aspirin on it.*

Off in the distance, the wup, wup, wup of an approaching helicopter became audible. The sound made Tony remember there was a bit of business he had to attend to before he sent Celeste and Honey off to the doctor's office in Rio. The group looked in the direction the sound was coming from and watched as the chopper appeared over the trees. Tony explained the situation with Celeste.

"So, let me tell you about Celeste. We all watched her get sick last night in the arena theater. Unfortunately, she woke up feeling ill again this morning."

DeShunta spoke up and said, "I told you. She need a pregnancy test and a ultrasound."

"I hear you," Tony agreed. "You could be right. We don't know. Normally we wouldn't talk about someone's private health information but out here…well, you guys signed waivers and authorizations back in the States, so yeah. Our problem is that we don't have any pregnancy test kits, plus an ultrasound machine was not in the budget even if it was possible to bring one here, which it isn't. We have secured a chopper to take her to a doctor in Rio if we deem it necessary. Do you think we should take Celeste for a pregnancy test and, if the doctor agrees, an ultrasound since she doesn't have access to it out here?"

Mystic Origin, the newly-appointed queen, voiced a resounding "yes." Annaliese vigorously agreed, as did DeShunta, Peaches, Aston and the Senator. When not everyone spoke up, Annaliese looked at each one who remained silent with incredulity. Her look pried an unenthusiastic "I agree" out of the rest. Now it was unanimous. Satisfied, Annaliese turned back to Tony, who acknowledged the will of the people.

"The people have spoken," Tony said. "Your compassion is admirable. So now, how to pay for her doctor's visit? The doctor will most certainly require payment at the time services are rendered. They aren't going to treat her for free in the hope she'll pay after they mail a bill to America. Celeste hasn't won any contests yet. She didn't bring any money with her; therefore, she can't afford the visit because she can't pay. The silver and gold coins in the chest are out. Brazilian doctors don't accept sovereigns and shillings for payment. They want reals, which we don't have. We don't have any printers out here, so we can't print money. That leaves us with two options. You can sell DeShunta's diamonds, or you can sell the gold bar jointly owned by Aston, Chaz and the Senator. There are places to do that in Rio. They have everything from diamond brokers to pawn shops. After you sell it, you can use part of the money to pay for Celeste's visit."

Chaz growled. His brows furrowed and his jaw tightened. His lips were drawn so tight they became a barely-noticeable thin line between his nose and his chin. Clarence noticed the change in Chaz's posture and began to slowly move out of harm's way. He was not eager to face the rage of a psychopath again. Aston fairly yelled at Tony.

"What kind of nonsense is this? You have to pay—Jungle Money has to pay! It's not our job! You've got all the money you need right there in that treasure chest! Use some of it!"

Tony confidently shook his head.

"Oh, no sir. By contract, everything in that chest goes to one or more of the competitors standing right here to be determined by who wins the contests. You signed that contract, too, remember? Jungle Money does not own the treasure; rather, Jungle Money is merely the steward of someone else's treasure until they meet the necessary prerequisites to claim it. Nevertheless, there are currently four people here with the means to pay for her doctor's visit."

Aston, who had had quite enough, said, "Oh, for god's sake, we can sell our gold bar to a broker in Rio and split the cost of her…"

The Senator, his voice quavering, broke in before Aston could finish.

"No! I am not handing a solid gold bar to some person I don't know and trust them to take it to an honest broker in Rio de Janeiro, get full value for it and bring the money back here. Are you insane? No! We're talking about Rio here! Rio is a dangerous place, people! Violent crime and armed robberies every minute of every day. I don't care if it was Tamper and Bones and an armored car who went, for that matter. Even if the person was honest and wanted to bring back the money, there's a good chance they'd be robbed and shot, and we'd never see either them or the gold bar again. So no! Forget it! Not going to happen. And don't look at me like that, Governor Parkman. I know you. You are the most generous person in the world…with other people's money."

Tony didn't respond. He merely turned his eyes to look at DeShunta, the fourth person with the financial means to pay for a medical visit. She felt the eyes upon her, but she didn't care. She wouldn't be rushed. She needed a minute to think. After a considerable amount of time had passed, she looked at Mr. de Cortinas.

"How much one of those gold coins I got worth? And them silver ones, how much?"

Before the gemologist could answer, Peaches stepped in and said, "What you ought to do is take one of your…"

"You shut up, diva!" DeShunta yelled. "Don't be talking to me about what I ought to do! Here I am, ain't got no money and you talking about what I need to do? How many millions you got, diva? All the time on TV, sitting around on your couch with your messed-up family getting your picture took, cashing those checks and you telling me how I ought to spend my money, and it ain't even been in my hand five minutes?"

Peaches, visibly shaken by the unforeseen attack, said, "Sheesh!"

DeShunta glared at her and said, "What you got to say now, diva? Where your money at? Telling me how to spend mine—where yours at, diva?"

Peaches took a couple of steps backwards, folded her arms and said nothing more. DeShunta glared at her, calmed herself and then turned to Tony.

"Take four or five of my coins I gave you to hold for me yesterday, enough to pay for the visit, and give them to her. But make sure you keep it all locked up in a lockbox. Diva here ain't got no check this week and she starting to look at everybody else's."

Mystic Origin, wanting to make peace, said, "DeShunta, thank you for modeling the heart of a true giver."

Tony looked around to find Stephen and Richard to make sure they were catching all the events on video. As he did, he noticed G standing in the back of the crowd. G was smiling behind his sunglasses, and Tony knew why. He smiled every time the topic of DeShunta's winnings came up. The bet at Bert's place was getting interesting. The gates had opened, and the horses were off and running. G's horse was ahead of Bert's horse in the secret side bet standings. As for Tony, he was out of the running altogether. He couldn't even find his horse.

The competitors were given a break so Tony could meet with Celeste, Honey and the pilot and see them off. Tony regretted having so many helicopter flights in and out of camp, but it couldn't be helped. Honey was thrilled. Tony was sending her on an important mission. She was no longer just a dancer. She was needed to care for someone. Being bilingual made her that much more valuable. Her face lit up like a Christmas tree as Tony explained the logistics. Summer, the youngest member of the film crew, would accompany them on their trip. She was instructed to video everything. Everything. Honey nodded taking mental notes of all the things Tony said.

Tony gave Honey one last instruction. He gave her a stern warning to make sure that no one other than Summer filmed Celeste. Tony and the production team must have exclusive control and possession over all video. This was television. This trip was part of the show, though an unplanned and unexpected part. If anyone tried to point a video camera at them or share video of this visit in any shape or form, Honey was to demand that they stop. If they refused, she was to call the police immediately. Unauthorized publication of video of Celeste's personal healthcare decisions and medical treatment would violate her HIPAA rights, and no amount of pre-signed releases would shield them from liability if they allowed it to happen.

Tony made Honey promise to follow his instructions. She promised. Tony was not satisfied. Honey had not said it as though she understood the importance of what he said. He placed his hands on her shoulders, made her look him in the eyes and promise. She looked at him with alluring eyes that could melt a corpse's heart at a January funeral. She grabbed his face and squeezed his cheeks. She promised. Tony was confident she understood him. Well, reasonably confident. Nothing could jeopardize the show more than a breach of confidentiality. He would have to trust her. He had his hands full right where he was.

After everyone had been briefed and understood their assignments, the travelers made their way up the steep climb to the plateau above the waterfall where the helicopter was waiting for them. Its rotors violently whipped the trees and flattened the grass. Celeste had packed her few belongings into a duffel bag. She held it with one hand while shielding her eyes with the other. Honey had her arm around Celeste waiting for the okay to walk to the chopper. Summer struggled to carry a large black case filled with her camera gear in addition to a piece of carry-on luggage. Honey felt sorry for Summer, who was not a big person, having to carry so much.

Tamper came from out of nowhere. He pulled Summer's duffel bag off her shoulder with one hand, lifted her case with the other and marched them to the chopper. Honey couldn't help but marvel at Tamper's physique as he walked. His sleeveless t-shirt revealed well-developed muscles covered in inked artwork that must have cost him thousands.

The pilot handed each of them headphones to block the noise. Celeste and Honey both tried on their headphones. Satisfied they would fit and be comfortable, they laid them in their laps. The pilot showed them the on/off switches on the headphones which would block out the ambient noise but still allow them to hear each other speak. Honey smiled at Celeste.

"How you feel?"

Celeste smiled a tight-lipped smile. She placed one hand in the air parallel to the ground and shook it side to side, like a plane dipping its wings, and said, "So, so. Actually, not great."

Honey felt for her. She felt a strange urge to pat Celeste's tummy, but resisted and patted her knee instead. Honey then asked the question she had been wanting to ask all morning.

"So boyfriend America?"

Celeste nodded and smiled. When things in Brazil got bad, whether it was bugs, heat, thirst, hunger, boredom or whatever, there was one surefire remedy. She thought of home. Aurora, her adorable little Havanese, was the first to come to mind. What she would not do to have Aurora jump up in her lap, tail wagging her whole body, climb up on her chest and lick all over her face. Her second thought was of the one she missed the most. Her man. What she would not do to have Trayton take her in his arms right now and hold her. In her mind, she buried her face in his shoulder and they swayed back and forth, back and forth. That was her happy place. Knowing she had him to come home to was all that got her through sometimes.

Honey watched Celeste's distressed face turn from worry to wishful to something close to contentment. She knew what Celeste must be thinking. Home. Her man. Honey leaned back in her seat and smiled. She would not let Tony down. She would do everything she could to make sure Celeste received the best healthcare possible.

Summer had her small video camera trained at both of them. She was excited to be on this trip as well. This was the first time she had been truly unsupervised and on her own. Summer was up to the task. She would do her very best to make sure she captured it all. The pilot climbed back in the chopper, turned to the ladies behind him and asked, "You ready?" They all smiled and nodded. Soon they were flying over the Brazilian rainforest on their way to an appointment with destiny.

Chapter Thirty-Five

Before the helicopter arrived that morning, the rainforest was tranquil and quiet, especially a mile downriver where the jungle was slowly but surely coming to life. From high atop their leafy perches, colorful parrots began to lift their heads out from under their wings to watch the morning light. Baby monkeys began to nuzzle their sleepy mothers' teats in a quest for milk. Out of necessity, the night insects ceased rubbing their legs together because their chirps would draw the hungry red worm lizards, the black and white Tegu lizards, the leaf-toed geckoes, and a myriad of other predators looking for the first meal of the day.

A footstep disturbed the quiet. Another footstep. Leaves crunched. A twig snapped. Senses on high alert, a mother monkey gripped her baby tight as she craned her neck to see the source of the noise down below.

A greater rhea stepped into view, searching the ground for its morning meal. When you are the largest bird in South America, standing close to five feet tall, and you can't fly, you make noise when you walk. The mother monkey, fears allayed, returned to her resting position and allowed her baby to continue nursing. The parrots, unconcerned by the giant flightless fowl, began to look at one another to see who would be the first to fly down to make a breakfast run.

Watching them all, silent and still, was Bones. He was taking advantage of the break called by Tony to do a little hunting. Bones was a ghost in the shadows—a watcher in the mist. He could disappear at will, having the uncanny ability to hide in plain sight. His movements were small when he moved at all. In the iron grip of his left hand he held a recurve bow made of maple wood. In his right hand he held the shaft of a razor blade-tipped cedar arrow. He had eaten plenty of ostrich back home in South Africa but rhea was a taste unknown to him. A guide in Argentina had once told him the meat was delicious, not like a turkey as one might expect, but rather with a flavor somewhere between beef and lamb.

Bones pulled the arrow out of the pouch on his back upon first hearing the footfalls well before the source of the sound made his appearance. After the impressive bird stepped into view, Bones relaxed the muscles in his right arm and radically slowed the arrow's approach to the bowstring, not wanting his movement to catch his quarry's sharp eyes. As the rhea's head went down to dig under a pile of leaves, Bones quietly nocked the arrow. When the bird raised its head to scan its surroundings, Bones froze, still as a statue in the shadows created by the canopy overhead.

The rhea, completely unaware of the man who stood not thirty feet away, was an impressive specimen. Bones eyed the claws at the business end of the bird's feet as it drew near. If it was anything like an ostrich, it used those claws as weapons when the need arose. *Turn sideways*, Bones told the bird in his mind. A straight-on shot was not ideal. He wanted to put the arrow through the bird's heart or lungs or both, but he couldn't unless it turned. *Turn, curse you.* The bird, oblivious to the man's presence, walked straight at Bones. *Turn before you step on the toe of my boot!* If it came any closer, Bones was going to be able to jump on it and go for a ride.

A tiny frog jumped before it was stepped on, catching the bird's attention. The rhea quartered away from Bones, giving him just enough time to draw back the arrow. Bones focused his gaze on a single feather on the bird's breast, just under the wing. His father's sage advice came to mind as it always did on a hunt. *Aim small, miss small.* Bones released the arrow. Twang thump. He saw the arrow skitter into a thicket on the other side of the bird. A complete pass-through. The rhea jumped and sped off into the jungle, spewing bright pink, foamy lung blood. Bones knew it couldn't go far. His heart was pounding as he finally allowed himself to breathe. The adrenaline rush of a close-range bow kill never grows old.

Bones did not chase it. He remained still and listened. The bird had disappeared into the jungle but alas, it was a noisy runner. He could hear branches slapping and twigs snapping, the noise growing fainter the further it ran away. Suddenly the sounds stopped. Bones leaned forward, listening intently. While his blazing blue eyes couldn't see it, his mind's eye saw it all perfectly. *Wait for it. Wait for it.* And then it came. He heard a fall followed by thrashing. He knew the bird had stood as long as it could, fighting the dizziness, battling the sleepiness brought on by the loss of blood. Now, he had fallen and was thrashing on the jungle floor as his life ebbed away.

Bones moved quickly now that his prey was down. He did not want to delay and risk confronting a hungry jaguar who might be drawn by the smell of blood. He did not have to go far. The bird had piled up less than fifty yards away. Bones kept a safe distance between himself and the bird. He held his bow by one end and used the other to gently poke the bird in the eye. No movement. Bones smiled as he exhaled. *Yes!* Keeping himself away from the powerful feet, Bones kneeled and placed his hand on the bird's chest. He patted it, almost a caress, then rested his hand on the coarse feathers. He looked at the rhea's now sightless eyes and felt the old familiar feeling—hunter's remorse. This kill, like every kill he had ever made, was bittersweet. The prey gave its life to sustain his. Such a gift deserved a word, even when there was no one to hear it but monkeys and parrots. He spoke quietly and reverently.

"Hey guy. I'm sorry. So you are a greater rhea, are you? You are a beautiful bird. Yes, you are. I have never seen a bird like you before, not in the wild anyway. Wow, look at your wings. They are strong. And look at those legs. And your feet! I am so glad you didn't stab me with those toes. You are quite the specimen."

Bones pulled back the wing in order to see the entry wound. It was small, not much bigger than the diameter of a pencil, with two slits evidencing the path of the broadhead.

"Right where I was aiming. I wanted it to be quick, mate. I'm glad you didn't run far. Thank you for living. You are going to feed at least six people. Thank you. Thank you, God, for creating him. You do amazing work. Now I've got to clean you."

Bones pulled his knife from its sheath. The edge of the sharp blade shone bright silver, gleaming in the ever-increasing light of day. In less than ten minutes he had butchered the rhea, placing each of the breasts in resealable gallon-size plastic bags, then harvested the rest of the meat in similar fashion. As he came close to finishing the job, he looked around at his surroundings, mindful of the need to remain watchful for the feline apex predator of the rain-forest. As beautiful and free as jaguars are, they were also terrible and fierce and hard to see. He had no desire to cross paths with one while carrying fresh meat.

Now, what to do about the carcass? He knew scavengers of all types, those that walked, crawled, slithered and flew would soon be paying it a visit. Bones scanned the terrain for a suitable place to dump it. He noticed a drop in the terrain off to his right. If it led to a deep ravine, that would be ideal. Before he dragged the carcass, though, he first wanted to take a look at the spot to make sure it was suitable. His steps were quick and light. Just before he hopped up onto the trunk of a fallen tree, he froze. Bending down to take a closer look, Bones' eyes widened.

A broken arrow shaft was sticking out of the tree trunk.

It was not his. He worked the arrow loose and examined the arrowhead. Bone. Crudely-fashioned bone. He touched his thumb to it. The edge was sharp. It would not produce quite the surgical strike as would one of his stain-less steel broadheads, but it would be effective nonetheless, especially if it was coated with slime from the back of a poison arrow tree frog. He wiped his thumb on the side of his pants and looked around him.

They were not alone.

Bones disposed of the carcass as quickly as he could. He dropped the remains of the broken arrow into his pouch, threw the plastic bags containing the rhea breasts in his backpack and double-timed it back to camp. *I need to find Tamper*, he thought. He had gained much respect for his teammate during the short time they had spent together. Tamper had known war. Not that Bones expected any such trouble with whoever had made the bone arrowhead...but just in case, Tamper needed to know. Tamper would know what to do.

Chapter Thirty-Six

An unnatural stillness had settled in over a dark clearing less than three days' walk from the arena theater. The usual cacophony of noise made by untold numbers of birds and insects had temporarily hushed. There was no visible explanation for the eerie silence, but the absence of sound commanded the attention of a band of monkeys that had, until a few moments ago, intended to cross the clearing in search of ripe mangoes. They stopped their progression through the boughs of the upper canopy and settled in where they were, waiting and listening, listening and waiting.

A chameleon left the direct sunlight and entered the shade which changed its bright green coloration to a dull brownish-green with hints of yellow. The lizard crawled unhurriedly over tree roots and leaf litter on the forest floor. It paused for a few moments when it climbed up the next obstacle. The surface was different than any other he had been on before. His new perch injected warmth into his cold-blooded feet and tail.

The chameleon stood atop the bare foot of a man.

The lizard lingered for several seconds longer, then clambered down to seek a tasty meal of worms under a fallen tree or rotten log. Next to the unmoving foot, pressed into the dirt, was the butt of a spear. An ant quietly made his way up the shaft of the spear, periodically veering to the left and to the right, wiggling its antennae as though trying to pick up a radio station, then resuming its vertical march to the top. Had he been looking to see what was next to the spear, the ant would have seen a man's leg, hairless and brown, with painted stripes of black and red. Naked with the exception of a cord fashioned from braided vine wrapped around his waist, the man stood as still as a statue. His head was invisible, cloaked in a headdress made of intertwined limbs, twigs and leaves. His camouflage was perfect. When he froze in position with a backdrop of trees and underbrush, even the sharp-eyed monkeys could not spot him.

To the naked eye, the clearing had no signs of life. In reality, there were twenty-three Javari warrior each adorned just like the first. They were masters in the art of disappearing. They stood at attention, ringing the perimeter of the clearing. They had been waiting like this for much of the morning. If necessary, they would remain that way all day. They would not display any signs of weakness or fatigue, not after hearing rumors that Kanapitu, the great warrior chieftain of the Awa people, was making his way here at this very moment.

The stories of Kanapitu were the stuff of legend, known by the Javari and all the other forest tribes. No one was quite sure if the stories were true because the hallmark of the mysterious Awa was their ability to stay hidden. They were invisible when they willed it, mist without substance, living without a trace. No one knew where they were, though everyone knew the part of the jungle they claimed as their home.

Kanapitu was said to have been born of a jaguar and was welcome in their dens. Kanapitu climbed to the upper canopy each night and rode on the wings of a harpy to survey the entire world before dawn. Kanapitu had been to the spring at the head of the Amazon and had seen the underground vaults which held the waters of the world. Kanapitu had been the one to teach the howler monkeys how to swing through the forest, and their howls were cries of thanks to their teacher.

There was a dark side to the legend which all the Forest People knew. Kanapitu was the one who kept The Outside away. All the world knew his name, and wisely stayed away, but there had been a day, long, long ago, when The Outside came. They could not find the Awa, because the Awa did not wish to be found. Nevertheless, while looking for them, The Outside cut down one of the Awa's trees. Kanapitu knew. Kanapitu knows all of his trees. The trees called to Kanapitu, and he answered the call.

Kanapitu filed his teeth into points and his nails into claws. He found the tiny colored frogs and dabbed the tips of his darts on their backs. He stalked up behind The Outside and paralyzed each one with a dart. He built a great fire in their midst and chose the largest of The Outside to cook and eat. The rest of The Outside had to sit and watch, paralyzed but still breathing and aware. Kanapitu had named the meat of The Outside "long pig," for that is what it tasted like. He then released the rest of The Outside to go back to their homes because it was more valuable to the Forest People that The Outside teach their own not to return than to eat them all. In all the reckoning of time since then, no one from The Outside had ever returned to the land of the Awa.

At least, not until two moons ago.

One day, without warning, a bright, shiny, giant bird which roared like a jaguar and flew without moving trespassed in the land of the Forest People. Its feathers reflected the sun. One of the men from the Javari tribe and his son happened to be standing in a small clearing when the bird started to land in the trees overhead. The giant bird shook the treetops but must have decided they were not strong enough to hold his weight because it flew away again. Before it flew away, however, the Javari and his son saw a man sitting in the great bird's eye.

No one would have believed the fantastical tale if they had not all heard the bird. A few of the men even caught a glimpse of the bird. The men had been quite a distance from the village on a hunt at the time. They were descending into a deep valley with trees so thick and so tall that they nearly blocked out the sun. Despite the overwhelming and terrifying noise, some of the hunters had scrambled up trees in order to get a look. They all came back with the same report. It was real, it was here, and most frightening of all, it was coming back again and again, day after day, staying longer and longer each time.

The various tribes of the Forest People kept to themselves and did not associate with one another. Chance meetings in the jungle, or on the banks of the mighty river, were always tense. Most of the time they ended quickly enough without significant consequences, but there were times when punishment was meted out due to violations of real or imagined boundaries. On rare occasions, women were abducted, with the justification that serious transgressions demanded a high price. There was almost nothing that could unify the tribes, since bitterness caused by old conflicts was remembered generations after they had occurred.

This new threat was different however. The giant bird with a man in its eye threatened them all. This was something big enough to make the tribes set aside their differences. As a matter of fact, it was already happening.

At great risk to themselves, two Javari warriors entered Awa territory to send word of the great bird. They found Awa men and told them the fantastical tale. Much to their relief, they were permitted to leave and return to their village. Within days, an Awa runner entered Javari territory to deliver a message.

Kanapitu had heard.

The legendary warrior of whom stories were told from one end of the forest to another would rise to lead a war party and kill the great bird with a man in its eye. All men from all tribes would see his bravery, his prowess, and his anger unleashed. The Javari had a mental image of the feared man they had never seen but who gave them hope. Hope had a name.

Kanapitu.

Chapter Thirty-Seven

Tony looked at his watch as he walked back to camp. It had been close to an hour since Celeste and Honey had taken off in the helicopter. The camp was fairly quiet and everyone seemed to be getting along nicely. People were milling about their huts or returning from the direction of the mango trees where they had enjoyed breakfast. Mother Nature was following Mystic Origin around holding her hand when she would allow it, having taken a liking to her. The conflicts from this morning seemed to have dissipated.

Bones had taken Tony and G aside and quietly showed them the piece of a broken arrow he had found. G said nothing, thinking through the possible ramifications. Tony was not concerned. It looked very old to him, like a fossil. He dismissed the threat. Tony's mind was on the day's festivities. Today was going to be a good day. He would make sure of it.

"Hey everyone, listen up," Tony called out. "We need everyone over here by the river. That is where we will start contest number two. Pass the word. We need everyone by the river in five minutes. Time waits for no man. Or woman. Or orangutan. Down by the river in five."

Tony flashed his trademark smile, turned and started walking toward the river. One by one the contestants made their way to the rendezvous point. They were glad to have a new chance at winning a fortune. Peaches mentioned how glad she was that there would be no climate change tax this round. Willow popped her hand over Peaches' mouth but in a playful way.

"Shhh! Do not let Mystic Origin hear you. Don't give her any ideas."

Tattoo, who was listening to their exchange, turned to Willow and asked, "So, where's your brother?"

The smile disappeared from Willow's face.

"I don't know. They said they are looking for him. I'm pretty worried. He should have been back by now."

Tattoo was less than sympathetic.

"Well, I hate to say it, but your brother's not very smart. He shouldn't have jumped when he did. Doesn't look like all that praying did much good now, does it?"

"That was totally uncalled for!" Peaches retorted. "What a mean thing to say! Nobody wants to hear from the Grunge! Go somewhere else. Willow, don't listen to him."

Tattoo called both of them names and left. Willow walked in silence the rest of the way, looking down at the ground. Peaches tried to assure her they would find her brother, but it was clear that words would not be enough to comfort Willow.

As they gathered at the edge of the river, Bones and Tamper were standing by a stack of logs and boxes. Miguel de Cortinas was standing by the treasure chest, which was closed. Tony counted heads. Once he was satisfied everyone was there who needed to be there, Tony began the day's proceedings.

"Good morning everyone, and welcome to Jungle Money contest number two! Before we begin, I would like to make you aware of a rather startling discovery that Mr. de Cortinas made just this morning."

Tony nodded at the gemologist, who unlocked the chest and opened the ancient lid. The hinges shrieked in protest. When the sunlight hit the horde of treasure inside, all those assembled leaned forward and gaped at the beauty before them. Flashes of morning light sparkled off the mounds of diamonds, jewels, silver and gold as they expected. This morning however, a new sight greeted their eyes. Loose pearls, some moonlight white, others midnight black, lay atop the mounds. Peaches, eyes wide with surprise, was clearly impressed.

"Well, would you looky there! We've got pearls!"

"I thought you might like that," Tony laughed. "We only thought we knew everything about that chest. Mr. de Cortinas was inspecting the diamonds, trying to get a feel for all the different sizes and grades, and as he did so, he noticed an irregularity in the surface of the underside of the lid. He brought it to G's attention, who gave him permission to do a little destructive examination while still preserving the integrity of the chest as a whole."

The competitors crowded around the treasure chest so they could see what Tony was talking about.

"He cut the inside lining of the lid, just a small cut right where he felt a lump that the rest of us had missed. Carefully, carefully he fished out the mystery objects hidden behind it without further tearing the lining. Lo and behold, he found a cache of pearls that had been secured behind there who knows how long ago. Most were solid and pristine, just like they came from the oyster. A few were pierced, having been made into necklaces. Miguel, can you give us an idea of their worth?"

He shook his head.

"Unfortunately, I cannot. I have consultant in Belgium that I trust who help me evaluate the worth of diamonds and precious stones, who is expert in pearls. He will have to see them in person, under special lights with magnifying lens to give accurate appraisal. Based upon what my eyes see, I can tell you they are very good, very good, and would bring the winner very high price."

Mystic Origin had a studied look on her face. She looked down at the trusting face of Mother Nature, who was holding her hand.

"What should I do, Mother Nature? What should I do?"

Mother Nature had a placid and contented look on her face. Upon hearing the small woman's voice, she gazed up at Mystic Origin, then looked back down. Evidently, she had no opinion on the matter. Mystic Origin looked back at Tony.

"Tony, as queen, I have made a decision about what we are playing for today. Money has no value to me here. I cannot give the trees money to bear fruit for me. I cannot give the river money to bring fresh water to me. I cannot give the birds money to sing for me. I cannot give the sun money to shine for me. I cannot…"

Clarence had had quite enough of this monologue.

"For crying out loud, would you shut up with the fairyland gibberish and just tell us what we're playing for? It's hot. It's buggy. Let's get on with it. Chop, chop."

He popped his palms together. She gave him a withering look and continued with her address to Tony.

"Tony, today we shall play for the pearls and only the pearls. They came from oysters who are beings as worthy of respect as we are. The pearls were labors of love begun with only a single grain of sand. The fact that the pearls are in this chest instead of in the oysters who gave them birth means that they were taken from their bodies at a high price. They are used to adorn women and appeal to their vanity. Should I win them, I plan to wear them without ceasing until one day I shall find their birthplace and return them to where they belong."

No one understood what she said. As was becoming a common occurrence, her listeners had their eyebrows lifted and their mouths were slightly ajar. After a moment of silence, Clarence laughed a derisive laugh.

"Do you mean to tell me that you have a treasure chest opened up in front of you and the only thing you want to do with it is take the pearl necklaces out and chunk them in the ocean?"

Mystic Origin was not pleased with his wording, but she was pleased that her pure motives had been plainly, if crudely, explained.

"Yes, in a matter of speaking. Our ancestors came from the sea. Corporations rape the sea in their eternal pursuit of fossil fuels. The least I can do is try to restore balance. Our mother will cease her weeping and be comforted, if only for a moment."

Annaliese, one of those who failed to understand her meaning, asked, "When you say 'our mother,' who are you referring to? Mother Nature? What are you saying?"

Mystic Origin shook her head. Annaliese wasn't getting it.

"No, not Mother Nature. Our mother. "The Earth" as you call her. She is 'our mother' to those of us who know her well."

Annaliese's mouth formed a silent "O." Tony grinned his trademark Hollywood grin. He liked crazy. Crazy made life worth living. Crazy also made for good TV.

"Pearls it is! So, here is the game. You have all experienced the magnificence of the Amazon rainforest in your quest for gods and animals. No visit to Brazil is complete however, without an intimate encounter with the power and majesty of the mighty Amazon River. Behind me is the source of life for the inhabitants of Brazil, both man and beast. The Amazon is the largest river in the world in terms of volume of water discharged, supplying 20 percent of all the fresh water discharged into the ocean. It is the second longest river in the world, second only to the Nile River, although some would argue otherwise. The Amazon demands respect. It is beautiful but just as deadly as it is beautiful. You must always be on the lookout for trouble."

Aston slapped a mosquito on the side of his face and then asked the question on everyone's minds.

"So, what are we doing in the river?"

Tony bowed a little bow.

"So glad you asked, Aston. By now you may have had all the mangoes you would ever care to eat. You are now going to have the opportunity to add a little protein to your diet. How do you feel about a little fishing?"

DeShunta spoke up and said, "I like to fish. My grandmama took me fishing since I was a just a child. We would bring home a mess of catfish and have us a fish fry. Cornbread hush puppies, fried catfish and homemade cole slaw. Mm, mm."

"Well, I think you might like our second contest then. Here are the rules. The one who catches the most pounds of fish by tomorrow at sundown wins all the pearls in the treasure chest. If you catch one giant fish that weighs thirty pounds, you might win. If someone else catches forty little fish each weighing a pound a piece, their forty pounds of little fish beats your thirty pound lunker. What kind of fish can you expect to catch? I'm going to ask our fishing expert Bones to educate us. Bones?"

Bones stepped forward, tipping his broad-brimmed boonie hat with a sunburnished hand. He smiled and said good morning. Peaches, who had fallen in love with his rugged good looks and engaging South African accent, returned his greeting with an exuberant "good morning" of her own. Her enthusiasm elicited a chuckle from Bones, but he turned his attention to DeShunta.

"Miss DeShunta, you'll be pleased to know there are catfish in the Amazon River. One species is armor-plated if you can believe it. What else is swimming around in there? The biggest fish of them all is the arapaima. It's a predatory beast that can get up to nine feet long and weigh two hundred pounds. It is the world's largest freshwater fish. They swim close to the surface so you might actually catch a glimpse of one. Good luck reeling one in, though."

Chaz rubbed his hands together as he looked at the river. He wanted to catch an arapaima. Bones continued his fishing lesson.

"The pacu is a bit smaller and much tastier—probably the best-eating fish in these waters. They'll get up to three feet and a hundred pounds. My personal favorite is the peacock bass. Fishermen from all over the world come here to tie into one of those. They are gorgeous, brilliant green, bright yellow, black stripes and orange fins. They can get over three feet long and weigh over twenty-five pounds. They will tear your tackle up, a big one will. Line snappers they are. I have been peacock bass fishing a few times in my life, and I will tell you honestly, it is without a doubt the most fun I have ever had fishing, fresh or saltwater."

The group was clearly excited at the prospect of catching Bones' favorite fish.

"Now, you'll be interested to hear this. This may shock you, but probably the most common type of fish that will be checking out your bait is the red-bellied piranha. If you catch them at feeding time with the right bait, you'll pull them in one right after the other. Might want to be careful taking out the hook, though. They've got these little teeth, you see."

Before Bones could utter another word, DeShunta broke in.

"Wait, hold on! Hold on! What are you talking about, piranhas? Ain't nobody told me about piranhas when I been getting in that water!"

She looked accusingly at Bones, her voice getting higher and higher. Tony was enjoying the moment and not concerned in the least. There was no reason for worry in his mind. No one had been bitten. No harm no foul. DeShunta felt violated. Unsatisfied with Bones' reaction, she marched over to Tony.

"Why haven't you told me about some piranhas? Answer me!"

Tony involuntarily took a step back. He had never been on the receiving end of an angry DeShunta before. It was terrifying. Before he could formulate an answer, Bones stepped in.

"Miss DeShunta, I think I can calm your fears. Believe it or not, piranhas get a bad rap. They aren't like the ones in scary movies. Just think of bream, bluegills, whatever you call them back home. There are several species of piranha that are strictly vegetarians. The only time the red bellies get in feeding frenzies is when the water gets unusually low and they start to run out of food because too many fish are competing in too little water. As long as none of those things are happening, though, you are as safe as you can be with them swimming right next to you."

Tamper spoke to him in low tones. Bones continued.

"Well, yeah, Tamper here reminded me. They will go a bit haywire if an animal starts bleeding out in the water. That will trigger them, too."

All the ladies looked at each other, eyes wide, thinking about the time they had spent in the water, completely ignorant of the danger all around them. Dr. Jane, standing behind the circle, thought about her experience when she went for a swim and shuddered. Bones finished his remarks and looked back at Tony.

"Thank you, Bones. So, there you have it. As Bones just shared with us, you have many opportunities to win this contest. Swimming right behind me is everything from the biggest of the big to the smallest of the small and everything in between. Now, what will you use to catch these fish and how do you get to the honey holes where they're hiding out? Here to answer those questions is our logistics man, Tamper. Take it away, Tamper."

Tamper stepped forward, rubbing his hands together as he approached an imaginary podium. With every movement of his hands, Tamper's chest, shoulders and biceps rippled. As he stepped, his thigh muscles and calf muscles flexed and released, flexed and released. Even the front of his shins were muscular. Peaches and Willow said in unison what the rest of the group was thinking. "Wow." Tamper was cordial but very businesslike. He gave a quick smile but did not otherwise acknowledge the compliment.

"Thank you, Tony," Tamper said. "As you begin your next challenge, my goal is to equip you with the tools you need to succeed. Let's start with transportation. You can't catch the fish unless you can get to them. You may have noticed this stack of logs behind me here. If you will look closely as Bones flips one over….thank you, Bones, these are not merely logs. These are the trunks of jackfruit trees, sawed in half longways, then hollowed out to make a dugout canoe. Bones and I made these the way the indigenous tribes make them. We burned out the middle with small controlled fires and then dug out the burned wood with an adze. They are not as aerodynamic as a professionally-made canoe, but they will definitely get the job done. We have personally tested each one to make sure none of them leak. They are the best boats that money can't buy."

Chaz was beaming. Kayaking was one of his favorite leisure activities. As soon as he realized the boats were made especially for them, and he was about to get in one, he could not wipe the silly grin off his face. He didn't care if he caught a single fish as long as he got to paddle a dugout canoe down the Amazon River. Tamper watched Chaz's reaction and knew he had a fan. He then addressed the issue of gear.

"Now let's move to fishing tackle. You have choices. First of all, we have cast nets. You can use them to catch small fish either to eat or to use as bait. I can show you how to throw a cast net. The technique takes a bit of practice but with patience you can learn it pretty quickly. Secondly, we have bowfishing rigs. These are essentially bows and arrows with a line tied to the arrow which you retrieve with the reel…"

Chaz could not contain his excitement any longer.

"I can't believe this! Bowfishing from a dugout canoe on the Amazon River? This is the coolest thing ever! I am so stoked!"

Tamper smiled.

"I'm glad you like it. One bit of advice. I would not even think about sticking an arrow in an arapaima. One of those monsters will drag you and your canoe straight to the bottom of the river. Keep in mind that there is a possibility you might encounter some competition out there. You may be reeling in a fish and have a giant river otter or a caiman snatch it before you can get it back to the boat. Make sure that what you are shooting at is a fish. You don't want to stick an arrow in a caiman. They will not count toward your total catch if you happen to stick one and reel it in."

DeShunta was growing concerned about the limited selection of tackle.

"Is that all you got for us, some nets and bows and arrows? You ain't got no regular fishing stuff like some rods and reels?"

Tamper nodded.

"DeShunta, just for you we also have regular old rods and reels, hooks, sinkers, pocket knives, needle nose pliers, stringers and even a few lures. Everything a traditional fisherman could want."

"But what do you got for some bait?" she asked.

"You have an unlimited selection of bait," Tamper smiled. "There are frogs and lizards all along the riverbanks and under just about every leaf and rock. You can dig worms. You can use the cast net to catch yourself some baitfish. You can use whatever kind of live bait your heart desires. You just have to gather it yourself."

DeShunta had no intention of grabbing a frog or a lizard or a worm and touching it with her hands. Her grandmama had baited her hook when she was a little girl. Grandmama had also taken the fish off the hook. Catfish whiskers could sting you—at least that's what DeShunta's brother Jaquez had always told her. Her grandmama told her to pay no attention to him, but DeShunta was taking no chances. She didn't touch any of it.

Grandmama kept telling her that this was the last time she was going to bait her hook, and this was the last time she was going to take the fish off her hook, but DeShunta knew better. Even as a small child, DeShunta had an iron will and was a force to be reckoned with. She would get her way, or there would be hell to pay. Her grandmama didn't want to go fishing by herself, and DeShunta was the only family member that would go with her. As a result, Grandmama baited every hook, and Grandmama took off every fish. That procedure had worked just fine when she was a little girl, and it would work just fine today.

DeShunta turned to Chaz and pointed at him.

"You going with me."

Chaz froze. Terror exploded throughout his body like a dye pack in a bank robbery. His joints locked. His vertebra fused. His tendons and ligaments became hardened cement. The spit in his mouth solidified into polyurethane. His heart stopped mid-pump, the blood in his aorta refusing to move any further, leaving his atria and ventricles to fend for themselves. He fought to remain conscious, but the shock was too great. His eyes rolled back in his head, and he dropped like a stone. Before the first person could cry out for help, Dr. Jane was already kneeling by his side, cushioning his head and elevating his feet. Tamper only hesitated for a moment before continuing.

"You can form teams if you would like, or you can fly solo. Sounds like DeShunta has already formed her team—if her teammate is up for the task, that is. How do team members get credit for the fish their team catches? You can divide the weight evenly by the number of persons on the team, or you can come up with a different method, however you would like. I would strongly suggest that you work out the formula with your teammates before, repeat, before you catch the first fish. Bones and I will be going from fisherman to fisherman and from team to team checking in with you and seeing how you are doing. We will not physically help anyone fish, nor will we reveal how your competitors are doing. We will give advice upon request, but only if you ask."

As the Senator thought through the possibilities, the lawyer within him compelled him to raise his hand.

"What if we have a disagreement as to giving credit for fish that we cannot resolve? For instance, what if a team member fishes for fifteen minutes and quits, and then his teammates fish all day and catch enough fish to win but without the first guy's help? What if that guy wants credit for fish he didn't help his team catch?"

Clarence had been totally disinterested up to this point. Fishing was boring. He was not a fisherman; he was a catcherman. All the sitting and waiting for a fish to bite was unbearable. He was not inclined to try his luck on a tiny dugout canoe, either. He may as well go ahead and dive in the water now rather than try to balance his bulk on the twigs they were calling boats. The primary reason for his lack of interest, however, was the prize.

Pearl necklaces. They were playing for pearl necklaces.

They let the crazy hippie chick make the rules which was a huge mistake in Clarence's mind. *All that money and all those diamonds sitting right there in that chest and all the hippie chick wants is pearls. Who cares about pearls?* But as he listened to the Senator's question, a light bulb went off in his head. Clarence cleared his throat and took a step forward.

"Senator, I have the perfect solution for your dilemma there. In the event of any disagreements, the parties will come to me for an arbitration. Each side will present its evidence. I will hear evidence and arguments and render a fair decision as to who gets credit for the fish. The supervisors and non-catchers have the burden of proof, while the workers who did the work get the benefit of the doubt. This is what I do day in and day out. Easy peasy lemon squeezy. Handled. Next."

Annaliese was skeptical.

"I would assume you would be doing this as a free public service, right? And you would recuse yourself if the dispute involved your own team?"

Clarence's tone changed from cheerful problem solver to menacing mob boss.

"You assume? Someone obviously never taught you about assuming. When you assume, you make an ass out of you and me. Don't assume anything, Governor Parkman. When big numbers are at stake, the litigants will be more than happy to pay for the services of a highly-trained arbitrator like me."

Annaliese bristled at his words. Clarence saw that he had struck a nerve. Like a neurosurgeon, he excelled at identifying inflamed nerves, but he had no intention at all of repairing them.

"You focus on you, Governor. Stay in your lane. You got more than your fair share when you were in office. How is it that your salary as Governor was, what, $129,000 a year, and yet after a four-year term your net worth was $3.7 million? How did that happen? Did you throw magic beans out on the front lawn of the Governor's mansion? Who was sliding you unmarked envelopes? Do you want to share now that you apparently think it is share time in the jungle?"

Annaliese's face turned red. She regretted stirring the pot with such a lout as Clarence Humberton. How did he get her numbers? Her accountant had some explaining to do. Either him or the IRS. This was an outrage. She would make darn sure that she never had to bring any disputes to Clarence Humberton to decide. She looked to Tony for guidance. Surely he wouldn't let Clarence have such a pivotal role in the outcome of this contest. Tony could see the question in her eyes.

"I am confident that you recall the rules of the game. Rule number one: You make the rules. Rule number two: See rule number one. That's it. Those are the rules. So, in order to permit Clarence's conflict resolution proposal to take effect, we must ask our Queen for a Day. Mystic Origin, would you like for disputes between team members, should any arise, to be decided by Clarence?"

Tony had barely gotten the last word out of his mouth before Mystic Origin answered, "No! He will not be the decider! I will be. Actually, Mother Nature and I will be."

Clarence was incredulous. He looked at her with utter disgust, then began checking the faces of those around her. *Are they really going to let an ape decide their disputes?* He got no help from anyone. Tony smiled and nodded.

"The Queen has spoken. Any questions? If not, time for you to fish, starting right now! You have until tomorrow at sundown in which to fish. We will call it 8 p.m. for those of you wearing watches. All fish brought back to camp before 8 p.m. will be weighed in. Any fish brought into camp at 8:01 or later will not be counted, no matter how much begging and pleading you do. So, it is important for you to be on time. Don't be late. There will be no exceptions. If you understand what I am saying, say, "Uh huh.""

Half of the contestants said, "Uh huh." Tony was not satisfied. He yelled, "Repeat after me! Arrive by eight and don't be late!" The contestants said, "Arrive by eight and don't be late." Tony screamed, "Louder! Arrive by eight and don't be late!" The contestants, by now all engaged, screamed, "Arrive by eight and don't be late!" Tony screamed, "At 8:01 the game is done!" The contestants were all in synch by this point. They yelled, "At 8:01 the game is done!" Tony yelled, "At 8:02 the game is through!" The crowd screamed, "At 8:02 the game is through!"

Tony couldn't think of what happened at 8:03, so he stopped. Another thought occurred to him.

"One last thing. I don't want to frighten you, but be on the lookout for anacondas in shallow water near the riverbanks where there is lots of floating vegetation. They put the "squeezy" in easy peasy lemon squeezy."

DeShunta gave Tony the stink eye. Tony, who had recovered his mojo after losing it to DeShunta earlier, grinned and gave her a stink eye right back. The first order of business for DeShunta was to check on her fishing partner. She walked over to Dr. Jane, who was waving smelling salts back and forth under Chaz's nose, talking quietly to him as she did. DeShunta put her hand on Dr. Jane's shoulder for support and leaned down for a better look. His eyes fluttered open. The first face he saw was the same one who had voluntold him to be her fishing partner.

"Here, let me help you with him," DeShunta said matter-of-factly

With that, she popped Chaz on his left cheek with an open hand and yelled, "Hey! Get up! We going fishing!" Dr. Jane protested and threw her arm up to stop her, but there was no need. Chaz suddenly revived, did a fireman's roll and jumped to his feet. DeShunta, having worked a medical miracle, ambled over to the fishing tackle to pick out a rod and reel.

Aston declined the Senator's offer to form a team. He remembered all too well the Senator's meager contributions to the victory attained in the first contest. Admittedly, he was the one who spotted the snake god, but Chaz had climbed up and gotten it, Aston had carried it most of the way through the steaming hot jungle, and Chaz was the one who killed the Brazilian rainbow boa. The Senator had watched…and from a distance at that. Most significantly, the Senator was all too ready to abandon Chaz and leave him when he fell behind. Aston originally intended to team up with Chaz, but DeShunta had derailed that plan. He had no trouble turning down the Senator, though. He would rather fish alone than get stuck with him again.

Tattoo was the first one in the water. He wore a bright, fluorescent green life vest with the words Jungle Money in bold black letters on the back. After sticking the blade of his paddle into the soft river bottom to steady himself, he managed to get seated in his dugout canoe without tipping it over. Bones waded out to him and handed him a net, a rod and reel and a small tackle box. Tattoo stayed anchored to the same spot while Bones waded back to the bank. Bones returned with a fluorescent green and black drink cooler. Tattoo opened it up and looked inside. His eyes were greeted by the sight of bottled ice water and plastic-wrapped snacks. He cried out in joy.

"Yes! Cheese crackers and granola bars! Something besides mangoes!"

Peaches and Willow formed a team. They were the next ones to hit the water—literally. Willow had not quite gotten seated before Peaches tried to swing a leg in, throwing the canoe out of balance. Willow went under as did Peaches. Their Jungle Money life vests quickly propelled them back to the surface. Willow came up out of the water spluttering and gasping for breath. Peaches apologized profusely as she wiped her finger under her eyes to determine if her eyeliner had run. The cool water actually felt very good. Despite the unexpected dunking, the two women retained their sense of humor and laughed along with those on dry ground who greatly enjoyed the spectacle.

The proverbial elephant in the room, which no one talked about unless they were sure she wasn't around, was Willow. Her brother had been missing for almost three full days. How could she possibly be mentally and emotionally stable enough to participate in a fishing contest, much less laugh? She told one of the ladies that remaining engaged in the contests helped keep her mind busy so she wouldn't dwell on her worst fears. Everyone was glad she was doing it, but no one could believe it. Interestingly, no one thought she was doing it for the money. The consensus was that she would break down sooner or later, and when she did, it would be bad.

Mystic Origin was glowing. Being crowned Queen for a Day had energized her. Being given the authority to make the rules had empowered her. Unexpectedly becoming Mother Nature's source of comfort and companionship had elevated her status in the eyes of her peers. Even now, Mother Nature held her hand and placidly watched as the others began their fishing adventure.

Now that it was time to fish, Mystic Origin was torn. An animal lover and self-avowed vegetarian, she prided herself in never having bought meat. Anytime the topic of diet arose, she made it clear to everyone that she had never bought a piece of meat in her life. Her statement was technically true. Fortunately for her, no one ever asked her about the reclaimed food she and Leaf ate from the dumpsters behind Burger Doodle, Steak and Lake, Pizza Me and The Rooster Coop. That technically didn't count in her mind since she was neither the killer nor the financier of the killing. As such, she remained guilt-free while indulging. Out here in the jungle however, there were no back alleys behind restaurants where she could make her midnight rounds, searching for what others left on their plates.

It was in that moment that Mystic Origin became a pescatarian.

Tamper saw her and Mother Nature slowly walking his way, hand in hand. He had just handed out a bowfishing rig and was about to show the user how to shoot when Mystic Origin, in her small person voice, asked a question.

"May I have a net?"

"Certainly," Tamper nodded. "Here you go. If you will give me five minutes to give this gentleman a tutorial on bowfishing, I'll be right back to show you how to cast the net."

Mystic Origin watched as Tamper gave Clarence Humberton a lesson in bowfishing. Clarence informed him he wanted to learn to bowfish because he could not stand to sit idle and wait hours for a bite. If he could actually be doing something, he might enjoy fishing.

She thought about his words. She could not bear the thought of causing a fish pain by piercing its lip with a sharp hook. If she could catch fish with a net, however, there would be no pain for the animal. It would experience mental anguish, nervousness, fright and despair of course, but no agonizing injuries. She silently chided herself for discounting a fish's capacity to experience emotional loss deeper than physical discomfort. If she really caught one, though, how would she dispatch it? She considered striking it in the head with a rock but then quickly discarded that idea. A fish doesn't have eyelids. It would see her hand raising the rock. It would see her hand coming down with the rock. It would wonder what it had done to deserve such a dastardly deed. Perhaps an arrow would be the quickest and least painful way to transition the fish from life to the divine river underneath the rainbow bridge. As Mystic Origin agonized over her dilemma, awash in psychological turmoil, a screech of anger, shock and pain suddenly echoed across the Amazon River.

"Son of a…!"

The horrendous screams were coming from Clarence Humberton. He had literally just shot himself in the foot. The arrow had not completely passed through. About four inches of the end of the arrow was sticking out, a sight so gruesome that Clarence was on the verge of passing out. His cries were so loud and so vile that a terrified Mother Nature leaped off the ground and climbed atop Mystic Origin's shoulders, wrapping her body around her human out of pure fear. Clarence screamed a host of obscenities at Tamper. His words fell into three main categories—assessments of Tamper's low IQ, suggestions that Tamper attempt anatomically-impossible acts, and a fervent wish that Tamper would go straight to hell. Tamper fired right back with all the ferocity of a battle-tested Army Ranger.

"Don't blame me you…!" At this point, Tamper inserted the names of various and sundry body parts, alternating between organs and orifices. "Why in god's name did you point the arrow at your foot two seconds after I told you to always point your arrow downrange?"

Not until much later, when Clarence was once again lying in Dr. Jane's medical tent, would he disclose that as he drew back the arrow to test the draw weight of the bow, a mosquito buzzed loudly in his ear canal. In hindsight, he wished he had not tried to shoo it away with his right shoulder while at full draw. After Dr. Jane started an IV drip and injected the top of his foot with local anesthetic all around the protruding arrow, she was able to examine it and determine that it had missed the bones, going straight between them. They discussed treatment options. Clarence just wanted it out.

Under Dr. Jane's guidance, Tamper carefully sawed off the shaft two inches above the entry wound and then, with much effort, pulled the point of the arrow out through the bottom of his foot. Clarence passed out cold as the arrow was finally extracted, which provided a few moments of much-needed relief for Dr. Jane. While he was unconscious, Dr. Jane aggressively scrubbed and disinfected the wounds.

After witnessing Clarence's injury, Mystic Origin's decision about how to fish became easy through the process of elimination. Hooks were out. Arrows were definitely out. That left the net as her only remaining option. She decided that she would take any fish she caught, lay it down on the ground, cover its eyes with a cloth or a leaf and allow it to breathe air, and only air, until it expired. Others would have to clean it for her. Pangs of longing for her partner Leaf overwhelmed her. She wished she was back in the safe confines of her yurt in the tent city underneath the Glade Parkway overpass. She turned to the only source of comfort available. She turned to Mother Nature and hugged her. Thankfully, Mother Nature hugged her back.

When Tamper returned from Dr. Jane's tent, he didn't find Mystic Origin near the dugout canoes where he expected her to be. When she saw that Tamper would not be available to teach her how to fish for a while, she decided not to wait. She wanted those pearls. For that reason, she picked out a net and walked down to the deep pool at the base of the waterfall. When Tamper found her, she was standing knee-deep in the water, throwing the net like it was a giant Frisbee. She was using her whole body to throw it, demonstrating surprisingly good form for someone with no prior experience. Tamper waded out to her. She proved to be a quick study. Her small stature and short arms somewhat limited her effectiveness but she nevertheless caught a small fish while Tamper was watching, which delighted her to no end.

Just when Mystic Origin had succeeded in throwing enough successful casts to make her feel comfortable enough to go out on her own, they heard a succession of slapping noises coming from the base of the waterfall. Something was floating, so they waded closer to investigate.

"Hey, what do you know?" Mystic Origin cried. "It's a fish! And there's another one! This is awesome! Why are they floating on the surface like that?"

As they watched, the fish floating on its side the furthest downstream from the falls began to move its body ever so slightly. Within a few seconds it righted itself in the water and disappeared beneath the surface. Thinking quickly, Mystic Origin waded upstream and grabbed the next floating fish before it, too, revived and swam away. She screamed in excitement when it began to wriggle in her hands. Tamper pieced together what he was seeing.

"Do you know what just happened?" he asked. "Those fish swam over the falls! They surely did. They must have been stunned when they landed and smacked the water. Man, did you ever luck out! I wonder how often they do that? If I was you, I wouldn't tell anybody your secret. You may have just found the honey hole of all honey holes!"

Mystic Origin smiled. This was one of the best days she had ever experienced. Tamper waded back to shore and left her alone to fish. Mother Nature, who was sitting on the bank watching them, studied his face as he approached. She reached her hand up as he neared her. Though it felt quite odd to him, Tamper took her hand and held it as she accompanied him back to the dugout canoes.

Meanwhile, back at the starting point, DeShunta Jackson sat by herself in the bottom of her dugout canoe, floating ten feet from the bank, glaring at Chaz.

"Look me in the eye, boy. I said, look me in the eye! Don't make me say it again."

Chaz could not bring himself to do it. He stood awkwardly, holding a paddle, looking into the water beside the canoe. His fight or flight instincts were firing on all cylinders.

"Look at me!"

Chaz could not resist but neither could he fully comply. He raised his eyelids enough to see her knees. It was as close as he could get. Terror kept him from lifting his eyes any higher.

"Get in the boat right now," she growled. "You going to paddle."

Reluctantly, Chaz stepped in the water. One foot, then the other foot. His eyes still averted, he waded ever so slowly to the canoe, drawn by the irresistible force that was DeShunta Jackson. He wished he was Daniel walking into the lion's den. He wished he was Shadrach, Meshach or Abednego stepping into the fiery furnace. Their trials were child's play compared to what he was about to do. He was about to drift down the Amazon, alone and unprotected, in a boat with DeShunta Jackson. He reached out to put his hand on the boat as though he was about to touch a live wire. He was greeted with a murderous threat.

"Don't you flip me over."

Chaz pulled back his hand. Of all things in life he did not plan to do, flipping DeShunta Jackson into the water was at the top of the list. He closed his eyes and breathed. It was going to take him a minute to work up the courage to touch the boat.

Chapter Thirty-Eight

Bert dialed the number that G had written on the back of the Senior Living magazine when they had last seen each other at Bert's house. Tony and G had given him unshirted grief about having the magazine. Bert told them he was always on the lookout for new material to work into his routines, plus some of the ladies were hot. Tony grabbed the magazine and started flipping through it, trying to find the hot ladies, but all he found were grannies with one foot in the grave and the other slipping. He found a full-page picture of a pleasantly plump old woman in a mobility scooter and asked Bert if she was one of the hot ones. Bert stepped over for a closer look.

"Yes, lord!" Bert cried out. "That's Miss September! She's also Miss October. They couldn't fit all of her in one centerfold, so they had to spread her out over two months. The pages are only 8 ½ by 11 you know. She likes biscuits."

Bert smiled as he remembered the fun they had that night. As he finished dialing 55 for Brazil, he waited for the odd dial tone he knew he would hear before he could punch in the rest of G's number. Anytime he placed an international call that required inputting a country code, there were always unusual pauses and strange electronic sounds. He had a bit in his routine where he talked about the FBI's investigation into the source of the noises, which turned out to be Betty White tapping his phone to see if he was cheating on her.

"Hello?"

"What's up, G? So tell me, because I've got to know. How much jungle money has my boy the Senator extracted from the treasure chest since we last talked? Is there any left? Did he at least leave the rest of them a quarter so they can call home? Tell me, tell me!"

"No, he hasn't won any more yet," G replied. "They are just starting the fishing contest. He's trying to talk Tamper into fishing for him by offering him a 10 percent finder's fee."

Bert howled. "Yeah, baby! That's my boy! You go, Bradford! Work it baby, work it!"

G chuckled, then asked Bert whether he'd had any success in finding a network or station with an open channel they could use to broadcast the trailer that Jason and Wally had put together.

"Well, yes and no," Bert answered. "I have good news, bad news and worse news. The bad news is that I have struck out getting us a cable channel or regular TV channel to broadcast it on such short notice. The worse news is that I have royally ticked off the bigwigs at MBC by even looking around because they have exclusive broadcasting rights. Olan Riggs wants you to call him. Sorry. I know how much fun that will be. The good news is that I found us a loophole we can totally exploit. The contract didn't say nothing about Jungle Money merchandise! We are free as a bird to market and sell neon green Jungle Money t-shirts on the shopping channel! Of course, nobody will have a clue what Jungle Money is yet since the trailer hasn't aired, but once it does, booyah! Mo' money, mo' money, mo' money!"

"Well, that doesn't surprise me," G sighed. "Maybe streaming is our best option. I just hope we can keep the wheels from coming off long enough to get it aired. If not, we may all be bunking in with the Senator when this thing is over."

"I'd rather sleep in a dumpster with your girl Mystic Origin than spoon with the Senator, but don't tell him that. Speaking of which, how is our favorite hippie doing?"

"She is actually Queen for a Day today," G answered. "Last time I saw her on the monitor in the video production tent, she was leading the orangutan around by the hand…or it may have been the other way around. Hard to tell. The video feed wasn't great. It was a little glitchy."

"Which reminds me," Bert interjected, "there is supposed to be a meteor shower or comet or asteroid or something like that circling the earth in the next day or two. The news guy said it may interrupt signals or destroy satellites or end the world or something. I didn't pay attention. I'm pretty sure I just made up the end of the world part, but he really did say something about interference with satellite transmissions."

"Okay. We'll be on the lookout. Hopefully we won't need to make any phone calls when it passes by."

The men ended the call and went back to what they were doing. G looked at his phone and saw that he had a message. He knew who it was from. He didn't want to talk to Olan Riggs right then. If Olan asked him, "Didn't you get my message?" G was going to tell him the meteor shower must have interrupted the signal.

Chapter Thirty-Nine

After paddling a mile or so downstream, Chaz and DeShunta found themselves in a tropical paradise. The river was calmly flowing by. The unlikely pair made their way to a small inlet shaded by beautiful trees, with multiple roots as thick as your arm extending above the water's surface, perfect for tying a rope and anchoring the boat. Colorful birds flitted from branch to branch overhead, twittering and chirping their happy jungle songs. While DeShunta stayed in the boat, Chaz crawled up on the bank and searched for bait. He found a stick suitable to use for raking back the leaves and ground cover. He found at least one or two worms or lizards with every rake of the stick. Occasionally, he found a small mud-colored frog. When he uncovered a bright yellow and black frog, though, Chaz quickly raked the leaves back over it and moved several feet upriver. He was pretty sure it was a poison arrow tree frog. He didn't want to die digging bait.

After filling the plastic bait bucket with delicacies that would tempt any fish, Chaz waded back out into the river where DeShunta was waiting. Although he was the one guiding the boat, there was no question as to who was captain of the ship.

"Hey, I need some bait on my hook. What you got in there?"

Chaz trembled at the sound of her voice. He answered but could not bring himself to raise his eyes.

"Worms. Lizards. Two frogs. Mostly worms."

"I want to start off with a lizard," DeShunta declared.

She swung the end of her fishing pole over to him. There was nothing but line. No hook, no sinkers, no float, no nothing. Chaz sighed. He climbed back in the boat, carefully so as not to tip it over. Thankfully, everything he needed was in the Jungle Money tackle box. He began rigging up her pole. They sat in silence for the next several minutes, listening to the beautiful sounds of nature all around them. Presently, DeShunta broke the silence.

"Sure is beautiful. I never seen nothing like this before."

Chaz's mind agreed, even if his throat locked up when he tried to vocalize it. He held the hook between his index finger and thumb as he bit down on a split shot sinker designed to help drag the line down into the depths where the big ones were. Once he finished with the rig, he turned his attention to catching a small black lizard in the bait bucket. Much to his horror, it wriggled out of his hand, jumped into the floor of the boat and dashed underneath the nearest available cover—DeShunta's derriere. Chaz began to hyperventilate. He was afraid to tell her for fear it would make her jump and spill them both into the water. He was definitely not going to reach up and try to recapture it. Although he knew remaining silent was not the best plan, it was the right plan right now. He didn't say anything. He just dug another lizard out of the bait bucket. Using extra concentration this time, Chaz was able to hook it through the underside of its bottom jaw, just inside the rim of bone that held its teeth.

"You are all set," he whispered.

"Speak up when you talk to me."

DeShunta swung the end of her pole around so she could inspect the shiny black lizard dangling from her hook. Satisfied with what she saw, she reached way back and cast with all her might. Her backswing brought the hook whistling by Chaz's ear. If he had not done a fast Matrix-style backbend, he would be wearing a new earring right now—either that or DeShunta would be fishing with a new, flappy, flesh-colored lure.

DeShunta's first cast went down the river without attracting any visible attention. She aimed her second cast more upriver at a forty-five degree angle. Chaz could tell she had done this before by how far she cast. Her bait splashed down just before reaching the far bank. Chaz watched the thick twenty-pound test line glide under overhanging limbs, through a collection of floating vegetation, past a fallen tree…

Suddenly, the rod bent double in DeShunta's hands. She screamed as the line made a mad dash downstream, slicing the water as it went. The reel started singing as the fish peeled off line. Chaz was glad he had checked the drag to make sure it would give out line if they hooked into a big fish. Chaz encouraged her to keep her rod tip pointed up so the fish would have to battle the bend of the flexible pole rather than having all of its line-snapping force applied straight to the inflexible reel. DeShunta, who had never hooked into a fish like this before, willingly accepted all the advice he could give. The battle continued unabated for several minutes. She was glad the boat was still tied to the tree root; otherwise, the fish would have pulled them way downriver.

Suddenly, the fish broke the surface and tail-walked across the water before plunging back into the depths. Chaz and DeShunta both cried out an excited, "Whoa!" The fish was big, and it was different from any they had ever seen. A violent yank on the line let them know the fish had seen them when he surfaced and had no intention of ever seeing them again. As her rod tip dipped into the water, DeShunta began yelling.

"Get back here, fish! You ain't going nowhere! I got you! You might as well give up! I got you! Come here! I said come here!"

The fish surfaced again but did not leave the water this time. His second run for the bottom was just as vigorous as the first. DeShunta almost lost her balance when he reversed course and swam hard downriver, using the current to aid his escape. She grabbed the side of the boat with her right hand to steady herself, then went right back to the battle. She fought through the fatigue in her arms and began to reel, gaining line slowly but surely. Chaz could tell the fish was starting to tire. The runs were getting shorter. The dives were getting shallower. DeShunta managed to complete fifteen or twenty turns on the reel without being interrupted by a run.

Suddenly there it was, floating on its side on top of the water. A beautiful green-backed, yellow-sided, orange-bellied, tiger-striped monster of a fish. Chaz reached out with his right hand, grabbed it by the bottom jaw and tried to lift it. Nothing doing. He couldn't lift it. He reached down and grabbed its jaw with two hands and lifted. Nope. Couldn't do it. Without releasing his grip, Chaz struggled first to his knees and then to his feet. He lifted again. This time he was successful. He pulled the fish out of the water and into the boat. DeShunta screamed with joy.

"I did it! I did it! I got you! Yes sir, I did! I got you!"

Chaz laughed. DeShunta turned to face him and asked, "So, what is it?"

Chaz shook his head and answered, "I have no idea. It looks like a tiger with all these stripes. Maybe it's a tiger fish? I don't remember what Bones said. Wait a minute, yes I do. I sure do. It's a peacock bass. This is the one he said was his favorite to catch."

The fish suddenly convulsed, hit the bottom of the boat with a thud and started flopping, causing DeShunta to scream. Chaz grabbed its bottom jaw again and held it still. They watched the fish's gills move in and out, in and out, as its fins continued to wave back and forth. Every so often it partially closed its mouth before opening it wide again. Chaz was stunned by the size and the beauty of the fish.

"DeShunta! That is the biggest, most beautiful fish I have ever seen!"

DeShunta burst out into joyous laughter. She stuck up the palm of her hand and held it up to Chaz. At first his eyes went wide with fright, but when he realized she was merely asking for a high-five, he high-fived her. She laughed even harder when she saw she had scared him. Chaz even managed to laugh a little himself. DeShunta wiped her eyes and tried to catch her breath.

"I think I'll be wearing some pearls tomorrow night!"

Chaz laughed and nodded. His smile faded a bit when he thought about the fact that she had just said "I" and not "we." He was certain she meant to say "we," but in the excitement of the moment she had merely slipped up and said "I." *Surely that's what she meant to say, right?* Of course she did. Chaz was certain of it.

Chaz was not certain of it. Not certain at all.

He started to ask but shut that idea down as soon as it popped in his head. He was alone with DeShunta Jackson in a tiny boat on the Amazon River a mile away from the nearest human. There was no way on God's green earth that he was about to risk starting a fight with her under these circumstances. He thought about addressing it with Tony when they returned to camp but suddenly he remembered Tony wasn't the boss.

Mystic Origin, the Queen for a Day, is the decider. She said so herself. She made the rules. There was one thing that Chaz knew about Mystic Origin. She hated DeShunta, and the feeling was mutual. Suddenly he felt better about his chances. He was thinking through the possible outcomes when DeShunta interrupted his thoughts.

"I'll let you wear some pearls, too. You did half the work, so I'll give you half the pearls."

Chaz's face didn't change, but his insides sure did. He closed his eyes, turned his face to the sky and exhaled. *Thank god.* Problem solved.

Meanwhile, Tattoo had decided to buck the crowd and go upriver to a side stream he had seen from the shore the day before. Eager to get out of the current, he turned left when he found a small tributary feeding into the main river. The foliage overhead was dense and nearly blocked out the sun. Once his eyes adjusted to the low light, he could see dark waters burbling past tangles of tree roots, ferns and moss-covered rocks worn smooth by thousands of years of water flowing over them.

The quiet unnerved him at first. He had grown used to being surrounded by noisy people and cameramen in the bright Amazonian sun. Back here though, he was alone. No cameras, aside from his Mini-Go. No Bones. No Tamper. No Tony. No women. Just Tattoo. Actually, he wasn't completely alone, not if you count squirrel monkeys, toucans, and all other manner of creatures. Nevertheless, he was acutely aware that he was on his own. As he rested his arms for a moment, he absentmindedly scratched the knuckle where the bullet ant had stung him. He intended to be vigilant this time and not allow his zeal for treasure to dull his awareness of the dangers around him.

Tattoo found a short stretch of the stream where the canopy opened enough to allow sunlight to hit the water. The light penetrated the depths and lit the dark water in such a way that he could see way under the surface. Every submerged branch, every leaf, every twig that was lazily drifting by could be easily seen. It was almost like an underwater spotlight. He was mesmerized by the beauty of what his eyes beheld. It was like a painting. He started to make his way to the bank when his eye caught movement.

A fish! He was in luck! He continued studying the water, keeping his eyes fixed on a submerged root while looking for movement around it. His heart skipped a beat when he realized he was not just looking at one fish. There was movement all around that tree root. They were not that big, but man, there was a bunch of them! A smile crossed his face. He tore his eyes away from the water and looked for a place to climb ashore so he could dig some bait.

Tattoo paddled to the shore as quietly as he could and began reaching for leafy branches to steady himself as he climbed out. The bank was higher than he would have liked, but the tree roots and a big exposed rock beneath looked like they would provide a good base for pushing off. As he got closer to the rock, he noticed it was wet and had tendrils of moss clinging to it which were pulled downstream by the water. He looked up and down the bank. This was still the clearest spot. Resigning himself to the fact that exiting the boat gracefully might be a challenge, he put the paddle in the boat and pulled himself as close as he could to the shore. While gripping a tree limb with one hand, he put the other hand on the hull of the boat and carefully, ever so carefully, began to stand up. With one foot on the boat, he stepped off into space with the other. When his foot touched rock, he breathed easier.

I made it, he thought to himself.

That pleasant thought had barely formed in his mind before it was no longer true. Tattoo made the mistake of having all his body weight on the foot that touched the slick river rock without first testing it to see if he could get any traction on it. His foot slid straight across and off the river rock, plunging him down into the dark water. Somehow he maintained his grip on the tree branch and did not go all the way to the bottom. The Jungle Money life vest cushioned the blow to his ribs. Unfortunately, his right arm got skinned all the way from the top of his bicep to the middle of his forearm, first by the tree branch and then by the rock.

Tattoo spluttered and cursed as he fought his way up and out of the water and onto the bank. So much for peace and quiet. With his back to the river, he held his injured arm out in front of him and used his other hand to twist the skin up so he could see the extent of his injuries. Not awful. It hurt worse than it looked. There were two scrape lines dripping with watery blood, but it wasn't much. His arm would survive. Then he turned his attention to what was really hurting—his leg. The fall had taken off every bit of skin on his right shin when his foot slipped off the rock and he slid down the side. It was throbbing to beat the band. Thick, dark blood was forming on the wound. He needed to see Dr. Jane. This was going to require medical attention—possibly stitches.

At that moment, a thought occurred to him. *The boat!*

Tattoo spun around as fast as he could. The boat was no longer within arm's reach, but he was relieved to see that it had not yet gotten out into the main current. He frantically looked around for something to reach it with but saw nothing other than a fallen log too big to lift and some small branches too short to be of any use. There was no time to waste. That boat was life. He regretted having to disturb the tranquil fishing hole a second time. *Hopefully, the fish will still be hungry when I'm done*, he thought to himself. He cannonballed down into the water, came up and began to dog paddle, trying his best not to make waves and push the boat further out into the river.

The wound on his arm only stung a little when he hit the water, but his damaged right shin hurt a lot. He tried to curse away the pain without much success. He toughened up and focused on getting to the boat as quickly as possible. Suddenly, he felt a sharp pain on his shin. It brought an involuntary cry to his lips. *What was that?*

Then he felt another…

Chapter Forty

Meanwhile, back in the main river channel, unaware of Tattoo's plight, the Senator had already been out and then paddled back to where he first got into his boat. When he spied Tamper, he began to wave.

"Mr. Tamper! Mr. Tamper? Oh, Mr. Tamper!"

"Yes sir, what can I do for you?"

The Senator wiped the back of his neck with a handkerchief.

"My good man, I need to ask for a little assistance. I can't quite see well enough to tie a hook on my line. Old eyes, you know. You'll know one day when you get as old as I am and your arms are too short for you to read a newspaper. Anyway, can I ask you to rig me up a hook and a bobber? And can I buy some bait from you?"

Tamper noticed reading glasses dangling from the Senator's neck.

"Senator, I think I've solved your problem. I've found your readers. They're hanging from your neck. Right there they are."

The look on the Senator's face let Tamper know the Senator already knew their location before he asked.

"Well yes, I've got these, but they don't help me see close, you see."

Tamper raised an eyebrow but otherwise didn't answer. The Senator decided to try brutal honesty.

"Look, I don't know how to tie a fish hook on this type of line, okay? I asked the ladies. Willow and Peaches. I thought they might have some sewing experience even if they had never been fishing, but somehow I made them mad by asking. They told me to get out of their spot. I have never seen a grumpier group than this one. Women just can't be pleasant when you take them out of the air conditioning, I guess."

The Senator gave a conspiratorial laugh. Tamper's face never changed. The Senator's smile faded.

"Look, will you tie my hook or won't you? You are the help, aren't you? Well, how about helping?"

Tamper shook his head. "I have helped you, sir. I made your boat with my own hands. I brought the life vest you are wearing. I brought the cast nets and the bowfishing rigs. I brought the rods and reels. I put together everything in your tackle box including hooks, sinkers and extra line. I brought the little cooler and even fixed the sandwiches that are in it. The rest is up to you, sir."

The Senator's face exhibited a level of disgust usually reserved for caddies who brought him the nine iron when they should know he needed the eight iron. Completely fed up, he spat out his rebuke.

"Well, aren't you just the cat's meow? Mr. Muscles, Mr. Army man, with nothing to do right now but kill time, and you can't find it in yourself to help somebody tie a stupid hook? I am not sure you realize this, but you wouldn't have a salary if I hadn't appropriated the funds to pay you with. I'm the reason you get paid, Mr. Ungrateful! The least you can do is show me some gratitude by tying me a hook!"

Tamper was not intimidated by the Senator. His blood pressure didn't rise even a single point while listening to his tirade. Tamper had searched dark caves all across Afghanistan with a Belgian Malinois named Hondo looking for Osama Bin Laden. He had disarmed roadside bombs without any protective gear when there was no EOD unit nearby and they needed to get a Humvee through a narrow pass in order to survive the night. He had seen battle buddies die from a sniper's bullet while kneeling right next to him. He had seen things and done things that his wife and two daughters would never, ever know about. Listening to a pampered politician complain didn't faze him in the least.

"Sir, let's talk about gratitude then," Tamper said with a trace of heat in his voice. "I served you for sixteen years, most of which was either in Iraq or Afghanistan. While I did, sir, you slept soundly in your bed at night because rough men like me stood ready to do violence to those who would do you harm. For that reason, I have two things to say to you. Number one—you are welcome. Number two—grow a set and tie your own hook, pansy."

The Senator's mouth formed an "O" as his eyebrows rose to his hairline. Unused to such a display of disrespect, the Senator made a mental note to lodge a complaint with Tony and G. Suddenly feeling like the distance between him and Tamper was a bit too close for comfort, the Senator held his hands up and backed away slowly, never breaking eye contact. Tamper's eyes, narrowed to mere slits, were inscrutable.

Thirty feet away, Mother Nature sat on an upended dugout boat on the shore watching the men with calm, serene eyes. Though she couldn't understand the meaning of the words, she understood the tone and didn't like what she heard. She slid off the boat onto the ground and ambled along the path in the direction of her small human friend. Maybe she was out of the water. Maybe she had some fruit.

Chapter Forty-One

Celeste was a bundle of nerves. Lying on her back on a gurney in a semi-private room with the curtain open enough to allow her to see people all the way down the hallway, listening to everyone babbling away in Portuguese, was not how she wanted to spend an afternoon. Even though she had been accompanied by two women, she felt very alone. She was filled with an intense longing to have Trayton here with her. She needed his touch, his reassuring tone, his calm demeanor. But there was something more she wanted. She could say this in her mind and no one would hear her or make fun of her. She wanted her mom.

Celeste was still a little nauseous though not nearly as bad as last night. She felt like it could be due to air sickness since the helicopter dropped suddenly from time to time and then circled for what seemed like forever when they reached the hospital. She felt her forehead, hoping she had a fever because a virus would be much less inconvenient than if she was...what everybody kept saying. She remembered that Summer was sitting in the corner, camera trained on her, not speaking or interacting in any way. It was easy to forget she was there. Celeste guessed that was the way Summer wanted it. About that time, the woman she knew as Hyacinth reentered the room. She was pleased—you could tell by her expression. In broken English, the only kind she spoke, she explained the reason for her smile.

"I find woman speak English and Portuguese. Help us, doctor."

Honey was beaming. Celeste smiled, grateful to know a translator was coming. After a few minutes, a nurse entered the room followed by another woman in street clothes. The woman in street clothes introduced herself as Fernanda. She did not work at the clinic. She was just a friend of the nurse who happened to be there waiting for her friend to get off work. Fernanda asked if Celeste would be okay with her remaining in the room in order to translate. Celeste nodded appreciatively.

The nurse took Celeste's temperature and blood pressure and recorded her vital signs. Celeste was almost disappointed when the nurse said her temperature was normal. The nurse gave her Phenergan for the nausea, then handed her a specimen cup and pointed her down the hallway to the restroom. Celeste had a near-irresistible desire to run out the door. What if she was really pregnant and experiencing morning sickness? Celeste looked at the cup in her hand. This was huge. This was it. Her whole life could change in the next few moments.

She brought the sample back to her room and handed it to the nurse. Fernanda told her the nurse said it would only take ten minutes to find out. Celeste took a deep breath and blew it out slowly. Honey patted her arm reassuringly and then held it.

"You just breaths. In, out, breaths. Is all okay."

Honey smiled a warm smile as she reached up and tenderly pushed Celeste's hair away from her eyes. Honey was so very beautiful and confident. Celeste felt neither beautiful nor confident. She laid on her back and put her arm over her eyes so she would have a few minutes to pretend she was back at home holding Aurora while watching her favorite TV show. Much sooner than she expected, the nurse returned with the verdict. She gave her the results herself without a doctor and without the assistance of Fernanda.

"You mama."

The nurse showed her the oval-shaped window which displayed two very clear pink lines. Celeste stared in open-mouthed disbelief. Honey hugged her, kissed the side of her head and said, "Congratulations!" Celeste said, "No, way." Honey said, "Yes, way!" Celeste burst out in tears. Fernanda joined in the group hug with Honey. Together they rocked Celeste back and forth, back and forth as she sobbed.

While they were comforting her, a doctor wearing a white coat walked in. He smiled at Celeste, whose tear-stained face was like many he had seen before. He held a clipboard with her intake form in one hand while he reached out to her with the other hand.

"Hello, Miss Shhh…"

"It's Schneiderman," she sniffed.

"I am sorry, Miss Schneiderman, very nice to meet you. I am Dr. Bortolazzo. And these people are…?"

"Okay, well, let's see, this is Hyacinth…"

The doctor smiled broadly at Honey and said hello to her with a warm two-handed shake, slightly more enthusiastic than he intended his greeting to be. When Celeste introduced Summer, he saw she was pointing a video camera at him. His face revealed his misgivings about having her in there during the visit. Celeste assured him that it was okay. He was clearly skeptical.

"No, really, it is okay if she is in here," Celeste said. "Believe it or not, even though I am crying, I want her to film all this. It's okay for her to be in here. So, go ahead."

Celeste started to tell him that they were filming for a reality TV show called Jungle Money but then thought better of it. There was no telling what kind of uproar that would create. The doctor might run out. Summer's youth and quiet affect gave no hint that the video would be used for anything other than Celeste's personal use. Satisfied with the explanation, Dr. Bortolazzo proceeded with the visit.

"So, as you already know, you are pregnant. Congratulations. You will be a good mama. Would you like to see your baby today?"

Celeste was stunned into silence. Honey answered for her.

"Yes, she would like see!"

The doctor nodded to his nurse and stepped out into the hallway. The nurse wheeled in a large machine next to the bed. After plugging two cords into outlets, she flipped a switch and the monitor came to life. Celeste tried to calm her racing heart. Her mind could scarcely take it in.

I am about to see my baby.

Chapter Forty-Two

Day two of the Jungle Money fishing contest, which Peaches dubbed "fishing for pearls," was drawing to a close. The Amazon rainforest was once again living up to its name. Aston stood under a thick stand of trees waiting for the usual afternoon rain shower to subside. He was wet from head to toe. Water dripped off the bill of his black and neon green Jungle Money baseball cap onto the front of his black and neon green Jungle Money life preserver. The branches overhead slowed down the velocity of the downpour before it hit him. Peering through the foliage above him, he could see bits of blue sky beginning to appear between the clouds. It wouldn't be long until the rain passed.

The weather pattern was the same every afternoon. When Aston first landed in the Brazilian rainforest, he sprinted inside his or someone else's hut at the first hint of an afternoon deluge and changed out of wet clothes into dry clothes multiple times a day. Now however, it was his new normal. The rain no longer kept him inside unless there was severe thunder and lightning. He simply rotated back and forth between the two dry-fit shirts and athletic shorts he had brought and no longer gave a second thought to being wet.

The rain washed off most of his mosquito repellant, which was unfortunate. The high-pitched sound of hundreds of mosquito wings would haunt his memory of this place forever, long after he returned to civilization. At this moment however, "mozzies," as Bones called them, weren't even a blip on Aston's radar screen. He was much too excited to be bothered by something as trivial as a bug bite.

Aston had hit the mother lode.

He stumbled across this honey hole of honey holes quite by accident. He had no intention of fishing here. His original plan, before DeShunta began giving orders, was to team up with Chaz, paddle to a remote part of the river in separate boats and try their luck. Without his buddy Chaz however, he was not quite as adventurous. The Amazon rainforest and the Amazon River were intimidating enough when you were in a group. The intimidation effect increased exponentially when you were all by yourself.

Aston had originally declined the Senator's offer to team up. He had the distinct impression that if he fished with the Senator, 90 percent of his time would be spent getting the Senator unhung, unhooked, and untangled, and only 10 percent of his time would be spent fishing. After a disappointing first day of fishing by himself, which had resulted in exactly zero fish despite his best efforts, Aston changed his mind. There had to be better places to fish which were farther downriver, but quite honestly he was scared to go by himself. If he was going to find one of the good spots a long way from camp, it was wiser to be in the company of an annoying person than to be alone and risk getting snatched out of your boat by a chupacabra and no one knowing where your body went. For that reason, he told the Senator they could start off together, but it was every man for himself when it came to catching and counting fish. The Senator was so happy to have a friend that he would agree to almost anything.

Not long after they started, things got a little testy. As Aston predicted, they hadn't gone a hundred yards before the Senator began making requests for help that really weren't requests for help at all—they were thinly-disguised ruses for Aston to do it all. "Hey, help me put the rod and reel together, would you?" "I can't see well—would you help me run the fishing line through the eyelets?" "Do you know how to tie a hook on? My grandfather taught me seven different ways but he used different line than this." "Hey, I don't have any pliers. Can you come over and put a couple of sinkers on the line? I promise I won't ask you for anything else." "I'll let you in on a secret. The best bait is a big fat grub worm. My grandfather swore by them. I'll bet there's a million of them under the leaves on the bank next to you there. If you hand me one I'll show you."

Aston hadn't fished many times in his life, but he knew enough to know that constant yakking, especially the loud kind that the Senator incessantly produced, was no bueno—it was a surefire way to scare the fish away. He went through one round of being the customer service attendant behind the Amazonian help desk, doing everything the Senator asked, before he lost his cool.

"No offense, but I am not trying to be your personal fishing guide," Aston said. "I'm trying to take care of me, which is hard enough without me having to stop and take care of you. If you want to fish beside me—great. If you do, though, you are going to have to fix your own stuff. I'm not being mean—I just barely know what I'm doing myself."

The Senator then explained for ten solid minutes why Aston had him all wrong—of course he knew how to fish, he's been salmon fishing with the best guide in all of Alaska; he's used a fly rod to catch bonefish in knee-deep water in Florida when he took the assistant prime minister of Japan out to butter him up for talks on a renewed trade agreement, blah, blah, blah. All Aston knew was that the Senator didn't know how to tie a hook on a line, and Aston had no intention of doing it for him all day. He had already shown him once, but it was obvious the Senator wasn't watching and had no interest in learning how. Why should he when he had somebody like Aston around to do it for him? Aston listened to him politely for as long as he could stand it before running out of patience.

"You know what?" Aston asked. "The one thing I know about fishing is that you scare the fish away when you talk. If that's true, you are putting us behind with every word you say."

The Senator started to speak again, but Aston put one finger to his lips and shushed him. Taken aback, the Senator started to retort when Aston shushed him again, this timely forcefully. Thoroughly disgusted and having exhausted all efforts to persuade Aston to do anything useful, the Senator announced a change of plans.

"Alright. Well, I'm going to have to paddle back to the start and see if Mr. Tamper or Mr. Bones will refresh my memory on how to tie this thick line, which I think is too large to go through the hook. Unless you will, which wouldn't take you two minutes to do because I've already seen you do it two or three times now."

Aston didn't say a word. He paddled away from the Senator towards the opposite bank and pretended he didn't hear him. The Senator tried one last time.

"You know, when they tie my hook on, the hook won't come off because they are professionals, and I'll have the advantage over you. Once they refresh my memory on how to do it, I'm not promising to share their technique with you. I don't want to be cutthroat about it but after all, we are in a contest."

Aston held his tongue. He was not going to take the bait. He simply pointed to a new place, well away from the Senator, and began to paddle.

"You know, I think I'll try fishing from the bank over there."

That was how Aston found himself sitting on the bank not three hundred yards from the starting line in a very nondescript, shallow, unremarkable-looking stretch of river that every other competitor would be paddling back and forth through all day. While waiting on the Senator to return, Aston opened his Jungle Money tackle box and found a spinnerbait. It had a garish rainbow-colored skirt made of rubbery strings that caught his eye. It had a yellow lead head with a painted eye on each side. It had a long wire like a straightened paperclip, bent in the middle, with two blades, one leaf-shaped and painted gold and one much smaller made out of silver. It didn't look like anything a fish would want to eat. Nevertheless, he tied it on and cast. As he reeled it in, it sounded like a helicopter chopping up the water after a crash landing. He laughed out loud at how ridiculous the thing was.

Boom. Fish on.

As the rod bent double, Aston looked downriver. The boats manned by Annaliese, Peaches and Willow were still within sight. He was certain they would paddle back to his spot if they saw. He did not want to have three more needy Senators to deal with. *Please don't look this way*, he thought. *Please don't look this way*. He reeled in a good-sized silvery fish of unknown make and model. He had no idea what it was. It didn't have rows of sharp teeth, so it wasn't a piranha. It wasn't ten feet long, so it wasn't a pikachu or whatever Bones had called it. It looked like money to Aston. He chuckled when he got it out of the water. *Why did you bite that, fish? What were you thinking?*

Aston got the hook out of its mouth easily enough. *Now, what do I do with it?* He looked inside the tackle box for help but saw nothing that looked useful. His eyes traveled over a tightly wound bundle of cord wrapped in plastic which just looked like heavy fishing line. He had no experience with stringers, so he didn't know that was exactly what he needed. He wished he had a bucket or an ice chest or something. The Jungle Money cooler was too small, plus it held his snacks and drinks. Looking around, he spied a hole in the ground at the foot of a massive fallen tree. Aston tossed the fish in the hole for safekeeping. *Why not? It's not like I'm going to eat it,* he thought to himself. *I just need to keep it long enough to bring it to the weigh-in.*

Mist hovered over the surface of the river. The rain ceased, the clouds parted and the air temperature began to change. Aston wiped his hands on his shorts to get the fish slime off and cast the helicopter monstrosity again. As soon as he engaged the reel and heard the click, it happened again.

Boom. Fish on.

There is no way this is happening, he laughed to himself. *What could they possibly think this thing is?* Aston looked downriver again. Was Peaches looking his way? Aston lowered his rod tip and stopped reeling. He didn't want to attract attention. He casually backed up until a tree was between him and Peaches, then he began furiously reeling again. It was another silver beauty, a little smaller than the last one, but hey, it was a fish. He unhooked it, tossed it in the stump hole and cast out again.

Boom. Three casts, three fish.

Thankfully, the ladies had floated further downstream, so he didn't have to hide this time. He reeled in fish number three and tossed it in the hole along with the others. By this point, Aston was a big believer in the power of the "helichopper," as he began to call it in his mind. The fishing slowed down in his first spot, so he walked twenty or thirty steps downstream and cast.

Boom. Fish on.

Aston repeated the pattern over and over again. When the bite slowed down he would simply walk a short distance and try a new spot. Purely by happenstance, Aston was in the right place at the right time with the right bait. Each time he caught another fish, he would dutifully walk back to the shallow hole in the ground and drop it in. A squadron of blood-sucking jungle flies covered the top layer of fish. They dashed away long enough to avoid being squashed by a falling fish but then returned to their feast immediately thereafter. After an hour's exposure to the sweltering heat, the smell became ripe. Aston did not like to think about having to shove his hands down into the pile in order to transfer the stinky fish into his boat for weigh-in, so he thought about something more pleasant. *How much do you guess that stash of pearls is worth?*

It dawned on Aston that despite the passage of a considerable amount of time, the Senator had not returned. He couldn't know that the Senator had become completely flabbergasted and quit after getting no help with tying hooks for the second day in a row. Bones was gone when he got back. Tamper was not in the mood to play camp counselor tying on a six-year-old's hook at Camp Sunshine. The Senator didn't appreciate being told to "grow some hair on your peaches." He realized he wasn't going to win, and he didn't like being out in the rain, so he quit and went back to camp. Whatever the Senator's reason for not returning, Aston didn't mind. He didn't mind at all.

After an indeterminate amount of time had passed, the bite grew cold. Aston noticed that the shadows were growing long. By this time, he was the furthest downriver that he had been. A thought occurred to him. *What time is it?* He looked at his wristwatch. *Whoa! Twenty minutes to eight. Son of a gun! Time to go! I don't want to be late to the weigh-in*, he thought to himself. He double-timed it up the riverbank, making a beeline for the hole in the ground which was by now filled with fish.

As he speed walked to his destination, something in the water caught his eye. Aston stopped dead in his tracks. *What is that? Is that a person in the water?* He saw what looked to be a small person swimming from the opposite side of the river to his side. Long arms came up out of the water, one after the other, in a perfect Australian crawl. Was it a child? The person was in no hurry. He continued walking up the bank towards his destination, keeping his eyes on the swimmer as he walked.

Something didn't look right. What was the child holding in his hands? As Aston neared and got a better look, he stopped. That was no kid. He had fur on his face. Those were long, curved claws at the end of his long arms. *It's a sloth! Who knew they swam like a person?*

At that moment, Aston heard rumbling out of his left ear. It was barely audible. His eyes left the river and searched for the source of the sound. He started to take another step towards the fish hole when the rumbling became deep, loud and menacing. When he saw the source, his blood ran cold.

Aston was staring into the luminous eyes of a black panther crouching over the pile of fish.

Its head was square, as big as a cinder block. The panther clearly outweighed Aston, who was slight of build. If Aston had been able to look anywhere other than the malevolent yellowish-green eyes boring holes in him, he would have seen the faint pattern of a jaguar under the black coat. The volume of the deep bass growl increased. The animal lifted its upper lip to reveal white, three-inch-long canine teeth that had pierced the skulls and brains of many victims.

Aston froze. He had no gun or weapon of any kind. He was defenseless. He wanted to scream for help. He was not that far from the starting line. He heard faint laughter coming from upriver as his fellow competitors gathered for the final count to see who won. *Help me*, he pleaded in his mind. He didn't yell for fear of triggering the animal. Although he was within ear shot, he might as well have been a million miles away. He and the jaguar were in a stand-off. If the beast charged, Aston knew he was dead.

The panther's attention turned to the river. The sloth. He had seen the sloth. The panther jerked his head back to Aston and lifted his lip even higher, exposing all of his cruel teeth. His tail whipped back and forth. Aston had seen that look before. His house cats did the same thing right before they pounced. His heart sunk. This was it for him. Aston silently begged the big cat for mercy. *Eat the sloth, man. Eat the fish. Eat anything you want, just not me.*

Suddenly an ear-splitting blast of sound assaulted their ears. Someone at camp had an air horn. The panther ceased its growling and raised its head, uncertain as to its next move. Aston was the first human he had ever seen. The loud noise which came from upriver startled him. It was unlike any noise he had ever heard before. Reluctant to leave his stockpile but unwilling to remain, the panther grabbed a large fish in his mouth and vanished seemingly into thin air. Aston looked desperately into the surrounding jungle, certain the big cat was circling around to attack him from behind. He strained his ears, listening for the slightest sound, but he was unable to hear anything. No footfalls. Nothing.

It was now or never.

Aston broke into a run and leaped into the waiting boat he had loosely tied to a low branch overhanging the water. How he didn't flip it over he didn't know. He untied the boat and began to furiously paddle upstream as hard as he could go. He did not look back. He didn't know if the sloth made it or not. He didn't care. He paddled as though his life depended on it, because it did.

Aston hove into view of the group, which was standing in a semi-circle. He was greeted by a cacophony of cheers and jeers. Someone yelled, "Glad you could join us!" Someone else yelled, "Arrive by eight and don't be late!" The group laughed heartily. Tony's voice rose above the din. "At 8:01 the game is done!" When Clarence saw that it was Aston coming in, he gleefully screamed, "At 8:02 the game is through!"

Aston didn't say a word. He was completely winded by his herculean efforts to escape the jaws of death. He was simply glad to be alive. Bones and Tamper could tell by his terrified look and obvious exhaustion that something untoward had happened. They waded out to help him out of the water. Bones got to him first and looked in the boat.

"No luck with the fish, eh?"

Still out of breath, Aston's voice was not loud.

"Actually, I did. Thirty-seven fish. They're all piled in a hole just down the river on the other side. But you won't believe what hap…"

Clarence, who was bracing himself with a pair of crutches to protect his heavily-bandaged foot, interrupted Aston's story.

"Thirty-seven fish? Ha! No sir! Uh, uh. Time's up, chief. Do you think you are special? There are no extensions of time just because it's you and you are special. You have blown it, buddy boy. You can tongue kiss your fish goodbye because they don't count. You, sir, are too late!"

Aston didn't have the energy to argue. He used the last of his strength to wade out of the water, then collapsed at the water's edge. Alarmed, Dr. Jane rushed over to him. She helped him sit up and called for a bottle of water. Peaches hurried over and handed him hers. Aston's hand and arm shook when he tried to hold the bottle. Dr. Jane poured a few sips into his mouth. He swallowed wrong which caused a coughing fit. Everyone crowded around. Dr. Jane instructed them to back up and give him some air, but no one moved. They had to know what happened.

Presently, Aston recovered enough to tell his tale. Eyes grew wide as he told of the apex predator prowling nearby. Everyone cut nervous glances across the river. When someone suggested that they relocate to the huts back in camp, not a soul protested. Almost as an afterthought, someone informed Aston that DeShunta and Chaz had won the fishing contest. DeShunta was not around to accept the praise. She had already beaten a path back to camp. As they were gathering up the baskets of fish, the scale, the tackle boxes, the life vests and the coolers, Tony turned to Aston.

"Say, you didn't see Tattoo out there by chance, did you?" Tony asked. "We were hoping he was with you. Nobody has seen him come in."

Aston shook his head no. Bones and Tamper cut eyes at one another, then spoke to Tony in low tones. Without another word, they each got in a dugout boat and headed to the middle of the river. Their night was just beginning.

Chapter Forty-Three

Honey was so used to not having cell phone service deep in the rainforest that the thought of using one never occurred to her. When the doctor stepped out of the room, it hit her. *Hey, is my cell phone in my purse?* Yes, it was. She powered up her phone. "No service," it said. She walked to the nurse's station and asked if there was a Wi-Fi password. There was. When she found the network, her phone began to beep, bing, vibrate and chirp. A week and a half's worth of unreceived messages, texts, reminders and updates began lighting up her phone. There was even one from Tony.

That's when it dawned on her. She knew exactly how to cheer Celeste up.

Celeste had expressed several times while in the jungle, in the helicopter, and in the clinic lobby, how much she missed Trayton. Honey felt sorry for her. There was nothing she could do except express her sympathy and understanding. Or was there? Then it struck her like a bolt from the blue.

FaceFone!

If Trayton had the FaceFone app on his cell phone or laptop, and if Honey knew the name Trayton went by, she could surprise them both by livestreaming one lover to the other. How exciting would that be? What if Honey could use technology to create a virtual reunion between Celeste and Trayton so they could look at the monitor together and see their baby, even while thousands of miles apart? How will Trayton react when he learns he is going to be a father?

Honey performed a quick social media search. She found Celeste's page quickly enough and scrolled down to Friends. Trayton was one of the first photos shown. She clicked on his picture which took her to his page. She looked at his profile, skimmed down the list of likes and dislikes, music, books, videos…and there it was. His FaceFone handle! sTraykat_strut. Yes! It was so easy to find. She tapped on her FaceFone app and opened it. Fingers flying, Honey searched for sTraykat_strut. Two seconds was all it took. Up it popped. There was his name and profile picture! A smile spread all over her face at her success.

Now, all she had to do was click Connect, hope he was near his phone or laptop, and the magic would happen. She held her phone carefully, as if she was balancing a stack of crystal glasses three feet high, terrified she would touch something and accidentally click out of the app. Pulse racing, she slipped back inside Celeste's room.

Celeste was absentmindedly pulling a strand of her hair while staring off into space. She had always been terrified of what it would feel like to give birth to a baby. The pain must surely be unbearable. She felt overwhelmed and alone, which caused her to vocalize the words she had been repeating to herself all day.

"I wish you were here."

A cart clattered out in the corridor when Honey reentered the room, which drew Celeste's attention. She saw a big smile on Honey's face and an expression that looked as though she knew something. Honey clicked on her phone as she walked towards her. The screen lit up. Honey held it up so Celeste could see.

"Celeste, you know FaceFone? Yes? My phone FaceFone Trayton! Trayton come here! Trayton face eyes see Celeste see baby!"

The thought had never occurred to Celeste. She too had grown used to not having a phone in her hand. It was actually a freeing experience, although at first she had experienced withdrawal symptoms when Tony took them away from everyone the night before they boarded the helicopters. *FaceFone! Yes, of course! I can FaceFone Trayton!* They could share this incredible moment together.

Summer quietly recorded everything being said from her spot in the corner of the room. She began to ponder how in the world she could capture Trayton on the cellphone, the ultrasound monitor and Celeste's face all at the same time. She thought about possible shooting angles and solving the audio challenges, wishing Richard was here to guide her.

The nurse and the doctor returned from the hallway. The nurse unceremoniously lifted Celeste's shirt, squeezed out a liberal dose of personal lubricant and rubbed it all over her belly. The cold caused Celeste to suck in air, but the gel warmed quickly. The nurse moved the transducer wand around her abdomen, which created a series of moving black and white images. As she was doing so, the doctor scrutinized the monitor. After a few seconds of searching, the nurse honed in on one particular area until the doctor said, "Stop." Both the doctor and the nurse gasped.

Celeste was alarmed by their reaction and searched their faces for any hint as to why they acted so surprised. The doctor began to speak to his nurse in Portuguese, which resulted in sudden squeals from both Honey and Fernanda. Celeste was desperate to know.

"What? What do you see?"

"Young lady," the doctor said, "you are going to have twins!"

Celeste burst into tears, the sobs wracking her body. All the women in the room save Summer, who was capturing it all on video, rushed over to comfort her. As the doctor watched the reaction his words generated, a wry grin appeared on his face. He knew that in a few months, Celeste would have two more who sounded just like her. After a bit, Celeste lifted her head and looked into Honey's eyes.

"I've got to go home. I can't be out in the jungle anymore."

Honey smiled and nodded sympathetically, trying not to show the extreme disappointment she was feeling inside. She knew what this meant. She and Tony had discussed it. If for any reason Celeste decided to go back home to the States from the clinic rather than continuing with Jungle Money, Summer was to accompany Celeste on the plane ride back home to Atlanta. Honey would simply stay in Rio because she would be home already. She was just a dancer. It was not worth the time and expense to fly a dancer all the way back to camp without a contestant flying with her. Honey's time was over. Celeste had just decided it without even knowing what she had done.

Tears welled up in Honey's eyes. No one but her knew they weren't for Celeste.

Chapter Forty-Four

Karena was lying in the bed, her golden hair splayed across all of one pillow and partially across a second. She was wearing only a t-shirt she had found in one of Trayton's drawers. She kicked the covers off. It was hot under there. The cool air felt good on her legs. As Jimi Hendrix looked down upon her from the poster above the bed, she reached her arms toward the ceiling and stretched a long yoga stretch. Rubbing her eyes felt good.

Trayton's little dog was awake. She could tell by the sound of its nails going clickety, clickety, clickety from the bed to the front door and back, over and over again. It was starting to annoy her. He should be taking his annoying little dog outside. *If it pees on the floor, I swear I am not cleaning it up,* she thought to herself. *He should be in here asking if I want coffee and a Danish. Instead, here I am awake, no coffee, no Danish, having to face morning alone without the necessities of life.*

She sat up and arranged the pillows behind her head so she could prop up and check her phone. *Which of you witches are posting photoshopped pictures of yourselves today? Fakers. Always trying to look like someone you aren't. Pathetic.* Karena loved the editing tools for these applications. She loved choosing the best pictures of herself and adding a sparkle to her eyes or a sparkle to her white teeth. Where was the one she posted yesterday? Scrolling, scrolling, scrolling, scrolling. *There it is. Ah, one hundred and sixty-six likes so far. Good, good. Now, what comments did people leave?* "You are so beautiful, Karena. Just like a fairy princess!" *Oh Candace, sweet girl.* Karena's thumbs tapped the keyboard. "Thank you!!!! UR 2 sweet!!!" *Who else? Okay, those are all girls. Girl, girl, girl...*

Whoa, back up, what did Edward say? "You is HAWT girl! Cant wait 4 Bikini thurs and lonjeray Friday!" Karena smiled. Edward is a cutie. Her thumbs were momentarily stymied. She couldn't write that he would have to come in person to see more. Her friends were watching to see what she would say. Finally, she found the words. "No 1 wants to see all that Mr. dirty mind! U post urs 1st!" She would have to check her phone all day to see the replies. Of course he would want to see all that. So would the other seven hundred something guys on her friends list. Thank you Edward for giving them a thread to express it. This would be a fun day for reading comments.

Trayton was in the bathroom brushing his teeth. He was humming a tuneless song. *Yikes. Not good. Note to self—don't ask Trayton to sing a love song to me.* Speaking of love songs, Karena bet he was brushing his teeth for a reason. He would be back in here any minute to spend some quality time with her before he headed to work. Did she want to have her legs on top of the covers or under the covers when he walked out? Did she want to flip over, pull the covers back up and pretend she was asleep? Decisions decisions.

About that time, Trayton's phone started vibrating. He had left it on top of the comforter on his side of the bed. Karena picked it up to see who it was. *A video invite from Hyacinth? Who is Hyacinth? What kind of a name is Hyacinth? Why is she trying to videochat with Trayton? Is he meeting new girls online? He better not be.* Karena brought the phone close to her face so she could see the profile picture. *Wow. Not your average Buymart greeter, that's for sure. Let's see what you look like.* She tapped the picture to enlarge it.

Holy crap.

A portrait of an exotic, dark-haired beauty appeared. She had pearly white teeth, an impossible body and hands overhead in some kind of dance pose. She looked to be in the midst of a performance before a crowd. The words on the wall behind her were clearly not English. *She can't be real. Trayton is being scammed. Somebody is trying to catfish him. She looks like a movie star. No one like her is chasing Trayton...unless he is paying her by the minute. Is he paying hot girls from other countries by the minute to videochat with him? If he is, I am out of here*, she thought. *I don't have time for this.*

The phone stopped vibrating. Karena was irritated. Trayton should be answering his phone, not her. She should be drinking a caramel Macchiato right now; instead, she was playing receptionist for Trayton's girlfriends. Speaking of girlfriends, why were so many of Celeste's belongings still on the dresser and shelves and end tables? If they had broken up and moved on with their lives, as Trayton claimed, why hasn't she picked up her things?

By now, Karena was wide awake and highly suspicious. She was feeling played. *I'll get to the bottom of this,* she thought to herself. *I'll tell him about the video invite and then watch his face when he picks up his phone and sees who it was. If he looks at it and takes it to the other room, or worse yet, if he shoos me out the door, I'll know he is talking to other girls.* The more Karena thought about it, the angrier she became.

On the other hand, she really liked Trayton. He was cute, he has a cute house, he has a cool car, he has a good job and he likes yoga. If she squinted real hard, she could see herself with him, at least for a while. She didn't want to blow up a promising relationship just because the guy got a video invite. So, how could she find out the situation without an ugly confrontation?

Then it hit her. She should have engaged the mute stalker function. She had an iPhone while Trayton had an Android, but she was sure his phone would do it, too. When you receive a video invite and want to see the caller but don't want them to see you, you answer but immediately press and hold the power button, the volume button and the function button, all at the same time, then release the first two and continue pushing the function button. All the caller can see is a black screen. They can't see or hear a thing. You can watch them and hear them until they hang up. It may only be a few seconds because who is going to stare at a black screen, but sometimes that's all you want or need. *I should have thought of that*, Karena said to herself.

Trayton's phone vibrated again.

Karena quickly turned to see what Trayton was doing in the bathroom. It sounded like he was tapping his toothbrush on the edge of the sink while gargling mouthwash. She looked back at his phone. Hyacinth again. Her heart rate tripled as she weighed her options. *Should I?* The thought of him paying some two-bit trollop by the minute gave her the jolt of adrenaline that tipped the scales. *Trailer trash is trailer trash, no matter what country she's from. I'll just pick up, look at her real quick, see if she says anything and then hang up.*

Karena answered the video invite and immediately activated mute stalker. *Press hold power button, press hold volume, push function, release the first two, hold function button. And...wait a minute. What's this?* Karena was surprised to see her screen go black instead of vice versa. *Where did the caller go? This is not like an iPhone.* She had killed the call. But why didn't the home screen reappear?

"What the hell?"

Karena stared at the phone, not wanting to release the function button just yet, just in case. She heard Aurora the Havanese whine to go out.

"Shut up, stupid dog."

Trayton came out of the bathroom. Startled, Karena started to drop his phone back on the comforter but then changed her mind. Instead, she went on the offensive.

"So, who is Hyacinth?"

Trayton was confused. What was she talking about? Why did she look mad?

"I give up. Who?"

Karena could spot a liar from a mile away. *Don't look innocent, buddy. You know exactly who she is.*

"I don't know. I figured you would. She just sent you two video invites. And by the way, you need to take your dog out or it is going to pee all over the floor."

Trayton felt a panic attack coming on. *Who is Karena talking about?* He chatted online with lots of girls but never by video chat. *Crap.* He must have forgotten one, or this was a new one. Karena interrupted his thoughts.

"It would be nice if you got me some coffee, too. Waking up is hard enough as it is."

Trayton grabbed his phone out of her hand and looked at the screen. Black. Was it on? Trayton tapped the screen. Nothing. He tapped again and ran his finger across the screen. The black disappeared, replaced by bright light.

Trayton found himself staring full into the face of Celeste.

Celeste's mouth was open. Some woman with an accent said, "Oh god." Celeste didn't say a word—she just stared. Trayton's heart stopped. An irresistible urge to throw his phone against the wall overwhelmed him, but he fought it. Instead, without a word, he clicked END VIDEO.

Oh my god, he thought to himself. *Wait, what?* Another prompt popped up. "DO YOU REALLY WANT TO END VIDEO?" *Sweet mother of pearl, yes!* He never spoke. The last thing Celeste, Honey and Summer saw before the video link ended was Trayton's panic-stricken face. Well, his face and the Jimi Hendrix poster above the bed.

When the video link dropped off, Celeste tossed the phone on the bed. Honey picked it up and closed the FaceFone app. The room was deathly quiet. The hum from the ultrasound machine was the only sound. The doctor and the nurse were still as statues. No one spoke a word.

Celeste, not knowing what to do, looked at the monitor. As soon as she looked, she could see a little head. A tiny arm moved, then a leg. She had just laid eyes on her baby for the very first time. The doctor looked at her. He was about to tell her she was much further along than she realized but changed his mind. She needed a minute. He spoke quietly to the nurse, who moved the wand slightly. The image on the monitor changed. There was another little head. Another baby, this one not moving…no, there it goes. It was moving, too. Honey and Fernanda wanted to cheer, congratulate, squeal, something, but they were stunned into silence by what had just occurred. Instead, they averted their eyes from Celeste and focused on the monitor. Finally, Celeste spoke.

"Call him back."

Honey started to ask if she was sure but held her tongue. FaceFoning Trayton had been a horrible mistake. She could not have done anything worse to Celeste than what she just did. She was not proficient enough in English to understand everything the pretty woman with Trayton had said, but she understood enough. Now the poor girl wanted to call him back? Honey was torn, but Celeste was insistent. She dutifully opened the app and sent the invite.

Trayton had just finished calling an Uber for Karena. She was furious that he was throwing her out like yesterday's used tissue, and he couldn't blame her. He was. He knew Celeste would be calling back, and he was a wreck because of it. Karena could fend for herself. She was in the bathroom peeing with the door open, loudly excoriating him when his phone began vibrating again. The dreaded second video invite had arrived.

"Hey, shut up, would you?" Trayton said curtly to Karena. "I can't hear."

There goes that relationship, he thought to himself. *Goodbye, Karena.* He held his vibrating phone in one hand while the index finger on the other hand hovered above the screen. He had to take it. He didn't want to take it, but he had to. He touched the screen and swiped. When he did, Celeste's tear-streaked face appeared. Pangs of guilt turned his face blood red. He tried to think of the right words to say. *Start small, Tray.*

"Hey babe."

"Hey," she said in a small voice. "I'm in Rio de Janeiro. You'll never guess what I'm doing."

"Tell me."

Rather than answer, Celeste turned her phone around so that it was pointed at the ultrasound monitor. Trayton squinted at the bright light, trying to make sense of what he was seeing. The black and white images meant nothing to him.

"What am I looking at?" he asked.

Celeste laughed a sad little laugh.

"Your babies."

Trayton peered at the screen. There was more than one person with Celeste, he could tell by the voices. Then it hit him. *That is an ultrasound I'm looking at. Oh, god.*

"Is that an ultrasound? Where are you?"

"Yes, Trayton, that is an ultrasound. I am in a clinic in Rio because I've been puking my guts out the past three days, and when I got here they gave me a pregnancy test and it came up positive, and then they asked me if I wanted to see my baby, and it was real sudden so I didn't have time to think, but I said yeah, and they brought a machine, and the nurse rubs this goo on my belly and then I'm looking and the doctor tells me I'm having twins."

Trayton stared at his phone without speaking. Celeste broke the silence.

"We're having twins, Trayton."

After an uncomfortably long silence, Celeste turned the phone back around so she could see his face. Trayton had his head down and was furiously running his hand through his hair, self-soothing his angst as best he could.

"Don't you have anything to say?" Celeste asked plaintively. "Are you happy? Are you surprised? Talk to me, Trayton. I need you to talk to me."

Now was not the best time, Trayton knew, not by a long shot, but now was as good a time as any—when the fetuses were still tiny, and she was not showing, and all options were on the table.

"Babe, I don't know how to tell you this, but it's just not working out. We're not working out. It's just not meant to be. I mean, it's been really good living with you, and we've had some really good times, but there has been some distance. I know you've felt it. People change, babe. I want you to have your soulmate…but it's not me. I wish it was—I really do. And just so you know, this has nothing to do with…the ultrasound. I was going to tell you this a couple of months ago, but then you got the letter, and you were all excited about Brazil, and I thought the time apart would be good for us and I could clear my head and think about what I truly want and you could, too. It didn't change, though. I still feel the same way. I'll always love you. I hope you understand."

Summer felt guilty filming. She knew that any minute she would be instructed to stop. Did Celeste remember the invisible observer was there? She had an overwhelming desire to ask Celeste if she wanted her to stop filming, but that was not her place. Richard's rule governed her conduct. *Catch it all. Don't get in the shot.* Summer kept the camera trained resolutely on her subject.

Panic rising, Celeste asked, "Are you serious right now? You are not giving up on us, are you? I mean, these are your babies, Trayton. I can't do this on my own! I can barely afford to put gas in my car."

She didn't know what else to say. She watched his face—the handsome face that she had kissed so many times. What was happening here? Finally, he answered.

"Look, you are in a clinic, right? You can just get an abortion while you're down there or when you get back, either one. It's your decision, and I'll support you. I can wire you some money if I can figure out how."

Celeste could not believe what she was hearing.

"What are you saying, Trayton? Are you crazy? No, I'm not having an abortion! I just watched them move! You just saw them! They are alive. No!"

The look of compassion fell from Trayton's face, replaced by disappointment.

"Look, Celeste, I can't raise two kids on what I make with all I have to take care of. I mean, look, I've got to rent a new apartment, I've got a car payment, car insurance, my cell phone…"

"You have got to be kidding me right now, Trayton! Of course you are going to help me raise two kids on what you make because we don't have a choice!"

Trayton shot back immediately.

"Yes, there is another choice. The government, remember? We did not have access to healthcare because they were not giving out free condoms at the health center, and the health insurance companies were not paying for birth control and we couldn't afford it. Just like you said in Congress when you were testifying. The government should pay the cost of raising a child to the age of eighteen because the government didn't give us a choice. They took our choice away, and they need to own up to it."

Celeste's blood vessels were about to pop.

"Trayton, why should the government pay when you are the dad? You chose to make the baby…babies, in me. You have a job, for god's sake!"

By now, Trayton was not pleased with where the discussion had gone. He had tried to keep it rational and professional, but she was clearly hysterical and not to be reasoned with.

"I don't know what to tell you, babe. You need to decide which side you're on. I've got to go to work. We'll talk later."

Trayton hung up. *No sense prolonging that conversation. She was acting stupid.* When he ended the video chat, he breathed a huge sigh of relief. She was no longer in his face. She was once again five thousand miles away. He remembered Karena. *Has the Uber come yet? Maybe she is still on the front porch waiting for her ride. Is there any chance she is still here? Is there any chance of salvaging the relationship? Maybe I could give her a ride*, he thought. Trayton jogged to the front door and opened it.

When he opened the door, there before him stood Mrs. Jankowicz, holding Aurora in her arms.

"Aurora got out, but don't worry; I got her before she went in the street. Who is the girl?"

Chapter Forty-Five

Dawn was approaching. The nearly imperceptible brightening of the sky quietly proclaimed that a new morning had arrived. Mist hovered over the trees as long as it could, sheltering the humans sleeping underneath but ultimately lost its battle to the rays of the warm Brazilian sun. Peace reigned in camp. No fights overnight. No early-morning confrontations in the latrine. All was quiet.

Until Willow screamed.

Willow's cry conveyed a very clear message—something was terribly wrong. Her fellow competitors were rousted out of their beds by the shrieks. They stumbled out into the light in various degrees of dress to see what was happening. Willow stood on the other side of the campsite, chopping her feet, pointing at Tattoo's vacant hut with a trembling pointer finger.

Chaz grabbed a good-sized stick and ran to the hut. It had to be a snake, probably venomous. Aston trotted up beside him. They slowed to a walk as they neared the entrance, neither one eager to be bitten.

"People!" Willow cried out.

Chaz and Aston looked at each other in shock. Aston went no further. Chaz swallowed his fear and took another two steps forward. He peered inside what should have been an empty hut. Much to his surprise, a diminutive old woman and a shriveled old man, both bent with age, looked at him from where they crouched against the back wall. The old man had a crudely-fashioned knife hanging from a cord around his waist.

"He's got a knife!" Chaz exclaimed in a harsh whisper.

A few seconds later, Annaliese screamed and bolted away from her abode. Behind her hut stood a tiny brown woman, near-naked, wearing adornments on her ears, neck, wrists and ankles but scant else. At first she appeared to be alone, but then a tiny little boy, not much taller than the grass behind him, peeked out from behind her legs. Mystic Origin called out in a tone that hinted at recognition.

"Well, aren't you the brave one coming all the way into camp today! What are you doing back there? That's our house, you know."

Annaliese was incredulous.

"Wait a minute! You sound like you've seen them before! Have you? Answer me! Have you seen them before?"

"Maybe, could have, possibly," Mystic Origin smiled.

"And you didn't tell anybody?" Annaliese demanded.

Now on high alert, the entire group began peeking in and around every hut. Aston saw movement out of the corner of his eye and quietly said, "Whoa, look." A group of women were standing behind his hut. When Aston realized that he had been surrounded by an indigenous tribe of South American natives last night as he slept, he almost fainted. Chaz checked behind his hut. None there, but that provided little consolation in light of the other visitors. His heart pounded as he surveyed the people who could have killed him in the dead of night.

Tony and Dr. Jane were standing outside the mess hall tent, sipping cups of coffee, when they heard Willow's cry. Tony tried to run without spilling his coffee, but to no avail. The hot liquid sloshed onto his hand, causing him to yelp and toss his cup to the ground. They arrived in camp just as the bulbous form of Clarence Humberton exited his hut.

Clarence was clearly not pleased at having been awakened by a woman's scream at dawn-thirty. He could only see the wrinkled old man peeking out. He did not realize there were others. The words that followed gave the distinct impression that Clarence would have liked a few more minutes of sleep.

"What in the hell are you doing here? You think you can march right in and make yourself comfortable in somebody else's bedroom? Are you kidding me? Get the hell out of here! Get out! Go! Don't stand there looking at me, you sawed-off little runt! Where are your clothes anyway? You just prance around wearing nothing but a smile and make yourself at home wherever you want? No! Get out!"

Clarence's height and girth dwarfed every normal-sized American he encountered back home. When he stood over the tiny brown man before him, the size difference was comical. When he realized there were others, though, he quickly stopped his tirade.

Despite the less-than-warm reception the natives received, they did not run. The old man pointed at the jungle. He began to speak in a tongue foreign to his listeners. He talked to Chaz and Aston, who were too petrified to run. As he spoke, his terrified American audience conjectured about the meaning behind his unintelligible words. The Senator speculated that he was telling them to leave and in which direction he wanted them to go. He then made haste to comply with those perceived instructions, not slowing down until he reached the far side of the clearing. Peaches disagreed. She had the impression he was telling them something was in the jungle. Willow said it almost seemed like they were fearful of something. The rest agreed that the latter was a distinct possibility based upon the man's attempts at sign language. The man continued to speak uninterrupted for another minute or so and then stopped and looked at them. Clarence said the only thing that made sense to him.

"Shut up! Shut the hell up!" Clarence shouted. "I don't want to hear any more gibberish from you, you chattering savage! You are not welcome here. Leave!"

When all eyes turned to Clarence, Aston used the opportunity to slip away from the huts and hide on the backside of the pergola. Chaz joined him in short order. As they tried to catch their breath, Chaz pointed out that the Indians didn't appear to look mad. Even though the old man had a knife, at least he wasn't pointing it at anybody.

Elise LeFleur, who was hiding behind Tony, pleaded with him to radio Tamper and Bones. Dr. Jane, distressed at the appearance of their visitors, asked Tony to send them away. Tony looked around to see who was there and who wasn't. Of course G wasn't around when he needed him. Of course he wasn't. Nevertheless, he knew what G's first question would be. Was Richard there? To his great relief, Richard was dutifully filming the magic moment, catching all the action.

Much to everyone's surprise, Willow broke ranks, stepped forward and knelt down beside the tiny boy. She began talking to him in a sweet, disarming tone of voice. The onlookers held their breath, waiting to see how the natives would react. As two or three tension-filled minutes passed, they were relieved to see that none of the Indians seemed overly disturbed by Willow's boldness. They began to breathe again.

Mystic Origin had not been terribly frightened when she thought it was only the little mother and her baby boy that had walked unbidden into camp, but once she saw the old man and the knife, she was genuinely afraid. Angered by Tony's inaction, she strode up to him, and in uncharacteristic fashion, punched his chest with her index finger.

"You have got to protect us here! I am not a big person! I had armed people all around me last night, and I didn't even know it! What am I supposed to do if they come at me? You need to do something! We need to be inside the big tent you are sleeping in or inside a fence or gate or something. This is unacceptable!"

Peaches echoed her concerns. The diva within her made its appearance. She demanded that Tony assign either Tamper or Bones to overnight guard duty outside her hut "because some of the women just naturally arouse a man's animal instincts." Annaliese, who had just returned from her hut to retrieve a pair of pants, stared at Peaches in disbelief.

Tony's face looked stern, but despite the gravity of the moment, there was an unmistakable twinkle in his eyes.

"Mystic, remind me what your rule was again?"

"Sir, my name is Mystic Origin."

She trembled with fear and rage. One corner of Tony's mouth turned up ever so slightly, betraying a hint of mirth.

"I distinctly remember a certain Queen for a Day announcing there would be no walls. Does that ring any bells for you?"

Mystic Origin was rendered momentarily speechless. Tony had clearly gone insane.

"Sir, I mean no disrespect, but please don't be a smartass! This is our safety we're talking about!"

The staring contest between Tony and Mystic Origin ended abruptly when one of the natives shouted in surprise. The competitors looked around frantically to see what was happening.

Mother Nature had arrived.

Denise Milton had missed all the uproar. She had been in the mess hall tent where the noise from the air conditioner blocked out all other sounds. She was blissfully ignorant of the confrontation taking place by the huts. Had she known, she would not have taken Mother Nature by the hand and strolled up the path on a leisurely walk into camp. When she saw the intruders she froze, eyes wide and scarcely breathing. Mother Nature stood calmly next to her, content to walk when she walked and stop when she stopped. After gathering herself for a few moments, Denise exhaled and found her voice.

"Okay, I wondered if this might happen. All right, guys. Wow. Okay, so like here is the situation. There are no orangutans in South America. This is the first time our visitors have ever seen a creature like her. They are probably freaking out right now because she is so big. The biggest monkey they will be familiar with is the muriqui or woolly spider monkey, which gets up to like thirty pounds. Mother Nature is like twice that size—actually more than that, more like three times that size."

The competitors studied the faces of their visitors, who were clearly amazed at the beast standing before them. Mother Nature detected nothing out of the ordinary. She was used to being the center of attention when in the midst of a group of people. Oblivious to the tense situation playing out in front of her, Mother Nature grabbed the crown that Denise held and walked her bow-legged walk up to the human who struck her fancy. Willow, who was still kneeling near the little boy, was the easiest to reach and therefore the only logical choice. Mother Nature placed the crown on her head.

Willow was now the Jungle Money Queen for a Day.

"Congratulations, Willow," Tony said from across the clearing, trying to project calm in the midst of chaos. "You are our Queen for a Day. Now, you remember our chant? Mother Nature decides who will wear the crown, who will make the rules until the sun goes down. So, it's your turn. What will be your rule for the day?"

Willow, well-liked because of her quiet demeanor and positive outlook on life, had already planned out what she would say if she was ever chosen to be queen.

"Okay. So, as Queen for a Day, I have decided that whoever gets something valuable out of this next adventure will give a third of it to the homeless. I have been homeless before myself and know what it's like to have nothing."

The Senator, who was standing behind a distant tree but still within earshot, rolled his eyes. He thought of the haggard old man who came out of the woods to stand at the end of the exit ramp near his home holding a cardboard sign that couldn't be read because the words were too small. Every day, the Senator pleaded with the traffic light to stay green when the man was standing there. His worst fear was having to stop for a red light, a prisoner in his own car, while the man looked in his window. The man made him feel guilty and uncomfortable. He meant to call the police to clear out the homeless camp near the interstate but always forgot by the time he got home.

Willow wasn't finished with her rules.

"The other rule I have is that this afternoon, whenever we finish whatever we are supposed to do today, we are all going to look for my brother and for Tattoo. All of us. That includes you, Tony. You and Tamper and Bones and G and Dr. Jane and…I'm sorry, I forget your name, ma'am…Denise. Yes, sorry. Denise and the photographers and the dancers—all of us are going to look. I am worried. I thought my brother would have shown back up by now."

Tony bowed his head in deference to the queen. When Clarence noticed that Tony was apparently done with the morning's business, at least for the moment, he took the opportunity to speak.

"I'm sorry about your brother, Willow," Clarence said. "And Tattoo, too. Hey, 'Tattoo too.' I like the sound of that. Anyway, it's breakfast time. Tony, what are our chances of getting bacon and eggs this morning?"

Tony could not believe that the contestants were talking about bacon and eggs when indigenous Indians with unknown intentions were standing in their camp.

"There is a breakfast buffet all around you, Clarence," Tony replied. "All the mangoes and bananas you can eat. Free, too. Trees everywhere. All you've got to do is pick them."

"Yeah, but I'm looking for the bacon tree. You got one of those planted around here?"

Clarence laughed and, despite the tension in the air, so did almost everyone else. This was a breakthrough moment in Tony's eyes. *Maybe Clarence is warming up*, he thought. It would be so much better for everyone if he did.

The Indians stopped trying to communicate with the white strangers and moved away from the campsite. Under any other circumstances, the contestants would almost certainly stay in camp and not even think about venturing out alone. In the surreal atmosphere created by the filming of a reality TV show based on the pursuit of priceless treasure however, they were willing to risk their own safety to win. One or two even suggested the natives were a planned part of the show.

Tony was nervous, but he had a lot of time and money invested in this project. He needed the show to go on. Thankfully, everyone seemed willing to do that very thing. Relieved, Tony dismissed everyone until ten o'clock. The competitors set about the business of finding breakfast and getting ready for the day.

Meanwhile, DeShunta Jackson continued to peer wide-eyed out of her crudely-fashioned window from the smallest of gaps between two elephant ear leaves. This was not the first time in her life she had heard early-morning screams from neighbors. She had no intention of leaving the relative safety of her home under the stage until she was certain all danger had passed.

"Starting to feel like home," she said quietly, a hint of sadness in the words that no one else would hear.

Chapter Forty-Six

The wizened old man watched as The Outside turned and walked away, having ignored everything he said. He had explained the impending danger awaiting them all, making it as plain and simple as he could. He knew right away they did not speak the language of the Forest People, so he used hand motions as he would with a child. Unfortunately, it was all for naught. They did not understand, and even worse, they did not seem to care.

Koa was a Sewat elder in a tribe ruled by Chief Peltu. Their tribe was small, consisting of twenty-two people counting the women and babies. They were peaceful hunter-gatherers and had been so since the beginning of time and human reckoning. When Koa was a younger man they were a much larger tribe with close to fifty men and women. That had all changed when the Javari came.

The Javari were the Sewats' nearest neighbors. They were a territorial and disagreeable people, protective of boundaries often changed to suit their purposes. They were quick to punish real or perceived trespasses. They used any pretext to raid the Sewat village and take their food and any tools or implements they could grab. As annoying as they were, their occasional conflicts never escalated to actual fighting—at least not until five summers ago when the Javari raided Chief Peltu's peaceful village in the dead of night. They took away several of the Sewat females of childbearing age and killed the men who protested. Unprepared and outnumbered, the Sewat stood no chance against the Javari that fateful night.

Chief Peltu knew it would be years before they could recover. They were not defenseless, but they were severely weakened. As a result, he moved the village far from their ancestral home, away from the marauding Javari, where they could find peace and have time to rebuild. They found a place near a waterfall with plentiful mango and banana trees. Over the course of four summers, the young girls grew old enough to bear children, and the Sewat tribe began to grow again. The waterfall retreat began to feel like home.

At least it did until the giant bird with the man in its eye began to come.

When the first giant bird came, the Sewat were terrified. The noise was deafening. Some scattered while others hid where they were. After it left, they regrouped and tried without success to make sense of what they had just witnessed. When the giant bird returned a second time however, they fled their village and sought refuge deep in the jungle. As much as the leader of the Sewat hated the prospect, Chief Peltu considered migrating back in the direction of the Javari. It had been four summers. Maybe the Javari had moved on.

He pondered the possibility of building a new village where the old one had stood.

The chief sent two Sewat men on a hastily-organized scouting mission. They had almost made it back to their former home when, much to their disappointment, they chanced upon a gathering of Javari warriors. The smallest and stealthiest of the two scouts crept close enough to pick up some of their conversation. He learned the Awa were coming to find the great bird and kill it along with the man in its eye. They suspected the great bird was bringing The Outside. If so, the Awa would kill them, too.

The Javari were torn. They wanted the great bird and the man in its eye to die, and the quiet of the rainforest to return, but now they were second-guessing their decision to involve the Awa. The ferocious Awa tribe made the Javari look loving and kind. They were the worst of the worst among the Forest People. They would exact a heavy price for ridding the Javari of the monster that came by air.

The Sewat scouts were greatly distressed at the news they overheard from the Javari. The Awa were coming to find the nest of the great bird. When they did, they would almost certainly find the Sewat and do as they always did—rape, pillage and kill. The scouts slipped away unnoticed and ran as fast as they could to tell Chief Peltu.

The chief weighed his options. There were too many pregnant women and young mothers with babies. The greatly-respected elder and his wife were too old to run anymore. The Awa would likely reach their village within the next two days—three at most. In a moment of desperation, Chief Peltu decided to do the unthinkable—he sent Koa the elder with a few of the women to seek the help of The Outside. If The Outside required a gift of the women in exchange for their help, so be it. Better that than extinction at the hands of the Awa.

Koa bowed to the wishes of his chief. He conquered his fear and led the chosen group into the camp of The Outside. He tried explaining to the strange-looking people that they were in mortal danger, but The Outside could not comprehend it. The big one with loud words had come dangerously close to catching a spear in his belly from a Sewat warrior hidden just inside the thicket behind the huts, but Koa made him stay his hand. They would need the big one when Kanapitu came. They would need him and every other able-bodied man if they were to survive. There would be no negotiations. The Awa were not known for leaving survivors. Kanapitu would not allow it.

Having failed at alerting The Outside to the danger they faced, the elder Sewat was perplexed as to what to do. For the moment, he and his people were safe. At least as of now, the Awa and the Javari did not know they were there. From what the scouts overheard, the other tribes did not know exactly where the great bird made its nest. The next time the great bird returned however, they would see, they would hear, and they would know. Fleeing might still be the best option, but there was one undeniable fact that made Chief Peltu and Koa consider staying. The men of The Outside were giants. They were far bigger than any of the Forest People. Perhaps they were great warriors. They had tamed the great bird. Maybe they could defeat the great Kanapitu.

After deep reflection and meditation, Chief Peltu's mind was made up. The Sewat would seek refuge and protection from The Outside. It was their only chance to survive.

Chapter Forty-Seven

Chaz was the first to hear the distant thrumming of the helicopter. It was 9:45 a.m., fifteen minutes before the group learned what the third Jungle Money contest would be. Willow noticed him standing stock-still, listening, and then she heard it, too.

Celeste had returned.

Rejoining the group had been totally out of the question for Celeste right after learning she was pregnant with twins. She had to consider her health and the health of her babies first and foremost. In line with Tony's instructions, Honey needed to arrange a flight to Atlanta for Celeste and Summer. Fortunately, she spotted a travel agent's office practically across the street from the clinic. A smiling woman welcomed them inside and began the process of purchasing two one-way tickets. They hit a snag when they learned the next available flight would not be for another two days. Celeste told her to hold on before booking the flight. She needed a minute to think. Celeste left the other two women inside and stepped out for some air. Her mind was swirling. Life was coming at her so fast. She felt like she was standing at the edge of a cliff looking down.

What was waiting for her back in Atlanta? Heartache and pain, for sure. Trayton sounded so dispassionate, so distant and disconnected. He reacted like she was calling to sell him an extended car warranty rather than telling him they were going to be mommy and daddy. He wasn't going to help with the babies. She could hear it in his voice. She could see it in his eyes. He had moved on already without even telling her he was moving. She was going to have to do it all on her own. Support them, raise them, feed them, clothe them, care for them.

It was in that moment that she decided to go back to the jungle. She had just learned the harsh lesson that in this life, she couldn't depend on anyone but herself. Her babies couldn't either. That was a problem. The jungle was the answer. A fortune waited for her there. She only needed to step up and claim it. Celeste set her jaw and decided right then and there what she was going to do.

I am going to win Jungle Money.

During the flight back to camp, Honey could hardly conceal her joy. When the waterfall finally came into view, she clapped her hands excitedly. She had never seen a sight so beautiful in all of her days. All the competitors were waiting when Celeste, Summer and Honey landed. Even DeShunta scaled the steep path leading to the plateau above the waterfall to greet her. She was covered in sweat from the effort when Celeste stepped out of the helicopter.

DeShunta would not go to such lengths for just anybody. It was clear she had developed a great affection for the young lady during the short time they had known one another.

When DeShunta learned that Celeste was expecting twins, she reacted as though it was her own daughter. When DeShunta learned that Trayton had broken up with Celeste over the phone when he got the news, she erupted. The unspeakable acts of violence that DeShunta promised to inflict on him were so graphic that Celeste decided not to reveal that Trayton had another woman in her bed when she called him. They could talk about that later.

It was almost 11 a.m. when everyone made it back down to camp. Tony briefed the three ladies on their unannounced guests, so they would not be surprised if they saw new faces in or around camp. Despite his warning, Celeste still screamed when she noticed three small, brown, near-naked people standing not three feet from her when she was walking to the latrine.

When she finished her business, Celeste exited the privy and headed toward the meeting place. Annaliese was jogging down to the privy for a last-minute pit stop. She had not heard the details of Celeste's trip other than that she had learned she was pregnant with twins.

"Hey! Congratulations, Celeste! Twins! Wow! So, are you excited to tell their daddy?"

Celeste's facial expression instantly changed. Since they were headed in opposite directions and would be out of earshot of one another within seconds, Celeste said the first thing that popped into her head.

"I hate men."

Annaliese responded without hesitation.

"I've been saying that for years!"

It took another thirty minutes to get everyone gathered around Tony. Between the natives and the helicopter, there were simply too many distractions to stay on schedule. Finally, everyone was huddled up and ready to hear his instructions. Tony flashed his best Hollywood smile when Richard and Summer gave him the nod.

"Alright, alright, alright. Ready to get started? Let's do it. Celeste, welcome back! So glad you could join us! We understand there may have been one or two little reasons why you have been feeling a little sick?"

Celeste, knowing the cameras were rolling, forced herself to appear more cheerful than she felt.

"Yes, I am going to have twins! Yay! I'm terrified!"

Everyone laughed and cheered, which made her feel a little better. Tony clapped and extended his congratulations.

"Well, we are excited for you. So Celeste, let me catch you up on what you missed this morning. Mother Nature crowned Willow as our Jungle Money Queen for a Day. Willow, as queen, has given us two rules. First rule:

One-third of anything received today goes to benefit the homeless. Willow shared that she has been homeless before and knows what it is like. She wants to help others in need."

Celeste nodded, indicating her approval of Willow's philanthropy.

"Her second rule," Tony continued, "is that everyone will help search for her brother Boedy and for Tattoo this afternoon."

"Tony," the Senator asked, "don't you find it highly disturbing that we have two missing persons? I mean, should we even be doing this contest right now? Shouldn't we be calling the authorities?"

Tony cut his eyes over to G, who was observing the proceedings from a respectable distance, making sure he would not be seen in any of Richard or Summer's video. His expression was inscrutable behind the ever-present sunglasses, giving no hint of whether he was concerned or content.

"Of course, I find it disturbing," Tony answered, "which is why Willow's plans for the afternoon are so perfect. We are all going to pitch in and help look when we finish up our activities. With this many people looking, I am certain we will find them both."

Tamper and Bones stood stone-faced at the back of the group. They had searched for Tattoo until the wee hours of the morning and came up with nothing. Tamper had burns on his fingers from holding a white-hot spotlight while they looked everywhere imaginable. Neither one held out hope for finding them, but neither one would ever say it.

"Alright, so here's the deal," said Tony. "Our first order of business is to handle the queen's business. How many of you took the opportunity this morning to gather some extra mangoes and bananas to store in your hut for later on today or tomorrow? Let me see a show of hands."

Nine of the ten competitors raised their hands. Celeste would have if she had been there. Tony took mental note of the yeses.

"Very good. As you know, we have guests who showed up in our camp early this morning who are clearly homeless. The elderly man and woman took up residence in Tattoo's hut, at least until Clarence told them to leave. The others, including a mother and her baby, couldn't get inside. They could only stand near a hut."

His listeners' faces showed varying degrees of attentiveness. The men seemed somewhat confused, impatient to hear about today's contest.

"Everyone, please go into your huts and bring out one-third of your food stores," Tony instructed. "Put it on this table by the fire pit right here."

No one moved; instead, they stood with mouths open, staring at Tony, trying to comprehend the meaning behind his words. Annaliese, momentarily stunned into silence, found her voice at the same time she lost her composure.

"Are you insane?" Annaliese cried out in frustration. "No! I'm not giving away the food I spent my time and energy gathering. I have to take care of myself. I am not depending on anybody to feed me and neither should anyone else. These strangers are clearly better at living in the rainforest than we are. This is their native land! They are one hundred times better at gathering food and living off the land than we are!"

For once, Mystic Origin agreed with something Annaliese said. Her mind raced to the stash of juicy mangoes she had gathered immediately after Willow was crowned queen. She did not wish to part with them so soon. Her dreadlocks shook as she voiced her opinion.

"The obligation and privilege to share food extends only to us, each other—not to outsiders. They are able to care for themselves. We could learn from them."

Tony's jaw was set. He shook his head and pointed at their tents.

"There were no such stipulations, exemptions or limitations when Willow made the rules. As Queen for a Day, her rules are law. They shall be enforced and will be enforced. Please return to your huts and bring out your fruit. We will have a monitor go with you to make sure you have correctly assessed yourself."

Clarence squared up in front of Tony.

"I'd like to see somebody walk in my hut and take my food."

Tony, nonplussed, answered the big man matter-of-factly.

"Very well, Clarence. Dr. Jane? Would you please assist Mr. Humberton in complying with the very compassionate rule put in place by our Queen for a Day? Elise and Denise, would you help the others? I am certain that our homeless guests are ready for breakfast."

Clarence was caught off guard. He couldn't bring himself to get physical with Dr. Jane. She had been caring for him the entire trip. Mystic Origin's temperature was rising. Her voice trembled as she spoke.

"How do you know they are homeless? They probably have a home somewhere back in the jungle!"

Tony did not answer her. He walked over to Clarence's hut to watch Dr. Jane bring out an armload of bananas. Denise exited Aston's hut carrying a double handful of mangoes, trying to make it to the table without dropping one. Willow brought her fruit out without a fuss. She didn't mind helping out people, natives or otherwise. Things were different when Elise LeFleur and Tony approached the former Governor's hut.

Annaliese, teeth bared, planted her hands on either side of her crudely-fashioned doorway to bar the entrance. She paused there for a moment, then disappeared back into her hut. When she reemerged, she was holding a club of sorts, made out of what appeared to be a thick tree root. She began to tap the head of the club into her open palm.

"I don't know what kind of trick you are trying to pull here, Tony, but I've had it," Annaliese announced. "Nobody is coming in my home. Nobody is taking my food—not a single mango. I'm done playing nice. This is ridiculous! Taking out taxes? Feeding the homeless? For crying out loud, we're in the jungle and all we have to eat is fruit! Give me a break!"

Mystic Origin, seeing an opportunity, said, "Annaliese does have the most food stored up of anyone. If anyone can afford to give, it's Annaliese."

Annaliese turned her wild-eyed glare from Elise to Mystic Origin and asked, "How could you possibly know that unless you are breaking and entering and snooping around?"

Mystic Origin held up one finger in an accusing fashion and said, "One percenters. It's always the one percent that don't want to pay their fair share. Always."

With that, Mystic Origin walked in her hut, reemerged with three mangoes and placed them on the table in front of the natives, never breaking eye contact with Annaliese. Annaliese's breathing sped up. She began rocking from side to side, popping her club into her palm even harder, like a tennis star preparing to receive an opponent's serve. Elise stopped in her tracks and walked no closer.

Tony's demeanor changed. The charming, handsome, fun-loving game show host was gone. In his place there appeared a Tony that none of them had ever seen.

"Annaliese, we let you do absolutely anything you want to out here. Anything. You make the rules. But when you grab a weapon and threaten to use it on your fellow competitors, we will shut you down. If necessary to protect someone, you will be forcibly removed from the contest and placed in confinement. Lest you think your new lifestyle in jungle jail will be an upgrade, understand that it won't. Unless you can persuade the others to work for you and feed you while you are inside, you will have two pieces of bread and water in the morning, and two pieces of bread and water in the evening. We will bring you one piece of fruit a day from the ones you personally gathered. That is it. Now, hand over your weapon or prepare to go to jungle jail."

"She wouldn't really ever get violent," Aston conjectured. "Would you, Annaliese?"

Peaches timidly raised her hand and said, "Look, I don't want to have anything to do with drama, but I feel like I need to share this. Annaliese has been keeping a journal and writing about how she wishes…okay, I'm just going to say it. She wishes she had a gun, but a club is the best she can do. She said if anyone tries to take it, she'll give them the fight of their lives. I didn't snoop—you left the book open, and the wind must have blown the pages."

No one, least of all Annaliese, believed Peaches' cover story about how she knew what was written in Annaliese's private journal. At this moment, though, no one besides Annaliese cared.

"I don't feel safe around angry people with weapons," Peaches continued. "Conflicts can always be resolved without resorting to violence. Sorry, Annaliese."

The look of betrayal on Annaliese's face was unmistakable. She screamed and made wild gesticulations with her hands and arms. Faced with jail if she didn't hand over her weapon and part with her food, she had no choice. She threw down her club and stomped back into her hut. A banana came zinging out like a boomerang in the outback. A mango fastball hit the table and exploded. A bunch of bananas flew out and split apart. Mango. Banana. Banana. Mango. It appeared that Mystic Origin was right. Annaliese did have the most fruit.

Tony let her have her tantrum without interruption. He struggled to keep down a chuckle. Mornings were always an adventure here in the rainforest. He turned his attention to their indigenous guests. Tony stepped behind the huts and loudly cleared his throat, drawing the attention of the elderly man who seemed to be their spokesman. He gestured to the table full of fruit. Tony motioned to the young mother, encouraging her to eat. She took her little boy by the hand, walked over and selected a piece. Tony's gestures and warm smile made the other little people feel at ease enough to help themselves. A semblance of peace returned to camp.

Tony became the game show host once more.

"All right, Jungle Money competitors, gather around. Today, the crown that Mother Nature placed on Willow's head has even greater significance. Not only is our Queen for a Day permitted to tell us what the rules for the day will be, but also something no other has been allowed to do. Today's crown bearer will also tell us what the next game will be!"

Gasps came from everywhere. The thought of creating their own game had never occurred to them. Tony smiled as he heard the excited reactions all around him. This should be interesting. Back during the planning stage, Bert had come up with the crazy idea of letting a single contestant run Jungle Money for a day. It could be chaos. It could be anarchy. On the other hand, it could be outrageous fun and run as smooth as silk. The possibilities were endless. Either way it would be raw, real and completely unscripted. The more Tony, Bert and G talked about it, the more they liked it. Why not? Let them have a go. Today was the day.

Willow's eyes were as wide as her smile. She shrugged her shoulders.

"I have no idea. May I consult with the others?"

"Sure, you can do whatever you want," Tony replied.

The men and women formed a tight circle around Willow. Clarence began to give options in a sort of stream-of-consciousness fashion. Other people would try to make suggestions and Clarence would talk over them. Willow could not think for listening to Clarence. She politely asked him to stop with the suggestions.

"Thank you for sharing your ideas, Clarence. Right now, though, I would like for just the ladies to help me. Gentlemen, would you be so kind as to go over there?"

None of the men took their expulsion kindly, especially Clarence. Nevertheless, they complied. Willow had the power. None of them wanted to get on her bad side. Quietly, so the men couldn't hear, the ladies began their pow wow.

Peaches said, "Willow, you have a great opportunity here. The first contest was geared towards the men. To win, you had to run through the woods and kill animals. That's a man's game. Second contest—fishing. Tying hooks and digging bait and reeling fish and battling jaguars. That's also a man's game."

"Yeah, but a woman be winning," DeShunta smiled.

Peaches laughed and nodded.

"Yes you are, DeShunta. You are doing awesome. But they are hard for the rest of us. I know they are for me. So, whatever you make the contest, Willow, make it something that the ladies stand a good chance of winning."

The other ladies agreed with Peaches' strategy. Willow nodded solemnly. She looked around, lost in thought. She watched an Indian girl play with the baby boy. The girl yelped when the boy grabbed one of her hoop earrings with his fat-fisted hand. That's when it came to her. She had the game in mind.

"Okay, I have decided."

"Tell us what our contest will be, Miss Queen for a Day," Tony said.

"Well, what we are going to do is have a costume contest. You have all day to make a native outfit as close to those guys as possible. Top, bottom, earrings, necklace, arm things, leg things, carrying pouch, makeup, stripes or tattoos or whatever those markings are, just like them. Then at the end of the day, everyone will wear what they make, and we will judge whose is the best. The best outfit wins the prize."

Mystic Origin clapped as she was quite crafty. This contest was one she intended to win. Tony was pleased with her idea but felt the need to clarify one detail.

"So, Willow, you do realize that the natives are mostly naked. You're okay with that?"

"Yes!" Willow laughed. "That's exactly why I thought it would be fun. If you don't wear what you make, you are not in the running for the prize. We are in the jungle after all. Why not get the full experience? Besides, it's hot. Less clothes will keep you cool!"

The groans that emanated from Clarence and the Senator were heavy laden with disdain and despair. Neither one had a crafty bone in their body.

The true reason for their angst however, was pride. Neither one was excited about the idea of exposing his belly for all the world to see. The ladies were thoroughly delighted to hear two of the men giving up before the contest had even begun.

"I'm not done with the rules," Willow declared. "I'm announcing one more. Whoever wins this contest wins the entire treasure chest and everything in it. We're playing for it all, Tony."

Tony's eyes grew wide. He did not intend to answer yes or no to this one. He had said from the beginning that the king or queen got to make up the rules, but this was not a rule he had anticipated. He chose his words carefully.

"Whoa! A high roller! So, you want this contest to be for all the marbles?"

"And," Willow said, "and, and I want a cheeseburger!"

Tony laughed along with all the contestants. He wondered how long it would take before somebody asked.

"Okay, Your Majesty. What you say goes. We'll fire up the grill."

Right then, Tony saw G waving to him from the back of the group. G held a pretend phone up to his ear and mouthed the word, "*Bert.*" Tony mouthed the word, "*Now?*" G mouthed the word, "*Now.*" Tony nodded and turned back to the competitors standing before him.

"Hold on to that thought for right now, Willow. The judges are going to need to confer. You can be at ease until…the judges confer."

Tony made a beeline for G. When he reached him, G said, "I got Beth on the phone. She and Bert are having a birthday party for their six-year-old. That's why they didn't answer earlier."

They hustled down to G's tent near the mess hall. G grabbed his satellite phone and sat in a chair as Tony plopped down on G's bed. When Bert answered, G put it on speaker. Loud disco music played in the background. Shouts from children followed by a big splash let them know Bert was having a pool party.

Bert yelled into the phone. "What's up, fellas? No, don't tell me, don't tell me. Let me guess. My man the Senator has cleaned out the treasure chest, your wallets and the Central Bank of Brazil, and President Villa Silva has told you to discreetly ask me for a loan to carry him through Tuesday. How close am I?"

"Not very," said Tony. "Bert, you won't believe this. We got natives. Yes, you heard right. Little bitty naked people running around camp. They haven't tried to kill anybody yet but two of them were sleeping in Tattoo's hut."

"Holy smokes, you have got to be kidding me!" Bert shouted. "Did they smell the barbecue and invite themselves over? Did they at least bring pound cake?"

"Nope, sure didn't," Tony answered. "They've got this tiny baby boy. Willow wants to take him home with her."

"Has Clarence tried to eat him yet?" Bert asked. "Is he chunky? Don't let Clarence eat that boy. The mama might not like it."

"Hey Bert, another thing," G said. "They are acting squirrelly. Not like we know what normal natives act like, but these guys keep pointing at the jungle like they are trying to tell us something."

"Well, they are probably telling you to get the heck out of their jungle, would be my guess," Bert offered.

"Maybe," Tony said. "Hey, we are doing the thing we talked about, which is let the contestant come up with a contest. It's actually good. Willow is our queen. She came up with a challenge for them to each make a native costume with necklaces and ankle bracelets and loincloths and stuff, and whoever makes the best outfit wins everything in the chest. The men are flipping out. None of them want to do it, but they've got a treasure chest full of reasons why they'll do it anyway."

"Man," Bert laughed, "I'd be telling everybody I'm heading to the Gas'An'Go to grab a bag of ice and a lottery ticket, BRB, and then I'd slip on down to the Berzins Brothers on Amazon Avenue and tell them to hook me up with a three-piece banana hammock and some nipple rings!"

"Oh my lord! I just had a mental image of that," Tony protested. "Does Dr. Jane do counseling? G, do you know?"

"Hey, on a serious note," Bert said in a somber tone, "please tell me y'all have found Boedy and Tattoo."

"Bert, we can't find them," G answered. "Tamper and Bones are exhausted from looking. They are getting maybe four hours of sleep a night. They are looking everywhere. They cannot be found. They are gone. Just gone. Willow is Boedy's sister, right? She has actually been pretty calm about it up to now, but now she is getting worried. She is okay with playing our costume contest thing today, but then this afternoon she wants everybody here, including me, Tony, the team, the dancers, everybody to go look for them. If we don't find both Boedy and Tattoo this afternoon, and Tamper tells me there's a 99 percent chance we won't, they are going to mutiny on us. They might not. The treasure chest may keep them going, but who knows?"

"G, what about the cameras? The Mini-Gos? Beth was asking me last night. Can't Jason and Wally pull up their cameras and see where they are?"

"We've tried," G said sadly. "Oh, have we tried. Jason and Wally—those poor guys have watched and rewatched every video from every stationary camera and from every Mini-Go at least four times each, looking for anything that might give us a clue. Nothing. We've already told you about Boedy. As for Tattoo, we've got him in the little boat fishing. Nothing exciting, he's not doing anything stupid, he's taking his time. He decides to put on a stupid do-rag that blocks the Mini-Go's view so you can't tell where he is, then we lose the video feed when he is close to a riverbank. They think he dropped his Mini-Go in the river. Either that or he drowned. Either way, they can't find him."

"That's not good, boys," Bert lamented. "I hate to say it but…"

"Don't say it, Bert," Tony warned.

"…we may have to pull the plug on this thing. We are just snakebit."

"No! Absolutely not!" G responded angrily. "We are here. We are filming. We have Indians and orangutans and helicopters and fist fights and jaguars and diamonds and rainbow snakes and drama and excitement and we are riding this train all the way into the station! Do you know why? Because there is a waterfall of gold as big as Niagara Falls waiting for us when we get there. All we've got to do is finish this thing and get it on the air and boom! I've got too much invested in this thing to quit now. You guys do, too. Don't go getting all weak kneed and soft on me now. Hang in there with me. We've got this. We can do this!"

G paused. He watched Tony's face. He listened to Bert's silence. It only took a few seconds before he knew. He still had them. They might be hanging by a thread, but he still had them. G's uncanny ability to sweep people up into crazy ventures had done its magic yet again. Before they could reconsider, he spoke.

"Bert, I just wanted to keep you posted. We are going back now. Enjoy your pool party. Later."

With that, G clicked off the phone, stepped through his tent door into the bright sunlight and disappeared, leaving Tony alone inside. Tony smiled, shook his head and talked to the ceiling.

"G, you are insane. Absolutely insane. That's why I love you."

Tony popped up from the bed and shouted, "Yo, hold up, man! Wait up! Don't be leaving the superstar behind!"

Chapter Forty-Eight

Tony trotted up the path back to camp where the contestants were awaiting his return. He flipped the bill of G's baseball cap as he ran past him and laughed when it hit the ground. He was delighted to hear G's insults, most of which involved the question of whether Tony's parents were ever married.

The contestants jumped up in excitement when they saw Tony coming. The ladies had spent their time efficiently while Tony and G were talking to Bert. They knew they couldn't start making their costumes until Tony said "Go," but no one said they couldn't gather supplies while they were waiting. They scoured the camp looking for long blades of grass, broad leaves, pretty flowers, colorful rocks, peelable bark, pliable vines, straps and cords from backpacks, pieces of tarps, colored shoelaces, and anything else they could find. They raided the fishing tackle boxes where they procured shiny gold, silver and bronze blades from spinner baits, multicolored feathers and yarn from lures. They took every article of clothing they were willing to part with, tore them and made strips of cloth. They had all of it spread out on the table as they waited for Tony's signal. He was impressed with all they had done in the short amount of time he was away.

"Wow! Looks like you are ready. Alright, people. You know the game. You know the prize. You know the rules. Ladies and gentlemen, let the Jungle Money Costume Party begin!"

Fingers flying, the ladies began assembling the eclectic collection of parts and pieces into what they hoped would be a winning outfit, complete with eye-catching bling and accessories. Their happy conversation and laughter foretold of hours of enjoyable work ahead. Willow could not have been more pleased with the reception her contest was receiving.

The men, however, were behind. They had wandered around aimlessly while they waited, not knowing where to start. Once they observed the women and the way they were doing it though, they took off on a hunt for raw materials, determined to catch up.

DeShunta, unlike all the rest, made no effort to gather supplies and materials. She seemed to be in no hurry. She could not have moved more slowly and casually than she did—a stark contrast to the frenetic pace everyone else was setting. Tony stared at her as she plodded along. He was mystified. She was walking away from the table where the ladies sat. *What is she doing? Does she even want to win? Is she satisfied with her first two wins? Is she sitting this one out?* Tony couldn't see DeShunta's face to tell what she was thinking. It was almost like she was intentionally turning her face away so he couldn't see.

Tony was right. DeShunta *was* intentionally turning her face away. She didn't want him to see her smile.

DeShunta realized soon after arrival in Brazil that she did not especially enjoy the company of the other contestants. With the sole exception of Celeste, they were not the type of people she would ever hang out with. When she made her home underneath the stage, she did not realize that the others would choose a build site on the other side of a stand of trees. When they did however, she was quite alright with it. She was content to stay in her shaded living room under the stage and let the rest fuss, fight and act the fool.

As a result of the distance between their living quarters, no one saw what DeShunta liked to do during her down time. No one had any idea that DeShunta had already made a grass skirt, grass anklets and a grass necklace before Willow was ever crowned queen and told she needed to dream up a contest.

DeShunta's grandmother had taught little DeShunta to sew, weave, stitch and quilt before she was ten years old. Her granddaughter was not athletically gifted, which suited her grandmother fine since she didn't want to sit by a ball field anyway. She did not have the money to put her granddaughter on a bus every night to meet with some club that would undoubtedly require fees she didn't have. DeShunta's grandmother loved quilting. Her granddaughter needed something to do. It was inevitable that DeShunta would become a seamstress whether she wanted to or not. Spending time quilting and sewing with her grandmother was one of DeShunta's happy places. Because of her background, it was not peculiar at all that DeShunta would seek solace from those memories while confronting the stressful world of Jungle Money, especially when her roommate left her alone to fly to Rio for a doctor's visit.

After arriving in the jungle, when she needed something to do between contests, DeShunta made authentic-looking clothing and accessories. She started by weaving three different grasses, each with a different coloring and width, into an intricate pattern. It had taken a lot of grass to make a skirt that would fit her ample figure, but she was surrounded by it. There was no shortage of grass. She had threaded flowers all around the bottom of the skirt to make it pretty. As luck would have it, on the flight to Brazil, DeShunta had found a gaudy pink psychedelic necktie in the sleeve on the back of the seat in front of her, left behind by a fretful and harried man trying to catch a connecting flight. The neon pink necklace and anklets she crafted from the necktie, which made a beautiful contrast against her black skin, were prime examples of her creativity and resourcefulness.

DeShunta knew where a dead parrot lay on the far side of the arena theater. It had not survived the opening ceremony when the flock of captive birds exploded up from the stage. Its vivid red and green feathers would look fantastic dangling from some handcrafted hoop earrings. She had admired its colors earlier in the day but hadn't touched it because it was a dead parrot. With the siren song of a pirate's treasure calling her however, she was sure she could get over her squeamishness and find it within her to pluck a few feathers.

For all these reasons, it was all DeShunta could do to suppress a smile when Willow announced the contest.

Back at the craft table, slowly but surely, jungle-worthy attire began to take shape. Richard observed the creativity of the contestants behind the lens of a camera. When the Senator began to walk towards the Indians, Richard quietly told Summer to stay with the ladies while he followed. The Senator began trying to convince the native women to make a craft for him. He held out a handful of grass to first one and then the other without success. "Help me make clothes?" he asked. Each woman shook her head to indicate she didn't understand. The Senator decided to try a different tack since his initial efforts weren't successful. He approached a nursing mother and repeated his request, but this time he said it much louder, apparently believing that she would understand if he yelled loud enough. She turned her back and continued caring for her infant. Undeterred, he asked her again, keeping the volume the same, but this time he spoke much more slowly, over-enunciating each word. Maybe he was speaking too quickly, he thought. After his third try, the oldest woman stepped over and inserted herself between the Senator and the young mother. The look on her face made it clear to him he needed to move on. Frustrated, he threw up his hands in exasperation.

While the rest of the contestants busied themselves with their work, DeShunta walked back to the stage in the arena theater and ducked inside. She found a towel, a washcloth, a bar of soap and a bottle of lotion. Tony gave her a quizzical look as she walked by him on her way to the river. DeShunta didn't care. She knew what she was doing. She wanted to get a bath while she knew there would be no one watching. If she was going to be wearing a revealing outfit tonight, she wanted to be all clean and lotioned up for the show. She headed to the beautiful pool at the base of the waterfall. Happy in the assuredness of victory, she sang as she walked. The voice of an angel came from her lips, though no one was there to hear her.

Chapter Forty-Nine

The competitors, consumed with the task at hand, were oblivious to the world around them. They had no idea they were being watched. If Mystic Origin had turned around and walked into the rainforest not even five paces, she would have quickly discovered—they were not alone.

Chief Peltu and eleven Sewat warriors stood under the canopy of trees ringing the camp of The Outside, hidden, not moving, invisible to the naked eye. They each held a spear as they watched their women. Each had a bow strapped to his back and a crude knife tucked in his waist band. Bantu had started to throw his spear into the back of the big man when he raised his voice and shouted at Koa the elder, but Chief Peltu had stayed his hand. He discerned that the big man was all thunder and no lightning. It had been the chief's idea to send Koa, the women and two of the smallest children into the camp of The Outside. It was the only way he could think of to keep the weakest and most vulnerable safe for the night. Though he had not personally seen the danger, he had incontrovertible proof of its existence.

Saltu had found a dart.

Two days ago, the Sewat men were on a hunting expedition. Their intended quarry was capybara. A single one of the world's largest rodents would feed them for days. Game had been scarce near the mighty river, so Chief Peltu sent a scouting team deep into the rainforest to a stream bed he recalled from years past. As he remembered it, there was a wide pool with plenty of sunlight and succulent plants growing on top of the water—prime habitat for capybara. Saltu, Bantu and Torok were chosen. They went without another word, honored the chief had selected them.

The chief's memory proved to be quite accurate. At the end of a day-and-a-half journey, the scouting team reached the pool. It was indeed lush and green. The slippery banks were littered with capybara tracks pressed deep down into the mud. The hunters smiled with anticipation. They melted into the riverside jungle and waited. Sure enough, just before evening, their prey emerged from the rainforest, waded out into the water and began to feed. Saltu and Torok silently pointed at the one furthest downstream. They would shoot simultaneously and put arrows in the beast's heart and lungs. Bantu, who was the best shot among all the Sewat, motioned that he would arrow the one immediately upstream. It was critical that they all release their arrows at once, since the capybara would scatter in all directions once one was hit.

Saltu quietly counted down, nodding his head as he did so the others would know exactly when to shoot. They all released their arrows in unison. Twang thump. The arrows hit their mark. Two capybaras began to thrash about in the water, one upstream and one downstream, as the others made their escape. Success! The hunters leaped into the water to dispatch their game with their knives before they could climb the banks and flee into the rainforest. They pulled them out of the water into the protection of the jungle and busied themselves with field-dressing. Once the body cavities were eviscerated, they chopped off the heads as well. The thick skulls weighed a considerable amount, and they had to carry them a long way. They worked quickly, mindful that the smell of blood would soon attract hungry jaguars and pumas. Once the butchering was complete, they began the arduous task of hauling them home.

When night fell, the three men made camp, unable to travel any further without risking becoming lost or injured by stumbling in the dark. They hung the meat high in a tree a hundred paces from camp. They did not wish to be in close proximity if any big cats came in the night. Fortunately, when they awoke just before dawn the next morning, the meat was untouched aside from a few scavenger birds. A good roasting over a fire would take care of any contamination.

The men set out at a fast clip, determined to make it back to their chief before nightfall. They took turns carrying the two capybaras. One would rest while the other two would labor—then they would switch. It was hard work, but then again, these were hard men. This had been their lives since birth. It was still morning when Saltu heaved his capybara onto Torok's shoulder. As he was stretching his tired arms and back, he glanced to his right and saw something that caught his eye. A monkey was lying still on the ground. As Saltu got closer, he could see the monkey's chest rising and falling ever so slightly. Very curious. Why was it not jumping up and running now that it could see a human standing over it? Saltu could see no blood or bite marks.

When Saltu's eyes fell upon the cause of the monkey's plight, he whistled to his companions. Bantu and Torok dropped their loads and hurried over to him. Together they examined the monkey and saw what Saltu was seeing.

Protruding from the monkey's side, just under its arm, was a dart.

It was not Sewat. Like their darts, the shaft was made from the stiff middle rib of a palm leaf. That was where the similarity ended. Sewat used cotton from the kapok tree for fletching. They always used cotton. This dart did not have cotton. It had bird feathers. Someone was in the far end of Sewat territory. That someone was not Sewat.

The hunters crouched down and looked all around them. The monkey was paralyzed by toxins from the slime of a poison arrow tree frog that someone had rubbed on the tip of the dart. They could not know if the monkey had been hit and traveled a great distance before collapsing or whether the owner of the dart was watching them even now. They quickly and quietly discussed their plan. Chances were good that they had not yet been seen. They could not leave their game lying here. The field-dressed animals would be a dead giveaway that someone was near. They had no choice. They had to run as swiftly as they could back to their chief and pray they avoided detection. Chief Peltu would know what to do. The men did not discuss who had darted the monkey. Each knew what the other was thinking.

Kanapitu. Eater of men.

Chapter Fifty

Bones and Tamper sat in silence, looking out across the river. The engine of Tamper's Paleo Growler was off but still hot, making popping noises every so often as drops of liquid landed on super-heated surfaces. Bones propped a boot up on the dash panel and retied the laces. Satisfied with the double knot, he picked up his other boot, retied its laces and dropped it down on the dash panel as well. He lifted his boonie hat with a permanently-tanned hand, ran a hand through his longish hair and dropped the brim down over his eyes. He laid his head back on the seat, closed his eyes and exhaled, continuing until he had expelled all the air in his lungs. To the untrained eye, Bones looked as though he was enjoying a leisurely nap by the river.

Tamper scowled at the world. Unlike Bones, he was incapable of hiding his frustration with himself. Holding a blade of grass in his hands, he snapped off short lengths of it and threw them down, one after the other. Brows furrowed, he scanned the surface of the water. Nothing. Nothing and nobody. He scratched the top of his buzz-cut head in the hope it would help him think.

No man left behind. That was Tamper's motto and creed. You stay until you find them, then you bring them home. Period. Tamper had dutifully followed that procedure in hellholes all across the Middle East. He always brought them home. For some reason though, this cursed rainforest was kicking his ass. First Boedy, now Tattoo, gone without a trace. It was maddening.

He and Bones had covered miles of water and jungle over the past twenty-four hours looking for Tattoo. Riverbanks. Stream beds. Game trails. Thickets. Back to the riverbanks, then more stream beds, game trails and thickets. Nothing. Absolutely nothing. Oh, they had found his boat quickly enough. It had lodged against a fallen tree where it was pinned and held in place by the never-ending current. Once they found the boat, they began methodically searching the water both upstream and downstream from where they found it. Every man-sized object under the surface got a thorough inspection. Tamper would swim out while Bones watched from the bank, then they would switch when they came across the next object downstream. Bones had upset a rather sizeable anaconda in a particularly still stretch of river, causing it to swim away across the surface of the water in serpentine fashion. Other than that, their search had yielded nothing.

Had he drowned? Had a caiman gotten him? An anaconda? Tamper had a growing fear that he would never know and not knowing was unacceptable for an Army Ranger.

Tamper stared at his ATV. It was his pride and joy. Mounted on the roll cage above and in front of him were two small but powerful speakers. Above and behind him were two subwoofers firmly bolted into the frame. The magnitude and quality of sound they produced was worthy of any band playing any stadium in the world.

Back home, one of Tamper's favorite pastimes was extreme off-road riding with his buddies from the service. Tamper was a serious and intense man in virtually every facet of his life. When he got together with his buddies however, a side of Tamper that few people knew would surface. They would load up the Paleo, leave the concrete jungle behind and find where the pavement ended. Life began where the pavement ended. Tamper would flip the switches on his sound system, insert the cord into his phone and plug it into the jack. Suitably armed, he would find the steepest incline or the deepest descent around. Just before he plunged into the off-road insanity his mind and body craved, Tamper would find the loudest, most raucous song on his playlist. The war cry he would yell right before his right thumb clicked Play was legendary. People back home reported hearing his music up to three miles away.

They called it "Tamper Jam."

Life was hard and then you die, but joy could always be found at Tamper Jam. There had been no Tamper Jam in Brazil however. Jungle Money was, by design, set in pristine, untouched and undisturbed rainforest. The cameras were always filming and the microphones were picking up every sound. Tamper Jam was not an option. As difficult as it was, Tamper would have to forego fun until after he returned to the United States.

But how to find Tattoo? Tamper turned it over and over in his mind. He thought about cranking up his Paleo and giving the jungle a blast of music in the hopes that Tattoo might hear it and come to the sound. He decided against it though. First, his music would spoil the audio of anything being filmed for sure. Secondly, he had the distinct feeling that Tattoo was not able to come to the sound even if it reached him. All the signs pointed to drowning. Tamper intended to spend the afternoon searching downstream as many miles as it took to locate the body. The grim reality was that Tattoo's body consisted of so much buoyant fat that it would surely bob to the surface sooner or later. He just couldn't understand why it hadn't happened already.

Tamper looked behind him at the gun rack. The AR-15 rifle hanging above him accompanied him everywhere he went. He closed his eyes and shook his head in muted frustration as he thought about the confrontation back at Customs when he first entered the country. The Brazilian government was as relaxed and unconcerned about what he brought into the country as one could ever hope for. As the supply and logistics guy who brought everything into the jungle that was brought, it had been great at first.

When Customs discovered he was trying to bring an AR-15 into the country however, their attitude totally changed. He tried to explain that he and he alone was responsible for the safety of dozens of people deep in the Amazon rainforest. The only thing standing between the reality show contestants and hungry jaguars, pumas, anacondas and countless other beasts was him and his gun.

He argued to no avail. Brazilian Customs officials explained that they had a no-gun policy whenever international travelers declared their intention to explore areas known or suspected to have indigenous tribes that had no previous contact with the civilized world. Tamper had escalated the conflict all the way to the ambassador at the U.S. Embassy in Brazil. No luck. If he had been on a guided hunt of two weeks or less where his guide took control of the rifle when each day's hunt ended, that would be acceptable to the government. Bones was a guide, Tamper had argued. They were unpersuaded. Bones was not an official government-sanctioned guide. They needed to have that application submitted months ago.

Tamper looked at the official dead in the eyes and demanded to know, "What am I supposed to use if a jaguar attacks me? Harsh language?" That remark had almost gotten him thrown out of the embassy, not because of the words but because of the tone he used to convey them.

Tamper's efforts were not completely in vain. When he came back a second time, he managed to curry favor with a Customs official by means of an unmarked envelope filled with cash. He could bring the rifle but no live ammunition—only dummy rounds. Rubber bullets. In other words, Tamper could bounce rubber balls off the jaguar while it was chewing on a contestant. The jaguar would still fill its belly, but at least it wouldn't enjoy its meal. He begged and pleaded but the official didn't care. Tamper was at his mercy. No live rounds, period. End of story.

As Tamper sat in the Paleo by the river, he knew he needed to be doing something; otherwise he would just sit and stew. He looked over at his companion. Bones' chest rose and fell, rose and fell as he took a mid-morning siesta. He wished he had Bones' ability to find the calm within the maelstrom when facing problems beyond his control. Bones could go to sleep in the middle of a Fourth of July parade. Tamper kicked Bones' nearest boot.

"Hey Sleeping Beauty, wake up. I want to go downriver and look for Tattoo. His body has probably surfaced by now."

Bones inhaled deeply as he came back to consciousness.

"I was dreaming," Bones said. "I was standing in camp watching all the people waiting for the treasure chest to be opened. They unlocked it, but it was completely empty. There was a hole in the bottom of the chest leading to a tunnel that went straight down. Everyone was screaming, 'Where's the money?' It wasn't dark in there, though. Sunlight was coming up from the hole. There was a ladder made out of bamboo so I started to climb down."

Tamper, by this point intrigued, asked, "So, what happened next?"

"I have no idea," Bones replied. "You kicked my shoe and woke me up."

"Maybe Tattoo was down there," Tamper said dismissively.

Bones shook his head as he repositioned his hat and said, "Don't think so. Hole was too small. He wouldn't fit. Too fat."

Tamper turned the key in the ignition and the Paleo came to life. He took a swig of Gatorade and dropped the bottle back in the Jungle Money cooler. Bones followed suit. Tamper put it in drive and headed downriver, hoping they would have better luck this time.

Meanwhile, back in camp, the costume contest was in full swing. The men may not have been thrilled, but the ladies were having the time of their lives. Mystic Origin was the first to successfully coax one of the Sewat people to assist her. She focused her efforts on the elderly woman. The breakthrough came when Mystic Origin ran to her hut and brought back a woven grass bonnet she had made. She showed it to the woman, who studied the bonnet. There did not seem to be any comprehension or interest at first. After a few minutes, though, the woman walked to the table. She never nodded or verbalized her agreement to help—she just started helping.

When the elderly woman sat down, Peaches immediately squealed with delight, scaring the woman half to death. Peaches quickly grabbed and hugged the woman to comfort her but only made it worse by doing so. The Indians did not publicly display affection one to another, much less to a strange-looking woman who appeared to be a giantess to them.

"MeeMaw," as Peaches named her, backed away from the craft table after Peaches' outburst. It took several minutes of Southern belle baby-talking to persuade MeeMaw to come back to the table. When she did, she hit the jackpot. MeeMaw was the craftiest of the crafty. She worked quickly and assuredly. Unfortunately for Peaches, MeeMaw made a bowl instead of a bonnet. When Peaches realized what she was doing, she was disappointed but didn't try to stop her. How often does one get their own custom-made bowl handcrafted by a woman from an uncontacted tribe in the Amazon rainforest?

Peaches oohed and ahhed over the bowl. The elderly woman did not overtly acknowledge the praise, but there was a sparkle in her eyes that let everyone know she was pleased with the appreciation of her work. Peaches tried to think of how to ask MeeMaw to make her some native clothing. She tapped MeeMaw's woven bracelets and said, "Oh, how pretty!" Then she showed MeeMaw her naked wrist. MeeMaw understood. When she started weaving a bracelet, Peaches began to clap. When MeeMaw got up and left the table, Peaches worried she had offended her again. Presently, MeeMaw returned with an armful of tall grasses. She placed them in front of Peaches. Message conveyed. MeeMaw was a teacher as well as a craftsman.

Celeste walked over and quietly sat down next to MeeMaw. She was pleased when MeeMaw placed several long blades of grass in front of her.

MeeMaw was not just Peaches' private tutor—she was willing to teach a whole class. A thought occurred to Celeste.

"We're going to have all these great bracelets, but what else are we going to wear?" Celeste asked Peaches. "What if she doesn't teach us how to make clothes?"

"Well," Peaches laughed, "the boys are going to get quite a show, aren't they?"

It was at that moment that Chaz sounded the alarm.

"Hey, hey, heads up! Everybody look! Men!"

There they were. Five small men, not much bigger than the women, appeared seemingly out of nowhere. Each had bangs cut straight across their foreheads and necklaces made of reeds. They wore loin cloths. Each had a string running from across their shoulder down to the opposite hip, which secured either a bow or a blow dart gun hanging behind their backs. They were barefoot with grass anklets just above their brown feet. What drew the most attention, however, were the long spears they carried, each one longer than they were tall.

The Sewat men had decided to join their women.

An unspoken but palpable panic set in. Everyone looked around for help but saw none. Tony had left several minutes ago, headed in the general direction of the mess hall tent. Clarence, who had been the first to lose interest in arts and crafts, was last seen headed towards the medical tent. The Senator was nowhere to be found. It was just them—Chaz, Aston and the ladies. When Annaliese noticed that Chaz and Aston had retreated behind the women, she scolded them in harsh but hushed tones.

"Where do you think you are going? Get up here! Be a man!"

It was evident from the looks on their faces that Chaz and Aston did not want to be men right then. Chaz was frozen in place, his feet rooted firmly right where he stood. Aston, shamed into action, reluctantly took one step forward with much fear and trepidation.

"Hello? Hello?"

The Sewat men looked at him, stone-faced and unmoving. They did not look friendly at all. Perplexed as to what to do, Aston turned back to the ladies.

"They don't speak English."

Annaliese, her neck beginning to turn red, said, "Well, of course they don't speak English, stupid! They aren't English!"

Feeling a vacuum of leadership which someone needed to fill, Annaliese reluctantly stepped forward and said, "Um, welcome? So, this is our camp. Are you guys in the same tribe as the ladies? What am I saying? Of course you are. Sorry, I'm nervous."

They noticed three more men standing in chest-high grass at the edge of the wood line. Their faces were dispassionate and cold. The native women stopped weaving and watched. The contestants felt a sense of impending doom. Chaz's heart raced. He debated bolting for the distant tents. Where were Bones and Tamper when you needed them?

Peaches decided to make a move. She slowly stood up from the table and walked around to the other end where there was a small pile of fruit. She picked up two mangoes and slowly walked toward the men. Her voice trembled as she spoke.

"Okay y'all, here's what I know. Men like to eat and they like women to fix it. Are y'all hungry? Please don't kill me."

She stopped a few feet away from the nearest man and held out a mango. The man did not react, and neither did the rest. They simply stared. Peaches felt lightheaded. This had been a big mistake. In the silence that followed, she heard Clarence's loud cough way off in the distance, followed by the Senator's faint laugh. Peaches wished terribly that they were here, standing between her and them, but they weren't. They may as well have been a million miles away.

After an uncomfortably long silence, the old woman said something from her seat at the table. The armed man in front of Peaches did not move, but he did cut his eyes over to the old woman. He uttered a one-syllable sound in response, then reached out his hand. Peaches gasped involuntarily. Breathing heavily, she placed the mango in his open hand.

"Oh lord, I'm shaking, y'all."

The man holding the mango bit into it. Peaches didn't quite know what to do with herself while he ate. She decided to slowly walk back to the table where she had been sitting.

"Okay mister, so I hope you like your mango. I'm just going to stroll back over here next to MeeMaw, and we're going to have us a time making us some bracelets. Don't kill me, m'kay?"

Everything within her told her not to take her eyes off of the men with the sharp weapons, but something else told her to go back to weaving like nothing was wrong. She eased down next to MeeMaw, picked up her grass and resumed weaving. She watched MeeMaw's hands out of the corner of her eye. She breathed a sigh of relief when she saw that MeeMaw began weaving again as well.

The man closest to the front took a step forward, catching Aston off guard. Aston flinched hard.

"Oh god, you scared me."

Much to Chaz's horror, the man walked past Aston and headed right for Chaz. He tried his best not to hyperventilate. Chaz's eyes went wide in abject fear when the man stepped in front of him and stopped. The man was a foot-and-a-half shorter than Chaz. When the man locked eyes with him, Chaz was visibly shaking. The tense stand-off seemed to last forever. Strangely, the Indian began filling his cheeks with air until they were stretched and distended.

"Pok!"

The blast of unexpected sound from the Indian's mouth felled Chaz like a tree. He landed heavily on his butt. The Indian burst out laughing. The rest of the natives broke out in laughter as well, including MeeMaw. The other contestants, still in shock, realized they were not going to be eaten. The comedy cut the tension. Everyone, whether American or Amazonian Indian, shared a hearty laugh.

Except for Chaz, who had passed out.

The head man walked past Chaz and continued up to the nearest hut. He took the bow off his shoulder and laid it, along with the sheath holding his arrows, up against the side of the hut. The other men did the same. The head man turned and walked back to the contestants. Much to everyone's surprise, he grabbed a handful of grass and began weaving. The speed of his hands was amazing. It quickly became apparent that he was not making a bracelet or anklet. His creation got wider and wider the more his fingers worked. Peaches stopped working so she could watch him. After a couple of minutes, it came to her what he was doing.

"He's making a shirt, y'all! Not a shirt, but you know, one of them little vest things they're wearing. Hey, I got dibs on the vest. I'm the one that gave him a mango, so I've already, like, paid for it. And let's face it," Peaches grinned, "I've got the most to cover. Now that I look at them, though, I think I need one for each side."

Mystic Origin, unlike Peaches, Celeste and Annaliese, who were giggling, found nothing funny about their situation. The blood drained from her face when armed men came into the camp bearing weapons. *No one needs to have a weapon,* she thought to herself. *Weapons kill. They cause war and pain and death.* She had attended marches in support of banning assault rifles, advocating gun control and repealing the Second Amendment. Their rainforest encampment had been relatively tranquil until today, but now the balance and harmony had been upset when these native men introduced weaponry into their camp.

Once she saw the warriors lay their weapons on the side of the hut, Mystic Origin hatched a plan. She knew how to restore the peace they once had known. When everyone's attention was diverted, she would slip over to the side of the hut, gather up the weapons and carry them to a safe place—perhaps the river where the water ran fast and deep. She wasn't sure yet. Either way, she would show them the nonviolent way was the best way.

Chapter Fifty-One

A fuzzy black-headed caterpillar undulated across the forest floor. Why it left the succulent leaf it had been devouring to find one exactly like it was unexplainable, but it made perfect sense to the caterpillar. There were no bad food choices here. All the dining options for insects were green, succulent and tasty, kept moist by the perpetual mist emanating from the beautiful waterfall only a short distance away. The tiny creature made its way across the usual flora and fauna, but then came to unfamiliar terrain. Halting momentarily, it used its limited senses to assess the new obstacle in its path. It was warmer than the usual surfaces on which he tread, but otherwise there seemed to be nothing amiss. The caterpillar resumed its trek, climbing up and over the hurdle before it.

There was a reason why the surface underneath the caterpillar's many feet was so warm. It was a heavily-veined brown foot. The foot belonged to Kanapitu. Eater of men.

Kanapitu's vision was not as sharp as it once had been, but it was sharp enough. His dark eyes were fixed on the singularly most unusual sight he had ever seen. A woman, whose skin was darker than his own, was standing in the pool of water at the base of the waterfall. She was bathing, but he could not tell what she was washing. After several minutes of observation, Kanapitu understood what his eyes were seeing. It was not a coat or covering she was bathing—it was herself. The quantities of fat were so vast that he could scarcely take it in. Mounds of flesh moved and jiggled underneath her hands. White bubbles appeared and reappeared wherever her hands went.

Even more remarkable than the sight of her was the sound coming from her throat. Beauty unspeakable poured forth from her lips. In all his years, during all the ceremonies he had witnessed and presided over, Kanapitu had never heard such a lovely sound. The pitch, the range, the sweetness was unlike any sound he had ever heard. He realized he was holding his breath in order to hear her better.

Kanapitu ran his tongue along his filed teeth. His tongue had traveled that path for so many years that it had become calloused, nearly immune to the sharp edges. Normally decisive, this time he was not. He could not decide what to do. Should he take her to himself and ravish her, or eat her? After another moment's reflection, he knew.

He would do both.

The Awa warriors behind him wondered how long their chief would stare. He was clearly transfixed. They were as amazed as he, but the novelty had worn off, at least for them. They were warriors on a mission—a mission to find the great bird with the man in its eye and kill them. The great bird had returned this morning, allowing them to pinpoint its nest. As soon as they heard it, they raced through the rainforest in a mad quest to reach it before it flew away again.

As they were running, the Awa war party found evidence of trespassers in the jungle. Their jungle. The Javari had warned them they might find Sewat if they came this way. The Awa and Javari alike looked down on the Sewat, a weak people unable to protect their women. Not an hour ago, they discovered irrefutable proof of Sewat trespassers hunting in their hunting ground. They found the severed heads of not one but two capybaras. Such a trespass was unforgiveable. All the Forest People knew the punishment that awaited those who dared enter the domain of the Awa unbidden. The penalty for such an offense was death. It was the warriors' duty to carry out the sentence. Their singular mission now had a dual purpose. Kill the bird. Kill the Sewat.

After the chief's eyes had drank their fill of the woman in the water, he turned back to the men who awaited his orders. Before they chanced upon the pool at the base of the waterfall, they had been tracking the Sewat trespassers. There were three as best they could tell. Their quarry was careless, leaving broken branches and drops of capybara blood in their wake. When they reached the area where they currently stood, the footprints of three became the footprints of many. The Awa warriors were taken aback by the size of the new footprints, but they were undeterred. They had found their intended targets. They remained hidden, as-yet-undetected. Perfect. It was time to creep close and make ready to spring, exactly as they had done to countless victims so many times before.

Kanapitu formulated their battle plan. He silently pointed to four of his warriors and made a wide, sweeping motion with his finger. They were to swiftly circle around the clearing where the trespassers had retreated. He pointed to the sun and stabbed it ten times with his finger. The men knew exactly how much time they had to get in position. Without a word, the four melted into the jungle.

Kanapitu pointed to five other warriors. Holding the palm of his hand horizontally, he spread his fingers wide. He looked at each warrior individually, making sure they understood. They nodded and disappeared into the trees surrounding them, each entering at a different point.

Kanapitu looked at the remaining warriors and pointed down the path where the footprints led. It was clear this path had been recently used. The danger of detection while following this path was great. Pressing his palms together near his chest, he pushed them toward the path, then separated his hands as he reached out. The men understood. They were to slink along the sides of the path concealed by the foliage that lined it, staying well out of sight as they went. The men nodded and instantly obeyed.

Left alone, Kanapitu turned his attention back to the voluptuous woman in the water. She fired every passion that dwelt within him. She was still bathing and still singing. Although he was past his prime by several circles of the sun, his loins stirred as though he was young.

Kanapitu reached around to his back and retrieved a long, cone-shaped object. It was stained orange by the purest river mud in Awa territory. The ornamental penis sheath, made of woven grass, was worn by Awa men during the annual feast to the fertility god and the animal spirits that did his bidding. It held great significance for them. Wearing it was not an automatic right or an entitlement—it had to be earned during the new warrior trial of becoming. When Awa boys had lived twelve suns, they left their weeping mothers at the appointed time for the trial. A nest of bullet ants was located and the boys were bound to the tree nearest the nest. They were left without food or water for two days and two nights. Despite the fear and indescribable pain, they prayed to be bitten. If the ants did not bite them, they were not worthy of becoming a man. If the ants bit them, however, the scars left by the bites bore witness to the fact they were worthy of becoming an Awa warrior. In the celebration that followed, they too gained the right to wear the sheaths.

Aside from the new warrior trial of becoming and the annual feast, there was only one other time the sheath could be worn, and that privilege belonged exclusively to the chief of the Awa. Following a great victory in battle, where many were slaughtered and no Awa were lost, the chief could wear the sheath. The chief anticipated today would mark the greatest victory in the history of the Awa—the killing of the great bird that roared and the man in its eye. For that reason, he had brought the sheath. He knew it was a breach of protocol to wear it before the battle had been won. He risked angering the spirits by doing so. Nevertheless, he wanted his victim to see it while she still lived.

Kanapitu positioned the sheath in front of his genitals and tied it securely around his waist with a triple-braided thong. The tip of the cone pointed directly at the woman in the pool. Satisfied with his appearance, he stepped out from the shadows under the canopy of trees into the open. Smiling a sinister smile, he quietly stepped down into the water without making a sound. Judging by appearances, he was certain the woman would be easy to take. Inwardly he hoped she would struggle. It would make the prize that much sweeter.

Chapter Fifty-Two

The afternoon passed quickly. Aside from Clarence and the Senator, who had all but given up on the third contest, the contestants could not remember a more pleasant day. While the spirit of competition was ever-present, a spirit of cooperation permeated the scene as well. In this setting, the two spirits were not incompatible. They learned that their visitors, who were playing a huge role in creating the warm atmosphere, were "Sewat," although some debated whether they were all named Sewat or just the old woman.

Under the tutelage of Chief Peltu, Aston had learned to make armbands almost indistinguishable from the ones worn by their visitors. Emboldened by his early success at making realistic jungle wear, and determined to win the contest, Aston decided to go all in. If he needed to look like an Indian to win, then he would look like an Indian. He asked one of the men to pierce his ears. Words were not needed to make his request understood. Aston conveyed his message quite effectively through playing charades. The man didn't give a verbal answer or even nod. He simply produced a crude tool which would do the job. He also appeared to throw a stick in the fire, but Aston paid no heed, preoccupied with the good-natured ribbing his companions were giving him about the pain he would soon endure.

Aston's earlobe was punctured, a common procedure that every woman in camp had endured. The piercing may not have been unusual, but the next step in the process surely was. While firmly holding Aston's ear, and without giving him time to object, the Indian grabbed the end of a slender stick glowing red from the embers of the fire and stuck it in the hole to cauterize the wound. Aston's scream reached the ears of Dr. Jane all the way down at the medical tent. She jumped up and started out the door, but the immediate and uproarious laughter from the Indians allayed her fears. Aston did not find it funny at all, especially when the smell of his own burning flesh wafted through the air. As a rule, the natives' facial expressions were stoic, but Aston's wild reaction and the dance of pain that followed tickled them all. As expected, the pain subsided quickly enough. Now Aston faced the prospect of getting the other ear pierced. The small brown man stood at the ready as the others chanted, "Aston! Aston! Aston!"

At that moment, a strange look came over the Indian's jovial face. His smile disappeared. His face blanched. The sharp tool fell from his hand. Bewildered, Aston looked down and saw an arrow protruding from the center of the man's chest. The man's eyes rolled back in his head and he dropped heavily to the ground.

Aston started to scream but his scream was cut short by an arrow that pierced his throat and severed his vocal cords. A rush of unchecked air replaced his cry. He died within seconds and collapsed in a heap next to his friend. The rest of the group screamed and ran for their lives. Some dove into huts. Some ran into the trees only to be cut down by the arrows and spears of the waiting Awa warriors.

The Sewat men sprinted for the hut where they had laid their weapons. They were shocked to see that they were nowhere to be found. Paralyzed by confusion at the missing weapons, the Sewat men's stationary figures made for easy targets. Arrows came from every direction, finding their marks time and again. By the time they recovered their senses and ran for cover, over half of the Sewat men had been fatally stricken.

Before the attack began, Dr. Jane was sitting in the medical tent having to endure a series of lewd suggestions from Clarence, who had given up on winning the third contest. Her patience having worn thin, she was just about to tell him off when she heard distant screaming. At first she thought it was more frivolity like she had heard only a few minutes earlier. When the screaming continued without being followed by laughter however, she knew something was terribly wrong. Before Dr. Jane could move, Elise ran in the tent with a look of terror on her face. She heard it, too. The sounds of death and dying were unmistakable. Dr. Jane grabbed her radio and frantically called for Tony.

The last thing Tony was concerned about at that moment was his radio. He had turned it off when he slipped inside Honey Hush's tent. The time apart from her while she was away on her medical trip with Celeste had been surprisingly difficult for him. He had very few distractions to occupy his mind here in the jungle. Her beautiful face, luxurious hair and intoxicating scent dominated his mind during every waking moment while she was in Rio.

There was something more than her beauty that called to him. Her resolve to remain pure both challenged and intrigued him. He used every technique he could think of to break down her defenses, but nothing worked. She did not seem to mind him trying, which gave him hope. Although he hated to admit it, even to himself, it made him want her love all the more. She was different than any other girl he had known. He begrudgingly came to respect the fact that she would not allow him to enjoy her fully without a ring and a solemn promise before God.

Last night while lying in bed, in the quiet moments before sleep took him, a calm came over him that he had never known before. He knew. He just knew. Whichever path he took when he left this jungle, Honey Hush was going to walk it with him. For now, Tony was content to spend alone time with his lady in whatever way she would allow. The love songs playing from his compact speaker were soft, but the window air conditioning unit was loud. No outside sounds could be heard inside her tent—not that either one was listening.

Tony could never have anticipated it, but his decision to turn off his radio saved his life and the life of Honey Hush that day.

Back at camp, the howls of the savages and the howls of their victims were nigh indistinguishable. The massacre was terrible and swift. The blood lust of the Awa warriors was unquenchable. Their intended target when they left their village on the other side of the great river had been the great roaring bird with the man in its eye, but the bird had flown once again. That left only the Sewat, the offending Forest People who had committed the unpardonable sin of entering Awa domain and taking their meat.

When the Awa war party first laid eyes on the white giants giving shelter to the Sewat, they were stunned. They had never seen people that large. They had never seen skin that white. The wonder and amazement passed quickly, though. The white giants were with the Sewat. They were in the Awa's jungle. They would die, too.

As the one-sided battle raged, one of the Awa warriors spotted Peaches peeking out of the door of a hut. She saw him looking and ducked back inside the dark hut, but it was too late. She had been seen. She was not what he had come for, but her curves caught his eye. He strode into the hut, caught her by the hair and led her out into the sunshine with a double fistful of her mane. He forced her down onto her knees, striking her forcefully when she tried to regain her feet. He worked his way around behind her with a malevolent gleam in his eye.

Suddenly, a wild scream cut through the jungle air. An enraged being, not quite animal but not fully human, launched himself at Peaches' attacker. He drove his full weight onto the head and shoulders of the Awa warrior, wrenching him loose from the sobbing woman, a handful of torn red hair as his only prize.

The Awa's attacker's name at birth had been Charlton Pinoir-Sinclair. When the gangly teenager became an awkward college freshman, he had assumed the name "Chaz." Almost without exception, he was a mild-mannered young man, at least when he was not in a junkyard with his girlfriend being embarrassed in front of a news crew. In this place of anguish and pain however, that mild-mannered young man ceased to exist. Instead, he was replaced by a ravening beast whose fevered mind went white with primal rage when he witnessed a sweet and kind woman about to be raped.

Before the Awa could react, his assailant had dug his fingernails deep into his eyeballs, eliciting shrieks of pain. So fixed was the Awa's attention on the agony of his eyes that he scarcely felt the teeth of his foe meeting and tearing asunder what used to be his ear. Chaz snarled and growled, bit and tore, scratched and ripped, screamed and thrashed in unrestrained fury without human thought or reason. Like a werewolf under a full moon, his teeth sunk deep into his quarry's throat. The Awa warrior knew not what manner of creature had torn out his jugular. He had only moments earlier lost his eyes. He gurgled a death rattle as blood filled his esophagus.

Another Awa warrior saw the unholy man-beast attacking his fellow tribesman. He unsheathed his knife and ran to the fray. His blade had almost reached Chaz's back when out of nowhere a massive arm clothes-lined him and knocked him flat of his back. The wind rushed out of the warrior's lungs from the impact with the earth. The owner of the massive arm lifted a size 16 work boot and stomped on the warrior's head, crushing his skull like an empty beer can. An enraged union boss from New York named Clarence Humberton had entered the ring and notched his first victory.

The Awa warriors were enraged when they saw the non-combatants become combatants. With blood-curdling war cries, they converged on Clarence and Chaz, who scrambled for cover. Seeing their opportunity, the women made a mad dash for the river. Celeste held her stomach as she ran, doing her best to protect the babies within her while praying to God she wouldn't trip and fall.

The women cried out in relief when they realized the Senator was running up behind them. Peaches was nearly out of breath, but she managed to form words in the midst of the sprint.

"Senator, oh thank god you're here! Chaz and Clarence need your help!"

The Senator made no response. He neither slowed, veered nor changed course. He simply continued his sprint to the river, leaving the women in the dust. His four years of track in college had prepared him for this moment, even if his old muscles no longer had the same spring they once had. The cries of dismay from the ladies did not dissuade him. They would get over it.

Things looked bleak for Clarence and Chaz, especially when one of the invaders grabbed a torch from the arena theater and set fire to some of the huts. Sadly, the craft table and all of their handiwork went up in flames. Energy and the will to survive can only do so much when one's assailants are armed and their victims are not. It was only a matter of time before the inevitable happened.

Suddenly the sound of an arrow's thump greeted the ears of the hunted, significant because it struck neither Clarence nor Chaz. An Awa looked down at his stomach in horror at the arrow that stuck out of him, which had passed almost completely through after entering just above his kidney. He tried unsuccessfully to stifle a cry, his warrior heritage trying but failing to mask the pain. His companions whirled around to see where the arrow had come from. They saw only warriors behind them. Maybe it was an errant arrow from friendly fire? They didn't have time to investigate. The white killers before them had to die.

Clarence and Chaz sought refuge in a thicket behind the huts. The biggest Awa, almost as tall as Chaz, produced a bone knife honed to a fine edge and slunk around to the back of the thicket. He had almost completed his stalk when an arrow pierced his ribcage, skewering both of his lungs. A spray of pink blood jetted out of the hole with every agonizing breath.

The marauding Awa were enraged at the back-to-back deaths of their fellow warriors. Two Awa were too many to lose. The leader of the war party spun in his tracks to face their unseen enemy. Nothing seemed amiss. No one but his own kind flanked him, yet the arrows were coming from somewhere. He traced the path of the arrows to determine their origin. Nothing. No one but…

Wait, who is that?

Bones was not like other men. A lifetime of hunting and tracking big game had equipped him to think like a savage. It was deep within him. When Bones heard the SOS go out over the radio, he was acutely aware he was unarmed, lacking any kind of firearm. He knew he could not dwell on it however, because dwelling on it wouldn't help. He needed to adapt, improvise and overcome, as Tamper liked to say.

Then it came to him. He knew what to do.

Years of exposure to the South African sun had permanently burned Bones' skin to bronze. His diet and exercise regimen kept him lean as a whip and hard as steel. Although his longish hair was not quite dark enough, he could nevertheless pass for an Indian at a distance, at least if one didn't look too closely. When he heard Dr. Jane's frantic voice on the radio, he yanked off his hat, ripped off his shirt and kicked off his boots. Grabbing his ever-present recurve bow, he sprinted to the sounds of battle.

Finding the melee, his bare feet allowed him to slip in behind the Awa unnoticed. He moved when they moved and faced the way they faced, always staying at least twenty paces behind them. He wanted to stay further back behind the cover of the trees, but the killing distance of his recurve was too short to allow it.

When the Awa discovered the deadly impostor in their midst, they howled in rage. Bones was badly outnumbered. With the element of surprise gone, he had but one option. He turned and made a mad dash to the river. The soles of his feet were not as calloused as those of his pursuers. His feet took terrible punishment from the uneven ground covered in tree roots, rocks and thorns, but Bones didn't feel any of it. His will to live gave wings to his feet and immunity to discomfort.

The first to reach the river was Mystic Origin. Her heart nearly pounding out of her chest, she stopped to breathe, glad to be out of sight of her pursuers. Her relief was only temporary. An Awa warrior materialized from out of nowhere. As he stalked toward her, she held up a finger and asked him to wait.

She pointed wildly down into the water. Although his pace did not slow, his face reflected curiosity. She hopped down into the water. The Awa, clearly under the impression she was attempting to swim away, prepared to jump in after her. He stopped when she resurfaced with something in her hands.

She held a dripping-wet Sewat spear in one hand, while in the other she held a wet bow by the string.

"See? We mean you no harm!" she explained. "Our ways are peace. Others brought the tools of violence into our camp, but I have removed them. They cannot hurt you. There is no need for you to be afraid!"

To show her sincerity, she turned and threw the spear as far as she could toward the deep water, then did the same with the bow. After watching them disappear beneath the surface, she turned back to the Awa and smiled.

"See? No war. No hate. Only peace."

Three Sewat men, fleeing from their Awa attackers, ran silently to the river. They stopped short when they saw the Awa warrior and the woman in the water. As-yet-undetected, the three men pulled back into the underbrush. As they tried to catch their breath, they watched in amazement as the white woman lifted their stolen weapons out of the water. When they saw her throw them into the middle of the river, their faces reflected pure, unadulterated shock. *Why? Why would she do such a thing?*

The Awa warrior watched dispassionately as the strange woman threw the weapons into the deep. He waited for her to do something else, but she didn't. She stood in the water, empty hands in the air, smiling at him. His face was stone. They stood that way for several seconds before Mystic Origin came to the disappointing realization that he was not going to return her smile. She began wading back to the bank. He met her when she began to climb out. The bank was high and she was short. She reached her hand up to him for help. He grasped her forearm and lifted her out of the water. Choosing to believe it was a show of courtesy, she smiled broadly when she stood to her feet.

"Thank you! What a gentleman!"

The Awa's expression did not change. He studied her necklace and earrings. They looked shiny when she stood in the water, but now he could see it was just because they were wet. Worthless. He reached around behind her head with his left hand and held it, almost tenderly. Mystic Origin smiled a coy smile, trying anything to save herself.

"Well, my partner Leaf is not here, and it has been a long time."

The Awa warrior calmly drew his knife across her throat and watched as the horizontal line became crimson. Mystic Origin's face reflected the betrayal she felt as she grasped her throat and tried desperately to close the grievous wound. The Awa placed a foot on her belly and pushed her back into the water.

The sounds of running feet reached the Awa warrior's ears. He turned and waited. A tall, gray-haired man was the first to appear. Upon seeing the knife-wielding Awa before him, the Senator slid to a stop, kicking up a cloud of dust. He yelled in fright when he looked to his left and saw other native men crouched under a tree but then realized they were his newfound Sewat friends. Their faces showed they were as scared of the Awa as he was.

Seconds later, the frantic women ran up next to the Senator and stopped. Faint hopes that the canoes might permit them to escape were dashed when they saw the menacing Awa warrior standing between them and the river. They were cut off. Cries from the enraged Awa warriors pursuing Bones came from behind them, growing louder and louder. The sight of a shirtless Bones running to help them would be a huge comfort in almost all circumstances, but not this time. They were surrounded and outnumbered. All hope was gone.

Chapter Fifty-Three

Back in the video production tent, Wally and Jason stared in horror at the bank of monitors on the table. Each screen was divided into four views from four separate cameras. Each was worse than the last. Death and destruction played out in real time before them and there was not a thing they could do about it. As they watched the band of marauding natives close the trap around the others, Wally said what both men were thinking.

"Oh my god! They are going to kill them all!"

The terrifying sound of the tent door being ripped open behind them tore them away from the screens. Wally dove under the table while Jason ran to the back of the tent, desperate to find any kind of weapon. Finding none, he turned to face his adversary, determined to go down swinging. The intruder shouted at them.

"Hey guys! We're under attack! We've got to hide somewhere!"

It was Willow. She had escaped notice during the melee and made a run for the crew's tents. The thin canvas walls provided scant protection, but it was better than nothing. The three of them alternated between barricading the entrance to the tent, looking for heavy objects to swing, and frantically debating over the best places to hide.

Suddenly, a noise like a jet taking off from a flight deck assaulted their ears. It came from every speaker on their computers. The monitors showed that the combatants were hearing it, too. The Senator, his face twisted in pain, pushed his palms into the sides of his head as hard as he could in an attempt to block out the sound. Flocks of birds erupted from treetops by the thousands, desperate to escape the sound blast. American and native alike jammed their fingers in their ears, trying in any way they could to protect their eardrums.

One of the contestants trapped at the river's edge noticed small trees whipping violently back and forth and cried, "Look!" The thrashing of trees got closer and closer and the sound grew louder and louder. Something was coming. Something big was coming. The noise was unbearable. At last, the vegetation split apart, and the source of the sound was revealed. A jacked-up UTV burst into the clearing, engine roaring and speakers blaring. A heavily-muscled man wearing sunglasses sat in the driver's seat, sporting a maniacal grin.

Tamper had arrived.

All his life, Tamper had heard people say music soothes the savage beast. To Tamper's way of thinking, they were all wrong. The flaw in the adage was that no one had ever put the savage beast in charge of the music. Tamper was in complete control now. The speakers mounted to his Paleo were designed for concert arenas. Tamper had twenty-two thousand watts of amplifier pointed at two previously-uncontacted Amazon Indian tribes at a distance of fifty feet. He knew the natives couldn't be expected to appreciate the chainsaw-shredding sound of an electric guitar as much as he did. He didn't care. After hearing Dr. Jane's frantic call over the radio, he felt the need to share a unique cultural experience with them.

Tamper turned down the music momentarily, pulled a winding cord down from the roof, held a microphone to his mouth and announced, "Ladies and gentlemen, boys and girls, it's time for Tamper Jam!"

Insanity in his eyes, Tamper wrenched the volume knob clockwise until it wouldn't turn anymore. The amplifiers blasted every monkey and toucan out of the trees for a radius of five miles. Tapirs gave premature birth. Turtle eggs burst open. Mangoes split and fell from trees. Singing the words to the song, Tamper snatched up his AR-15 and charged his weapon.

Let the games begin.

He pointed the barrel of the rifle at the nearest native, squeezed the trigger and stomped on the accelerator. Rubber bullets were not Tamper's first, second or third choice, but it was all he had. Feeling generous, Tamper served up a mighty helping of .223's for the natives to feast upon. *So many targets to choose from*, he thought. He lit up the back of a fleeing native. Three solid impacts took the native down. Tamper turned to the next one. Two shots—one missed but the second one hit squarely and put the Indian on his face in the dirt.

"Hey, this is fun!" he cried. "Just like the arcade at Chunky Monkey! A few more and I'll have enough tickets to get the stuffed polar bear!"

He had to stop firing momentarily so he could steer. Tamper turned the wheel hard left, floored it and drove straight into the back of a native at thirty miles an hour. Fortunately, his target sailed off to the left rather than flipping up and into the front seat.

"Sorry, dude! Did I forget to use my blinker? My bad!"

Natives dead ahead. Tamper took aim and fired. Boom, boom, boom! One shot one kill times three! Well, technically not kills, but since they were writhing in pain on the ground, Tamper counted them anyway. Detecting movement to his right, he spun the steering wheel and stomped on the accelerator. Spinning tires as he did a one-eighty, Tamper screamed a big "Yeehaw!" A running native looked back at him in terror…and centered a tree with his forehead. Tamper howled with laughter.

"Hey! Teach your buddies to do that! Saves bullets!"

Spying another fleeing suspect, Tamper mowed him down and drove over him with a big thump.

"Hey! If that doesn't buff out, I'm calling your insurance carrier!"

Tamper could not remember having more fun in his life. He drove at a threesome, firing as he went, but suddenly felt a terrible pain shoot through his right arm. An arrow pierced his right bicep and pinned his arm against the seat. He involuntarily turned loose of the steering wheel with his left hand to grab his wounded right arm. When he looked down at the arrow, he lost focus on his driving. The Paleo glanced off a forked tree at forty miles an hour, spun, flipped and hit a larger tree dead on with the back bumper while upside down. The impact with the first tree destroyed the engine, while the second tree obliterated the sound system.

The silence was deafening. All eyes, friend and foe alike, turned to see what had happened. There was no movement inside the driver's compartment. Whether Tamper lived or died was anyone's guess.

Clarence and Chaz reached the clearing to rejoin their compatriots. Both were badly wounded. Chaz was leaning heavily on Clarence, hopping on one foot. An arrow stuck out of his right calf, clearly causing him severe pain. Clarence, who had shot himself in the foot with an arrow less than two days ago, had one arrow protruding from his left shoulder and another lodged in his right butt cheek. They were no longer physically able to defend themselves, much less anyone else.

The Awa warriors' attention was completely focused on Tamper and the motorized monstrosity that brought him, which now lay sideways—quiet, smoking, and leaking black fluid. All were silent. The Sewat were frozen in place. The competitors dared not move a muscle for fear of drawing attention back to themselves. Suddenly, a voice broke the silence.

"Hey! What's happening? Why all the screaming?"

Tony had been reluctant to leave Honey's tent for multiple reasons, not the least of which was the window unit air conditioner. It may have been loud, but it sure was effective. When he went back for the sixth or seventh goodbye kiss, Honey was ready for him to go. She pushed him out the tent door with a shove—a loving shove, but a shove nonetheless. When he stepped out into the hot Amazonian afternoon sun, he heard a strange sound. It almost sounded like a…car crash, but of course, that was impossible. When he heard the screaming that followed, he took off in an all-out sprint to the river to see what had happened.

His timing could not have been worse. He slid to a stop and saw a terrible sight. He knew instantly that it was Tamper's Paleo wrapped around the tree. Tony called Tamper's name. As he called, movement caught his eye. Much to his surprise, a fierce band of Indians he had never seen before surrounded his group. Their body language, facial expressions and menacing weapons betrayed their evil intent. Tony seriously regretted leaving Honey's tent.

With Tamper gone, the Awa turned to face their quarry. Knives bared, spears pointed and arrows nocked, they prepared to dispatch their victims. There was no escape. All would die. None would be spared.

Jungle Money had come to a nasty and brutish end.

Chapter Fifty-Four

DeShunta Jackson bathed all alone at the base of a jungle waterfall in a tropical paradise, blissfully unaware of the eyes upon her. She had never experienced a finer moment in her life. She held sweet-smelling soap and a soft cloth in her hands. She had rich, creamy coconut butter lotion waiting for her by her clothes on the shore. The water swirling around her washed away the tough exterior to reveal a sweet side of DeShunta that was seldom seen. Song sprang from deep within her soul. A melody welled up within her as though from a spring, and it poured forth from her mouth as if from a fountain. She had heaven all to herself—not a care in the world.

The blast of noise from Tamper's speakers jolted her out of her tranquility and made her drop the soap. Instinctively, she bent to grab it before it sunk to the bottom. The water was fairly clear, so she was able to catch a glimpse before it disappeared. Upon recapturing the slippery bar, she stood and turned to face the noise…and found herself staring into the eyes of a nightmare.

A hideous, near-naked old man, sharpened teeth bared in an evil grin, stood not more than three feet away. His black eyes were wild. His body was marked with crude tattoos. A tooth necklace adorned his neck. One wretched hand wielded a razor-sharp bone knife. The other hand clutched the orange cone concealing his awaiting appendage. His loins prepared for triumphant entry. Kanapitu was determined to make this a ravishing worth remembering.

The events that followed could scarcely be followed by human eyes, so great was the speed at which they moved. The bar of soap, no longer needed, once again hit the water. DeShunta had a higher purpose for her hands. She bent her knees and dropped her hips, like an NFL linebacker preparing for a goal line stand. Her lips tightened. Her teeth snapped shut as she clinched her jaws. Her eyebrows dropped down over her bulging eyes. Her upturned hands and fingernails formed cruel claws. With the roar of an enraged lioness, DeShunta exploded up from the sandy river bottom. Talons extended, she grabbed Kanapitu's organ and proceeded to squeeze with all the strength and fury that she possessed.

The scream that erupted from Kanapitu's diaphragm was high-pitched. The agony in his cry was so loud and so clear that all who heard it hurt for the screamer, even without knowing the source of the pain. His scream lacked words, but the message was clear. "Kill her!" "Kill me!" "I don't care which!"

Kanapitu got a lucky break, for this reason—DeShunta had just dropped the soap. His frantic and desperate writhing allowed him to slip out of her angry but slippery hands. For only a moment, however. Chopping her hands like a hibachi chef at a Japanese steakhouse, DeShunta reacquired her target and began the assault again. Using the same technique she used as a child to single-handedly win the tug-of-war event on Field Day at the Meadows Elementary School, DeShunta punished Kanapitu. He dropped his bone knife into the Amazon River, completely incapable of using it. If he still held it, he would have plunged it into his own chest to end his misery.

Less than a hundred yards away, the blood-thirsty Awa warriors were seconds away from dispatching their victims in a most gruesome fashion when the anguished cries of their stricken leader reached their ears. They bolted and ran for the source of the sound at the base of the waterfall, leaving their surprised victims behind. Defying logic and common sense, the Jungle Money contestants trotted after them, inexorably drawn to the ghoulish screams.

When the natives reached the waterfall, their eyes witnessed the most horrible sight imaginable. Their highly-revered chief was held aloft by the massive arms of an apoplectic black woman whose fury knew no bounds. Kanapitu begged for death but none came. Unholy cries spewed forth from his lips. His followers plunged into the river, weapons waving, bent upon saving their leader. They would have thrown their spears from the riverbank but for the fact they might kill Kanapitu with an errant toss.

The competitors arrived at the scene. They cringed at the chief's unbearable agony. They covered their eyes, not wanting to see the swift and certain death that awaited DeShunta and then themselves. Bones tried in vain to persuade them to flee. None would listen. They couldn't bear to look, but they couldn't bear to look away.

Chapter Fifty-Five

Boedy Da had no idea how long he had been in the cave at the top of the waterfall. He knew he had been unconscious, but had no idea how long. Hours? Days? Weeks? He had no clue.

The first thing Boedy knew when he regained consciousness was pain. When his head hit the back wall of the cave, he had fractured the orbital bone around his right eye socket and his right cheekbone. The pain was unbelievable. He wanted to touch his face but couldn't. He tried to dip his face in the cold water that ran through the cave from under the back wall to bring down the swelling, but it hurt too bad. Whenever he leaned down, blood rushed to his face. He felt his heart pounding from between his eyes all the way around to his right ear. He stood and gently, gently pressed his face up against the back wall. The cool surface provided a small measure of relief.

The second thing Boedy knew was hunger. He was starving. He hadn't eaten in days—he wasn't sure how many. Thank God he had water. A little stream, originating from the very back of the cave where the ceiling was low, flowed through a small, defined channel, maybe eighteen inches wide, to the mouth of the cave, where it joined the roaring cascade. He had all the water he could drink but not a bite of food.

On the morning of the second day of wakefulness, Boedy lay on his back on the cool rock inside the cave, listening to the water falling outside. If he stayed still and didn't move his head, the throbbing in his face was almost bearable. As he lay there, he began to talk to God.

"Hey, God. Good morning. So, how did you sleep? Yeah? What? Me? Oh, I've had better, thanks for asking."

The only sound he heard in response, other than the roar of the water outside the cave, was water dripping from somewhere overhead. He talked quietly. He didn't need to raise his voice.

"God, your cave is cool. I wonder when you made it. Hey, I just thought of something. I'll bet I'm the only man in history to be in here. How cool is that?"

Boedy closed his eyes. If he listened really hard, he could differentiate between the sound of the stream near his head and the sound of the waterfall outside. A zing of pain ran across his right eye.

"Ow! Oh man, that hurts. Wow, that really hurts. Hey, if it's okay with you, I may just lay here for a bit. I'm not looking forward to sitting up. It really, really makes my face hurt."

Boedy laid very still until he dozed off again. A few minutes later, his stomach grumbled and woke him up.

"So, about breakfast, God. I don't want to ask you to make breakfast just for me, but if you were going to make you some, it sure would be great if you'd save a little plate for me."

A slight change in the sound of the waterfall was immediately followed by a breeze that stirred within the cave.

"Sounds like it's a little windy outside today. It may be sunny, too. Can't tell without sitting up, which is not high on my agenda right now since it makes my face feel like exploding."

Boedy reached up and tenderly touched his face. Yep. Still swollen. He felt his ribs. They were more prominent than usual. He never carried a lot of body fat, but whatever he had, there was less of it now.

"Hey God, thanks for always being with me. It helps to know I'm not alone even when I'm alone."

As Boedy stared at the ceiling of the cave, he saw a mosaic pattern of light playing above him. Sunlight reflected off the stream close to the mouth of the cave, allowing it to reach all the way to the back where he lay.

"So, God, about that breakfast. I've been thinking. Do you remember how Elijah had the big showdown with the priests of Baal? How Elijah said his God was the real God, and he challenged the priests of Baal to a cook-off? And how they took the bet, but Baal didn't come when they called because, well, it was pretty obvious, Baal wasn't you? Then you showed up…ow. Sorry. Ow. My face is throbbing. Hold on. There, okay. Anyway, so, you brought fire down from heaven, and burned up the sacrifice? Yeah, that was cool. I love that story. Man, I wish I could have been there."

A drop of water fell on Boedy's forearm. He thought about wiping it off but decided to let it stay.

"So, anyway, here's why I bring it up. I don't remember whether it was before or after, but I definitely remember you sent ravens to bring Elijah food. Remember? Yeah. That was amazing. So, yeah, if you have any spare ravens that aren't doing anything right now, could you maybe…?"

The light continued to play on the ceiling. Boedy watched it, hypnotized, until he dozed off again. A gust of wind blew a mist onto his face, which woke him up. He gently wiped the water off of his uninjured left cheek.

"Kind of wet in here. Man, I am so hungry. So, so hungry. Hey God, I just remembered another bird food story. Remember when the Israelites were wandering around the desert and all they had to eat was manna, and they were hangry, so you sent them quail? And apparently the quail weren't good at flying so they could catch them? Man, I could munch on some quail right about now."

The wind blew mist on Boedy again.

"So, if those ravens are all tied up, it sure would be cool if you would send some quail up here. Only God, I need you to make them really slow quail, because my face hurts if I move too fast."

Boedy watched the light on the ceiling. Try as he might, he could not bring himself to get up. He was very thirsty and very hungry, but there didn't seem to be any point in taking care of either. What did it matter? If he went back to sleep, maybe he wouldn't wake up and then he wouldn't hurt anymore. Suddenly, the patch of light on the ceiling went dark.

With a rush of wings, the harpy eagle that called the cave home flew in. The eagle was massive—as tall as Boedy when Boedy jumped up to his knees from his rocky bed on the floor. It was a toss-up as to who was more surprised at the meeting—the eagle or the man.

"Dude! You're so big!"

The plume of feathers around the giant bird's face fanned out when he saw the unwelcome intruder. Boedy had been wondering what the large collection of sticks, dried grass and leaves was all about. There were a few small rodent skeletons in and around the mess, but it was much too big to be a nest, at least in Boedy's mind. Now he knew. The eagle had a fish in one of its talons. Before Boedy could beg the bird to drop it, the eagle turned silently, leaned forward and flew away, never to return.

On the morning of the third day of wakefulness, Boedy was desperate. He was getting very weak. His mind was fixated on the fish. If only the eagle would bring him one. Water was the only way he could fill his belly, so he drank. As he leaned down to get a drink from the stream, he saw a silver flash in the dark water. A fish! Boedy watched the fish dart away when it caught the movement of his hand. It tried to halt its progress before plunging hundreds of feet down the waterfall. No such luck. The fish disappeared. Boedy wondered if it lived after falling from such a great height.

He pondered the question of where the fish had come from. The river behind the back wall of the cave must have worn a small hole in the rock through the relentless force of millions of gallons of water every day for eons. Fish didn't know what a bad idea it was to follow the current into the hole. Perhaps they realized they were at the top of a waterfall, and they were making a last ditch effort to save themselves by diving into the hole.

The cave was dark, and the light was poor. Boedy discovered that when he didn't look directly at the water, but rather to the side, he could catch movement and flash out of his peripheral vision. When he saw a second fish, his heart leaped. He tried to grab it, but it was too quick and elusive. It was like trying to grab wind. This wasn't going to work. How could he catch them?

Looking around the dimly-lit cave, he got an idea. He began to dismantle part of the eagle's nest. Despite the fact the eagle had no twine or baling wire when he built it, the nest was surprisingly difficult to take apart. Once he had a section broken loose, Boedy fashioned it into a fish basket of sorts. It took him a while to figure out how to place it in the water and hold it there without being washed down and out the front of the cave. Once he got it anchored however, he felt a glimmer of hope.

It was not five minutes before a fish squirted through the cleft in the rock and swam into his fish basket. Boedy capped his hand over the top to block its escape and lifted the basket out of the water. He had a fish! Boedy bit into it like a horse eating an apple. Despite his ravenous hunger, he did not enjoy the fish slime and scales. He ended up spitting out much of the contents of his mouth. He took a different approach on bite number two. He first used his teeth to pull off as many of the fins and scales as he could to expose the meat underneath. When he got a mouthful of raw fish, it was the best-tasting meal he could ever remember. It hurt to chew—there was no denying that, but the pluses outweighed the minuses. He managed to catch enough to at least partially fill his stomach by the afternoon. His eyes began to grow heavy. For the first time since he made the ill-advised decision to jump out of the helicopter, Boedy went to sleep and slept soundly.

When he woke up, somewhat refreshed, Boedy turned his mind to the big problem. Could he get out of the cave and down to the bottom of the waterfall without killing himself? He had no idea how high he was. He had no idea if there were rocks below that would smash him to bits or hydraulics that would suck him under to drown or rapids that would drag him to his death by falling over yet another waterfall. He couldn't see what was below the opening of the cave because of the curtain of water blocking his view.

Boedy had another problem. He couldn't see, at least not well. The retina in his right eye had detached due to the impact of his head with the wall of the cave. All he could see out of his right eye was a brown film and a little bit of blurry light. He still had good vision out of his left eye, but his right was gone, at least for the moment—maybe forever. He wished he could sit and wait for rescue, but the grim reality he faced wouldn't allow it.

No one would ever find him in this cave. No one. Ever.

Boedy was hidden from the world in a place where no search party would ever look. Even if they knew there was a cave and that he was alive inside of it, it was physically impossible for them to climb up and rescue him. Everyone probably thought he was dead. He wouldn't blame them for thinking that way. If it was him, he would have searched the water below the falls for a body, but if days passed without finding anything, he would have assumed the corpse washed downriver and was gone. Boedy knew he would no longer be looking if it was him, so why should he hold out hope that anyone else would do differently?

Willow. His sister was probably worried about him. The thought made him sad. He didn't want her to worry.

"God, I don't know what Willow is doing right now, but could I ask a favor? She is probably worried about me. Could you comfort her, hug her, something? I sure do love her. She's a great kid sister. Please bless her, okay?"

His face felt a little better today. He was actually able to touch his right eyebrow and cheek if he didn't press too hard. He looked around the cave.

"Hey Jesus, it just dawned on me. You were in a rock tomb kind of like this, weren't you? I know you had a big stone in front of yours, but was it kind of like this, without all the water?"

Boedy looked at the entrance to the cave. There was a gap between water columns, a clear area where no water was falling, which allowed him to see out just a little. He couldn't look down, but he could look out and see a little bit of sky and a little bit of treetops.

"You were in your rock tomb for three days. I'll bet you got tired of being in there, didn't you? So, on the third day, you busted out. That is so cool. That pretty much rocked the world. You kicked death in the teeth and said, 'What now, death? What now?'"

The wind kept blowing mist on him, so Boedy scooted back in the cave away from the entrance.

"You know, God, I've spent my whole life trying to get away from people and get close to you. They bring me down, just being honest. All those guys at Bert Redmond's house in Atlanta—did you hear them? They complain and they argue and they want stuff so they fight each other and all they can think about is getting stuff and more stuff. They never look up. They have no idea how close you are. You are all around them, and they won't even look up. I think I jumped as much to get away from them as I did to catch some air and fly."

Boedy pulled a twig off the eagle's nest and held it up to his good eye. A piece of a downy feather clung to it.

"Look how that worked out for me," he sighed.

He closed his eyes and listened to the water falling. Big water. Made up of tiny, individual droplets.

"Now, though, all I can think about is how bad I want to get down there to them. Especially Willow. I'm supposed to be sharing you with them, aren't I? I'm supposed to be helping them look up instead of keeping you all to myself."

Boedy sat in silence and pondered for a long time. In that moment, something changed in Boedy. He knew what he had to do. He had a new mission—a new challenge. People were his new challenge. They were his new mountains—his new skyscrapers. He smiled a one-side-of-his-face smile. If he wanted to meet his new challenge, he had to get down there to them. But how? Boedy sat on the floor of the cave and thought. An idea came to him. It wasn't a good idea, but it was an idea.

He was still wearing his wingsuit.

Boedy thought through what he knew. On the first day after he woke up, he had leaned out of the cave as far as he could to see what was below him. A huge updraft of wind hit him as he leaned out. He couldn't see anything below, and it wasn't safe to lean further, so he didn't try it again. There was no way to climb down.

But what if? What if he jumped and caught the updraft? It was windier today than the previous two days. Could he catch enough air to slow his fall so as not to get killed upon impact with the water or the rocks? He felt silly even entertaining such a thought. He needed to be miles high to safely wingsuit, if there was such a thing. Hoping it would work was foolishness, but hope was all he had. As if he didn't have enough worries, there was one other fear that played havoc with his mind.

What if they had left him?

What if he was a million miles away from everyone and everything? What if he survived the jump only to find himself alone, lost in the Amazon rainforest? There was no way to see whether anyone was still around. The wall of water blocked his vision. There was no way to hear anyone. The roar of the waterfall was deafening. If no one was down there, even if he lived, he died. No one would be there to help him if he landed badly. No one would be there to be his eyes and lead him out. If only there was some way to know if they were still near. He sat on the damp ground, dejected, trying to dislodge a fish scale that was stuck between his teeth. He finally got it loose. Just when he was about to spit the scale out into the darkness…

He heard a different sound.

Yes, he definitely heard something. The sound made no sense to him. Not out here. He wasn't ready to listen when the sound came, but if he had to put a name to what he heard, he would have to say…

Heavy metal?

He only heard it for a short time. It could have been a figment of his imagination. He could be losing his mind. But then again, maybe he wasn't. Boedy walked to the front of the cave, as close as he dared without slipping and falling, hoping to hear, but the water falling in front of him was too loud. He walked to the back of the cave, which filtered out at least some of the sound, and listened with all his might.

Come on, man, make the sound again! Let me know somebody is down there, he pleaded in his mind. *Let me know I'm not going crazy. I'm ready to listen now! Give me some guitar! Give me just one chord, man. One note. Just one.*

But no more electric guitar sounds were to be heard. After waiting and waiting and waiting some more, Boedy grew despondent. He had dreamed it.

There was nobody down there. He cursed himself. *There are no electric guitars in the jungle, you idiot. There are no outlets to plug a cord into. What was I thinking? Idiot.* Boedy sat down on the floor of the cave, leaned forward and carefully, carefully put his wounded face in his hands.

Then came the cry.

Boedy jerked his head up. It was an inhuman cry. A cry of unspeakable pain and agony. Even through the roar of the water he could tell somebody down below was badly, badly hurt. The cry was bad for someone, but it was a godsend for Boedy. Now he knew. Somebody was down there. That was all he needed.

Boedy took five running steps, spread his wings and leaped out into space. There was a small opening in the curtain of water caused by a protruding rock above the mouth of the cave which split the water and left a clearing. When Boedy realized he had nailed the launch, avoided the deluge and was even now flying into the bright sunshine six hundred feet above the pool of water below, he screamed for joy as loud and as long as his lungs would allow. Tarzan himself couldn't have given a better jungle cry. As he plummeted toward the pool of water below, he felt no fear. He dove with the confidence of a man who had done this a thousand times before. He trusted. He had faith.

Just when it looked like he was plunging to his death, an updraft of wind filled the fabric of his bright red wingsuit and puffed it out as pretty as you please. His trajectory changed from dropping like a stone to rocketing down the river like a fighter jet. Within the blink of an eye, Boedy was doing his favorite thing—riding the air mattress and surfing the cloud pillow.

He was not going to die. He was going to live to tell the tale. No archangel in heaven ever flew with such joy. Boedy gave a Tarzan yell even bigger than the one before. He cried out the words that exploded from his soul.

"Thank you, God!"

Chapter Fifty-Six

The Awa warriors stopped cold when they heard the strange and terrible cry overhead. All eyes flew to the heavens. What they saw struck fear in the center of their superstitious hearts.

It was a bird that was a man. It was a man that was a bird. It was the man in the eye of the bird.

They had angered the bird god. This was his waterfall. A vengeful god was flying down to kill the Awa. Spears and arrows are useless against a god. None of them would be spared. All of them were going to die.

Blood-curdling screams came from every Awa warrior's mouth. Fear consumed them. They ran for their lives, lifting their knees as high out of the water as they could while running to the bank. They jumped out of the river and fled into the jungle. The Sewat tribe members who had survived the slaughter vanished into the rainforest as well. As quickly as the indigenous peoples had come, they were gone.

All except for Kanapitu.

His terrified warriors left their chief there, stricken, to fend for himself. Whether he lived or died remained to be seen. If he lived, one thing would never be the same. Formerly known as eater of men, he would now and forever have a new name.

Kanapitu. Eunuch.

As soon as the Jungle Money contestants saw the wing-suited man jumping out of the waterfall, they knew instantly who it was. Willow cried out with joy.

"Boedy! Oh my god, it's Boedy!"

Boedy made a tremendous splash when he hit the surface of the water downriver. The impact knocked him senseless. When he surfaced, he was floating facedown. Tony's mind was reeling from all that he had just witnessed. Bones broke the trance by grabbing Tony's shirt and yanking him towards the water. Willow was way ahead of them. Together they waded out and rescued Boedy from the river. He regained his senses just as they prepared to lift him out. He sputtered and coughed. When he came to himself, he thanked them profusely for saving his life. Everyone came over to hug Boedy, marveling at his feat of daring. The Spider Monkey truly was a real-life superhero. As Boedy thanked the last hugger, Tony made an announcement.

"Guys, I'm calling it. We are done."

Annaliese was incredulous.

"Oh no, we're not! After all we went through to get here, and after all that's happened, do you think we're just going to quit? No sir! You can't end this early! There is a treasure chest back in camp, and I'm not leaving until I've had my shot at it!"

"No, we are done," Tony said, shaking his head. Jungle Money is officially over."

"So, who won?" Annaliese demanded angrily.

"No one," Tony retorted, "because no one is wearing an indigenous Indian costume."

Suddenly someone cleared their throat very, very loudly.

"Excuse me! Did you just say no one got a indigenous Indian costume?"

DeShunta Jackson, the owner of the voice, stood on the riverbank with her feet planted and her hands on her hips. She was dripping wet and as naked as the day she was born. Everyone's eyes got wide. Some looked away out of respect, but most just stared. Tony, who was in no mood to play, spoke dismissively.

"That is a birthday suit, not a costume."

DeShunta was unfazed by Tony's objection. She did not argue. She pointed. Peaches was running towards her with the woven garments she found on top of DeShunta's folded beach towel lying on the bank.

"Lord help, DeShunta, put these on, darling! When did you make these? These are fantastic! I think they may be better than MeeMaw's!"

DeShunta put them on and struck a pose. Tony was not satisfied.

"Okay look. What you made looks cool, but it doesn't look like what the natives were wearing. The contest was to see who ended up with the most authentic-looking costume. I'm sorry, but that is not authentic-looking."

DeShunta's face displayed supreme confidence, which puzzled Tony. She didn't reply with words. She didn't need words. She merely pulled something out from behind her back and held it aloft for all to see. Her pinky was raised while the rest of her fingers held tightly to her prize.

Dangling from DeShunta's right hand was Kanapitu's orange cone. As she watched their eyes, and their open mouths, she posed a question.

"You want me to put it on?"

Chapter Fifty-Seven

Bert Redmond's game room was normally a place filled with laughter and games, but not today. The gloom hanging over the place was almost palpable. The three men holed up in its confines were the very epitome of sadness and defeat. G leaned back on the couch, his eyes hidden behind his ever-present sunglasses. Tony was sprawled out on the floor, one forearm covering his eyes. Bert slowly wandered around the room, glass in hand, with no destination in mind other than somewhere other than where he stood now.

"Well boys," Bert said sarcastically, "that was a riproaring success, wasn't it?"

"Without a doubt," G answered. "Let's see. Forget today for a minute. Let's run down the numbers, shall we? Out of twelve contestants, we've got two dead, one missing and presumed dead, two shot with arrows and another one blind in one eye. Out of the staff, we've got one with a broken neck who is still in rehab from crashing into a tree after being skewered by an arrow. We had seven Indians from the Sewat tribe killed in our campsite, although those weren't our fault. We killed five or six murderous psychopaths from the other tribe. Plus, we had an old chief with fangs get his balls torn off, courtesy of DeShunta Jackson. We barely got out of Brazil before being charged with crimes against humanity for disturbing previously-uncontacted indigenous tribes. If the United States ever decides to extradite us back to Brazil to face charges, we are screwed."

"Oh, and let's don't forget," Tony added, "our airtight release and hold harmless agreements weren't so airtight. They should have been but for a stupid, corrupt, bribe-taking judge denying our motions to dismiss Aston's family's wrongful death lawsuit. We were forced to settle. That was just wrong."

Bert's ice clinked in his glass as he took a drink.

"Look man, it was either that or their attorney said they wouldn't settle, and they'd let a jury decide it," Bert lamented. "You know and I know we would have gotten popped. It wasn't like we had liability insurance to cover this stuff, either. Who knew our insurance company had a policy exclusion for claims not occurring in the U.S.? I want to sue our insurance agent! If we got hit with a huge judgment, we'd have nobody to pay it but us. At least we got everybody's claims settled and released."

"You know what still puzzles me," G said, "is Willow. Willow took off straight out of the airport after the plane landed in Atlanta. I can't believe she didn't wait for the van to take her back to Bert's along with everyone else. Even her brother didn't know where she went."

They sat in silence for a while. After a bit, though, Bert started chuckling. He pointed at Tony and then started laughing in earnest.

"Then DeShunta wins the whole thing with that nasty orange cone. Do you know where that cone had been, Tony? And you touched it, you big dope!" Bert laughed. "You touched it! I hope you washed your hands with soap. Wait, you know what? Hey Tony, you want an ice cream cone? Hey G, grab an ice cream cone out of the freezer for my man Tony, would you? I think he's in the mood for an ice cream cone!"

Tony couldn't defend himself. He was totally incapacitated laughing. Even G joined in. Then Bert remembered the question he kept forgetting to ask.

"So, G, tell me again, where were you when nuclear war broke out?" Bert asked. "Why weren't you out there letting the Indians turn you into a pincushion along with everybody else?"

"Migraine," G answered. "I was sound asleep in my tent. Medicine knocks me out. Slept through the whole thing. That's why I wear these sunglasses. Sunlight triggers them."

"That's awfully convenient," Bert said suspiciously.

"But G," Tony said, "as bad as it gets, at least you have one bright spot out of this whole thing. Here is me and Bert in the depths of despair. Nothing good came out of this whole thing for us. But then there's G, Mastermind G, G the puppet master, just like the wizard behind the curtain, pulling knobs and spinning wheels and making smoke so his girl DeShunta would win the whole thing. Here's us in financial ruin, but then here comes G, smiling big with his hand out because he bet on DeShunta Jackson who takes Brazil literally by the gonads and wins it all, just like he said she would."

G put his hands behind his head and sighed contentedly. He had bet on DeShunta to win Jungle Money for a reason. He knew right from the start she was a force. He just had no idea how big a force she would turn out to be.

G smiled behind his sunglasses and said, "Pay up, boys."

Tony jumped up off of the floor and cried, "Man, I ain't paying you nothing! I didn't make no money to pay you with!"

"Quit crying, whiney britches," G taunted. "Pay up. What, are your widdley feewings hut? You want your pacifier?"

"Screw you!" Tony screamed. "I ain't paying!"

"Pay up, Tony," G repeated. "One hunnit thou, baby. Pay up. You too, Bertrand."

"That ain't happening!" Bert protested. "I'm the one who put up the most cash to start this whole thing, remember? I ain't paying you!"

"Pay up," G repeated, "unless…"

Bert and Tony looked at him intently, then Tony asked, "Unless what?"

G smiled underneath his sunglasses and said, "Unless you want to go double or nothing."

"What are you talking about?" Bert asked.

G pulled off his sunglasses and sat up.

"Island Money, that's what I'm talking about. There's this island chain near Bora Bora and Tahiti. Gorgeous place. My buddy just got wind of a shipwreck nobody else knows about. We could have a show where the contestants are flown out to this island and they dive down to the shipwreck and look for treasure. We'll have contests just like Jungle Money, except people don't get killed this time. We'll call it "Island Money." It's got a ring to it, doesn't it? So, what do you think?"

Bert threw a handful of cashews at him and cried, "G, are you kidding me right now? You are crazy in the head. Insane in the brain. A living, breathing, walking lobotomy. No! Not a chance!"

"G, you are mental! We just lost everything we own!" Tony yelled. "Well, a lot of what we own, anyway. We have Wanted posters with our pictures on them in South America, and you want us to do it again? G, I have bars of soap with more brains than you have!"

G simply stared with the hint of a devilish grin appearing at the corners of his mouth.

"No! Not going to do it," Bert vowed.

G continued to stare and grin.

"G," Tony warned, "you can stop looking at me. No!"

G stared and grinned. Bert sighed, shook his head and hid his face. Tony fell backwards, pushed his fingers in his ears and kicked his legs like a pesticide-filled roach. G continued to stare. And grin. Finally, after a long minute of silence, Bert spoke.

"Double or nothing, huh?" Bert asked.

G just smiled. He knew he had them. Again.

Chapter Fifty-Eight

Morton Canfield pranced around his house like a five-year-old on a hobby horse. Cheri, his fifth wife, angrily stubbed out her cigarette in the ashtray.

"For crying out loud, Morty, what are you doing?" Cheri asked. "You're acting like an idiot. You are giving me a headache."

Morton was undeterred. He galloped around his living room, holding a pretend horse's reins in one hand while slapping his own butt with the other. He reared up, gave his best horse's whinny and stopped his wild ride.

"Whoa there, big fellow!"

Unfortunately for Morton, his back seized upright then, which knocked him to the floor. As he gingerly stood back up, Cheri looked around to see if there was a clean shot glass lying around. It may only be 9:30 a.m. but she needed some liquid help to deal with her new husband. He was in rare form this morning. Morty's exuberance could not be contained.

"Look Ashlynn…I mean, Cheri. Geez! Sorry, sorry, sorry! Cheri…"

Cheri glared at him. This was not the first time he had called her by wife number three's name.

"Cheri, baby, you know what today is. You know what today means for our future. I finally get to sell the pawn shop! At long last, my ship has come in!"

Cheri was not nearly as happy as Morton. The prenuptial agreement she had been forced to sign kept her from being overly happy. Morton begged her for the ten thousandth time to ride with him to the closing attorney's office to watch him sign the papers. While she did enjoy riding in his new car, she declined. Mornings were just too early to be up. The world should not start until after lunch, at least in her opinion.

Morton looked at his gold watch. It was time to leave. He checked his look in the mirror. Exceedingly pleased with what he saw, he clucked his tongue.

"Looking good there, Morty boy. Looking good. What say you and I go on a ride with me, myself and I?"

Morton popped his favorite riding hat on his head and headed out the door. When he reached the driveway, he stopped in dramatic fashion and grabbed his chest.

"Oh, be still my beating heart!"

Standing in his driveway, wearing a custom-fitted tuxedo, was Anthony Williams, formerly known as Black Magic. Anthony had quit working for Morton not long after "The Pawn Man" went off the air due to poor ratings. As soon as Morton missed two paychecks, Anthony was out of there. Morton promised Anthony he would triple his salary as soon as another station picked up the show, but it never happened. America had quite enough of "The Pawn Man." Anthony resigned and never looked back.

Just yesterday, though, Morton called Anthony up and made him an offer he couldn't refuse. He said he was picking up a car that afternoon and offered to quadruple his former salary and buy him a tux to boot if Anthony would be his chauffeur. Who could resist such an offer? Anthony said sure and found himself working for his old boss once again.

The reason for Morton's racing heart was not Anthony's tux. It was the vehicle Anthony was standing next to while holding the driver's door open that had him thrilled beyond belief.

A shiny black 1967 Rolls Royce Phantom Touring Limousine.

This was not just any 1967 Rolls Royce Phantom, either. This was Jack Fontaine's 1967 Rolls Royce Phantom. Who is Jack Fontaine, one might ask? Only the most famous American actor of the 1960s. If he had not died in a tragic plane crash while on the way to Jackson, Wyoming one snowy winter morning in 1971, he would have most certainly continued his domination of the film industry into the 1970s and 80's.

Morton would never have dreamed of being able to buy such a luxury automobile, not with a price tag that hefty. This time last month, he was bouncing checks for his gas, water and sewer bills, and worst of all, for Cheri's wedding ring. Morton was down on his luck. He would have declared Chapter 7 bankruptcy but for the fact he already did two years earlier. But then came the magical day it all changed.

Out of the blue, Morton received a letter from a New York attorney stating that an unnamed client was very interested in purchasing his pawn shop in an all-cash deal. There was a catch however. The sale could only go through if all the inventory was removed and the closing took place within the next thirty days. Morton's cigar fell out of his mouth when he saw the price being offered.

Ten million dollars, cash money.

Morton could not call the attorney's number fast enough. He was referred to a local closing attorney who explained his limited role in the process. After hearing a brief explanation about electronic signatures, Morton told him he had heard enough. Time was wasting. Morton put his electronic signature on the purchase and sale agreement before five o'clock the same day. When the attorney asked what dates Morton had available for the closing, Morton said, "All of them!"

The day after signing the contract to sell, the Pawn Man woke up with future money burning a hole in his pocket. He knew that the smart thing to do was to wait until after the closing to start making purchases. He talked sternly to himself and thought he had made himself clear to himself. Himself didn't listen very carefully, though. All these great deals began popping up all around him.

For example, Stone Glover, the action movie star, was selling his ocean-front home for a mere $7.9 million. Morton couldn't risk letting such a bargain get away, so he signed a contract. Morton was smart, though. He expressly stated that the closing would take place no sooner than thirty-three days after acceptance of the contract. He wanted to make sure he got the money from the sale of the pawn shop first. Smart thinking. Morton was beyond thrilled to be buying the home of a movie star.

When Morton found Jack Fontaine's Rolls Royce for sale however, he was over the moon. He might have gotten a little overly-excited when the bidding started at the auction, and he may have possibly overpaid by more than a little, but did it really matter? It was Jack Fontaine's Rolls Royce, for Pete's sake. At least it used to be. Now it was Morton Canfield's.

Unlike the beach house however, he had to hand over a cashier's check for the Rolls at the time of purchase. He thought he could get a car loan and make payments, but after trying every lender in town, he realized that wasn't going to happen. The loan officers heard the little word "bankruptcy" and completely overreacted. He was not going to let a little thing like that stop him, though. No, sir. He just quietly liquidated his mother's savings account, borrowed the money his accountant had set aside for payroll taxes and income taxes and voilà! He marched up to the seller with the cashier's check and walked away with the keys to Hollywood history. He wasn't too worried about the borrowed funds. He was good for it. After the sale of the pawn shop, he'd replace everything he borrowed and then some.

As Anthony drove down the boulevard headed to the closing, Morton's head swiveled like a stool at a soda fountain as he tried to see who was looking at him and his Rolls. The more looks, the more it was worth it. People pointed. People gave thumbs up. People grabbed for their phones to snap pictures. Morton's joy knew no bounds.

"Hey, slow down, Magic. We're coming up to the light," Morton directed.

"Okay, first, my name is Anthony. I don't go by Magic no more. Second, why you want me to slow down? The light is green."

"Because I want it to turn red so we can sit at the light. Don't you see these girls in the VW next to us? They want me to stop."

"Yeah, I see them," Anthony answered. "They don't know you're a hundred years old because the windows are tinted so dark. They are having a great time guessing who's in here. You ought not spoil it with reality."

As they continued on their way to the closing attorney's office, Morton wondered again about the mystery buyer who had come out of nowhere and offered to buy his store. The New York attorney representing the buyer hadn't said anything about his client. The closing attorney had been extremely vague about the buyer's identity, simply because he hadn't met the buyer. He promised they could meet at the closing. After what seemed like an eternity, Anthony pulled into an office park. When Morton saw the placard with the law firm's name, he almost passed out from excitement. Every stint and valve in his congested heart felt like it was about to burst. He ordered Anthony to stay with the car and he walked inside.

The receptionist showed Morton into an ornate conference room decorated with paintings of men on horses chasing dogs and foxes. He asked if they had any bourbon. She apologized, brought him a bottled water instead and told him the attorney would be with him shortly. At eleven o'clock on the nose, a nicely-dressed man wearing a camel-colored suit and a red-striped tie walked into the room.

"Good morning, Mr. Canfield. Very nice to meet you. I'm Marty Vincent. I am the attorney you have been talking with about your contract, your e-signature, all that."

"Yes, how are you, Mark?" Morton asked. "So, before we start, take a look out that window into the parking lot and tell me if you see anything special. Go on. Look."

Mr. Vincent politely complied and walked to the window.

"I see…what is that? A Rolls Royce?"

"You nailed it. And guess who it belonged to before me. Go ahead. Guess."

Mr. Vincent, like every closing attorney, had his entire day booked up with one closing after the other. He did not have time for guessing games; nevertheless, he didn't want to be rude.

"I have no idea, but I'll take a wild guess. I'll say…"

Morton cut him off and blurted, "Jack Fontaine! That was Jack Fontaine's Rolls Royce! You know who Jack Fontaine was, right?"

"Um, he was like an old-time actor, right?"

Morton grinned broadly. This was the first person he had gotten to tell that he owned Jack Fontaine's Rolls Royce. He made a mental note to tell the receptionist on his way out. She was a cute girl and might want to walk out and see it.

Right then the conference room door opened. A sharp-looking young man wearing a charcoal-gray suit and a starched white shirt opened the door for a very well-dressed woman. She tried to enter but, as she was a rather thick woman, there wasn't enough room for both of them in the doorway. The young man apologized, quick-stepped through the doorway and held the door for her from the other side. The woman entered and walked to the table. Morton jumped up, eager to make acquaintances.

"Well, hello there, young fellow!" he said eagerly, grabbing the young man's hand and pumping it with vigor. "Wow, you must have done awfully well for yourself, being able to make a purchase like this at such a young age. Good for you! Is this your grandmother?"

The woman's nostrils flared almost imperceptibly. She started to speak, but the young man interjected before she could.

"No, no. I'm not making the purchase. Definitely not me. Let me make introductions. I'm Rodney Dixon from Dewey, Cheatham and Howe. You may recall the letter offer I sent to you? You and I spoke briefly when you called my law office in New York. This is my client, Ms. D'Amazon Jameson. She is the one making the purchase."

Morton was flabbergasted.

"Really? Wow. I never dreamed a…"

Ms. Jameson, whose eyebrows were furrowed, asked, "You never dreamed a what?"

Morton swallowed and thought about how to answer her question.

"I never dreamed a…woman of your caliber would be interested in buying my pawn shop. So, if you don't mind me asking, how do you make a living, Ms. Jameson? I don't often meet people whose assets are as big as yours."

The woman thought about her answer and said, "Let's just say I had a successful jewelry business in Brazil."

"You must have," Morton laughed. "You're paying me ten Brazilian dollars! Get it? Ten Brazilian dollars?"

Ms. Jameson just stared at him, clearly unimpressed at his poor attempt at humor.

"Yes, I did very well with my jewelry business," she continued. "As a matter of fact, I did so well I had to hire a lawyer to legally change my name. All of a sudden, I had more friends and relatives banging on my front door than I could tolerate. After the long hugs ended, they all asked me for money. As a successful businessman and TV star, I'm sure you know what I'm talking about."

The closing attorney tried to interrupt the conversation so he could begin the process of explaining the paperwork on the table before them, but before he could, Ms. Jameson asked a question.

"Mr. Morton, may I ask how you are planning on spending the money after I buy your pawn shop?"

"Well, that's kind of unusual, isn't it?" Morton responded. "I mean, I don't mind telling you, but it's really personal, isn't it? Aw, you know what? I don't care. Why not? Heck. Step to the window, and I'll show you."

The woman walked around the table and stood next to Morton at the window. Morton asked her if she noticed any particularly nice cars in the parking lot. As he turned to admire his purchase, he noticed Anthony standing next to the Rolls, waving his hands frantically and shaking his head.

"Huh? Wonder what's wrong with Magic," Morton mused. "I think I need to call him. Oh shoot. I left my cell phone in the car. Oh well. Do you see the guy waving? Do you see the car he's standing next to?"

Ms. Jameson smiled and said, "Oh yes, I see it. My attorney Mr. Dixon parked right next to it. I spoke to your friend on the way in. He said he thought he knew me from somewhere."

The closing attorney had waited as long as he could.

"All right, folks. I've got another closing at eleven thirty, so I need to get this one going. We will start with the closing statement and go down the numbers in the left-hand column, then we'll walk through the numbers on the right. First of all, Mr. Canfield, this here in front of me is the check, written out of my firm's escrow account, in the amount of ten million dollars payable to Morton Canfield, courtesy of Ms. D'Amazon Jameson."

Morton leaned forward as far as he could to see the rectangular green paper with his name on it. Saliva appeared on the corners of his mouth, requiring him to wipe it away with the back of his index finger. He was visibly shaking. For some reason, being around so many attorneys made him nervous, especially when he thought about his recent withdrawals from his mom's savings account, the payroll taxes and the income taxes. He promised himself that the first thing he would do after the closing was replenish those accounts.

A hint of a sly smile appeared on the woman's face, but with effort she erased it. The closing attorney tried to continue, but Ms. Jameson's attorney had a question.

"Excuse me," Mr. Dixon interjected, "but may we have a signed copy of the disclosures from Mr. Canfield? I don't have a signed copy in my package."

Morton was getting impatient. Who cared about disclosures? Nobody ever read those things. What does every seller do? They go down the checklist and check "no" on every box. Do you have radon gas? No. Do you have termites? No. Blah, blah, blah.

"Let's get on with the important stuff," Morton suggested gruffly. "You can get a copy of all the signatures afterwards. Let's go down the numbers, get the check, sign the deed, and let Mr. Vincent go on with the rest of his day. He's got other closings after this one, you know."

The closing attorney apologized for the oversight and handed Mr. Dixon the disclosure form filled out by Morton. After quickly glancing over it, Mr. Dixon spoke.

"Since we are just now getting this, my client Ms. Jameson has not had an opportunity to do our due diligence," Mr. Dixon explained. "Fortunately, Ms. Jameson and I have a certified building inspector on-site even as we speak. Let me give him a call."

Morton, looking very concerned, said, "Wait a minute. On-site? What do you mean on-site? You mean you've got somebody in my store right now?"

Mr. Dixon placed his cell phone on the table and hit speaker. After a couple of rings, someone picked up.

"Professional Building Inspectors, Ben speaking."

"Hey Ben, Rodney Dixon. Did you get the picture I just texted you?"

"Yes, I did," the voice on the phone answered. "I've got the disclosure form. The team is verifying Mr. Canfield's representations even as we speak."

"The team?" Morton demanded. "Who let you in my store?"

"Her name is Brittany," Ben answered. "Says she is the returns clerk."

"Morton, did you get that store cleaned out like I said?" Ms. Jameson asked. "Hey Ben, did he get all that inventory cleaned out?"

"Yes, I did," Morton growled, "and I paid dearly for it. I got a hernia and a slipped disc in my low back from lifting. It took us two and a half weeks to carry all that stuff out of there. You run a pawn shop for thirty years in the same place and it is unbelievable how much crap you can accumulate. I've got hernia surgery coming up next Tuesday, and then my orthopedist wants to schedule back surgery for me once I heal up from the hernia. I can tell you with 100 percent certainty—it's all cleaned out."

The closing attorney expressed his sympathy. They were still talking about hernias when Ms. Jameson asked Morton another question.

"Did you have a lot of TVs to move? A lot of big screens?" she asked.

"Oh my god, yes," Morton complained. "I have TVs coming out my ears. People bring their TVs in, I buy them on the cheap and sell them with a big mark-up, then those customers bring them back, new customers buy them, it goes on and on. Sometimes they last, sometimes they don't. I've had up to seven or eight transactions on the same TV."

The voice on the other end of the speaker phone returned.

"Hey Rodney, Ben again. Hey, we've got some problems here. The disclosure form says no asbestos, but guess what, we've got asbestos in the flooring and asbestos in the ceiling tiles. That's not all. The disclosure form says no mold, but guess what, we've got black mold in all the sheetrock in the basement at floor level, which probably means it has flooded here in the past and was not remediated. I'll bet there is mold all behind this sheetrock in the wall spaces and the studs."

Morton tried to keep his tone normal but he was starting to panic. The tension in his neck muscles almost locked up his vocal cords.

"Okay, so look—so we had some water damage in the basement," Morton protested. "Who doesn't have water damage in the basement? I probably lost thirty-thousand dollars' worth of inventory when the pipes froze and burst last winter. And that asbestos is nothing. We looked at getting it torn out and replaced, but do you know what it costs to get somebody out to do a simple job when the EPA or EPD or whoever starts sticking their nose into it? They don't let you just fix it—they require hazmat suits and all that stuff. It's outrageous!

So, my guy said he'd just put carpet over it and not worry about it. I wouldn't worry about it if I was you, Ms. Jameson."

Morton tried to stay calm, but the looks he was getting were making him angry. Mr. Dixon put his elbows on the table and leaned forward in a very lawyerly fashion.

"So, Mr. Canfield, do you mean to tell us you knew about the asbestos and the mold when you signed this disclosure form, knowing my client Ms. Jameson would be relying on you as the seller to be truthful when making her decision whether to buy this building or not?"

Morton did not like the accusing look on the young lawyer's face. He looked to the closing attorney for help, but found a cold, dispassionate face looking back at him. He turned to the lady across the table.

"Look, Ms. Jameson, surely you are willing to overlook trivial things like a little mold and a little asbestos. This building is a money-making machine! It's even been on TV! I'm sure you could get them back out there, the TV producers I mean, and do your own show. You could call it "The Pawn Woman." Doesn't that sound nice? "The Pawn Woman." You'd make a mint!"

Three faces stared back at him. Morton felt the situation slipping away from him.

"Okay, look here," he said, all pretense of cordiality gone. "We have a signed contract where you expressly agreed to buy my business for ten million dollars. I cleaned out that whole place in reliance on that written agreement. This is a binding contract, and you cannot legally back out of it now. That check right there has my name on it. Here are four sets of keys to every door in that place. They are yours. Here!"

Morton slid the keys across the table but used a little too much force.

"Sorry, didn't mean to slide them off the table. So, I've done my part. Now I want my check and I want it now! If I don't get it, I will sue you for everything you've got!"

Mr. Dixon looked at his client, who shook her head.

"Mr. Canfield," the attorney said, "you are guilty of fraudulent misrepresentations. You intentionally lied to my client in order to induce her to enter into an agreement under false pretenses. We've got the proof right here in black and white. This contract is null and void and unenforceable. No judge in the world is going to side with you over Ms. Jameson. You, sir, can keep your pawn shop. Mr. Vincent, I'm going to ask you to tear up that check to Mr. Canfield right here and now. We need you to refund Ms. Jameson's ten million dollars. You can certainly understand why we need you to make that happen right now, before we leave."

Morton was frantic.

"For god's sake," he cried, "I just put down a contract on a beach house! I'm supposed to close next week! This can't be happening!"

The woman across from him smiled a devilish smile. She put her elbows on the table and said, “You don’t remember me, do you?”

Morton shook his head and said, “No, should I?”

“Let me see if I can jog your memory,” she offered. “I changed my name to D’Amazon Jameson earlier this year. Up until that day, for the first thirty-four years of my life, I went by my birth name.”

Morton waited, uncertain as to where this was going. She paused for effect. He grew more and more irritated.

“Okay, so what was your birth name?” he demanded.

She leaned forward and said, “My birth name was DeShunta Jackson.”

A puzzled look came over Morton’s face. It was replaced soon thereafter by full-blown, unwanted, terrified recognition. He felt the ground crumbling beneath him. He switched tactics. When all else fails, beg.

“I need this closing! I borrowed a lot of money to buy that Rolls Royce!”

DeShunta patted Morton’s cheek in mock sympathy.

“Well, Morton,” she sneered, “I sure hope you kept your receipt.”

Chapter Fifty-Nine

Much to three men's disappointment, Jungle Money never aired. Years passed. People forgot and moved on with their lives. It was like the debacle in Brazil never happened.

Therrell Berry had no idea why his assistant Maya had set up an appointment with the girl sitting in his reception area. He looked at the monitor on his desk and maximized the window with the camera. *She is a little twiggy thing, isn't she?* He would be surprised if she was old enough to drive. *Why would she want a personal one-on-one with a television producer? More importantly, why did Maya say yes and put her on the calendar?* Therrell spoke to his AI assistant Applelonia.

"Applelonia, call Maya."

An electronic female voice said, "Calling Maya." In a few seconds, his real assistant answered.

"Yes, sir?" Maya asked.

"Maya, I just finished with my ten o'clock. It ran long. So who is this girl and why am I meeting with her?"

"Let's see. Her name is…Fawn DaVinci," Maya answered. "Does that ring any bells?"

"None. No bells ringing," Therrell replied. "You don't know anything else about her or why she's here?"

"Sir, I think it was you who said you knew her uncle?"

Therrell shrugged his shoulders and said, "I got nothing. If she's here to sell fundraiser cookies, she picked the wrong guy. Tell her I'm in an important meeting, and today is not a good day."

Maya didn't respond, which was unusual. She normally said "Yes, sir," and complied with his wishes immediately. It sounded like she was thinking. He decided to wait on Maya to give him more information if she had any. Finally, she spoke.

"I think you said he was a monkey or something? I might be going crazy."

Therrell laughed as he remembered.

"Oh yes! Yes, the Spider Monkey guy! He was way before your time. Free climber. Guy did crazy stuff like climb buildings without ropes. Insane stuff. Then he became a preacher and built some mega church out in California. Oh shoot, what was his name? His real name. Aw, it will come to me. Boedy! Boedy, that's it. Boedy Da. Yes, now I remember. This girl is his niece. Said she had something I'd like to see. Okay, I remember now. You are right. I did put her on the calendar. Okay. You can bring her in."

Therrell stood when Maya opened the door. The girl that followed her in looked even younger than she appeared on camera. She had slightly-tousled red hair cut in an attractive mid-length bob. She had pale white skin, bright green eyes, pixie features and a nervous smile.

"Hello there, young lady. I'm Therrell Berry and you are…?"

"Hi, Mr. Berry. I'm Fawn DaVinci. Pleased to meet you."

"Nice to meet you, too. Come in, Fawn. Sit down. Before we get to why you are here, tell me this. You are somehow related to the Spider Monkey, right?"

"Yes, sir," she smiled. "My Uncle Boedy was the Spider Monkey before he became a preacher. I heard all the stories growing up. My mom left me a box filled with magazine articles and newspaper clippings. There are old DVDs in there. Of course, I haven't watched them because I don't have a DVD player, and I haven't found a place to get them converted to digital."

"Wow," Therrell smiled, "I'll bet there is some cool stuff on those DVDs. I'll bet you can find somebody. Now, you mentioned your mom? How is she related…?"

"Oh, she was Boedy's sister. Her name is…was Willow DaVinci. I'm her only daughter."

"Okay. Okay. So, did she climb, too?"

"No, sir. She did a lot of outdoors stuff, and I found out just recently, when she was sick and in the hospital, that she did long-distance running when she was younger, like marathons and stuff. She mostly liked outdoors. She was kind of a hippie."

"Okay. Cool. So, Fawn, to what do I owe the pleasure?" Therrell asked. "What are we doing here today?"

The girl looked at the ceiling as she gathered her thoughts, then looked back at the man across the desk.

"So, this might sound a little strange," Fawn answered, "but my mother said to come see you."

"Okay. Why did she want you to see me?" Therrell asked.

"Well," Fawn began, "she and my uncle were apparently in this reality TV show that never aired. It was in Brazil in the Amazon rainforest. They had, like, contests and stuff. They were trying to win a pirate's treasure chest filled with gold and jewels and stuff."

Therrell pushed back in his chair.

"Okay, sounds very exciting. So, let me guess. Your mom wanted you to come pitch the idea to me? And she probably wanted you to be in it, right? I'll bet that's it. 'Go see Mr. Berry and see if he'll produce a reality show and let you star in it.' That would be a lot of fun, I'm sure, except I'm fresh out of treasure chests at the moment," he laughed. "So, why didn't the show ever air?"

Fawn looked at the ceiling as though it might help her remember the details her mom told her.

"Okay, so she said it was really exciting, and they put a lot of money into it, but they had some accidents. Like bad ones. Some people got killed during the filming. Apparently, they got attacked by a bunch of, like, indigenous tribe people, and people on both sides got killed."

By this point, Therrell was very interested in her story.

"Wow, okay. And so your mother was in it, you say? And your Uncle Boedy?"

"Yes, sir. The Indians stopped attacking because Uncle Boedy jumped off a waterfall and flew over them."

"What?" Therrell exclaimed. "He flew? Like in a hang glider or something?"

"No, sir, in a wingsuit."

"Wow!" Therrell replied. "That's amazing! I'll bet that was awesome."

"Yes, sir."

"So, did anybody win the treasure?" he asked.

"Yes, sir," Fawn answered. "This one lady did. It was a lot. Like, a lot."

Up to this point, Therrell had been entertained by Fawn's story but his interest was beginning to wane, particularly as he thought about a production deadline he had to meet by the end of the day.

"Well, that is a great story, Fawn. Thank you for sharing it with me. Unfortunately, I'm in the middle of producing the new season of My Doppelgänger Life, so I won't be able to film another reality show anytime soon."

Therrell stood and began to walk around his desk to open the door for his young guest. She remained seated. She had something more to share.

"You don't have to film it," she explained. "It's already been filmed. I have it all here in my purse. It's on these things."

Fawn reached into her purse and produced a handful of small gadgets.

"I don't know how to play them," she said. "I can't open them. They're not compatible with the software on my computer, so I've never seen them, but my mom says the raw footage is all on there. She said it's got the treasure, the contests, oh, and a monkey that crowned people king. It's got the Indians attacking and people being killed, and it's even got my uncle flying off the waterfall."

Therrell, by now intensely interested, grabbed one of the gadgets from the palm of her hand and held it close to his eyes for a better look.

"Okay, okay. I've seen these before," Therrell said excitedly. "These are flash drives. They used these back in the teens and twenties time frame. So, you say it's all on here? Or on all these? How full is your purse? Wow, it's packed! So, how did your mom get them? I'm not clear on why you have them and nobody else does."

"She told me she hid from the natives in the video production tent when they started attacking," Fawn replied, "and one of the video production guys handed a bag full of them to her and said it was the master and to save them in case anything happened to him."

Therrell was mesmerized. Fawn continued.

"Then there was a big lawsuit and a court case, and the producer was ordered by the judge to destroy them all. It was all confidential and sealed. The contestants all got money and had to keep it confidential. The lady who won the treasure had to keep it confidential. I didn't understand it all, but that's the way Mom explained it."

"So, why wasn't your mom part of all that?" Therrell asked. "Why wasn't she ordered to turn it in and keep it confidential?"

"Because she got in the contest late and she never signed the papers that everybody else did," Fawn answered. "Then after they got back to America, she like took off and lived outdoors for a few years, like in California, and the lawyers couldn't find her. I guess they gave up and did it without her."

"Really?" Therrell exclaimed. "Wow, what a story! I'm sure there's some cool stuff you have on there. Unfortunately, I don't have anything that will play flash drives. I'm sure somebody somewhere does, but I don't have time to spare right now to research it. It's a great story you tell, though."

Therrell stepped past her and opened the door. Still the young lady didn't take his hint that he wanted her to leave. Instead, she was digging around in her purse. She found something and held it out to him. In spite of himself, Therrell stepped over to see what was in the palm of young Fawn DaVinci's hand. When he got close enough to see, he sucked in air.

There in her hand lay a massive, uncut diamond.

"Is that what I think it is?" he asked.

"Yes, sir, it's a diamond," Fawn answered. "It's big, right? Mom told me she got a jeweler to look at it one time. She said he told her how many carats it was, but she forgot how many he said. It was a lot."

Therrell was incredulous.

"So, how did your mom get this massive diamond?"

"She said the lady who won the treasure chest gave it to her on the plane ride back from Brazil," Fawn explained. "She had a treasure chest full of them. All the other people were kind of mean, but the lady who won it said my mom was a good lady, and she wanted her to have one."

"Wow," Therrell exclaimed. "What was the lady's name? The one that gave the diamond to your mom?"

"I want to say DeShunta Jackson? Something like that? She had to change her name once she got back to America because people were trying to get her money, and I don't know what she changed it to, but yeah. That's how my mom got the diamond. And supposedly it's all here on these flashdrives."

Therrell quickly stepped back to his desk.

"Applelonia, call Dexter."

The electronic voice said, "Calling Dexter." Presently a man answered.

"Yeah, Boss?"

"Dexter, I need you to drop everything you are doing and find me something that will accept flashdrives. I've got some old video I need to watch."

"Flashdrives? Are they not digital? Wireless? Bluetooth?"

"No, these are from back in the twenties we're guessing," Therrell replied. "You actually have to plug them into a port to download the information. I need you to find me one ASAP."

"Okay," Dexter answered. "Any ideas where I can find one?"

"That's why I pay you," Therrell stated. "Get busy."

"On it, Boss."

Therrell turned back to the girl in his office.

"Did your mom ever tell you what the show was going to be called?"

"Yes, sir," Fawn smiled. "Jungle Money."

"Jungle Money, huh?" Therrell chuckled.

"Yes, sir."

"I kind of like the sound of that," Therrell mused. "Fawn, you've got my interest. You've definitely got my interest. I think I can find a little time to look at this after all."

Acknowledgements

This book could not have been written without the time and talents of some very special people. Erik Sikorski, you were the first person to read a chapter and laugh. You have no idea how much that meant to me. Tara Parker, Melissa Moore and Julie Welborn, thank you for reading an unorganized mountain of paper a foot thick and helping me find the story buried within it. Tara, thank you for teaching me about skydiving and wing suits. Quin Lyles, thank you for teaching me about rubber bullets. I'd like to thank Mariana Figuero and Hilton Head Helicopter Tours for flying me over the shooting location for jungle movie scenes and allowing me to use the picture as my own.

Dan Lorton, you introduced this disruptive high school student to Chaucer and The Miller's Tale, opening my eyes to a literary world of entertainment I didn't know existed. Now all these years later, you kindly agreed to read your student's writing once again and help him make it better. Thank you so very much. If my book is a failure, it won't be your fault!

Jason Lyell, thank you for using your video production talents to minister to countless children in summer camps, and teaching me your craft in the process. Ty Wheeler, thank you for being a veteran author willing to help a novice with your insight and experience. Julie Pollock, I cannot thank you enough for the time and energy you put into reading my work and giving me your thoughts and encouragement. When you laughed while quoting a passage from memory, it was medicine to my soul. Sherrie Poirrier, you were the final test. Hearing you laugh when you retold me my story was the greatest gift. Thank you and Philip so very much for your friendship.

Ken Kelly, I am still reeling from the fact that a world-class artist like you would agree to paint the cover of my book. I asked the very best and, much to my surprise, he said yes. As I tell my children, you never know until you ask. I am so very glad I asked. Frank Frazetta would be proud of you, Ken. You produced a masterpiece. Thank you.

Julie Welborn, I love you best of all! You have listened to me talk about a book that existed only in my mind for years, and never once told me you were tired of hearing about it. Your editorial suggestions were so very good and made so much sense, whether you were reading the very first draft or the final version. You have been so patient with me on beach trips when I spent all my time in front of a laptop writing while you enjoyed the beach alone. This next trip, I promise, I will leave the laptop at home.

Made in the USA
Columbia, SC
02 February 2022